Kat Scratch Fever

Karen Kijewski

HEADLINE

First published in Great Britain in 1997
by HEADLINE BOOK PUBLISHING

First published in paperback in 1997
by HEADLINE BOOK PUBLISHING

10 9 8 7 6 5 4 3 2 1

ISBN 0 7472 5475 3

Printed in England by
Clays Ltd, St Ives plc

HEADLINE BOOK PUBLISHING
A division of Hodder Headline PLC
338 Euston Road
London NW1 3BH

For Tom Jessen, for everything . . .

CHAPTER 1

Merry Christmas

In death there was no love in his face. Or kindness. Or peace. There had been little of any of these in life either but I had not known him then and would not learn that until later.

What they say about the dead – that they look peaceful – is a lie. Or perhaps the undertaker's magic. When I saw him, he was flung out across the floor – bloody and destroyed – as though carelessly tossed there by a lackadaisical giant.

He did not die immediately. There was time to think and feel and, perhaps, regret. I could not imagine that someone would choose a death like this. I could not imagine it but James Thomas Randolph had. I could not imagine what Randolph had thought, felt, regretted in those agonizing minutes as he lay alone and dying. But I needed to. That was the job.

'What the hell are you doing in here, Kat?'

I looked at homicide detective Bill Henley. The sickness in my heart and mind was, I knew, written on my face.

His voice softened. 'They shouldn't have let you through.'

'Suicide.' It wasn't a question; that wasn't one of the questions in my mind then.

'Yeah. That's my guess. But it's early yet. Catch up with me later.'

I left before he threw me off the crime scene. Timing is a funny thing, is everything, they say. I wondered if it was the same 'they' who said the dead look peaceful. If so, what did they know? I threaded my way through plainclothes and uniformed police officers and crime scene equipment and out into an early-winter night, the darkness split by revolving police lights.

'Hey ducky-lucky.'

Lean, compact, and wiry with blond – almost white – hair, he was slanted, hands in pockets, against a black-and-white. He wore a shit-eating grin and was casually, disingenuously gorgeous and charming à la a dissipated Robert Redford.

'Hey news-slime,' I replied halfheartedly. Blood and death had taken the starch out of me. A uniform lifted the yellow *POLICE LINE DO NOT CROSS* tape and I scooted under with a quick nod of thanks.

'Buy you a drink.'

'Lost my taste for hemlock.' I shoved my hands into my pockets and started for my car.

'Was it murder? Did you see a body? A shapeless woman with a black silk designer warm-up suit and an avid look plucked at my elbow.

'Was there blood? Huh? Huh? Did they blow his head off like on TV?' The child was *Sesame Street* age. His words echoed his mother's, as did his empty, avid eyes.

I could taste the bile in the back of my throat. I pulled up the collar on my jacket.

'C'mon tootsie-pop.' J.O. tucked his arm through mine. 'You look like you need a drink.'

I sucked in a breath, walking fast now. It was cold and damp. And dark. At six it was still clear. By ten the fog would clamp down on the city. I hate winter in Sacramento.

The Bronco was parked at the corner of American River Drive and Ashton. I shook off J.O.'s hand and unlocked the car. 'Okay,' I said to him. I didn't want to be alone with my thoughts. Not yet.

'Atta girl.' He started around to the passenger side.

'You take your car.'

'You got it, baby-cakes.'

'Kat. Not ducky-lucky, or tootsie-pop, or baby-cakes.'

'Sure. babe.' He winked at me.

I didn't say anything, just got into the car. So now you know how bad it was. J.O. was nothing to what I had witnessed: the blood, the pieces of red and white and gray things falling out of the body and blasted around the room. The empty staring eyes that mutely testified to horror. *If the eyes are the windows of the soul, what had his been open on?* 'Where?' I asked, trying to turn away from the eyes.

'The Sacramento Bar and Grill?'

'No.'

'Great atmosphere.'

'Cheap drinks,' I corrected. And probably full of newspaper people. He shrugged. 'Paragary's? Zelda's?'

I nodded at Zelda's. *Why would someone choose to die slowly and painfully? To make others suffer? To do penance?* And it was a choice, not an accident. Randolph had been in Vietnam; he knew about guns, he knew about death. It was a long time before I turned the key in the ignition.

J.O. beat me to Zelda's. A full beer and an empty shot glass sat on the bar in front of him.

I pulled out a stool and ordered a chardonnay. 'Get out a credit card, weasel.'

'Kat,' he reproached me. 'Like I'm not good for it.'

'Exactly,' I replied. 'Like I'm going to fall for that one again.' I stared at him until he got out a credit card and then, after a short tussle, I handed it over to the bartender. 'See if this is good for fifty.'

The bartender nodded, her eyes blank and uninterested. *But not dead.*

'Hey!' J.O. protested the amount.

'All set.' The bartender gave me a thumbs-up sign so I ordered stuffed mushrooms and garlic bread. Grease as comfort food. And all on J.O.

'Dammit, Kat.' He said it glumly.

I smiled. 'Remember the two extra-large pizzas with everything and the three pitchers of beer you stuck me with?' *Payback is a bitch.*

'Tell me what you saw.' He ignored my question and signaled for another shot of Gold.

My smile disappeared. 'Not until I have a couple of drinks. What do you know about Randolph?' *The dead man. The suicide.*

It is important, with J.O., to get information before you give it. And J.O. has information. J.O. Edwards has been in the newspaper business for over twenty years. He says J.O. stands for John Osborne; rumor says it stands for Jerk Off. So far rumor has gotten more votes for truth than J.O.

He worked in Texas before he came to California to write for the *Sacramento Bee*. J.O.'s a very good reporter, his stories cutting-edge and solid, but he doesn't give a good goddamn how he gets his information. Doesn't give a damn how he lives his life either. His loose brawling ways are more suited to Texas than California and nobody who knows him can understand why he's never been fired or killed. But he knows everything: hears things, sees things, and remembers both the trivial and the profound.

The bartender plunked the shot down. There were limes and a saltshaker on the bar already. J.O. drank the shot, sucked a lime and stared at me for a long moment. On general principles – which are the only kind he has – J.O. hates to part with information. Especially for free. And never – these are his words – when he's buying. The food had arrived, reminding him of this. I ate four stuffed mushrooms before they started looking like empty eyes; then I stuck to the garlic bread and waited for J.O. to get over his snit and start talking. Which he did.

'Randolph was a decent enough guy. Well liked and respected, known for the right reasons. Had his own business, been in insurance forever, I guess. Good family man, loved his kids, belonged to Rotary and went to church, did charity shit and coached kids' basketball.'

'Fuck you, J.O.' I stood, reaching for my purse and jacket.

'Katy, c'mon, what's the matter? Sit down. You haven't even finished your wine.'

'Fuck you, J.O.,' I said again, too exhausted to fight.

'Okay, okay. I'll tell the truth. I promise.' He held up his hand like a Boy Scout.

I happen to know that he was kicked out of the Boy Scouts three times in two cities. I started putting on my jacket. It was slow work, like the sleeves were full of Jell-o. God, what a day.

'I swear on my mother's grave,' he said, the sadness and sincerity clear in his voice.

'Godmother's, you lying sack of shit,' I said, the fatigue clear in mine. He hated his mother who was still living, his godmother was

4

the one he loved – as much as he was capable of loving anyone.

'Godmother's,' he corrected.

I sat down and let him pull off my jacket.

'What was it?'

'It?'

'That tipped you off?'

'You always lie.'

'There must have been something?'

'He wasn't in insurance, he didn't have kids, and he wasn't that good a family man.' I tossed in a lie myself.

'Yeah? What did you hear?'

I shook my head. 'Your turn first, remember.'

J.O. ate a mushroom. 'He was the last guy I would have pegged for it, Kat.'

'It?'

'Suicide.'

'Why?'

'I dunno. He wasn't a sensitive guy. I can't imagine something getting to him enough to make him want to kill himself. He struck me as the kind of guy who'd shrug and ride out the bad times. He'd seen his share of shit, too. Vietnam. A failed marriage, maybe two of 'em come to think of it. He's in a successful partnership now but he had earlier ups and downs.'

'Is he really in Rotary and involved in charity stuff?'

'Yeah, though I didn't get the feeling it was because he cared. More that Rotary was a place to make business contacts, and charity work a way to look like a good guy.'

'Which he was, or wasn't?'

J.O. shrugged. 'Depends on your definition. He never committed a felony, filed for bankruptcy, or screwed a client in a way that wasn't strictly legal. So, yeah, I guess he was an okay guy.'

'What charity?'

'Some sob-sister shit about dying or fucked-up kids.' He signaled the bartender for another shot and a second glass of wine for me.

'Did he ever lose a child?'

'Dunno.' Mr Warmth and Compassion shrugged again. 'Anyway, you wouldn't figure a guy like that to commit suicide, would you?'

5

'I don't know.' I watched the faces in the mirror behind the bar smile and laugh and talk. 'I never thought about it. Maybe anyone will commit suicide if they get pushed too far.'

'No.' He was emphatic. 'There are some people who would never consider the possibility.'

'Like you?'

'Yeah – as long as we're not counting suicide by alcohol. And I would have said Randolph too.'

'His marriage happy?'

'Never heard anything else.'

'He get along with his business partners?' Randolph had been a partner in Bradshaw, Bellows & Emerson, a prestigious law firm. As I well knew – Richard Carter, a partner in the firm, had put me on the payroll to check out Randolph.

'Yeah, so far as I know. Maybe a disgruntled client got to him.'

I laughed. 'In probate work?'

J.O. smiled. 'That what it was?'

'Wills, living trusts, probate matters.'

'And the dead don't cause trouble.'

I thought of Randolph's eyes and wasn't sure. And I thought that death, and the dead, cause plenty of trouble.

J.O. eyed my wineglass and the empty plates. 'Time to sing for your supper, Kat. Spill your guts.'

Pictures of Randolph again. *Guts literally, not figuratively, spilled. Ugly. Horrible.*

'Thanks for the drinks.' I stood, pulling on my jacket. 'And the snack.'

J.O. half stood, his mouth open. 'Well, I'll be a son of a bitch.'

I smiled. 'Night, J.O.' *Payback is sweet.*

Driving home I listened to a medley of Christmas carols: 'Joy to the World,' 'Hark, the Herald Angels Sing,' and 'Silent Night.' But with suicide there is neither joy, nor singing, nor silence.

CHAPTER 2

Dear Charity,
I lost my job just before Christmas and we can't hardly afford
any presents. My kids are good kids who will understand but it
saddens me to miss Christmas.

Brokenhearted in Battlefield

Dear Broken,
Presents are not Christmas and gifts from the heart cost
nothing. This is a good thing to learn at any age.

Charity

It was after eight when I got home. The message was formal but
slightly distraught. When I returned the call the phone rang only once.
Richard Carter must have been hovering over it, like a buzzard over
a corpse.

'Mr Carter, Kat Colorado.'

'You won't believe this, Ms Colorado.' His voice was somber,
subdued now.

I was a jump ahead of him. 'Yes. I will. I just came from there.'

'He's dead. *Murdered.*' The subdued tone was gone.

'The cops think it's suicide. They won't know for sure until the
coroner's verdict is in.'

'Cathi, his wife, said it was murder.' Puzzled now.

'Suicide is a difficult thing for a family to accept.'

Silence while he thought that one through.

'Do you wish me to continue this investigation, Mr Carter? Now
that the police are on it . . .'

7

'Absolutely! It is all the more imperative now. I was worried that something was wrong with Jim, and clearly that was accurate. I was, and I remain, deeply concerned that whatever was personally impacting him could negatively impact the firm. That is unacceptable. In order to minimize the effect, I need the best and most complete information possible. And I need it fast. Do whatever you have to do – cost is a secondary consideration – to get that information.' His voice was harsh and authoritarian now, a lawyer ordering a hired minion about.

He had a dead body on his hands and his first concern was damage control. Business as usual. Interesting.

He cleared his throat. 'Please, Ms Colorado,' he added politely. He had caught himself.

'All right, Mr Carter.' Mentally I tacked on a significant fee just for dealing with attorney arrogance.

'You were at Randolph's house. What did you ascertain?'

'Nothing. The cops kicked me out. Actually, I shouldn't have gotten in in the first place.'

'How did you?'

'I was following Randolph, waiting to see if he was in for the evening. I managed to slip in with the ambulance and the first wave of cops. They assumed I belonged there; I didn't correct the assumption.'

'I'm going over to the Randolph house now. Cathi has called several times. She is extremely upset.' There was a note of distaste in his once again calm voice. 'You'll meet me there, I hope.' A statement, not a question.

'Yes. Thirty minutes.' Legal crispness was catching.

'Good.'

I listened to the phone disconnect.

It was almost nine when I got there. The cop cars were gone. The yellow police tape was down. A few neighbors milled around outside and the fog was drifting in. A van from a cleaning service was parked in the driveway.

The body was downtown in the morgue and the process of trying to erase the ugliness had begun. I parked the Bronco and walked across the quarter acre of lawn to the front door. I had no desire to speak to the curious who started to close in on me.

There are parts of my city, as in any city, where violent death, screams in the night, and police sirens are common, where such things no longer even raise an eyebrow. American River Drive is not one of those areas. It is exclusive, sedate, elegant, and controlled. Crime is neither expected nor tolerated.

The fog fuzzed the edges of everything and made the house look smaller than it was, although I guessed it to be between five and seven thousand square feet. Outside, the lawn was manicured and the camellias were a gorgeous profusion of color. Sacramento is known for tomatoes in the summer and camellias in the winter. A blood-red camellia spilled over into the entryway. I rang the bell and listened to a few bars of muted music I didn't recognize.

Carter opened the door and nodded briskly at me. I stepped out of the grayness and fog and into a house where every light seemed to be on – a desperate effort to banish fears and nightmares that I readily recognized. Carter shut the door and shot the dead bolt. Another such effort.

'If you'll follow me, please.'

I looked around this time. I remembered nothing from my earlier visit but Randolph's body. The house and the furnishings screamed money and sophistication in a stylish and impersonal decor. I followed Carter through the living room, past a formal dining room, modern kitchen with pantry and breakfast nook, music room with piano and harp, and into a cozy sitting room. The style here was Laura Ashley run amok, very different from the rest of the house. It was hard not to feel mugged by pastels and prints, silk flowers and lace pillows.

A crying woman was curled up on a pillow-laden sofa watching a silent TV. Humphrey Bogart and Ingrid Bergman looked deeply into each other's eyes and spoke and kissed in Paris. The woman didn't look up as we entered. I could see tear streaks in her makeup.

Carter glanced helplessly at me, then cleared his throat. 'Cathi, my dear, I'd like to introduce you to . . . uh . . . Kat Colorado, my associate.'

Cathi flicked her eyes up and stared in our general direction without focusing. There were tears in her eyes, streaks of mascara on her cheeks. She did not look like a woman who ordinarily let her makeup get messy.

'How do you do.'

I looked at the wads of soggy tissue in her hands and decided to skip shaking hands. 'I am sorry to be meeting you at a time like this. My condolences on your terrible loss.'

Her eyes strayed to the television screen. 'It was our favorite movie.'

'*Casablanca*?'

Carter rolled his eyes.

'Yes. It could always make me cry.' She started crying in earnest. 'It's so romantic, the sacrifices a man will make for the woman he loves.'

'I'm sure your husband made sacrifices for you.' From condolences to investigation, just like that.

'Oh yes.' She looked at Carter, then back at me. 'But I can't talk about that now.'

'Have you eaten today, Cathi?' I asked, with only a slight ulterior motive.

She shook her head weakly.

'Rick.' I dropped the Mr, dropped the Richard, trying to sound like an informal associate. 'I wonder if you could find something for Cathi to eat, maybe make some coffee.'

'Tea,' Cathi corrected.

'Tea,' I agreed.

Carter looked at me, slightly outraged and definitely ruffled. And then comprehension dawned. He left the room, left 'us girls.'

'You don't look like a lawyer.'

'No?' I queried, deliberately vague. *And you don't look like Randolph's wife*, is what I thought, but didn't say. *Or rather*, I corrected, *not the original wife*.

Jim Randolph had been forty-five, Cathi was twenty-five. I looked past the swollen eyes and tear streaks. Maybe. Maybe twenty-three or four. As trophy wives go, she was a humdinger. Not beautiful exactly, but striking and dramatic. She was a slim woman, about five eight I thought, though it was difficult to tell when she was seated, with short, sculptured black hair. Her eyes were dark and huge, her complexion creamy, her lips red and full. *Snow White with short hair.* She wore jeans, an expensive sweater, and loafers. There was a rock the size of a lima bean on her ring finger and an innocent sexy look about her that I imagined men found irresistible. Some men.

'Were you home when it happened?' I asked gently.

'*Oh no!*' A flood of tears again. 'If *only* I had been here, it never would have happened. *Never.* I just can't forgive myself for not being here.'

'You couldn't have known.'

'Today's my day to volunteer at the hospital.'

'Did your husband know that?'

'Oh yes, it's the same day every week.'

'Did you find him?' My heart dropped, the way your stomach does in an elevator. I hoped she hadn't.

She shook her head. 'No. The maid did. She ran outside screaming. Finally a neighbor came over and called nine-one-one. By the time I got home, the police were here. He died before I got home, I didn't even get to say goodbye.' The slowed-down tears picked up again. 'Does Rick know what's in my husband's will? Did he take care of me? How will I get by?' There was a desperate streak in her voice.

On the TV Bergman's plane took off into the fog and Bogie faced life without his love. Was Cathi worried about her lost love or her meal ticket?

There was a small crash from the general direction of the kitchen. We both ignored it.

'What was your name again?' Cathi asked me.

'Kat.'

'Kat,' she repeated vaguely.

'Do you know why your husband . . . why this happened?' I asked.

She shook her head.

'Was your husband experiencing financial difficulties?'

'No. At least . . . Oh God, I *hope* not. I wouldn't know though. Jim never spoke of those kinds of things to me. I don't even know how much he made.'

11

'Do you have children, Cathi?'

'No. I wanted to but Jim didn't. We fought about it sometimes. God, that seems so unimportant now.'

'Did your husband have any enemies?'

'Enemies? What are you talking about? What do you mean? Of *course* not. I mean there were some people who didn't like him very much, but he was a tough businessman. You know.'

But I didn't. 'Like who?'

'I don't know exactly. Just people. It was nothing important.' She ran her fingers through sculptured black hair. It ruffled, then settled exquisitely into place. 'And his exwife, but she's a bitch.'

'Would any of these people want your husband dead?'

'No. Of *course* not.'

'Did your husband have any personal troubles you were aware of?'

'What are you talking about?' she whispered. 'You're starting to sound like the police. What are you people getting at? My husband was a good person. We had a good life. We didn't have troubles. Not that everything was perfect, but it was fine, not what you're talking about. We were getting ready to go to Mexico for a vacation.' She started crying again.

'Was your husband's health good?'

'Yes.' She gave me a wan, puzzled look through her tears. 'Why would you ask that?' Comprehension flickered in her eyes. 'He didn't kill himself. He wouldn't. He *wouldn't*!'

Rick Carter pushed open the door of the sitting room holding a tray with a teapot, mismatched china cups and saucers, and a plate of oddly shaped sandwiches. Cathi was sobbing. I was somber. Girl talk had not gone as well as I had hoped. Carter put the tray down, jingling cups and spoons. A sandwich fell off the plate. It looked like ham and peanut butter, a combination I had always hoped was beyond a sensible person's comprehension.

But that was foolish. If murder was possible – and suicide – then so was ham and peanut butter.

Carter poured tea, handed Cathi a cup, and thrust the plate of sandwiches at her. 'You must eat, Cathi, keep your strength up.'

'What *are* they?'

'Ham and cheese with mustard.' He sounded a little defensive. I was relieved, though definitely puzzled that cheese and mustard could look like peanut butter. Carter thrust the plate at me. *Bon appétit.* I shook my head.

'Cathi, did Jim . . . Did your husband leave a note?' I spoke very gently.

She set her teacup down with a crash. Her face was white and her eyes two black bottomless holes.

'No!' she cried. 'No, no, no!' She covered her face, her horrible eyes, with slim white hands. The fingernails were long and scarlet.

So there had been a note. Did the police know? I wondered.

'The police said it was a note, but it wasn't. I mean it wasn't what they said. 'It *wasn't*.'

'What did the note say?'

Carter glared at me and shook his head. I ignored him. It wasn't harshness or callousness; truth is neither. It just is. And it is important.

'What did it say, Cathi?'

'It said "Sorry" and that he loved me, and he signed it Jimmy. That was my pet name for him.' She stood and walked to the window, looking out on blackness. 'Do you know what dead means? It's not just a word. It means I'll never again see him walking across the yard and waving to me. It means I'll never see his smile, or feel his arms around me, or watch *Casablanca* cuddled up next to him.'

She turned and faced us. 'Dead does not mean sorry. It means over. Finished. Done. Kaput. Dead means never. Never ever again.'

She walked over to the coffee table, picked up her teacup, looked at it, then carefully and deliberately threw it at the fireplace. The teapot followed. Carter moved to stop her but I held him back. Our teacups and the sandwich plate sailed and crashed.

'Right now someone is in my husband's study dressed like a spaceman and cleaning up little bits of my Jim. That's what's left. I saw him. Oh God, I saw him. My neighbor told me not to go in there but I didn't pay attention. My husband, my Jimmy, needed me.' She ran her fingers through her hair. 'People who are in little bits don't need you. Did you know that?' she asked conversationally.

'Get a doctor over here,' I said to Carter, who nodded and left the room.

13

'He said he loved me and he said he was sorry but he got it all wrong. Dead doesn't mean love and sorry, it just means dead. It means no more love and no more second chances, or third, or fourth, or however goddamn many it takes,' she explained pleasantly. 'It just means dead. Dead as a doornail, stiff as a board, dead, dead, dead. Dead and gone. Gone.'

'Cathi, let me call your family and friends. Tell me who to call and where to find the numbers.'

She shook her head. 'It was just Jimmy. My Jimmy. And he's dead and gone. Dead as a doornail. Stiff as a board. Dead, dead, dead.'

I sat on the sofa and held Cathi's hand and listened to this cadence of death over and over. Nothing I said made any difference. It took the doctor thirty minutes to get there.

The ham and mustard clashed with the Laura Ashley.

The doctor gave her a shot and left us pills and directions. He and I put Cathi to bed. I would have left the room then but she started screaming.

'Don't leave me, don't leave me, don't leave me! Don't leave me alone with the bits of my Jimmy.' She grabbed at the doctor and tried to scramble out of bed.

So I came back.

'Don't leave me, *please* don't leave me,' she begged.

I promised I wouldn't. The doctor and I sat with her until she fell asleep. Then he left. Before Carter took off he said he would send someone over in the morning. He couldn't wait to get out of there.

'Are you Randolph's lawyer?'

'The firm is, yes.'

'Do I have your request and permission to look around?'

He hesitated for a long moment. The son of a bitch wanted me to act on my own, to stick my neck out.

'Without your permission, I don't do it.'

He nodded. Reluctantly. Another weasel, I thought wearily. They seemed to be everywhere these days.

The house was quiet after Carter and the spaceman and the cleaning van left. I sat by Cathi's bed and watched as she slept, white and silent, her face drugged and empty now.

The dead are dead and the living are alone.

14

Joy to the world.
Time to look into death.
Silent night.

CHAPTER 3

Snow White/Silent Night

It would be a lie to say that I've never tossed a place, but am I an expert? No. I had no idea how thorough the police search had been but I was betting not very. The apparent suicide would have deflected the kind of major investigation a homicide scene gets. And they hadn't been there all that long.

The obvious place to start was Randolph's study. I stood outside the closed door with my hand on the knob, taking deep breaths. Like Cathi, I didn't want to be alone with bits of Jimmy.

Taking a last deep breath and then holding it, I opened the door and snapped on the light. How long can you hold your breath? A minute? The room was impeccably clean. I was pretty sure that there had been draperies on the floor-to-ceiling windows overlooking the backyard; there were none now. Ditto a small Oriental rug in front of the windows. Ditto the gun.

And the body – which had been on the rug. When I finally sucked in a breath all I could smell was disinfectant, soap and chemical lemon and pine. I moved gingerly across the room, looking carefully before putting my feet down. I was headed for the desk. It too was pristine. Overly so for a working desk? I checked the huge, black leather desk chair before sitting down. Randolph's office was the opposite of Cathi's sitting room, masculine and dark in oak, leather, hunter greens and burgundies. And not a pillow or silk flower in sight.

Nothing of note in the desk except a checkbook and current bills. I set them aside for a careful look and turned to the computer setup on a smaller side desk, flipping the computer on and scanning the files. Much more interesting: personal finance records, recent correspondence, notes on cases at work. I marked everything I wanted, checked the printer for paper, set up the print jobs and started the computer.

From the desk Cathi smiled at me – young, beautiful, and happy – a Cathi I hadn't met yet. I looked at the clock. It had taken me an hour to go through the computer. The doctor had said Cathi was out until morning; I went upstairs to check. She didn't look like she'd moved, and except for the faint rise and fall of her chest, could have been a pale sleeping mannequin. She sighed and smiled as I turned to leave. A blessed and brief respite in dreams.

The filing cabinet was large and full. I eyed it glumly. It would take me a week to go through it carefully. In an hour I found pretty much what I had expected: careful records of a careful personal and professional life. If there was financial hanky-panky here I wasn't astute enough to spot it. Nor was there anything threatening or damaging: no letters from the IRS saying cough up a million dollars in back taxes or go to jail; no notes from cranky mistresses, illegitimate children, or partners in fraudulent schemes; no evidence of financial loss, collapse and/or destitution.

What emerged was a picture of a successful, organized businessman with strong ties to community, church, and charities. I looked at the letter of acknowledgment from Hope For Kids in his income tax file. The letter was grateful – no, effusive, almost groveling in its appreciation of Randolph's donation. Understandably so. The check had been for a hundred thousand. I whistled.

Randolph had obviously appreciated the things his money allowed him to enjoy, the fine house, the Lexus, the membership at Arden Hills Country Club, the pretty, well-dressed wife, but he had been generous too, opening his wallet to the Rotary Club, his church, the endowment fund of the Crocker Museum as well as Hope For Kids.

I pulled a number of things out of the files and made copies. Also copies of his checkbook register and current bills. I stuffed that and my printing job of computer files into a large manila envelope. I was suddenly tired and cold.

The thermostat, when I found it, was set to a nighttime sixty degrees. I jumped it manually up to sixty-seven and headed for the kitchen and something hot. The stuffed mushrooms and garlic bread seemed to belong to another day, another week, even another world. I made three slices of raisin toast. Someone was a gourmet cook – I perused the twenty or so cookbook titles as I munched on toast. There was a food processor, a bread machine, a pasta maker, and a refrigerator full of food.

And now, too few people to eat it.

I walked through the house. I didn't know who the cook was. Or the musician. The piano and harp were dusted and mute. The ten-foot Christmas tree had delicate ornaments and no presents. The house, though very expensively and tastefully furnished, was oddly impersonal. More a four-star hotel than a home.

Back in the kitchen, I made one more piece of raisin toast and headed upstairs. Cathi had bright, elegant expensive clothes in small sizes; Randolph had dark, elegant expensive clothes in large sizes. I made a note of two prescription drugs I found in the medicine cabinet. Also of the handgun I found in a bedside table. I thought it might be a good idea for Carter to take charge of that for now.

What else? I looked at the bedside clock next to the sleeping and still-immobile Cathi. One o'clock. Something was nagging me. Downstairs again, I put the raisin bread away and the water on to boil. Because I was watching it, it took forever.

Where would Randolph have hidden something? Crime – not that hiding something is necessarily a crime – is gender-related. Homicides by women are more likely to take place in the kitchen or bedroom, by men in the garage or family room. Women committing suicide will overdose on pills, occasionally use knives or razor blades; men use guns and cars. Hiding places? But you're with me now. Women will tuck letters under the lining of a drawer, jewelry in a flour canister, treasures in a shoebox on the top shelf of a closet. Men use garages, toolboxes, a sports bag or car.

I had forgotten the water so it boiled. Finally. I made the tea much stronger than I usually drink it. Or like it. One-thirty in the morning. Caffeine wasn't working anymore and two adrenaline rushes today had left me pretty wrung out.

Okay, I was wrong about that.

Wrung out was what I felt two hours later when I finished going through the garage and an attached toolshed. Unheated, both of them. It was thirty-nine degrees that night, which I know is nothing in Alaska, or even Massachusetts. But I wasn't dressed for those states, not even for the garage.

Not just wrung out, discouraged. All right, pissed. I had found nothing. Nada. Zip. I checked on Cathi. Same sleeping mannequin, same frozen Snow White. I made my way back to Randolph's study.

I must have missed something. I *hoped* I'd missed something. Something definite and factual, the kind of thing that would make a private investigator (me) and a lawyer (Carter) sit up and take notice; the kind of thing that would begin to make sense out of an apparently senseless act.

Three-thirty a.m. I looked at everything in Randolph's study again. The photographs. This time I skipped the ones of Cathi and looked at the ones of Randolph: a handsome smiling man with the governor of California, a handsome smiling man with a trophy fish, a handsome smiling man with a hunting rifle and a dead deer tossed on the hood of a car.

I had found rods, reels, flies, and other fishing things I had no knowledge of or names for. Where were the guns? Rifles took up space. I started walking the house again. I found the gun cabinet in the music room. Instruments of harmony and of death, an interesting juxtaposition. And sad, I thought. Although maybe the harmony, the beauty, lightened the pain of death and destruction. But I was too tired to play with that philosophical notion.

The cabinet was locked. I went back to the study for (a) a key I somehow hadn't noticed before but hoped would be there now, preferably conveniently labeled or (b) a paper clip, a letter opener, and anything else in the make-do tool department. I had to settle for b.

It took me ninety-six seconds. And we wonder why there are so many burglaries? Hah. Houses are even easier because burglars are considerably less scrupulous than I. The rifles were not, thank God, loaded. There were six of them, one shotgun. No handguns. Several large internal drawers held boxes of ammunition. I started lifting the boxes out and piling them neatly on the floor. Most were heavy; the light ones I set aside. I pulled the empty drawers out and found nothing behind, between, or beneath either.

Still not batting a thousand.

The light boxes were nearly empty, except for one. Almost full. I dumped out the. 30/06 shells and stared at the videotape. Bingo. Home run. Hot damn.

I didn't think it was a backup copy of *Casablanca*.

Four-fifteen a.m. It would have to wait. I repacked the ammo and closed the cabinet.

I slept that night in Cathi's room on a piece of furniture (fainting couch maybe?) of the sort that I associate with sinuously draped, statuesquely built Rubens nudes. I, however, was fully clothed and wrapped up in a comforter that I found in a linen closet. I started to borrow a pillow from Cathi's bed, then realized it would be her Jimmy's. Oh well. If Rubens nudes didn't need pillows, neither did I. I fell asleep listening to Cathi sigh in her dreams.

The doorbell rang at eight o'clock. Twice, actually. After three and a half hours of sleep my reflexes weren't that great. The middle-aged, middle-sized woman said she was there on Carter's instructions. I let her in, let her stand there with me in the hall while I called Carter's office to verify it. We were definitely in the Taking-No-Chances zone – an area strikingly similar to the Locking-The-Barn-Door-After-The-Horse-Is-Gone zone.

Carter verified the attendant, then ordered me to come to his office immediately.

Bad move.

First I sent the attendant upstairs to sit with Cathi, then I let him have it. 'Yo, Carter.' The 'yo' is not a good sign, as anyone who knows me will tell you. 'Yesterday I found a body, dealt with a hysterical woman, searched a house, got little more than three hours of sleep on an uncomfortable couch, and you are telling me to be in your office minutes from now?'

'Uh . . .' he said, in a most unlawyerly fashion.

'Right,' I agreed, and hung up.

I went upstairs to gaze at Cathi and wish the world were a different place, and that the smile that played – dreamlike – on her face would stay there when she awoke, but of course it would not. I considered waking her up to introduce her to the attendant, easing her shock at finding a stranger in her home, but I couldn't bear the thought of stealing whatever minutes or hours of oblivion remained to her. I left the attendant with instructions, pills, and phone numbers.

Then I went home. And to bed. Oblivion was welcome to me too.

CHAPTER 4

Suicide or Murder?

Sacramento attorney James Randolph was found dead in his home yesterday of a gunshot wound. Neither police nor private investigator, Kat Colorado, who was at the family home on American River Drive, would comment. Randolph, a partner in the law firm of Bradshaw, Bellows & Emerson, was well liked and respected in the community. He was a member of Rotary and a staunch supporter of local endeavors including the Crocker Art Museum and Hope For Kids.

A suicide note was reportedly found on the scene but police have not released the contents of the note. Cathi Randolph, the deceased's wife, was unavailable for comment and reported to be under a doctor's care.

All who knew James Randolph were both saddened and puzzled at the nature of his untimely and unfortunate death. The police investigation continues at this—

The scrambled eggs slid off my fork and hit the plate. Ranger and Kitten watched closely and hopefully. I glanced at the byline of the article. 'God*damn* it, J.O.!' I pushed back from the table and newspaper and stomped around the kitchen. Ranger and Kitten divided their attention between me and the abandoned scrambled eggs. 'Damn, damn, damn!' I stomped some more.

I had misjudged J.O. Weasel was too nice a term for him. Slimeball. Pond scum. Bloodsucker. Those were better. The milk of human kindness and compassion not only did not run in his veins, it didn't run anywhere near him. Didn't run? Hah. It curdled at the mere mention of his name.

The phone rang. I yanked it off the receiver and practically snarled a hello.

A calm, polite female voice asked if I was free to speak to Richard Carter for a moment. I took a deep breath and said that yes, I was.

'Kat? Rick here. Good morning.'

Death had taken us beyond Mr and Ms and into first names. Death, the great familiarizer and leveler.

'Did you have a chance to see the morning paper?'

'Yes. J.O. Edwards, the reporter, is known for this, for capitalizing on a private grief for public entertainment.' And for payback, I thought. Definitely for that.

'It is obvious that to avoid further unfortunate publicity, we must resolve this as quickly as possible.'

'Yes.'

'I did make my position clear? That expense is a secondary consideration to the resolution of this issue?'

This issue. Suicide. Or murder.

'Yes.'

'Did your . . . uh . . . research work last night bring to light anything of note?'

Research. Lawyers are so good at misleading euphemism and deliberate confusion, even at occasionally mislaying legal technicalities and the niceties of principle.

'Nothing definitive yet.' *Except the tape. Talk about deliberately misleading statements.* 'I found some things I don't understand the significance of yet.' *And deliberate oversight.* 'I made copies of a number of things in both written and computer files. I haven't had a chance to go through them.'

'Good. I'll expect to hear from you then.'

'Yes.'

'Good day,' he said, and hung up.

I scraped the rest of the scrambled eggs into Ranger's and Kitten's bowls. Ranger is my Australian shepherd and Kitten my full-grown cat with an outgrown name. They are both shamefully spoiled. I tossed Ranger the toast. No, not spoiled, loved. Ranger stood next to me and pushed his head up against my hand. And appreciated. He has come to Kitten's and my rescue more than once. Kitten sauntered by and arched his back against Ranger.

Is suicide about love, or lack of it? But Randolph had apparently been loved by his family and appreciated by his colleagues and community. Not a question with an easy answer. I headed for my office. I live in Orangevale – which is county not city – about thirty non-rush-hour minutes from Midtown where I have one of four offices in a refurbished Victorian.

The videotape was in my purse.

The phone was ringing when I walked in, just like in a B grade movie. I got to it before the machine did. 'Kat Colorado Investigations.'

'My name is Madeline Hunter and I think I may have information about the death of James Randolph. I saw your name in the paper, you see. May I come and talk with you?'

'Yes.'

'Good. I will be there in . . .' The precise voice paused. 'Thirty-five minutes. If that is all right?'

'Yes. I look forward to seeing you.'

She hung up on a gentle goodbye. It is usually a mistake to create a person from a voice but I did it anyway. I thought I had just spoken to an elderly woman, both educated and refined, most likely with financial security if not a good deal more.

I was interested. And curious. That was an understatement.

I turned on the lights, banishing the winter gloom, picked up the phone messages, ran through the morning's mail and faxes, and swallowed the impatience that threatened to choke me. Madeline Hunter was punctual, almost to the minute.

My guess was close.

She was in her seventies, perhaps late seventies, very petite and beautiful. A cloud of short white hair framed a delicate face with a creamy, soft complexion. Her eyes were wise and old and, I thought, tired or perhaps sad. She wore an elegantly tailored and expensive red suit, size four or six petite tops, with a silk scarf in pink, red, and cream swirls tucked in at the neck.

She gave me no smile, just an appraising look.

'You're not what I expected.'

'No? What did you expect?'

'I don't know.' She tilted her beautiful, small white-cloud head to one side and evaluated me. 'Seeing you has quite driven the other picture out of my mind. Does that ever happen to you?'

'Yes.'

'More and more I wonder whether such things happen to everyone or whether it is just age slowing me down.'

I gave her back her appraising look. 'I would guess the former, not the latter.'

She smiled then.

'Would you care to be seated?'

I walked out from behind my desk, offering her the most comfortable chair. I took the one next to it. She seated herself, smoothing her skirt over her knees. Her eyes met mine. They were a startling shade of blue, pale and icy and compelling.

'Are you good, Ms Colorado?'

'Yes. Very good. Is it Miss Hunter or Mrs?'

'Ms. I pride myself on keeping up with the times.' She smiled wryly. 'Over the years I have prided myself on many things, some of them quite unimportant and irrelevant, I now see. But I am here on a matter that is most important and relevant. And it is necessary that you be good.'

'I can give you as many references as you like.'

'Ah.' She smiled serenely. 'I have already checked you out quite thoroughly. I wished to know what you would say, that is all.'

I could not read the pale icy eyes, nor did I attempt to. This small determined woman would tell me in her own time.

'And I am quite satisfied.'

My phone rang. She startled and froze for a second, no more. The machine picked up the call in silence. I waited in the same silence.

'I am afraid for myself, very afraid. In reading about James Randolph I became, too late, afraid for him. If my fears are correct, and if they are connected, then I am afraid for others as well.'

Elusive. Elliptical. Fear puts that spin on things.

'Do you see?' Her voice was soft but strong. There was no fear in it.

26

'You perceive a similarity in Randolph's life, or a condition in his life, and your own. That similarity exists for others as well. Randolph just died a violent, ugly death. What perhaps before was only a concern, dormant or pushed to the back of your mind, is now of vital importance.' I tried to paraphrase her fears.

'I like you, like you very much, and I think you'll do nicely. May I call you Kat?'

'Yes.'

'And you will please call me Madeline. I want you to come to my home tomorrow. Tea at two o'clock. I wish you to meet someone. And I wish to continue our discussion in my home. Will you honor an old woman's whims?'

I laughed and she looked at me, startled. 'I find it difficult to think of you as an old woman or as someone given to whims, but yes, I would be glad to come to tea at your home.'

The startled look smoothed out. 'And to work for me.'

'Yes.'

'Good.' She opened a small leather clutch that lay on the chair at her side. 'I have taken the liberty of jotting down directions to my house and making out a check to you for a thousand dollars. I thought that would start us off. Is that acceptable?'

'Very much so.' I kept my reservations about a possible conflict of interest to myself for the moment.

'And do you find it difficult to think of me as afraid?' Her voice was strong and sure, her hand steady as she gave me the directions and the check.

'No.'

She nodded. 'One of the blessings of old age – and there are many – is that a number of life's earlier fears now have no power over you. What is there to fear? Tomorrow is short, the end is known. Do you not agree?' A slim white eyebrow shot up in a question.

'We do not only fear for ourselves.'

'Precisely. I am so glad you see.' The eyebrow went down and she stood. 'Tomorrow then.'

'Two o'clock,' I agreed.

There was a tap and a bump on my office door and then it exploded open. 'Kat, do you think—' Oh Lord, I'm *sorry*. I didn't realize you

27

were busy. I *do* apologize,' Tessie stuttered.

'Not at all.' Madeline was gracious in the extreme. 'I was just leaving.'

'I wanted to ask Kat something. Well, could I ask you too?'

Teenagers, I thought – and not for the first time – have a very limited and self-centered sense of timing.

'Of course.' Madeline, still gracious, beat me to an answer. I was going to throw Tessie out, and not all that graciously either.

'Oh good! Look—' She thrust a magazine at us. 'I want to get my hair cut like this. Blond streaks too. And I want a ring in my eyebrow. A little gold one. Maybe with a pretty stone in it. What do you think?' Her voice danced around excitedly, like a kid at a carnival. Her eyes matched her voice. 'Huh, huh?'

'The haircut is great, the eyebrow ring is gross,' I said. How's that for finessing a teenager?

Tessie wailed.

'Better than a nose ring though, much better,' I amended.

'I quite disagree,' Madeline announced formally.

Tessie slanted downcast eyes away from me and toward Madeline.

'I think the haircut will be most distinctive and that it is important for every young lady to choose attractive adornments for her person. And I congratulate you for having the courage to express yourself.'

I stared at Madeline.

'You think it's a good idea?' Tessie was amazed.

'Yes.' Madeline smiled.

Tessie gave her a shy little hug. 'Well, aren't you just the biggest dear!' And danced out, leaving behind her a slightly dazed person and a slightly stunned one. I was the stunned one.

'If young people could only express themselves and their individuality more often in such wholesome and harmless ways, they would make far fewer serious mistakes later in life,' Madeline pronounced, and nodded her goodbye to me.

And I wondered, as I watched her walk out, how she had been held back in her youth, and how serious the mistakes she later made were.

Tessie stuck her head back in my door. 'Who would have thought you'd turn out to be a fuddy-duddy and the old dear so with it? Jeez, Kat, and to think I thought you were the best. I'm sli-i-iping,' she said histrionically, and disappeared again.

I sighed. Tessie was the teenage daughter of the architect in the upstairs office. A recent divorce had placed Tessie with her father, a man who had a far greater affinity for building codes than for people, especially teenage people.

I punched the play button on my phone machine: 'How is payback tasting now, Kat? Still sweet?' J.O.'s voice asked me. There was a maniacal burst of laughter, the kind that comes from a gag shop toy. *Speaking of people who lack social skills.* Fortunately for society at large, J.O. is far too self-centered to have children. I flipped through my Rolodex and punched in a number.

'Henley, Homicide,' Bill snapped out.

'Hey Bill.'

'Kat, I got thirty seconds. What can I do for you?' But the snap was gone.

'Randolph.'

'Nothing from the coroner yet but I'd bet my grandkid's shoes it's a suicide. Position of the gun, powder burns, note, a shitload of things add up to it.'

'Reason?'

'Don't know. Note was an apology, not an explanation. Wife says they were happy. We haven't come up with financial problems or anything else that would explain it. Kat, I gotta run. Give me a coupla days, we may come up with something.' And he hung up.

I doodled the word 'payback'. And then 'suicide'. Did they add up? Not really. Fear? Not necessarily.

Blackmail?

Maybe.

CHAPTER 5

Santa, Baby Jesus, and
the Spirit of Christmas

The videotape was in black and white. At first I thought it was an old one, then I wasn't sure. The opening shot was of a newspaper. Only the name of the paper, *The New York Times* and the headline, 'More Troops to Vietnam,' stood out. Then the camera zoomed in, focused on the date, October 17, 1971. The newsprint blurred into a black-and-white smear and then exploded in a radiant flash. Then the newsreels and clips, occasionally interspersed with stills, began.

Planes taking off and airbases, crying wives and whimpering children. Then rice paddies and a wildly beautiful, lush countryside, a beauty that could only be guessed at in black and white. GIs, at first smiling and cocky and heartbreakingly young, and then sweaty and dirty and scared, shot up and bloody and in body bags.

Saigon. Bustling, teeming, thriving on the war and the Americans and the black market and the greed. And paying a price for it all. Many film clips: of city streets and temples and churches, of markets and vendors, of people – people old and young, walking, bicycling, and in cars, Vietnamese and American, healthy and dying – of jeeps and soldiers. Of men and women and then of just one woman.

The stills were photographs, snapshots that were framed, in time and cultural context, by the newsreels. The woman was young, Vietnamese, and strikingly lovely. She wore a simple, traditional, and modest dress for which I had no name. There was innocence and longing both in her eyes, and no smile on her face. It was a head-and-shoulders shot and hope seemed to surround her in a faint, bright aura. Hope and doom both.

The newsreel clip that followed was of a jeep loaded with young, carefree GIs, handsome in their innocence and youth. Hope and doom clung to them too. Or maybe it was just me. The hope was there, was theirs, I was sure of that. But the doom? Perhaps I brought that with me.

The stills that followed, always framed by newsreels, were of a child. A girl whose beautiful features were a gift from her Vietnamese mother and her American or European father. The baby became a toddler and then a school-age child and a teenager in a school uniform that bore a faint resemblance to ones I have seen in Catholic schools in this country. In the final shot the young woman, eighteen or nineteen I guessed, was in traditional dress.

I sucked in a breath. There was a click, a trick of light and dark and shadow on film, and then two snapshots were juxtaposed. Two beautiful young women, roughly the same age but a generation apart, the mother Vietnamese, the daughter Eurasian. Beauty. Hope. And doom. I could feel tears in the back of my eyes. We had brought that – all of it – to Vietnam. And left it behind, but not in equal measure.

The two young, beautiful, unsmiling women stayed on the screen for a long time. Their faces burned into my consciousness and I thought that I would recognize either one of them now. And then I remembered the passage of years and how life marks us, and I doubted. Their faces dissolved into a newsreel that was in a fast-forward blur. The blur dissolved into a bright explosion that dumped us into the next sequence.

It was in the present. And in color. I gasped in shock and surprise. The camera focused on Randolph, smiling, laughing, talking to someone whose back was to us. The power and vitality of the man was palpable. I could not reconcile this image with the one I held in my mind of him in death. Cathi's cry about 'little bits of my Jimmy' echoed in my mind. Though it was a close-up, I thought it had not been shot close. Randolph was relaxed, unaware; there was nothing on-camera about him.

The sequence dissolved into black-and-white newsprint: a stark shot focusing on the name of the newspaper, *The Sacramento Bee*, and of the date, October 17, one year ago. And then it slipped into a fuzzy blur of rounded pastels, soft pinks and whites. When the camera's focus tightened, the soft roundness became muscle definition, the young slim round smoothness of a beautiful woman/girl and the taut worked-for hardness of an adult male.

The stroking, the touching, the licking – by him and her both – the lovemaking and consummation was never pornographic. It was a soft, sweet seduction and then satisfaction (the aura of hope and doom – was I imagining it?) with overtones of love – but whether the love was in the camera or the people I could not tell.

The people. The young beautiful Asian woman and James Randolph.

The tangle of bodies and sheets blurred and then resolved into a rapid-fire sequence of the photo images of the baby/child/girl/woman growing up. Then we were thrown back out of black and white and into color, into the pathos and heart of the young Asian woman.

She gazed into the camera, her eyes large and lost and vulnerable, and spoke clearly but haltingly. 'I always wanted your love, Daddy. Always.'

The film ended.

The pain, the violation and grief I felt was unspeakable. Appalling. I could not imagine Randolph's reaction. It must, I thought, have been almost unendurable.

Distance – whether in time, space or emotion – is one of our greatest protections. I forced myself to think as an investigator. Not as a person. Or woman. Or daughter.

There was nothing else on the tape. I fast-forwarded it to be certain. Nor had there been anything with the tape. Nothing to prove the allegation the young woman had made, nothing to further explain, or justify, her actions. If such actions, knowingly undertaken, were justifiable, which I found difficult – no, almost impossible – to accept.

Seducing your father. My stomach turned. Still, it was one possibility. I swallowed hard.

And thought the story through. If you got the chronology right, and a little of the background, and then told a complete stranger –

one who fit the required profile – that he was your father, what would happen?

Randolph was a hard-nosed lawyer, neither naive nor a fool. He would demand proof: blood and DNA tests. Without that I thought he would dismiss the woman, an adult now – not a minor child – outright. He would certainly understand that neither society nor, most probably, his family would hold him accountable to an overly strict standard for a sexual liaison (perhaps a paid one) that had taken place in another country, in wartime, and over twenty years ago.

So for the woman – I wished I had a name – to appear and be recognized by Randolph meant relying on his generosity and integrity. *After* her allegation had been proven. If she had not cared to be at the mercy of his generosity or his interpretation of right, or if the allegation was false, then the seduction was masterful.

For perhaps then Randolph would not have demanded DNA testing. Perhaps the possibility of heinous certainty was worse than the possibility of deception. Perhaps he even welcomed deception/ delusion/illusion, almost anything but the certainty that he had had a sexual relationship with a woman who was not a stranger but his daughter. If that fact had come to light would people have been understanding? My stomach turned again.

We would understand with our minds but nothing else. It was a violation of such a deep taboo that the repugnance, the revulsion, was unthinking, unreasoned, and unreasonable. That reaction was not a risk but a certainty. Even a whisper would finish Randolph. The best legal reputation in the world, Rotary, church, and charity work until the cows came home, would not save him then. And if the revulsion did not destroy him, pity would.

Rarely had I seen a more perfect target for extortion.

Or a more perfect setup?

Carter was in a meeting when I called. His secretary was formal and snippy, a combination I found intriguing. I wondered if that was required of legal secretaries or a skill developed on the job.

'I suggest you interrupt the meeting and ask if he will take my call.' I spoke politely but firmly.

'I can't do that.'

I received her pronouncement in silence. She broke after only thirty seconds.

'Just a minute then.'

Richard Carter's voice came on the phone, rich and full and lawyerly.

'Rick, I need to know who benefits in Jim Randolph's will, and to what extent. Also anyone whom he might have specifically excluded. Addresses and phone numbers wherever possible, please.'

He greeted this with silence. I could feel the coming legal demur. 'You see the importance of this, of course.' And forestalled it, I hope.

'I'll see what I can do.' Short, clipped tones. 'Anything else?'

'Alert everyone on your staff about J.O. Edwards, the reporter. He's not only devious, he's a gifted liar, and one completely without scruples or principles. He'd seduce your secretary in a heartbeat.'

J.O. had told me this himself: 'What the hell – anything for a scoop. And, if they're really bad – a total dog – I make sure the light is out.'

'Anything else?' Rick was frosty now.

'How's Cathi?'

'As well as can be expected.' The question caught him off guard.

I doubted very much that he had inquired today. Or that, beyond keeping himself and the firm in the clear – he cared. 'May I have her number? I'd like to talk to her as soon as possible.'

'I'll have my secretary get that information for you.'

'What do you know about Hope For Kids?'

'Other than the name and the fact that it's a local nonprofit organization, nothing.'

He was as interested in this subject as in Cathi; it sounded as though he was looking at his watch as we spoke. Except for a brief chat with his secretary, the conversation was over.

I pulled out the newspaper and paged through looking for any mention of Randolph's death besides the news story (sic) J.O. had written. Nothing. I read J.O.'s story again. I had been angry because he mentioned my name, but it had brought me Madeline Hunter. I wondered what else, if anything, it would bring. Or who. I turned to the Scene section and the page with Charity's advice column.

Dear Charity,

What is Christmas Spirit? My dad thinks it's eggnog with a ton of booze. Spirit and booze, get it? Big laugh, huh, especially when he's passed out snoring on the couch. My mom thinks it's presents and Christmas cookies. We all smell like gingerbread.

My little brother thinks it's Santa and Baby Jesus and he won't believe it when we tell him that Santa is not Baby Jesus' daddy.

I think that Christmas Spirit must be something else but I don't know what. Do you?

Nicky

Dear Nicky,

The Christmas Spirit is love, peace and joy to the world. It can be in eggnog and cookies and Santa but mostly it is in people's hearts and hugs. You are a wise boy to see where it is not. Merry Christmas!

Charity

I remembered the huge, gorgeously decorated Christmas tree in Cathi's living room. I doubted that the Christmas spirit would be in that house this year. My heart twisted. *Please don't leave me, not with little bits of my Jimmy.*

I picked up the phone to call Cathi. The nurse/attendant answered briskly and updated me with enthusiasm.

'Mrs Randolph has been most difficult, I'm afraid. I'm going to have to ask for extra pay on this one.' There was a gleeful gloating note in her voice. 'Doctor's been here already and she's had another shot. Out like a light,' she announced cheerfully.

Peace on earth, good will toward men.

I disconnected, biting back the anger I felt, and called the doctor. He shared my concern, he told me, and had already requested another attendant. She would be there by evening and he would check in as well. About eight. Would I be there? I would, I agreed, and he hrumphed in approval.

I had a lot to do before evening.

CHAPTER 6

Dear Hope forr Kids,
Pleaze pleaze pleaze pick me for one of the kids. My mom
dusnt know I am writing this becuze she says we shud be happy
however GOD maid us and no matter whut we shud be thankful.
But how wuld you like it if all your lif peeple laff at you and
call you crosseyes and squinty and dummy face? It dusnt make
me laff it makes me cry.

Timmy

It took me three calls, home, office and car, to find Charity. Bingo on
the car phone.

'Katy, what's up? *Hullo Shit-For-Brains, this is not driver-training*
week! Let's have lunch. Are you busy?'

'Yes and yes,' I said.

'*This is my lane, that's yours, dimwit!*' Charity hollered.

Charity is a nationally syndicated advice columnist whom you've
probably read. Like most of us she's a whole lot better at other people's
lives than her own. Except in Charity's case, it's not better, it's brilliant.
She's been my best friend for years. And she's always acted out in
cars.

'Where?' I asked. I rarely make food decisions when I'm with
Charity, the food expert.

'Bernice's Cookery. Half an hour. Well, maybe forty-five minutes.
You know where it is?'

'Four Points.'

'See you.' A faraway horn blasted briefly in my ear and the phone
disconnected.

If Charity said forty-five minutes that meant an hour, maybe more. It was one now. I shifted into high gear. First was a call to a friend of mine at the *Bee*, Sacramento's only major newspaper. Chris is the chief whiz in Bee Search, an invaluable research resource open to the general public. I listened to her polite voice-mail recording and left a long message. Detailed. Specific.

And then I headed downtown. I found a parking place on 10th and G, the courthouse just down the street. One block and I ran up the steps and across the courtyard, threading my way through a cross section of this part of Sacramento: three-piece suits (male and female lawyers, prosecutors and defense attorneys both), everyday folks (witnesses, jurors, and victims), and dressed-up lowlifes (defendants).

In this state – and, I hope, the other forty-nine as well – you can't just set yourself up as a nonprofit organization. You have to have a charter, a board, and so on, and all that has to be verified, approved and registered. That was the information I was after on Hope For Kids. It took me thirty-five minutes, most of it waiting in line, to get it. And then I had no time to look it over carefully. It was a little after two and I was late for lunch.

Charity was sitting at the small bar in Bernice's sipping white wine and holding court. She smiled as she looked up and saw me, her beautiful blue-eyed, serene Madonna-like face framed in straight blond hair. She is short, a little on the plump side and – except when she is on one of the quarter horses at her ranch – always dressed impeccably and expensively.

We are a total contrast. I am five seven with a tumble of curly shoulder-length brown hair and green eyes, slim, and usually in blue jeans. Today was usually – although I was dressed up with boots, a cotton shirt I had actually ironed, and a wool blazer.

We are closer in personality, though I have a lot more everyday common sense than Charity. Not that you would know that from reading Charity's columns, which are packed with good, sensible, often very wise advice. She is one of the nicest, kindest people I know and I love her dearly.

'You're here! Good. I'm starving. I'll probably eat two lunches.' She picked up her wineglass and floated over to a table, leaving a bevy of disappointed courtiers in her wake.

I didn't try to talk until we had ordered. Experience had taught me this long ago. In the two-kinds-of-people breakdown, those who eat to live and those who live to eat, I am the former and Charity is the latter. I looked at the menu for thirty seconds and decided on the special, a yummy-sounding chicken or other. Charity perused slowly and carefully, ordering only after elaborate negotiations with the waiter and several exotic substitutions. I drank my diet soda patiently and waited.

'Is this work or fun?' Charity asked – no, twinkled. A Madonna twinkling – what are the odds?

'Work, mostly.' Charity's an absolute treasure house for certain kinds of information: restaurants, other people's love lives, the social comings and goings of Sacramento. 'Have you heard of an organization called Hope For Kids?'

'Sure. In fact I contributed ten thousand dollars to help it get going.'

'Tell me.'

'It's really a very special organization. You know how difficult it is to translate ideals and dreams into everyday reality, especially if you're committed to not compromising those dreams.'

'Difficult? I would think it almost impossible.'

'Yes. So often dreams and business are antithetical concepts.'

'But not in Hope For Kids?'

'No, it works amazingly well. The premise is very simple. If something is messing up the happiness or dream of a child, fix it. And guess what? Hope For Kids was pooh-poohed, even attacked at the beginning for being superficial.'

'Superficial? Why? It's hard to see anything superficial in helping kids.'

She shrugged. 'It's not an organization that deals with abuse or neglect or poverty, with drugs or severe medical problems. Their position was that these are huge socioeconomic issues that one small group couldn't change and that a lot of people were already working on anyway. However, what could be changed was how a kid looked.'

I blinked. Okay, now I saw where the charge of superficiality could come in.

'I loved and supported the group from the beginning.' Charity, who was born gorgeous and has stayed that way, smiled. 'Loved it.

41

You know how I have always believed that it is a whole lot easier to be a kind, loving person on the inside if the world around you is kind and loving to your outside?'

I knew that, yes.

'It's not Hope For Kids that's superficial, it's our society. We treat nice-looking people a whole lot better than we do plain ones. Study after study has shown that. And the ugly ones? The misfits and odd ones and different and hard-to-understand ones? We're *horrible* to them. We pay lip service to a different value: "Beauty is only skin deep." "Don't judge a book by its cover." "Beauty is as beauty does." Hah! Lip service, that's exactly what it is.'

I nodded. I agreed with her.

'Nice-looking people not only get treated better, they get better opportunities and jobs, more people are attracted to them as friends and lovers. Looks are really *very* important. We may not believe they *should* be, we may not say they are, but they are!'

Our salads came and Charity paused. She was so engrossed in her subject she didn't give her salad the usual once-over and waved away the waiter and the pepper mill.

'I bet you never even really thought about it, Katy.' Charity looked her question at me.

'I haven't, no,' I agreed.

'It's because you're extraordinarily attractive. You're tall and the right weight, with beautiful curly hair, green eyes, good skin and teeth, and dimples. You're a very pretty woman, so why on earth *would* you think about it?'

I stared at her bleakly, not feeling pretty at all, but unaware, unobservant, superficial, and lacking in understanding and compassion. Crummy person example A.

I'm as tough to read as a freeway billboard. Charity smiled at me. 'Don't look so stricken. It's hard to understand something like that unless you or someone close to you has experienced it.'

I opened my mouth to answer her.

'And don't start thinking you're insensitive for not knowing this. You are the *least* likely person in the whole world to judge someone by looks alone. I just wanted to point out how most of us react and how hard it is if you're someone who doesn't quite fit the prevailing standard of beauty. Especially if you're a kid someone.'

'Yes.' I nodded, understanding that perfectly.

'Okay.' She took a deep breath and a bite of her salad. 'Mmmm! This dressing is *superb*! I must ask Bernice for the recipe.' She looked around quickly but didn't see Bernice. 'Anyway, that was the idea. A few of us – I was one of the original board members – were really committed to getting Hope For Kids started.'

'What, exactly, do they fix?'

'Disfiguring scars and burns, ears that stick out, crossed eyes, bad and missing teeth. They get glasses and hearing aids and attractive orthopedic shoes, even leg braces. Acne and other dermatological problems. And more serious, but not life-threatening things. Do you have any idea how many children are born with webbed toes or extra digits?'

I shook my head.

'A lot more than you'd think,' Charity said matter-of-factly. 'The list of things Hope does is huge and growing every day. If there's a need, they try to address it. All services are provided on a volunteer basis: doctors, dentists, optometrists. There are pilots and limo services that donate transportation, businesses that donate supplies. Even beauticians and hairdressers who demonstrate how to make the most of who you are.'

Charity speared a tomato and ate it thoughtfully. 'I wish you could have seen the expression on a little boy's face as he watched the bandages come off his ears. They lay like little pink shells on the side of his head instead of sticking out like jug handles. All his life he had been teased unmercifully. *All his life.* And then it was over, just like that, and he was free to be Bobby, not the kid with stuck-out ears. He stood there for the longest time just looking and then he started crying and whispering thankyouthankyouthankyou over and over again. We made his dream come true.'

She smiled at me. I was practically crying myself.

'And you know what's really remarkable? Once you make a dream come true for a child, they dare to have other dreams, big dreams, and to work very hard to make them come true. It's really something.'

Charity popped a last bite of salad into her mouth just as our entrees arrived. 'Is that what you wanted to know?'

'Yes. Is Hope For Kids the same now as in the beginning?'

'In philosophy, yes. It's bigger now, of course, with a professional staff and coordinated volunteer and kid-outreach programs. *Sixty Minutes* did a piece last year and that helped a lot. The goal now is to go national.'

'Funding?'

'Grants and donations, mostly donations. And fund-raisers. There's a big gala this Saturday at the Hyatt. *Everyone* will be there.'

'Everyone?'

'The director and board members, major contributors, local entertainment and society people, people in the community who support the program. Probably a thousand or more people. Want to go? I'll get you a ticket at my table and introduce you around.'

'Yes please.'

'What is this all about? Should I ask?'

'Not yet.'

'Okay. It's formal.'

'Rats . . . hmmm . . . maybe I can borrow something from Lindy.'

Lindy is eighteen now and in her first year at Davis but she was a fourteen-year-old throwaway kid and hooker when I pulled her off the streets. Alma, my grandmother, adopted her, as she had me so many years ago. Lindy is a straight-A student, a great kid, and absolutely beautiful. Also a size 8. I'm a size 10; okay, sometimes a 12, but it's mostly muscle – not that Lindy isn't athletic too – oh . . . never mind.

'Get real, Katy. We're going shopping. You need a nice cocktail dress anyway.'

I made a whimpery sound.

Charity ignored me. 'And shoes, bag, and accessories too, of course.'

I left whimper in the dust and moaned.

'Katy, for goodness sakes, don't be such a big baby. You'd think that shopping was some kind of torture.'

Exactly. On a scale of 1 to 10, shopping is about a minus 13 for me.

'Let's see . . .' Charity was rushing through her lunch now.

Shopping is one of the few things that will get her excited enough to zoom through a meal. If she skipped dessert I was in big trouble. 'The Arden Fair Mall, I think – Nordstrom, Ann Taylor.'

The waiter cleared our plates and Charity waved the notion of dessert away. I was in big trouble. It wasn't just the shopping, it was the expense – Nordstrom and Ann Taylor for crying out loud. There was no way I could put this on the expense account. I thought about Carter's direction: Do what you have to do, the expense is secondary. Hmmmm. No. I sighed inwardly. I had morals and ethics. If I started billing like a lawyer, I was lost.

I paid for lunch – that was a legitimate expense – while Charity went off in search of Bernice and her recipes.

'Ready?' she queried a few minutes later. 'I'll meet you in the mall in front of Nordstrom in fifteen minutes.'

'No sequins.'

'Oh, puh-leeze.' Charity rolled her eyes. 'Sequins, how gauche, how passé.'

'An hour, tops. I mean it.'

'Katy!' Charity looked truly pained. 'We can't rush it like that.'

'Yes we can. I'm out of there in an hour, with or without a dress.'

'All right.' Charity's enthusiasm dimmed, but only momentarily.

I did nothing at Nordstrom but follow Charity around like a lost puppy and hold the dresses she collected. Oh, and veto some really improbable things. Charity put up quite a fight over a strapless, backless, plunging-down-the-front, slit-up-the-thighs one. 'It's gorgeous,' she breathed out in reverent tones. 'I could *never* wear it but *you* could.'

'Ask me again when hell freezes over,' I said cheerfully. 'Also when I've gotten more enthusiastic about stapling a dress to my body to keep it on.' I glanced at the price tag. 'Not to mention spending enough to keep a small Third World country afloat for a week.'

We finally settled on a tight, above-the-knee, off-the-shoulder, slightly low-in-the-back black number. No sequins, but a little jet beading.

Charity was pleased. 'Stunning, absolutely stunning,' she crowed. If she'd had a drum, she would have beat it like an Energizer bunny.

'You should wear pretty things more often, Katy. This is really becoming.'

And it was. Even though I was going for the undercover when-in-Rome look I refused to buy high-heeled sling-back pumps, though Charity managed to add an evening bag, jewelry, and hose to my fast-growing wardrobe.

'What, after all, are credit cards for?' she queried blithely. It is, naturally, far easier to be blithe about spending a friend's money than your own.

Amazingly, I was out of there in an hour.

Out of fashion and into sleuthing.

CHAPTER 7

'Tis the Season to Be Jolly

In the lobby of the *Sacramento Bee* at 21st and Q, I shifted impatiently from one foot to the other – like a little kid who has to go to the bathroom – while I waited for the guard to get to me. He was explaining in a slow, methodical, kind voice – top speed two and a half miles per hour – how to get to Highway 99 from here (not tough at all, trust me) to someone who had all the directional savvy of a lemming. By the third time through – they were in the mapmaking stage by then – I was ready to scream. Patience comes hard to me.

The lemming finally left, still confused, and the guard turned to – not me, though I had already opened my mouth to speak – a UPS person. I closed my mouth, lessening the temptation to scream, and reflected that life was giving me a second chance on this patience thing. Talk about special. Fortunately the UPS gal moved like greased lightning and was gone, leaving a pile of packages on the desk. The guard moved them, one by one, and stacked them neatly on the floor.

Somewhere Methuselah was getting much older. I hoped that the news never depended on this guard and then I wondered idly how early he had to get up to shower and brush his teeth and get to work on time. Or how long it took him to walk out to the mailbox and get his mail. Or . . .

'Help you?' he asked in his slow kind voice.

'Did Chris in Bee Search leave a package for Kat Colorado? Please,' I added with an effort.

47

'Well now, let's see.' He looked at the pile of UPS packages.

Please God, I entreated silently, don't let him go through those. Don't, don't, don't . . .

He picked up his coffee and sipped and ruminated. Well, I reflected sourly, I got what I asked for. Next time I'd have to be more specific. *Today*, I begged. Please let him find it today. It was almost four – he only had an hour – oh jeez, the flight of time, the psychological pressure, the unrelenting—

He reached for the out basket and looked through it, then extracted a thick manila envelope, my name scrawled across it in two inch letters. Even I could read it upside down and I can't read upside down. He held it thoughtfully, staring at my name in what appeared to be a deep meditative trance. If this continued much longer I would either learn patience or learn firsthand what it felt like to be booked into the Sacramento County Jail for assault.

'This looks like it,' he said at last.

I didn't make a move, just waited patiently (Life 1 – Kat 0) for the message to travel from his brain to his hands. Which it did a mere minute and a half later. I took the proffered package, smiled sweetly and said thank you (Life 1 – Kat 1), and was out of there like a bat out of hell.

Ten minutes later I sat at my office desk and looked at the stack of paper in front of me: the news files I had asked Chris for, the printouts from Randolph's computer and the copies of items from his files, copies of courthouse documents and handwritten notes – all of it calling my name. I pushed it away and turned to my computer, flipping it on as I dialed the phone.

If you have been paying attention at all, you know how much information is out there on anyone with a paper trail, which is everyone. Credit history, financial history, health history, legal history – births, deaths, marriages, divorces, civil suits, criminal records. Personal and family history. The list is almost endless.

What you may not know is how readily accessible and easily available this all is. There are very few laws protecting your privacy, and what laws there are are easily broken and, when broken, not enforced. The framers of the Constitution agreed upon self-evident truths and inalienable rights. They could not foresee this but I bet anything it would have scared the shit out of them not to mention being a violation of both the spirit and intention of the Constitution. This information is accessed every day, some of it legally, much of it illegally.

I could tell you exactly how it is done but I won't, a small, pitiful attempt on my part to stem the tide. If you ever thought about griping to your elected officials, now is the time and this the issue.

An hour later I added a smaller stack of paper to the large stack already on my desk. I reviewed the few things I needed to know now and filed the rest under Later. It was almost six by the time I locked up and headed over to Alma's. I had meant to call earlier but had forgotten. Not that it mattered. Metaphorically the door was always open; literally too, as I had a key. I could have walked – chased the cobwebs out of my mind and gotten fog in my eyelashes – but I didn't. Large parts of Midtown, after dark, are not that great a place to be in.

The lights were on and I could hear the inside racket that is common at Alma's. I rang the bell and, when no one answered, let myself in. I found Alma in the kitchen stirring spaghetti sauce, humming, tapping her foot and watching TV. The radio was on too. I have read about the slowing down of the elderly but this is not something you could prove by Alma, who at eighty-one is a firecracker – her word, not mine. The spaghetti sauce was made from last summer's home-grown tomatoes, not out of a jar with a picture of a gray-haired little old lady or a movie star on it.

'Katy dear!' Alma kissed me and hit the mute button on the remote, frowned when she heard the radio, and turned it off too. 'I'm *so* glad you're here. That Gary, somebody ought to kick him in the pants. Stir this will you, dear? And not the seat of the pants either, if you get my drift,' she announced darkly.

'What did he do?'

'He hops in and out of beds like they were a toaster and he was toast.'

I blinked at Alma's metaphor but let it go. Actually, it was more solidly constructed than many of her metaphors.

'I swear he has the sense of . . . of . . .'

'Dryer lint,' I suggested helpfully.

49

'Exactly! Thank you, dear. Anyway, at last count his girlfriend, who is madly in love with him even though he is just toying with her – that two-timing no-account bastard! – was pregnant. On purpose, if you can believe that, because she thinks that now he'll marry her. Hah! Gary's principles are just as dryer lint as his morals and common sense. Honestly, I have no patience with him. And now he's after a cocktail waitress who acts like she's a sweet girl but is really a little tramp – which is just the opposite of his girlfriend who acts like a tramp but is really a sweet girl – and she, the waitress I mean, is leading him on quite a merry little chase. And then guess what?'

I shook my head and stirred spaghetti sauce. Who could guess?

'One night when he's flirting with the waitress, whose name is Amber – didn't you know an Amber once, dear?'

'Yes. She was a tramp too.' Also a blackmailer after other people's (translation: mine) boyfriends. Not that I was angry. Or bitter.

'Well, he's flirting with Amber and then who should come in but—'

'Hi Alma. Hey Katy.' Lindy gave us both hugs.

I gazed at her beautiful smiling face in appreciation and relief. No eyebrow rings, no lip rings, no tattoos. Not even any makeup on her clear, healthy complexion. Lindy shrugged her backpack off and slung it on a kitchen chair, then headed straight for the refrigerator to graze. The refrigerator was one of her many natural environments. Good thing she had a metabolism that was always on the go.

'I'm thinking of getting a job,' Lindy announced as she emerged from the fridge with a chicken leg, a chunk of cheese, and some celery sticks.

'No.' Alma and I spoke simultaneously.

'I think I could manage easily. It'd only be about fifteen hours a week but I'd make a reasonable amount of money and—'

'Lindy dear, we've talked about this over and over. Kat and I both feel that school *is* your job now. We want you to work hard and do well and also have time to do things with your friends.'

Lindy gave us both a long solemn look. 'When I was younger I just took it for granted,' she said. 'The money, I mean. I don't think I've ever taken the love for granted.'

She looked at her chicken leg and we looked at her. Alma and I don't take love for granted either. Not by a long shot.

'But now I don't. Davis isn't cheap. Shoot, *feeding* me isn't cheap and I'd like to help out. It's not like you guys are made of money.'

'Yes we are,' I corrected her. 'We're eccentric millionaires who choose to live in a modest and humble fashion. Helping out a college student is a mere pittance to us.' I waved my hand in a grand fashion, dismissing the pittance.

'Katy!' Lindy giggled in spite of herself. And took a bite of chicken.

'And you do work, dear. You work every summer on Charity's ranch and buy all your own clothes and pay for your car insurance,' Alma said.

'On the car you and Katy bought for me. I just want to help out.'

'Okay,' I agreed. 'You can.' Alma stared at me. 'But later.'

'Later?' Lindy asked.

'When your kids are ready to go to college.'

'Oh *Katy*, and I'm not even *your* kid.'

'Sure you are.' I gave her a big hug. 'I *really* hope you don't get your nose, eyebrows or lip pierced though.'

'*Ewwwww*. Gross.'

I sighed in contentment. Davis, the land of Birkenstocks, tofu, herbal deodorants and wholesome whole-earth attitudes. Good choice. Expensive, but worth every penny.

'Thanks you guys,' Lindy said shyly.

'You're welcome,' Alma and I chorused, slightly out of key.

'Tricia and I are going to study together tonight.' Another quick forage and she was gone.

'Tricia?' I was puzzled. I know almost all of Lindy's friends.

'Patty. She changed her name to Tricia after the operation.'

'Operation?' *Jeez*. How did I get so out of touch?

'Oh Katy, for goodness sakes, don't you remember that awful port-wine stain all over her face?'

I did, of course, although I didn't remember it as that awful or all over.

'Poor thing, she was always so sensitive and embarrassed about it. It was hard to get her out, don't you remember? She hated the stares and comments. People are *so* rude. Her parents never could afford the treatment, it was a group called Hope For Kids that made

51

it possible. It changed her personality overnight, quite remarkable. She was always the sweetest thing but now she's outgoing and . . .

Lindy thundered down the stairs, dashed through the house, and stuck her head in the kitchen. 'Home around eleven. Stay out of trouble you two.' She grinned and waved and was gone.

Hope For Kids. I hadn't heard of it until recently and now . . . Mentally I shook myself. 'So what happened?' I asked.

'With what, dear?' Alma answered vaguely from the inside of the refrigerator. This seemed to be foraging hour. She emerged with broccoli and salad things.

'I'll turn the sauce down to simmer and make the salad. What happened with the Jerk and the Tramp, of course.'

'Oh. It was Coretta.'

'Yeah. So?'

'Goodness, Katy. Can't you remember *anything* tonight?' Alma sounded peeved.

I rolled my eyes. But carefully, so she couldn't see.

'She was the one Gary dated a year ago, the only woman he ever truly loved. She loved him too though at first it was just gratitude because he pulled her out of the burning car after that terrible accident. He saved her life. After the accident, because of the shock and all, she couldn't remember a thing. Not even her name. Total amnesia. Anyway they fell in love and were going to get married. Remember how beautiful Coretta looked in her wedding dress with all the pearls and the baby pink roses? And then, just as she was about to say "I do" she remembered *everything* and ran crying from the altar. She was *already* married, you see. Oh my, it was tragic. She refused to see Gary and left town right away without even speaking to him. And that's when he really started drinking and running around. Not that that is any excuse,' she added primly. 'Many people who are grief-stricken go to church or take a class.'

'Oh *right*.' I laughed.

'Okay,' she qualified. 'Not many maybe, but *some*.' She maintained pious for a few more seconds and then lost it in a laugh.

I cut up radishes and carrots and green peppers for the salad. When Hank was sort of fooling around with his Amber I hadn't gone to church or class. I had come unglued. And occasionally drowned my sorrows. *And* put Amber in jail on a felony charge. The paring knife slipped and cut my finger. I held it under cool running water. Some hurts take a long time to heal.

'Are Coretta and Gary working things out?' I asked as I wrapped a bandage around the cut.

'I don't know. It ended there. I can't wait for Monday's episode.'

I smiled fondly at Alma. 'My grandmother, the soapaholic.'

'Is Hank coming up for Christmas?'

'It depends.'

'Work?'

'Yes.'

Hank is a detective with the Las Vegas Police Department. We've been together for almost three years but recently things have been a little rocky. Amber had something to do with that. And Hank. And now me. We were fighting a lot. I wasn't positive that I wanted him to come up for Christmas. Or that he wanted to.

Deck the halls with boughs of holly
tra la la la la, la la la la.

Alma gave me a sideways look. She doesn't miss much. Besides, now my love life had a soap-operaish quality to it that made it doubly intriguing.

'Maybe not all work?' Alma asked.

'Maybe not,' I replied in my I-don't-want-to-talk-about-it tone of voice.

Later we had spaghetti. When Alma heard where I was going she insisted on loading up a plate for Cathi.

'That poor *poor* child. What a thing to happen! What a time of year for it to happen. Tell her to come over here. She sounds like she needs taking care of.' Alma gave me a hard look. 'You come over more often too, dear. You could use a little taking care of yourself.'

It was difficult leaving Alma's bright, warm, loving home for the death, desolation and despair at Cathi's.

'Tis the season to be jolly . . .

CHAPTER 8

Dear Charity,
Last year my husband got me a new radial saw for Christmas.
I am afraid of power tools. The year before he got me Forty-
Niner tickets. I hate football. This year I really hope he will
get me something I want (a racing bike!). What do you think?
                                        Stuck in Stockton

Dear Stuck,
Statistics are not in your favor. I would suggest doing your
own shopping or, better yet, getting him a woman's racing bike.
Merry Christmas!

                                                Charity

'Do you know what I wanted for Christmas?'

I shook my head no. We were in Cathi's kitchen and I was nuking the spaghetti and broccoli and toasting the garlic bread. Cathi was supposed to be eating the freshly dressed salad I had placed in front of her.

'Jimmy was always so generous. He couldn't seem to do enough for me. Last year he got me an emerald ring just because I admired one in a store window. And earrings to match.'

I watched Cathi in fascination. She sat at the table, almost primly, with her hands folded in front of her. Her eyes were dark and lifeless, her voice flat and without intonation or emphasis. The drugs she was on had sucked the life and emotion out of her. Her mind still worked – slowly and who knows how efficiently – but there was no heart, no feeling. Zombie person. The doctor had come and gone and said it was better this way, for a few days at least, and couldn't a friend or relative come stay with her?

'I didn't want jewelry or clothes or any of the expensive, fancy things Jimmy usually gets me. I just wanted him. My Jimmy. I mean it seems like I have him, he's here, I don't ever not know where he is, and if we go out it's usually together. But even though he's around all the time, he's not there. His body is but his mind is somewhere else, somewhere he won't let me go or even tell me about. I know. I asked him. Over and over I asked him.'

Jimmy was present tense, not past.

'And he told me that it was nothing, that I was being silly, that he was right there all of the time. He wasn't though, he really wasn't. I didn't feel like he was lying to me or trying to deceive me, more like he didn't want me to worry.'

Her voice droned on lifelessly.

'Like he did. At first it was just a little and then it seemed like it was all the time worry worry worry. He would go into his study but it wasn't work because when I went in I would find him just sitting at his desk, no work or anything in front of him. He was thinking, he said. Sometimes I would find him almost in the dark. Sometimes he seemed sad and sometimes he was angry and he started drinking more.' She paused and gazed at me, a thoughtful look superimposed on her blank face.

'Anyway, that's what I wanted for Christmas.'

'What?' I asked, lost.

'Oh, didn't I tell you?' She looked confused.

'I don't think so,' I replied gently.

'I asked Jimmy to take me to Mexico. We would get out of this awful fog and be in the sunshine. I wanted my Jimmy back, my old Jimmy, my fun, happy, loving Jimmy.' Her voice was low, almost inaudible, and she pushed lettuce, and tomatoes around distractedly as she spoke. 'I just wanted my Jimmy.' She put her fork down and stood.

'Is it cocktail hour yet? I can't tell. It's so dark here in the winter. I hate it. We were supposed to be in Mexico where it's sunny and bright.' She glanced at the clock. 'Jimmy and I always had a drink. I'll get us one, that would be nice.'

'It would be better if you didn't. The medication you're on is strong.'

'Oh.' Her hands dropped to her side and she looked around her helplessly, then sat down.

I cleared the salad away and put dinner in its place. She took a few bites and then looked at me.

'I know what I said and that it's wrong, stupid,' she stated. There was a slight emphasis in her voice now.

'What?' I asked, lost again.

'It can't be just like it always is. Was,' she corrected. 'Jimmy's gone and nothing will ever be like it was. Nothing. Ever.'

'Do you know what was upsetting Jimmy?'

'No. He wouldn't tell me. I told you.' She frowned. 'I did tell you, didn't I?' she asked fretfully.

'Yes.'

'Okay. Well, pay attention.' Petulant.

'Did he get any letters or phone calls or see unexpected people, anything that would—'

'No.' She interrupted me and then ate a few bites of her dinner. 'I'm not a child. Don't keep asking me the same question in different ways. If anything like that had happened I would have noticed. I would have tried to do something about it. Jimmy always wanted to take care of me but I didn't want to be taken care of. I think marriage is a partnership, not one person taking care of another. Don't you?' Belligerent.

'Yes.'

And I did, I agreed with her. I also remembered that right after Randolph's death she had asked what would happen to her, had wished to know if her husband had provided for her in his will. *If he had taken care of her.*

'I don't want to eat anymore.' She pushed the plate away. 'Or talk either.'

Her mood had changed. Or the effect of the drug was wearing off. Something.

'All right,' I agreed again.

She got up and marched out of the kitchen. I followed at a discreet distance, watched as she popped a video into the VCR and settled on the couch, drawing her knees up to her chin and pulling her robe over them and down to cover her bare toes.

She was off to Paris. And Casablanca.

J.O. called me at home that night. I have an unlisted number that I have never given him, so what does that tell you?

'How's my favorite dick?'

That was his opening line. I knew what it told me.

'I realize you have no manners and minimal charm, J.O., but don't you find it occasionally useful to fake it?'

'Yeah. Be wasted on you though, Kat.'

'Manners are never wasted,' I stated primly. 'Good thing Jane Austen can't hear you say that.'

'Who's Jane Austen? You mean the writer? That's just like you, littering up a perfectly good conversation with dead writers. Dead *prissy* writers.'

I refused to rise to the affront or point out the obvious errors: it *wasn't* just like me, it was *not* a perfectly good conversation, and Jane Austen is not *prissy*. Actually, knowing J.O., it was probably not even meant as an affront. Obnoxious is just standard operating procedure for him. 'You've got thirty seconds to say something that interests me or I'm hanging up.' Okay, my reply was a little testy. I stretched the phone cord so I could make it to a cupboard and get down a wineglass. 'Tick . . . tick . . .' I pulled a bottle of chardonnay out of the fridge and poured.

'Look, Kat, I figured we could work together, pool our talents. I have a feeling this Randolph thing is going to turn into a big story.'

'Tick . . . tick . . . tick . . .'

'I've got resources you don't; you have an in with the family that I don't. Symbiosis. Perfect working relationship.'

'You're right.'

'Good, Okay, you tell me what you have and I'll tell you what I have.'

I laughed.

'No, I mean it. We're partners. I wouldn't hold out on you.' His voice oozed, crawled with sincerity.

'Yeah you would, J.O.'

'I'd hold out on another reporter, yeah, but not on you, not on a partner in an investigation.'

'Really?' I made my voice bright, happy, and questioning.

'Really.' Serious, sincere, and definitive.

'Oh darn, I just remembered something.' Deep regret and sorrow.

'What?' J.O. asked, curious but complacent.

'I don't work with unprincipled dirtbags.' I hung up and took a sip of wine in a silent toast to that standard. I wondered, too, what to expect from J.O. He was a wild card with a mean streak and an imagination. It had been an ugly combination in the past and would be again in the future. I shrugged. He was also unpredictable so there was no point in worrying about it.

I curled up on the couch with my wine and the stack of files I had accumulated on this case. Ranger was at my feet, Kitten on my lap.

I was almost content.

The contentment didn't last long though, not with what I found.

Madeline's directions were good. I parked in front of the house in Land Park, an old, gracious, and pricy part of town. The house was the same: old, gracious, and costly. Madeline matched the elegance of her surroundings although today she was 'casual' in navy slacks, a teal sweater, and color-coordinated scarf, accessories, and pumps.

We were seated in what I took to be a library or study – walls lined with books and a desk with nothing but knick-knacks on it – in an informal chair-and-coffee-table grouping in front of the fireplace. On the table a large silver tea urn was flanked with delicate china cups and saucers and dainty tea sandwiches and cookies that looked homemade. The fire snapped pleasantly at us as Madeline determinedly chatted about trivial topics. I joined in and waited to see what was coming. A thousand dollars covers a lot of billable hours.

I was on my first cup of tea and my second teeny cucumber sandwich when I heard a door open behind us. Madeline undoubtedly heard it too – expected it? – but gave no indications. I eyed the plate of sandwiches longingly. It had been another day with no lunch and a caffeine breakfast. I thought Alma overdid it with her insistence on three squares but two certainly had my vote.

'Kat, I'd like you to meet my niece, Amy.' She smiled.

I was seated, facing the fire with my back to the room, so I stood and turned. I forget how automatic a reaction is until I have to adjust it. My gaze was at eye level, mine. I had to drop my gaze several feet to meet the steady scrutiny of the extraordinarily beautiful young woman in the wheelchair. Her hand was cool, her grasp firm as she reached out to take my hand.

'How do you do?' she queried politely. Her eyes were the same icy blue as her aunt's but her hair was blond and straight, falling in a shimmering fluid wave to her shoulders. She had a trim and slight build and wore jeans and a sweater. Small diamonds sparkled in her ears, a much larger one on her hand.

She tucked the wheelchair into a space on the other side of her aunt and graciously accepted a teacup.

'Kat, if you would help yourself to the sandwiches and pass them around?'

I did as I was bid.

'How was school, dear?' Madeline asked Amy, love in her voice.

'Hard.' Amy rolled her eyes and grinned affectionately at her aunt. 'I had no idea you had to take so many math and statistics courses as a psychology major. It's got me in a twist.' She stretched a hand out for the sandwich plate. The teacup rattled in her lap.

I looked away so I wouldn't leap up to offer help that was neither needed nor sought. We talked about school and sandwiches and the weather. If you can dignify what we have in the winter in Sacramento – rain or fog – by the term weather. And I wondered idly how long it would take to get to the purpose of this visit. Or if we would get there at all. Or even if there was a purpose.

After tea and sandwiches Amy kissed her aunt and, with a couple of cookies in her lap, took her leave. 'Statistics homework,' she explained ruefully, was calling her name.

Boredom was starting to call mine.

CHAPTER 9

Dear Charity,
I was an itsy bitsy bit indiscreet. Okay, it was a little more than
that. I had an affair with a married man I met at the office
Christmas party. Actually, he is my husband's business partner.
A woman I know found out and she says she will tell unless I
put on a charity fund-raiser. She says she is squaring my
conscience and doing me a favor. What do you say?

Careless Carol

Dear Careless,
The correct term for that is blackmail, not favor.

Charity

'Do you have any idea why you are here?' Madeline asked me in a
silence no longer punctuated by tea sandwiches or the gentle clinking
of cups.

'Oh yes.' Two could play the minimal-communication game.

She tilted her head to one side. 'Oh? And pray tell, what would
that be?' There was a delicate thread of wonder and, I thought,
amusement in her voice. Amusement at someone who thinks they
know the answer but – really – hasn't a clue. Or that was my
assumption about her assumption.

You implied you noted a similarity, or at least the possibility of
one, in your situation and Randolph's. And that you feared for others.'
I didn't specify the others; she hadn't either. 'I had already begun to
consider the possibility of blackmail in Randolph's case. Your
comment reinforced my interest, particularly when I found that you

61

were on the board of Hope For Kids and Randolph was a major contributor. I haven't had time to turn up anything definitive yet but my interest has increased considerably. I suspect you are a victim of extortion.'

The fire snapped and crackled, its warmth a startling contrast to the deep freeze in Madeline's icy blue eyes. 'My, my. And what, pray tell, am I presumed to be extorted about?' She ended on a tentative and hesitant note. Something was making her nervous. The subject? Ending a sentence with a preposition?

'I don't know specifically, though I'm sure – given enough time – I could find out. But I assume that you are paying me to find out what you don't know, not what you do? Or are we playing Twenty Questions?'

'Yes.' Madeline took a deep breath. 'Yes, of course.'

Yes? We *were* playing Twenty Questions? I thought it over quickly. Okay, I was going with animal for my first question. I was ready.

'I mean no, we are not playing Twenty Questions, and yes, you were quite right.'

I was a little disappointed, I admit it. At twelve I had been the neighborhood champion in twenty questions.

'Someone is trying to blackmail me – extort, is that the correct term?'

I shrugged. 'The legal term. They seem to be interchangeable in everyday usage.' We were still dancing around the edge of it.

'And James Randolph was being blackmailed?'

'Was he?' I answered a question with a question in a familiar two-step.

'Didn't you just say that?' She waltzed and twirled, graceful and serene. Her eyes were friendly, open and questioning now, not icy and bold.

We were playing Twenty Questions. Or Trivial Pursuit.

'Madeline, I am not here to discuss Randolph's or anyone else's life or problems with you. It is appropriate for me to make a general connection or statement but not to go into specifics.' Neither appropriate nor ethical. 'Perhaps you merely wanted me to be aware that blackmail is a factor in this case.' *Not true, of course, but I was sick of piddling around.* 'I am grateful for that information.' I shifted in my seat as though ready to leave. 'If that is the extent of your concern you do not need my services and I will return your retainer.'

She spoke immediately and without hesitation. 'I want you to work for me. I want you to discover who is doing this and stop him. I want you to protect my privacy and I want all this done as quickly and quietly as possible.' She took a deep breath. 'Please.'

'You don't need me.' I explained what I was certain she had thought through long ago. 'Extortion is a crime. The police will handle this.'

'No. I want absolute discretion.'

'An ongoing investigation is not a matter of public record. The police can be discreet and considerate; their approach is not the *National Enquirer*'s.'

She shook her head emphatically. 'No. Absolutely not.'

'All right. I have been retained by another client to look into the affairs and death of James Randolph. You understand that if there is any conflict my first loyalty will be to my original client?'

'Yes.'

'I would also be happy to refer you to another investigator so that no possibility of a conflict of interest could exist or will arise.'

'No.'

'You wish to proceed on the basis I have outlined?' I was leaving no room for misunderstanding.

'Yes.'

'Tell me what is going on. Everything. The subject of the extortion, how the extortionist gets in touch with you, anything you know about him or her, how many times contact has been made, what they want. *Everything*.' I emphasized the everything partly because I didn't think I was going to get it. You never do in blackmail.

'Money. He wants money,' Madeline said.

Duh, I thought but didn't say. 'How much?'

'A hundred thousand.'

'Do you have a hundred thousand?' The house, area, and furnishings screamed money but that was no guarantee.

'Oh yes. It is not, however, the way I would choose to spend it.'

Something in her voice. 'Have you already paid?' I kept my voice neutral.

'Yes.' Her eyes slipped away from mine. 'I shouldn't have, I know. I should have called you then.'

I agreed, but I said nothing.

'He gave me very little time and I was frightened.'

'He?'

'It wasn't the usual thing, you know?'

Again I said nothing. There is a need in us all to experience our lives and ordeals as unique. But blackmail is pretty standard: a victim and a secret, money and a payoff to a slimeball. I would be surprised if this case was different.

'Oh?' I asked finally, filling up the silence.

'I didn't send him the money. I sent it to Hope For Kids. He didn't want it for himself. He even made a joke about how it wasn't really a loss because I was helping children and I could deduct it as a charitable contribution on my income taxes.'

'Was helping the children in Hope For Kids important to him?'

She shrugged helplessly. 'I don't know. I'm usually good at figuring out things but I was too frightened, I couldn't pay close attention.'

'You say he? You are sure it was a man?'

'No. Is there something, a device of some sort, that you can use to alter your voice, make it sound higher or lower or very different in some way?'

'Yes.'

'I think he had a device like that. It did not sound like a real voice, did not sound very human.'

I ignored the oxymoron: blackmailer as human being. 'But you think it was a man?'

She shook her head. 'I have no reason to believe that. He never said anything to identify himself as a man or woman. I just say he because it was a deep voice, like a man's voice, but I don't know.'

'Were all your communications by telephone?'

'Yes. He called me. I had no way of reaching him.'

'No letters?'

'No.'

'Or attempts to arrange a meeting?'

'No.'

'How many calls?'

'Three.'

'Did you record them?'

'No.' Her voice was rueful. 'I thought of it later but at the time I was too frightened and nervous.'

'Over what period of time?'

'A week.'

'Was the hundred thousand a total payment or a partial one?'

'Total. That's what he said, anyway.' Madeline's face was a blank but the gnarled fingers twisted restlessly in her lap.

Blackmailers didn't usually stop at one payment. But I was more reluctant to jump to conclusions now than I had been. Maybe the secret to his success was the lack of personal gain, the one time hit, and the minimal personal contact. A hundred thousand was the amount of James Randolph's contribution to Hope For Kids as well. I stared into the fire and found no answers. When I looked back at Madeline her face was still blank, almost serene, her hands relentlessly twisting. The firelight played on us both as I asked the question Madeline didn't want to answer.

'Why was he blackmailing you?'

'There was something in my past that I really didn't care to have come to light.'

Surprise! I thought, and then I caught myself.

A calm, easy answer. Simplified and rehearsed. And without content. Most of us have things in our past we don't choose to share with others but they are rarely hundred-thousand-dollar-ticket items. Or more. Victims don't assume that a blackmailer will be satisfied with one payment. The guilty are not naive. *Guilty?* I caught myself again. I didn't know that yet.

'I need you to be more specific. I'm sorry. I know this is difficult and unpleasant.'

'Unpleasant, of course,' she acknowledged. 'But also irrelevant.'

I stared at the fire before answering. 'You are asking me to find the person responsible for this crime without giving me the necessary information.' Madeline started to make a comment but I spoke over it. 'You are concerned that there may be a pattern here involving you, Randolph, and others. Madeline, I can't figure out the pattern without knowing the details. The nature of the crime often leads to the criminal.' I looked away from the fire and back to Madeline.

'Yes, I can see that. You will have to accept my word that such is not the case in my situation.'

'Very well.' I smiled at her and she visibly relaxed. 'I do. May I suggest another investigator to you, or do you already have someone in mind?'

She stiffened. The fingers of her right hand rested lightly on her breast, her eyes paled to a light blue that was almost white. 'You are being most difficult, Ms Colorado.'

'I cannot work effectively in the way you have outlined. I respect your personal position; I ask you to respect my professional standard.'

'Very well.' Her lips were pursed with disapproval, even dislike. 'I will tell you then, but I do so under duress.'

I let it go. There was no duress, of course. We both knew that. But perhaps the notion made it easier for her to speak.

'Amy is not my niece. She is in her early twenties and the disparity in our ages alone makes that improbable. She is my grandniece, her mother and father both dead. And she is the unfortunate product of an incestuous relationship.' Her face softened. 'By "unfortunate" I mean in no way to reflect on Amy, who is a blessing to all who know her, but to refer to the circumstances of her birth. Her parentage was suspected by many though few indeed knew the truth, which was even more shocking than that which was suspected.'

Madeline stood and walked to a window where the gray winter landscape was as cheerless as the details of her story. 'Amy's mother was a sweet but severely mentally deficient woman who was passed around among her brothers and uncles. No one knew the father of the child and no one wanted her. When it became evident that the child was crippled, the rejection was complete. They would have killed her had I not intervened.'

She turned away from the window and met my look squarely. 'They were a harsh and cruel family, although perhaps death would have been better than growing up there, where she faced the same fate as her mother. I took the child and severed all ties with the family. We had an agreement that there would be no claims made. Ever. On either side. I hired an excellent lawyer to handle the adoption and erase as much of the past as possible.

'Amy knows I am her great-aunt but nothing else. I cannot bear that this foulness should fall on her. She has had challenges enough already in her short life. I have done all that I could to protect us and, until now, it has been enough. I am trusting you with this. It must go no further.'

Her voice almost beseeched me now. 'I will not claim to be selfless in this, to be acting only for Amy. It is for myself as well. I have never married, nor borne a child. I have no family save Amy. She is everything to me, more dear than life itself, and I would do anything to protect that, to protect us.' Her voice trembled as she crossed the room and sat next to me on the couch. 'Please help us. *Please*.' Her breath caught on something halfway between a sigh and a sob.

'After all these years it is still there, is as "wonderful and luminous" as ever.' The last – the wonderful and luminous – was a quotation.

Her forehead wrinkled in puzzlement as she looked at me. 'What do you mean? 'What are you speaking of?' Innocence and vexation chased around her face like children playing ring-around-the-rose.

'Surely you remember the reviews in the *San Francisco Chronicle*? "Lively and spirited with an air of both innocence and worldly wisdom that is captivating and charming." That was when you were still in the dance halls. Later, on the stage of more legitimate theater, they referred to you as "wonderful and luminous, sublime, witty and enchanting." You were the toast of the town in those days.'

The look of innocence and puzzlement had long faded from Madeline's face. 'You are better than I supposed,' she said coolly. 'You are much better. What else do you know?'

'That you were married to Alphonse Gordon. I believe that you bore a child to him. That marriage was annulled some years later. I found no subsequent record of the child. Amy was adopted by you as an infant but is no blood relation.'

In the silence of the room I could hear the ferocity of the storm. Rain now, as well as fifty-mile-per-hour winds. It was some time before Madeline broke the silence. There was sadness in her voice. And resignation.

'First I merely prayed that I could hide the past in all its hideousness and lovelessness. Then I thought I could forget it. And, for years, I did both. Even the long-ago nightmares were gone. Now it seems that they are all back: the past, the memories and the nightmares.'

For the first time since I had met her she looked like an old woman. To lose hope and the future is to begin to die.

'No. Not necessarily, but we must fight back from a position of strength and knowledge. Don't give up hope, Madeline. Don't stop fighting.'

'You are still willing to help me? Even after – I am ashamed to admit this – my lies?'

'Yes.'

'I am afraid. Of many things. But also of the truth. Perhaps you will not want to help me if you hear the truth?'

'Perhaps, but I don't think so. Not from what I know of you so far.'

'But it is a risk . . .'

'Life is a risk,' I agreed.

She nodded. Her face was calm once again but her hands still twisted relentlessly in her lap.

CHAPTER 10

Dear Santa,
Could you please bring me a brand new bike. And my sister
too. We have never had anything new. Lisa wants a red one
and I want a blue one.

Tammy Thompsen

P.S.
Could we have a coloring book and some crayons too. Please.
Thank you!!!

Madeline spoke quietly. 'I read in the newspaper the other day that a woman gave her eight-year-old daughter to a man in payment for a crack debt. Eight years old; he raped her. Women are sold more often than we know. I was thirteen and it was a gambling debt of my father's.'

The silence in the room was absolute.

'I hadn't led a sheltered life. My father was a gambler and a drinker and my stepmother an alcoholic who had died the year before. My mother died when I was a small child, I have no memory of her. Still, nothing in my unhappy and unloved childhood prepared me for what was to come.'

I could hear the wind outside, howling at us and shrieking around the corners and edges of the house.

'They lied about my age – this father and husband of mine – paid off the minister, I am sure. The man my father illegally married me to was as despicable as he.'

'Alphonse Gordon?'

'Yes. I did not know his full name until years later when I had a lawyer track down the records and annul the marriage. I never heard him called anything but Big Al. He was not a big man. Not in stature, or heart, or understanding. He was little and mean. And he was forty-five to my thirteen. The wedding took place at ten in the morning. By noon he was drunk. I was raped repeatedly that night. When he finally passed out I was too frightened and broken even to cry. Even to wash the blood from my legs.'

She looked at me dry-eyed. I could hear the winds pounding the house. The full force of the rains hadn't come yet.

'Over the years I have cried a great deal about that night but I didn't then. I was afraid he would kill me if he heard. I was always afraid he would kill me. Day or night that fear never left me. He did not love me, of course, nor even particularly favor me. I was nothing to him but strong arms and a strong back and the warm place between my legs. He worked me as one would a slave or an animal.

'I think I must have gotten pregnant almost immediately. I was too ignorant of womanhood to recognize or understand the physical signs and changes in my body. It was only when he started making coarse comments that I understood. I never saw a doctor. He said that if pigs and cows could give birth unassisted, then I could as well.

'I thought when he raped me that first night that my body was being torn apart, that my insides were ripped up and mangled and there was no pain I could ever experience that would equal it. I was wrong. I found that out when – alone and not yet fourteen – I gave birth in an unheated house on a freezing-cold January morning.

'The child was a boy. Again and again I have tried to remember his face but I cannot. I can only remember looking between his legs and seeing what he was.' Madeline put her hands over her eyes as if to blot out the pictures, the memories.

'I wish that I could say he was stillborn. Or that I can't remember what happened next. Or that I acted in pain and fear and madness. But none of that is true. I was filled with a deep, cold rage. I saw, not an innocent boy child, but the father and the husband who had violated my innocence and childhood; I saw, not his little face, but the maleness that had brought so much misery and pain into my life. I covered his face with a kitchen cloth. He was so little, he hardly struggled at all, it was over in a moment. By the time I had cleansed myself the small body was already cold.'

Her voice was passionless, as though time had wrung dry the emotion as well as the memory.

'I walked to the gully where we tossed the household garbage. And I left him with the debris. It was only a matter of time, I knew, before the feral dogs in the neighborhood would find it and destroy it. I called him it already.

'I padded my dress to feign pregnancy and pleaded female problems for the next month, and slowly I got my strength back. Then one morning when there was a brief break in the weather and Big Al was away, I put all of my clothes on in layers, took whatever money or valuables I could find, and walked six miles to a small town where I caught a bus. I bought a ticket to a large town several hundred miles away and then I bought another and then another until finally I reached a city in California. I thought California was a land of honey and oranges, of sweet dreams and rainbows and sunshine. Bakersfield was my last stop. I picked it for the name. It sounded so warm and homey. And I was almost out of money.'

She looked at me, Madeline now, and not that lost and frightened girl she had been once. 'It's a mistake, you know, to think that a city will be anything like the pretty picture you have imagined.'

'Yes.' I have made the same mistake. More than once actually.

'I couldn't believe how little money I had left. I had eaten almost nothing, trying to save my funds for travel. But when I reached Bakersfield I didn't have money enough for another ticket. The bus station was not in such a good part of town but I asked directions of a friendly clerk and set off walking, trying to ignore the hungry eyes of the men that I passed. There were many then, in those Depression years, who were unemployed with nothing better to do than stare and call out at an odd and frightened girl with raggedy clothes.'

'Directions to where? Did you know someone in Bakersfield?'

'No. I asked for the bakery. You see how young and naive I was.'

'But there was one? And you found it?'

'Oh yes. The woman behind the counter was the owner though I did not know that then. I told her I was looking for work and asked her for a job. I said I was a strong girl and a hard worker and would

71

do anything. She looked at me strangely. Many many people were desperate for work then, but they were mostly men. Rarely was it a woman. Or a girl.

'She asked me if I was hungry, and when I nodded, gave me a raisin bun and a cup of milk. She asked me where my family was and I told her my mother was dead and my father a drunk who had not used me well, and so I had run away from him.

'An odd look passed over her face then. I think perhaps she had a notion of what I had suffered. She was a kind and generous woman and it was a very great blessing for me that I met her, and a blessing I was sorely in need of. She put me in the back of the shop where a man and a boy were baking and told me to rest. It was warm and sweet-smelling and I fell asleep, tumbled over onto the bags of flour, with a sense of peace in my heart that I had never known.'

A quiet look crept over her face, of peace perhaps, or love.

'I stayed with Emily and her family for four years. She treated me like the daughter she had never had. Goodness knows I had never had a mother. I loved her dearly. I worked hard in the bakery and I had my own little room and pretty things and went to church and socials with the family. They told everyone who asked that I was a cousin from Missouri. Oh my but they were happy years. I might have stayed there forever had not their eldest son fallen in love with me. He wanted to marry me. Everyone wanted the marriage.

'Everyone but me. After Big Al I wanted no man as my husband. Though I came to like and even trust Emily's husband and sons, their minister and other friends of the family, I wanted never to be close to a man, nor to be in the power of one. I had to tell Emily the truth, some part of it. I think it about broke her heart, the hurt to me before and then to all of us. I made up my mind to leave.

'I decided to go to San Francisco and try to be a live-in governess, maybe someday a schoolteacher. Emily's husband found me a ride with a trucker who promised to take me to a respectable boardinghouse for young ladies. Emily gave me clothes and money and made me promise to come back if it didn't work out. And to write. There wasn't a dry eye when I left.'

I felt a sense of foreboding, even though Madeline's face was calm and things had obviously turned out well. It was impossible not to be afraid for that hurt child, then a young woman of eighteen, she had made so real for me. 'And San Francisco?' I asked.

'Oh, San Francisco!' she sparkled. 'What a beautiful city it is – the hills and the views, the old houses and churches, the waterfront and ferries and the parks and flowers, the museums and the Tea Garden, the stores and shops and cable cars and Chinatown and North Beach, the opera and theater! Oh Lord, how I loved that city. All the different colors and people and languages and sounds and smells. I loved it from the moment I saw it!

'And it loved me right back. The rooming house was decent and respectable and I made friends with a young woman there. And I got a governess job.' Her face darkened. 'The woman was very nice. The children were spoiled but we got on. It was the husband – I could see he was going to be a problem. I had turned into a very pretty young woman, you see. He started coming home when his wife was out. That one, he was not the gentleman or gentle man that Emily's son was.

'In tears I confided in my girlfriend who took me to the dance hall where she worked. She told me that a girl could make more money by being nice to the gentlemen but that there was no pressure to do so. And I found that to be true. I started off as a cigarette girl but in no time I was on stage singing and dancing. It all came so naturally to me. And then the theater. I loved it, and I was a hit. I, who had not been loved for most of my life, was adored by many. But I kept it all at an enjoyable distance; I let no one get close enough to hurt me.

'It was a wild, gay time of life and I was a wild, gay, almost happy girl. I forgot – I *made* myself forget – my father and Big Al. I re-created myself as so many come to California to do. In time I became the mistress of a wealthy man. He was kind to me, loved me well. Old enough to be my father. I wonder now if I didn't seek in him the love and security that I had never gotten from my father. I even came to tolerate his touch, though I never enjoyed or sought out physical intimacy. And I took great care never to become pregnant again.'

Her fingers, intertwined and twisted, were white-knuckled with her fierce grip.

'He taught me a great deal, manners and culture and the ways of society. He encouraged me to read and educate myself and bought me books and paint boxes. When he saw that I had a head for figures he taught me numbers and math. And then he explained to me how his business worked and let me learn whatever I would. He was a stockbroker and a commodities trader. He gave me money of my own to invest and let me manage the little house he had bought for me. I will always be grateful to him.

'As good as I was on stage, I was even better with investments. He told me that I had a natural genius for it and encouraged me greatly. That skill and training has stood me in good stead all my life, has brought all this to me.' She gestured with her hands.

'At thirty I stopped dancing and moved, with my dear friend's blessing, to Sacramento where I could join respectable society. I returned to church, became a patron of the arts and active in charitable work. I was content, if not happy.'

Madeline shifted in her seat, her hands stilled now in her lap.

'There is a little room here in my house with no furniture or adornment save a rug and a small table with a bowl of fresh flowers on it. Not a day goes by that I do not fall to my knees and pray for forgiveness and the soul of the little one whose life I smothered before it could even start. God is all-loving and forgiving, I know. He has forgiven me; it is I who cannot forgive myself.'

She sighed and there was a long silence in the room broken only by a log falling and sparks popping against the screen.

'I have always been attracted to charities for children. For many years I went as a volunteer to the orphanage. There I would hold and cuddle, sing to and love the little babies that no one wanted. There I met Amy. She had been abandoned as an infant, not only an unwanted child but one with a severe physical problem.

'I had never desired a child, a family of my own. I was content to watch life pass by as I stood in the wings. Giving up something – yes, I recognized that full well – but that was acceptable to me. No, more than acceptable, necessary – for I felt that I could not endure the pain that I understood and accepted as a necessary part of family life. And—' Her voice broke.

'And I feared something in myself too. I feared the part of me that had killed an infant. The adult I became could understand the terror, the desperation, the fight for survival that defined the child I had once been. And I hoped that that was the answer. And I feared it might not be. That fear is an awful thing. It has haunted me most of my life.'

She did not meet my eyes and I was relieved. The pain and fear of others haunts me too. I could hear the rain now. High winds lashed it against the windows in a furious pummeling. Trees flailed wildly in the wind and the skies were dark. It seemed a long time that I listened to the storm shriek and waited for Madeline to speak again.

'And then I saw Amy. And held her. And, much against my judgment and wishes, I came to love her. Those eyes. They are the same as mine. Perhaps you noticed?'

I nodded in unseen agreement. Madeline was gazing at the fire, not waiting for a response.

'Very soon she came to recognize me, my voice, even the sound of my footsteps, and her little head would turn when she heard me and her eyes seek me out. She didn't just smile then but crowed with delight and held out her arms to me, held her little face to mine when I picked her up. Even then her small legs dragged against me.

'I was lost. And afraid. For I had killed one innocent child. What right had I to allow myself to become close to another? I prayed to God every day. I prayed that He would harden my resolve, that a good and dear family would come for my Amy, that something, anything, would happen. But it did not. It was too late, of course. Already I thought of her as mine. God never spoke to me – I prayed for that too – but finally I came to believe that perhaps He had sent me this child to gladden my heart and help me make amends.

'I was in my fifties then and a spinster, not an ideal choice for a parent. But there was, and still is, very little hope for a child like Amy. Everyone wants a perfect child and the first requirement in that perfection is physical health and wholeness. I chose a child no one wanted and I was a respected and well-known member of the community, a woman of means. Gladly they let me adopt Amy.

'Now my prayers are different – not only for forgiveness but in thanksgiving. I thank Him for the loving gift He gave me. I thank Him from the bottom of my heart.'

Madeline turned and looked at me then. 'Do you know what Amy means?'

I shook my head, puzzled at the question, at her meaning.

'Her name means beloved. It was I who named her. She came to the orphanage unnamed. No home. No future. No past. No name. She is her name in every way, beloved not just by me but by all who know her. Dearly dearly beloved.

'Do you see?' She held my gaze and her voice was beseeching now. 'The blackmailer threatened all that. And I was afraid. Not for myself and my reputation. I am an old woman, and a sensible one – I did not think that those who had known and respected me all these years would suddenly change their opinions. By them I will not now be judged on one incident, however horrific, but on my character and a lifetime of achievement. You see,' she smiled wryly, 'how strong I can sound. And be. But not around Amy. There I am afraid. I could not bear to lose her love and respect. That is what I cherish and value most in this world.

'A hundred thousand dollars was, is, nothing to me in the face of that fear. I paid. Almost without thinking I paid. The thought came later, of course. And with that thought came another fear. The fear that it wasn't over, wouldn't be over, that the first payment was only the beginning of a nightmare that would destroy not just me – what did I care about that? – but Amy and the love we shared and had so carefully built. About that I cared. Deeply.

'Oh, I had so much, so very much to lose. I was the perfect target for blackmail, was I not?'

The question was rhetorical and I did not attempt to answer it.

'Sometimes those of us who are haunted recognize each other. There was something about Jim Randolph, something that I saw and recognized without being able to define. I said nothing, of course. One does not.' She paused in reflection. 'Jim Randolph was a very generous donor to Hope For Kids. Did you know that?'

'Yes.'

'I wondered whether he had given freely or under duress. Murder is an awful thing, to be sure, violence from the outside tearing away a life. But suicide? That is violence within tearing away, destroying a life. They both frighten me a great deal. Enough to call you. Enough even to tell the truth.'

There was a ripping, rending sound and then a crash as a branch outside was torn from a tree by the wind and carelessly, heedlessly thrown to the ground.

CHAPTER 11

Let Nothing You Dismay . . .

The band was loud and, I thought, not very good, but that was difficult to tell, musical nuance having been lost in volume. We were gliding around the floor, J.O. and I, to the tune of 'My Way,' a good song forever ruined for me by its association with Frank Sinatra. As it turned out, J.O. was a really good dancer and in his arms I was temporarily lost in the music.

And in my thoughts.

The Hope For Kids extravaganza was like every other posh fundraiser I've been to. First champagne and circulation. The circulation was supposed to involve bidding in the silent auction as well as evaluation of the major auction items; it was also time to see and be seen, to compare one's dress, date or spouse to everyone else's, and to talk.

Then dinner and more wine. The food and wines were superb. This was a given at two hundred and fifty a plate. After dinner winners of the silent auction were announced and then the big-ticket items auctioned off by TV news entertainers long on flash and slick looks and short on personality. And finally dancing.

I had kicked into high gear right away. I had a glass of wine in my hand but I wasn't drinking: I was working. Champagne is a great camouflage. Charity had seated us at a table that consisted, as far as I could tell from her hurried and whispered asides, of the head honchos within Hope For Kids.

'My dear, isn't this wonderful!' A slim hand with virulent red, polished nails and fingers dripping with diamonds reached across the table in front of me and gripped the wrist of the gentleman on my left. 'All these people! And the publicity – it's money in the bank!' She leaned toward him and I, apparently invisible, leaned back so as to be safely out of the way of the pointy, predatory breasts that were bearing down on me. A miasma of perfume engulfed me.

'Jackie.' The gentleman's voice was gently chiding. 'I am afraid that in the excitement we are forgetting our manners. Forgive me,' he added, turning to me. 'We were introduced but so quickly that I must confess that I have mislaid your name.' His smile, like his voice, was gracious and charming. Instinctively I leaned toward him, as a plant does toward the sun.

'Kat Colorado,' I responded in answer to his question.

'Sam Gunther.' That smile again. 'I am a fund-raiser for Hope For Kids. And you?'

'A good friend of Charity's,' I dimpled sweetly. 'She is afraid I don't get out enough and insisted that I come.'

'I'm so glad she did. Have you met Jackie Anderson, our director?'

I turned to Jackie to acknowledge the introduction and received a slight nod and a glacial stare. Talk about special. Before I could turn back to Gunther she deigned to speak. Since I was working, I deigned to listen.

'Then, you are not a supporter of Hope For Kids?'

'No. Not yet. I have just learned about your organization.'

Her lip curled. Have I mentioned that her lipstick matched her nails? There was a smear on her front tooth and it looked like blood. The diamonds in her ears and around her neck and descending into her cleavage winked at me. Her lip curled a little more. She was about thirty-five and, except for the sneer, sexy, vivacious, and beautiful in the ravishing kind of way.

'But I am here with a purpose. My godmother wished me to look into Hope For Kids. She is filthy rich and always looking for places to throw her money. "Better a good cause than the IRS" is her motto.' I smiled disingenuously.

Jackie smiled back, then laid her talons affectionately on my arm.

80

I felt suddenly like a sparrow caught in a hawk's sights. My smile wobbled a bit in her predatory glare. Forget cold indifference. Consider fearsome greed.

'*Really?* And what is your godmother's name?'

'She wishes to remain anonymous,' I said coyly, the power of my lies going to my head with great rapidity.

'Ah.' Jackie tried to look understanding. '*Not* that it matters, or that we would *ever* dream of badgering your godmother. Quite the contrary, although it is true that we would be most interested in her support and most happy to provide her with information and answer any questions she might have.'

'I'll tell her.'

'Perhaps I could take your godmother out to lunch? I would love to do that.'

'I'll tell her that too,' I said agreeably. And then I turned away. It's not that there wasn't more to be gotten from Jackie. There was. Or that I couldn't get it. I could. It's just that I was temporarily sickened and needed a break.

'Mr Gunther, do tell me about your work.'

'Gladly.' The corners of his mouth twitched. 'But I hope you will call me Sam?'

'Sam,' I agreed.

He was older than I by twenty to twenty-five years, mid to late fifties. His hair, once dark, was graying, thinning slightly and neatly trimmed, as was his mustache. The tux showed off his wide shoulders to advantage. He was stocky without being heavy and, I guessed, about five foot ten. He would be charming to everyone, I thought, but especially to women. This was not a guess.

'There are as many definitions of a fund-raiser as there are people who fill the job.' He reached across the table for a wine bottle, filled his glass, glanced at mine – still almost half full – and set the bottle down. 'Support can be solicited on three levels: through grants, corporate donations, and individual donations. My focus is almost entirely on the first two.'

'You don't look like a fund-raiser to me. Not,' I added hastily, 'that I have the least idea what a fund-raiser looks like.'

'I'm retired military.'

I let my breath out in a whoosh. Yes. That was *exactly* what he looked like.

'I am financially comfortable in my retirement but,' he shrugged, 'easily bored.'

'There is more to it than that, I think,' I said, reading his eyes.

'That is astute of you.' He smiled at me. 'When I was in the military, I saw a great deal of killing and destruction. I am proud of my career, proud that I had the chance to serve my country.' He sipped at his wine thoughtfully. 'And now I am grateful that I have a chance to do work that is healing in nature.'

'Sam, may I borrow you for a moment? There is someone I should like you to meet.' An elegant woman drifted into view and rested her hand on Sam's shoulder.

'I hope we will have the chance to continue our conversation.' Sam spoke warmly to me. His comment was not a formality and I did not take it as such.

'He's something, isn't he?' Jackie's voice cut into my thoughts, softer, warmer than I had yet heard it. 'Fund-raisers generally take a percentage of what they raise. He declines, taking nothing but the most minimal of expenses. I wish *I* could say that I was that altruistic.' She laughed.

'But one can't forget Number One. Of course Hope For Kids is a close second. I think I would do anything for money. And anything for this organization.' The diamond-studded pin nestled in Jackie's cleavage was in the shape of a huge dollar sign. 'And if people won't give willingly, why then they should be *made* to. Forcefully, if necessary.'

She laughed what I assumed was meant to be a happy little trill but really sounded like a buzzard at feeding time. I didn't laugh with her although I managed a feeble smile.

'Dear dear Sam is quite the exception but others can be encouraged to give, don't you think?' Another buzzard cackle. 'Oh Henry dear, do come meet Kat.' Jackie introduced us and then walked away, other fish to fry, no doubt. Or altruism to force?

Was forced altruism blackmail?

I chatted with Henry who, I was finally able to ascertain, was on the board of directors and was genial and good-natured to the point of coma, and only slightly more boring than Humpty-Dumpty, to whom he bore an unfortunate physical resemblance. Charity appeared just as I was feeling desperate.

'Oh Henry, do excuse us!' She flashed a dazzling smile and whisked me off.

And I wondered if there was the look of a blackmailer about Jackie or Sam or Henry. Only blackmail has no look. Neither does murder.

But both leave tracks. And it was time to look for them.

I followed Charity and switched over to cobra. Here is my definition of cobra: striking without warning – swift, silent, and deadly.

Here is how we worked: Charity and I had done the research, knew who the major contributors (defined as two thousand and up) were. Charity had even pulled strings and wormed out the names of many of the anonymous contributors. We would sidle (do snakes sidle? slither?) up to these generous souls and Charity would introduce me. We would be generally charming and then I would gush about how absolutely, *totally* wonderful I thought it was to be so giving but – I would add demurely – I did wonder, just a *wee* bit, why people gave. Was it human kindness and compassion, true generosity, a tax write-off (laughter on my part), or (a dramatic drop in voice) a guilty conscience.

Hisssss. The fangs in place, the venom released.

When the dancing started I changed tactics. Dancing, like champagne, is a good cover. On the dance floor J.O. pushed me away in a slow twirl, then pulled me back in and tucked me in his arms, nibbling on my ear.

'Cut it out, J.O.! Those earrings are expensive, never mind that I am revolted at the thought of any of your bodily fluids on me.'

Tact is wasted on J.O. Directness is too. He laughed at my comment as though my intent was to flatter and amuse. The band was playing 'Fascination.' He pulled me in closer and licked my neck.

'I suppose you think that because we're in a social situation with a thousand or so other people I wouldn't knee you in the groin?' I asked conversationally.

He chuckled but it had a nervous edge. And he pulled back. *The cobra strikes again.* Jeez. This band was forever stuck on slow songs. I glanced over the dance floor, found what I was after.

The band swung into 'Girl From Ipanema' and J.O. started flinging and twirling me about. I flung and slung and twirled in one direction only.

'Just a reminder, Kat,' J.O. said tartly as he caught up with me, 'the guy's supposed to lead.'

'No!' I exclaimed in astonishment., 'Really?' I picked up about five feet in a swing, J.O. trailing. 'That *can't* be. I *know* they would have told me in finishing school!' I winked at a reluctant J.O. and dragged him the last three feet, then switched over to cobra, poised and with prey in sight.

I had a great side view: blond head, broad shoulders, narrow hips, long legs and a killer bod. That was the man. The woman was a short, plumpish, drabbish type of person, plain and undistinguished. I reached out to tap him on the shoulder.

'May I cut in?' I dimpled prettily.

He looked at his wife, who first looked alarmed and then looked at J.O. and smiled. *Pretty Boy scores again.*

'Nibble on *her* ear, big boy,' I whispered as I transferred myself out of J.O.'s arms and into the big guy's. 'I can't believe how bold I'm being,' I said archly to my new partner.

He smiled at me and lifted an eyebrow, implying that he could believe it, and thought I could too.

'Okay,' I looked up through my eyelashes. 'I can.' I dimpled again, swayed in his arms just a little. 'Smoke Gets in Your Eyes.' Another slow song.

He laughed, subtly playing to me as I was to him. We were – by mutual consent, I thought – drifting away from his wife and J.O.

'May I confess something to you?' I was still arch.

'It goes with the territory.' He smiled down on me.

'I've always wanted to flirt with a minister.' Okay, I lied.

'This is your first try?' he queried. 'You do it well.' There was no note of condemnation or even toe-the-line in his voice.

'I find myself in need of counseling.'

Someone slammed into me from behind and sent me flying into his arms. He caught me, held me a nanosecond too long.

'Oh?'

'Do you minister just to those in your church or could I possibly

. . .' I let my voice drift off and my eyes drop for just a second before I raised them and stared boldly into his face.

He was looking down the front of my dress and didn't even blink when I caught him. 'Shall we say tomorrow, Sunday afternoon, after service around two o'clock?' he asked smoothly, his hand resting lightly on my hip, his thumb tucked into my waist.

'Oh, let's,' I agreed.

'At the church.'

A hand tapped my minister on the shoulder and J.O. reclaimed me. We switched partners smoothly.

'You definitely have a bitchy side, Kat,' J.O. said affably as he steered me away.

Bitch? No, I was still into cobra, had in fact made several hits tonight and was very pleased with myself. Big Boy was a good one. God's Word was not the only thing he spread, I was sure of it.

'Katy, do come, there's someone I want you to meet.' Charity was at my elbow. The last strains of 'Dock of the Bay' faded out.

'Not you, J.O.' Charity dismissed him with a gesture. 'You're rude and annoying.' Charity knows J.O. too well to waste courtesy on him.

J.O. laughed. 'And dry. I'm off in search of booze. If you want me back, Kat, you'll have to beg.'

'What are the odds?' I asked, as I followed Charity. 'A million to one? Two million? Ten?'

'Hush, Katy, and listen to me. Remember Delia? Her husband, Robert Melton, is a state assemblyman. Very ambitious. Remember?'

'Yes.'

'I looked up their contribution.' She arched an eyebrow at me.

'How much?'

'Ten thousand.'

Ten thousand. I whistled.

'And?'

'And I think she once used the stage name Delilah Delightful.'

'Stripper?'

Charity shrugged. 'Maybe. Maybe porn films?'

'How did you find this out?'

'I can't tell you.'

The reason Charity hears so much is that she is the soul of discretion.

'Is the information reliable?'

'I think so. Oh drat! Where did she go?'

The crowd was thinning out, but not quite enough to locate someone easily and quickly.

'Rats, I can't see her.'

I decided to go to the ladies' room. Call it a hunch. I struck out on those nearest to the ballroom, bingo on the third try. Delia was blotting her eyes and stabbing on a fresh layer of crimson lipstick in an ineptly orchestrated routine. It was smudged and uneven and she stared at it bleakly and then began swearing under her breath. The swearing stopped as the bathroom door swung shut and she looked up and caught sight of me in the mirror.

The bleak look changed to a stony stare and then her gaze dropped. She picked up her bag and got ready to depart, crimson smear and all.

'I'd like to talk to you.'

'Please.' She started to edge past me. 'You'll have to excuse me.' Her face was white and the lipstick stark and ugly. Her hand reached out to push the door open.

'Blackmail is a horrible thing.'

'I don't know what you're talking about.' Her hand dropped to her side, where it hung listlessly. She made no further move to leave.

'I do not mean to threaten you in any way,' I said gently. 'I am acting on someone else's behalf. I mean to stop it. This would be to your advantage. I hope you will assist me by answering a few questions.'

'I don't know what you're talking about.' Her voice was dull and toneless. The evening bag in her hand started to slip and she clutched it to her breast. Her eyes were huge and there were dark half-moons under them.

'I understand your husband is running for reelection.'

Her eyes, immense as they already were, widened. I wouldn't have thought it possible. 'He knows nothing about this,' she blurted out, and then a hand flew to her mouth. Too late she realized that sticking with a flat denial and ignorance was the better tactic.

God, I hate blackmailers. And bullies. I was feeling a little like a bully though I was trying not to act like one. I reached out a hand to reassure her, winced inside as she flinched.

'Please believe that I have no intention of hurting you in any way. I only want to stop this. Will you tell me what happened?'

'And that's the end of it?' Her voice was stilted.

'Yes.'

'Someone called me and said enough about . . . about something in the past that would . . . ummm . . . embarrass me – and my husband – if it came out, which it would, he said, unless I chose to make a ten-thousand-dollar contribution to Hope For Kids.' She smiled at me in an attempt to be brave and stoic that almost broke my heart. 'Naturally I was happy to contribute to such a good cause.'

Naturally.

'Naturally I—' Her eyes brimmed with tears. 'Oh shit, shit, shit,' she murmured. 'Please. I've got to get back. My husband is waiting. Please. I—'

I stepped back, out of her way. 'Was it a man – the blackmailer?'

'I don't know.' She shook her head. 'He had a low voice but it was odd-sounding. I assumed . . . but I don't know.'

She took the business card I held out to her without even looking at it and was gone. I washed my hands, feeling dirty, and went back to the ballroom in search of Charity. To say that I didn't feel like dancing anymore was an understatement. A huge one.

J.O. snagged me a little later as I waited outside for the valet to bring my car around. 'How about a ride, Kat?' He tucked his arm cozily into mine and gave me his two-hundred-dollar thousand-watt smile.

'No.' I shook the arm off and moved away from him in a message that J.O. chose to ignore. Big surprise there.

'I shouldn't drive, you know, had way too much to drink. You wouldn't want to read about it in the paper tomorrow.' He dropped his voice and intoned solemnly, '"*Bee*'s star reporter killed in traffic accident."'

'I wouldn't, no,' I agreed. How about: '"*Bee*'s loudmouth reporter jailed on drunken walking charges." You cooling your heels overnight in county accommodations – now *that* has appeal.' I smiled at the thought and moved forward, next in line now. A perspiring young man took my ticket and trotted off.

'Have a heart, Katy.'

'No.'

'I've got something to show you.'

I looked at him briefly and evaluated the odds. 'No.'

'Seriously.' He grinned at me.

'What?'

'A photo of Randolph and a young woman, a young woman not his wife.' J.O.'s grin widened. 'A very pretty young woman.'

My Bronco appeared in a squeal of tires and snarl of brakes. I handed the valet two bucks and climbed in the door he held open for me. 'Get in,' I said to J.O., and watched as he sauntered around to the passenger side. *Cobra*, I reminded myself as he climbed in. Cobra.

Still, it went against my better judgment.

J.O. lived in a dumpy little place in East Sac within walking distance of the *Bee*. The area was once nice but has gone downhill. The principle of urban renewal is at work around here, but actual accomplishments are hit-and-miss.

The inside of J.O.'s place wasn't dumpy; it was spartan. The furniture was scarce and simple. No curtains, just old-fashioned roll-up window shades. No knick-knacks or pictures though there were stories and photos tacked up everywhere. And it was cold.

J.O. flipped on a wall heater, tossed his jacket on a chair and made his way to the kitchen where he grabbed a bottle of bourbon and a water glass. 'What can I get you, Kat?'

'The photograph.'

'Hey! What happened to your manners?' He grinned at me. 'I seem to remember you chiding me on that very issue not so long ago. I thought observing the social amenities was de rigueur.'

'Oh for godssakes, J.O., cut the crap.' I sat in a straight-backed wooden chair, the kind that used to be – and maybe still is – in libraries, and eased off a pump. *Ouch*. I could see the blister right through the heel of my jet-black panty hose. 'The photograph and a Band-Aid,' I amended my request. '*And* cut the crap.'

'Anything for you, Kat.' He bowed in a courtly fashion and left the room, the same stupid grin on his face, the glass of bourbon in his hand. The bourbon level had already dropped considerably, I noticed. 'Allow me.' He had returned with a Band-Aid and was trying to open it.

'Don't even think about it, J.O. You'd have to put your drink down. Way too stressful.'

He grinned at me. 'You're right.' He lounged over to a threadbare sofa and draped himself on it, arm across the back, an ankle resting on his knee.

'Very manly,' I said in mock appreciation. I peeled the Band-Aid and plastered it on top of my panty hose, then eased my shoe back on.

'It's warming up in here now. Take your coat off, Kat.'

'I'm not staying long enough. Either you produce the photo or I'm out of here. Make up your mind, J.O.'

'Over there.' He jerked his head toward a desk covered with a number of more or less orderly piles of stuff. 'And it's photos, there're two of them.'

I sucked in a breath. It wasn't what I expected, not at all.

'"God rest ye merry gentlemen, let nothing you dismay . . ."' J.O. sang in a rich baritone.

CHAPTER 12

Dear Santa,
I want a bike and a dog and a million dollars for Christmas.
Then I'll be your best friend.

Love from Allie

'So?' I glanced at the pictures and then at J.O.

'Nice, huh? A picture's worth a thousand words, they say. Shit, these are the kind of pictures they had in mind. Sometimes one picture is worth a million bucks, too.' He grinned at me, looking more than ever like a slightly dangerous and inebriated Robert Redford. I don't understand how the world works – why weasely guys are so good-looking, for instance.

Two photos. The first was of Jim Randolph and a girl coming out of a downtown building. I wouldn't swear to it – there wasn't enough of the building in the picture – but I was pretty sure it was the jail. Randolph looked like a lawyer: three-piece suit, shined shoes, briefcase, grim expression. The girl looked like a scared college girl. The second was a booking photo. She wasn't scared here, terrified was more like it. The black-and-white numbers were stark across her chest.

'Hand me the bourbon, willya Kat?' J.O.'s words slurred together very slightly but his hand was steady when I held out the bottle to him. He was a trouper, all right.

I tossed the photos back on the desk in a gesture of disgust. 'A million words? A million bucks?' I made no attempt to keep the fatigue and irritation out of my voice. 'If there's something there, I'm not

91

smart enough to get it. You win, J.O. You suckered me into a ride home.'

'You're smart enough, Kat, but here's a hint. How often does a probate attorney bail a client out of jail? Hell, you can't get bailed out of where Randolph's clients go. It's a one-way ticket.'

'I don't know, J.O. Not often, probably.' I shrugged. 'Who cares? Maybe this came up and he couldn't get ahold of anyone. Who cares? Maybe we'll never know. Who cares? Am I making myself clear here? Do you catch my drift here?'

'This is different, Kat. Anytime you have a death, the differences in a life become interesting. It's important, trust me.'

'Yeah? Have fun, J.O.' I looked around for my bag, then remembered I'd left it in the car. My keys were in my coat pocket still. 'This is the kind of stuff you wanted to trade with me? Wow.' My voice was tired and bored.

J.O. poured more bourbon in his glass. I hoped he owned stock in sour mash. A lot of it. The slur in his voice was getting more noticeable.

'I forgot about your cheap shots.' He tossed down a heavy belt of whiskey.

'That's you, not me. You're the king of cheap shots, J.O.' I spoke gently.

'Acting like there's nothing there. Bullshit. Not that I wouldn't do the same thing in your place.' A long sexy grin. 'How better to discredit an opponent than by undermining his confidence.' Another slow, easy grin.

Lounge lizard meets *Streetcar Named Desire*, I reflected.

'We're not opponents and I can't touch your confidence. Nobody ever could. Go to bed, J.O.'

'I'll walk you to your car.' His walk was smooth, his voice a little husky now, a drawl with the memory of Texas.

'I'm okay, thanks.'

'Well then, I'll kiss you goodnight.'

He reached out and pulled me into his arms and kiss, a slow soft kiss. I swear I could smell honeysuckle, hear slow, muted melancholy strains of music. And the screams of Blanche DuBois. I could taste bourbon and smell aftershave and something primal and masculine and J.O. I pulled away and turned quickly on my heel. The Band-Aid slipped and the pain of the blister bit into me, a jagged reminder as I opened the door.

I made one hell of a cobra.

'Where are you going?' he asked softly. He made no move to close the distance between us, just reached out a hand and touched my lip gently. 'Pretty lady.' No smile on his face, no mockery in his eyes.

Something inside me shivered. 'Plan B?' I asked. My voice sounded husky and strange.

He raised an eyebrow and touched my cheek. 'Plan B?'

'I remember you saying you'd go to bed with anyone for a story. Even a dog.'

He laughed, the sound loud in the muffled midnight fog that drifted in on us. 'Get your facts straight, baby. Not anyone, just women. But that doesn't apply here. This is plan A, not B.'

'A?'

'You, Kat. I've wanted you for a long time. It was strong, dancing with you tonight. But that's not when it started. Desire starts between the ears, not the legs. Your independence, your strength, your go-to-hell attitude: I love it, I always have. And you're a beautiful woman.' His finger drifted along my cheek and across my lip and down my chin. The shiver in me became a tremble. 'It ain't the bourbon talkin', Katy darlin', it's me – coming out of hiding and telling the truth. Meet me halfway.'

He reached out with both hands for my waist. I stepped back. He dropped his arms to his sides. But his smile, that slow sexy drawling smile, stayed in place. The tremble inside me became an ache. I was suddenly sure that there was something deep and important in me that was unfulfilled.

And I remembered Blanche DuBois.

And that all is fair in love and war.

I left, this time for real.

''Night, darlin'.' J.O.'s drawl followed me out the door and into the fog. I turned to look at him. Standing in the doorway with his hands in his pockets, his legs crossed at the ankle, and his head tilted sideways at me. Black-and-white. He would have fit right in in Casablanca.

It was the kind of night and I was in the kind of mood where it

93

would have suited me to drive savagely and wildly, speeding through town and onto the freeway. It was the kind of night, the kind of fog, where that would have been suicide. I drove slowly and carefully, five or ten miles per hour in the deepest pockets of fog, hands tense on the steering wheel, eyes searching for the white lines on the road. I couldn't see the edges of the road. I couldn't see what was in front of me.

In the fog everything is quiet and muffled, not as much as in a snowfall at night, but almost. All the noise, all the violence and savagery and wildness, was within me.

And the questions and recriminations.

J.O. was right, of course. About the photos.

Dammit. He was onto the girl. Dammit, dammit, *dammit*. I hadn't looked at the photos for long – not wanting to give them any importance – but I hadn't had to. I recognized her as the girl in the videotape immediately. The girl? The daughter? The blackmailer?

The unknown factor.

And I had memorized the booking number.

All of it made me jumpy. I didn't want J.O. to figure this one out. He could, and would, do many things with it. Handling it discreetly was not one of them.

How had J.O. gotten those pictures? And what else did he know?

I turned on the radio. Linda Ronstadt singing 'Desperado.'

There was a single message for me when I got home. Hank's voice: 'I'm on my way, Katy. I'll be there by morning.'

I went to sleep in a foggy confusion of male voices: Jim Randolph, J.O., Hank, others that I couldn't distinguish. Too many men, I thought sleepily. I felt trampled by testosterone, or pheromones or . . . something . . .

I woke up to one voice. I thought it was a dream at first. Ranger had barked but only briefly, not enough to alert me, to wake me. It was still dark and it wasn't just the voice. It was the touch, the kisses. It wasn't a dream.

I woke up again at eight-thirty. The dogs were getting rowdy – Hank had brought Mars, his black Lab – and were eager to go outside. I let them out, turned up the heat and retrieved the paper from a bush across the yard. My paperboy is not only directionally challenged but a stranger to the concepts of practice and improvement. Then I got back into bed to warm up.

Hank woke up fast when I put my feet on him.

'Jeez, Katy,' he said sleepily, as he rolled over and tucked me into his arms. 'You been standing on ice cubes?' He groaned when I wrapped my arms around him. My hands were only slightly less freezing than my feet.

'Cold hands, warm heart,' I said cheerfully.

'Did you wear your slippers?'

Hank can be such a mom sometimes. He had gotten me fur-lined moccasins to keep my feet warm and toasty.

'I forgot. Anyway, I was just going to let the dogs out and turn up the heat but then I decided to get the paper. Walking through the wet grass was bad news.'

Hank's hand was under my, extra-huge T-shirt tracing delicate patterns on my back. I was warming up fast.

'I forgot something else too.'

'What?'

'How much I could miss you.'

'Show me.' He kissed me gently.

So that's what we did. I showed him how much I had missed him and he showed me how much he had missed me. It was ten-thirty, at least, before we got up. Of course it's important to dot all the *i*'s and cross all the *t*'s in Show-and-Tell.

'Okay, before *I* got up. I was all rested and peppy and ready to roll. Hank had driven all night, arrived at six a.m. and – counting our time-outs – had only had a couple of hours of sleep.

'C'mon,' I said. I was bouncing on the bed as I said it. 'Get up with me and let's have breakfast together. Then you can go back to sleep while I take care of some business.'

'All right,' he agreed, but his eyes were closing.

'Waffles,' I whispered in his ear. 'Going once, going twice . . . Do I hear . . .'

He yawned and tossed me and the covers back. 'Race you to the shower.'

I laughed. 'Like I'm going to fall for that again.'

Here's how this one works. Hank says I'll race you to the shower, and I'm in the shower all soaped and shampooed up before I figure out that he's back in bed asleep.

'No?' His voice was a little regretful.

'No. I'm right behind you, though.' Showering together isn't very efficient, but it's fun.

We didn't talk about much – that would come later – just caught up with things as I made breakfast and filled up my large, hungry boyfriend with waffles and juice and fresh fruit.

Then I tucked him back into bed and went off to meet a lawyer. And a minister.

Carter was a little testy. Although I am sensitive about a number of things, ruffling the feathers of a lawyer is not one of them.

'I don't like this, Kat, doing business on a Sunday afternoon at my home,' he grumbled.

'No?' I queried cheerfully. 'Well, too bad. You could have gotten back to me before this on Randolph's will. The timing was your call.'

'I don't see why it couldn't have waited until tomorrow.' More grumbles.

'Then let me tell you. A name: J.O. Edwards. He's got something he doesn't know the significance of yet, but he will if we give him enough time. I'm way ahead of him still; I'd like to keep it that way. And so would you.' It was a statement, not a question, and there was no mistaking the seriousness in my voice.

'Why don't you tell me about it,' he said, equally serious now, the grumpiness gone.

That was last thing I wanted to do. 'Why don't I do that when we have more time,' I stalled. 'I have a two o'clock appointment and I need to see the will. Translation,' I added. 'I need you to go over it with me and put it in English.'

Carter gestured to me to be seated across from him at his desk and pulled out the will. 'The bulk of his estate goes to Cathi. There are a number of charitable bequests and a provision for a lump sum to go to his first wife should he die in the time period when she was due alimony. Which he did.'

'Is Hope For Kids one of the charities?'

Carter gave me an odd glance. 'No. The largest bequest is to the Stanford University endowment fund. There are also bequests to a Vietnam vets organization and to a local scholarship fund for at-risk teenagers.'

'Personal bequests?'

He nodded. 'I thought that's where you were heading. Two items of interest. The first is not a bequest but a statement that, to his knowledge, he has no issue—'

'Issue?'

'Children. Further, if such a claim is ever made, such claim shall be settled by payment of ten thousand dollars upon receipt of proof of parentage. Such proof shall consist solely of DNA typing. Said payment will end any and all claims.'

'Would that hold up?'

'In my opinion it would.'

'And the second item: a bequest?'

'Also in the amount of ten thousand dollars, to a woman by the name of Moon Nguyen.'

'Is any reason given for this request?'

'No.'

'Did Randolph tell you?'

'No.'

'Do you have any idea?'

'No.'

Jeez, nothing worse than a gabby lawyer. This was like pulling teeth. 'Address? Phone number?'

He gave me an address.

'Anything else?'

'Of note? No. Everything else is standard.'

'Is this a large estate?'

Carter raised his eyebrow at me. 'Let me put it this way. It is Cathi's choice whether she works or not.'

'Does that include keeping the house?'

'The house and a Tahoe vacation property. Jim Randolph was a very sensible investor.'

Like me, I thought. Or rather, like I would be if I had any money to invest. I wondered which was scarier, growing old with no money or

97

dying young and not needing it. Right now I was a more likely candidate for the latter.

I stood, pushing back my chair, thanked Rick, and walked out into the chilling grayness of this winter Sunday afternoon.

One down, one to go.

I was looking forward to the minister.

CHAPTER 13

Dear Charity,
I told my husband if he gave me a two-carat diamond for
Christmas I would give him sex whenever he wanted. He was
upset but I don't see anything wrong with it, do you?
                                                    Sparkling Susan

Dear Sparkle,
Exchanging sex for money or goods is prostitution. Your
husband is upset because he doesn't want to be married to a
prostitute, especially at Christmas.
                                                    Charity

There are quite a few places of worship on Hazel Avenue in the stretch
between Madison and Douglas where Hazel turns into Sierra College
Boulevard. There is still room to develop out there and the land is
still relatively cheap.

The church I was looking for turned out to be a good-sized white
frame building with dark green trim, an older building that had been
recently repainted. It was surrounded by well-established trees and
set back from the road. The parking lot needed lines, leveling and
patching. A sign the size of a small billboard with movable letters in
the style of a theater marquee offered advice: *DIE NOW, PAY LATER!*
Or admonition. At one end of the building was a door with a sign,
Church Office, over it.

I parked and adjusted my attitude. Not private investigator, at least
not at first, but slightly simpering flirtatious woman in need of
'counseling.' I tucked my voice-activated minicassette recorder into

my blazer pocket, got out and slammed the Bronco door.

Sidney Johannsen. The Johannsen fit the blond Nordic-god good looks. And the Sidney? I've always disliked that name. Distrusted it. Sidney, the sideways sidewinder. Sidney, the smooth-talking, slick-walking, sleazy weasel. Sidney the— I reached the office door, turned the knob, walked in. A drab cluttered office decorated with sentimental religious pictures and gewgaws greeted me in silence. I saw no one and heard nothing. A round bell sat on the edge of the desk. I dinged it.

And waited expectantly for Sidney.

It wasn't a long wait.

He walked in looking smooth and dashing in cords, a heavy Scandinavian sweater and a high-volt smile.

I smiled back. Low-volt.

'Miss Colorado, how nice to see you. Won't you come into my office?' *Will you walk into my parlour?*

I stepped up my smile to medium-volt, threw in a little dimpling for effect. 'Oh yes, thank you.' I followed him demurely into an office that was a larger, more masculine, no-sentimental-stuff-here version of the outer office. It was furnished with a desk, two comfy chairs and – surprise! – a couch.

'Let's be informal, shall we?' *Said the Spider to the Fly.* He indicated the couch.

I seated myself there (translation: in the web), crossed my legs and folded my hands in my lap. *Hmmm. I hoped I wasn't overdoing the demure bit.* Sidney smiled at me. *Nope, I was fine.* And sat down about a foot and a half away.

'Since we're being informal, please call me Sid.' He leaned toward me; the web quivered and tightened.

'All right. Thank you.' I fluttered my lashes a little, hoping it looked sexy and not as though I had something in my eye. I made a quick mental note to practice fluttering.

'How may I help you?'

Sid sat a little sideways on the couch and leaned forward, elbows on knees, hands loosely clasped. His voice was low, smooth and sexy. It was good. I was positive he dropped women like flies. Okay, almost positive. Give me ten minutes and I'd be positive.

'I don't know really.' I let demure slip a little into flirtatious and seedy as I glanced out of the corners of my eyes at him. 'I just feel so lonely and sad all the time.' Pushing somber and solemn there. 'I really wish I had someone like you in my life.' I just spit that right out, didn't choke on the words at all. Good, huh? 'Exactly like you,' I qualified. 'I guess I'm just hoping, *really* hoping, that maybe you could give me some pointers on how to find a guy like you.' I looked him straight in the eye, opened my mouth ever so slightly and licked my lips like a shameless hussy. Hollywood, eat your heart out.

He shook his head. 'Sad? Lonely?' And slid down the couch, narrowing the distance between us to about a quarter of an inch. 'What you need is a *big* hug.' His arms wrapped around me. The snake.

Spiders, snakes – mixed metaphors, I know, but you get my drift. Just like I got Sid's.

It would have been hard not to. His hands were starting a full-body once-over, his lips delicately brushed my cheek.

'Oh Sid,' I breathed out.

'Go ahead, hug me back, it's all right.' His voice was soft and reassuring. He held me tightly now, his hands pressing into my back. 'Let me show you what love is between a man and a woman. Let me be your teacher about the sweetness of love between a man and a woman.' The tight pressure on my back was released. One hand drifted across my breast and landed in my lap, the crotch end of my lap, not the knee end. It was hard not to flinch. Never mind slap him silly.

'Let's take off some of these clothes, shall we? It's an important first step, an indication of openness and trust as well as closeness.' He smiled at me, then pulled the sweater over his head. No T-shirt, just gorgeous, muscled, male chest studded with blond hair.

I smiled right back. Nothing flirtatious. Nothing coy. 'If I were a vice cop, this is where I would flash my badge and read you your rights.' *Big* smile. I was enjoying this now. I've always loved the part where the worm turns.

Johannsen jumped like a stuck pig and scrambled to put his sweater back on. His eyes were hard and his face flushed in an ugly shade of red.

'I don't know what you're talking about.' He towered over me and tried out the Intimidating Male Routine.

'Sure you do. You're a minister. Being a minister and counseling people puts you in a position of trust – which you abused by making sexual advances to me. Abused big-time.'

'I don't know what you're talking about. I would *never* do that. I'm not that kind of a person.'

I smiled. 'I think we've established exactly who you are.' *Or what.* 'Sit down. We're going to talk about it.'

'I think you'd better leave right now.' He spoke through clenched teeth. And his fists were clenched. More Intimidating Male Routine.

Unfortunately this is not a routine that works well on me.

'We're going to talk about two things, first the one that interests me, then the one that interests you.'

'Nothing you could say would interest me,' he snarled.

I smiled back pleasantly. 'Really? I thought you'd be interested in what I'm going to do about your actions today.'

He sat down. Deflated. I was still smiling, adding insult to injury, no doubt.

'What?' The snarl was gone.

'Tsk, tsk,' I chided him. 'First we talk about what *I* am interested in.'

He stared at me in silence. Not much of a conversationalist with his clothes on, I guess.

'It has come to my attention that you made a contribution of three thousand dollars to Hope For Kids. How generous.' I smiled at him. 'How thoughtful. How mind-boggling. How out of character.'

'What's your fucking point?'

'There, you see? You're back in character.'

'Well?' He was snarling again.

'Why?'

'Why what?'

I ignored that and glanced at the clock. 'Pick up the pace, Sid.'

'None of your goddamn business.'

'Okay, shortcut.' I leaned forward slightly and looked him in the eye. 'I know why: blackmail.'

The starch went out of him again. He ran his fingers through his hair. 'Look, this is just between us, right?'

'Right.' Okay, I lied. Lying to slimeballs is not the kind of thing that keeps me awake at night.

'This guy had something on me. I figured if he blew, I stood to lose a lot, maybe even my position as a minister. He told me if I gave three thousand to Hope For Kids it was all over, I'd never hear from him again. I wasn't sure I could believe him but what choice did I have? So I paid. I don't get it. What guy in his right mind would blackmail for charity?

'What contact did you have with the blackmailer?'

'He phoned me. Twice. The first time he told me what he wanted and what he had on me., The second time he told me where to send it.'

'That was it?'

'Yes.'

'What did he sound like?'

'Odd, like he was doing something to change his voice.'

'But you think it was a man?'

He looked puzzled. 'I don't know. I guess I just assumed it was. It was a low voice.'

'What did he have on you?'

He looked at me and his face said: *Like I would tell you. Like I'm crazy.*

I sighed. Pushing around guys like this was not only annoying, it was time-consuming.

'How many women?'

'Women? What makes you think that? What are you talking about?'

One too many questions. Methinks the gentleman doth protest too much. Of course, as a general rule slimeballs don't read Shakespeare, so there you go.

'How many?'

'A couple. Not that I did anything. I didn't.' There was a note of outrage in his voice, the same one you hear in schoolyard bullies when they get caught.

'An innocent man paid three thousand dollars to a blackmailer? Right. Give me a break, Sid.'

'Even an unfounded rumor can ruin a good man's reputation,' he intoned piously.

'If those accusations came out, I wonder how many others would surface?' I asked conversationally. 'I wonder how many other women, how many other stories—'

He tried to maintain his pompous dignity but it was difficult. I was suddenly very tired of this man and his conversation. Nobody likes a blackmailer but the victims are sometimes difficult to sympathize with too. Madeline and Randolph were one thing, this scum bucket was another.

'Your preying on women is going to stop, Sid. The so-called counseling, the fucking around and fucking over, it's all going to stop.'

'Yes, yes, you're right. I know that. I'd come to that decision myself.'

'Really? I guess I missed that, what with your clothes coming off and all.'

He flushed.

'I'm not taking your word for it, of course. We'll have to work something out.' Translation: I hadn't thought this through yet. Or figured out how to handle it. But I would.

'What do you mean?'

'Keep your nose clean.' I thought about that one. 'And your zipper zipped. I'll be in touch.'

And I was out of there. Past the minister with Nordic-god looks and the morals of a sewer rat, past the smiling Jesus surrounded by simpering children and the bleeding Jesus on the cross, and through the door. I sucked in a breath of fresh air. The last half hour made fog and gloom look good.

DIE NOW, PAY LATER!

Did Johannsen read his own material?

The house smelled wonderful when I got home. Having a boyfriend who cooks is a definite plus. I set the table and opened a bottle of wine while Hank dressed the salad and grated the Parmesan for the homemade ravioli and marinara sauce. I also rescued the garlic bread from the broiler.

We lingered over dinner, talking about things and catching up – but not talking about the things between us. Nobody ever talks about

– never mind explains – the fine print: how difficult relationships are to build and maintain. And how tenuous trust – that hard-earned, hard-won bond – can be. After dinner we hit The Pause. The Silence. And that means you have face it or give up trying.

Hank poured the rest of the wine in our glasses. 'Let's go sit by the fire, Katy.'

I nodded. How many times had we sat there, me curled up in the circle of Hank's arm, talking, laughing, making plans for the future? I took a sip of wine. All right, it was a gulp.

We sat next to each other on the couch but it wasn't the same. It wasn't before.

'You weren't expecting me, I know, Katy.'

True. If he had called and suggested coming up, I would have said no. I had too much on my mind now. On my plate.

'I want to work this out, Katy. I want us to go forward, not be stuck. No.' He took a deep breath. 'I want more than that. I want us to have a life together and I'll do whatever it takes to achieve that. I'll get a job with the department here, sell my house and move. Katy, I want to get married.'

He smiled at me, traced my cheekbone with his finger, and waited for the answer I didn't have. 'Don't be such a chatterbox.' His voice was gentle, patient.

'It's a lot, Hank.' I was stammering.

'It's not a surprise.'

No. No, it wasn't. Hank had wanted to get married for a long time. I was the one who wasn't ready. And, until now, neither one of us had been ready to change jobs and move. So that was a surprise.

I held my wineglass tightly, as though it were a life preserver and I a drowning person. Drowning? Scared. 'Can't we go on the way we are?'

'No. For three years I've tried to do it your way. I can't do it anymore. I want a life together with you. Things don't stay the same, Katy, you know that. We're not going forward now so we're going backward. I don't want that. I want to come home to you, I want to share my life with you. I want to hold you, not just think about you. If you don't want these things then it's time for us to go our separate ways.'

I swallowed hard. 'Hank . . .'

He grinned at me. 'Shit or get off the pot, sweetheart.'

I giggled in spite of myself, then tried to sound outraged: 'Hey, is that any way to propose? I bet Elizabeth Barrett Browning got a much better proposal. Not to mention Juliet, Scarlett O'Hara, Cleopatra and a whole lot of heroines in romance novels.'

'Our lives aren't much like romance novels.' He put on his thoughtful expression. 'We could try, though. How about starting with a love scene?'

'Love or sex?'

'Both.' He hugged me.

'I don't have an answer yet, Hank.'

'Soon?'

I nodded. The love scene that night was a good one – hot and wild, romantic. *Much* better than a novel. New beginnings are wonderful, filled with hope and love and daring. Hank was right; you can't stay in the same place, and if you're not going forward, there's only backward.

So all I had to do was get through the old stuff, the fear.

Hank left with the first early-morning light and I curled back up in the warm spot we had made, the memory of his kisses on me, love and fear within me.

CHAPTER 14

Dear Hope for Kids,
I read in the paper where you help kids out. Like this girl who
needed a hearing aid or the boy who got plastic surgery cause
he was in a bad fire. Well, I need help too. My teeth stick out
and are all sideways and ugly. Please write and tell me when
to come in and be fixed. Thank you from your friend.

Bernadette

Unresolved emotion is a heavy hangover.

I slept late, until almost ten. A hot bath didn't set me straight
inside but at least it woke me up, and that got me dressed and rolling.
I was halfway through my pancakes before I lost it again.

Police Question Suicide of James Randolph

That was the lead-in. The article read well, smooth, easy, but then
J.O. was a pro and I expected no less. A pro can make garbage look
good. J.O. had done just that, building an article around speculation
and innuendo. He was careful not to tread too heavily on police
territory and/or toes, thus compromising an essential source, but that
was it. Compassion? Sensitivity? Kindness? Not in this article. Not
in J.O.'s repertoire. I cursed him at great length under my breath.

Lot of good that did.

So I finished my juice. And hoped vitamin C was a stress mitigator.
(You know, of course, what they say about hope.) Ranger got the rest
of my pancakes. Maybe I should eat breakfast before reading the
paper?

I picked up the calls from my office; Delia and Sid both. Delia on Sunday, Sid early this morning.

Moon Nguyen was on my list too. And Henley. And Hank, only he didn't belong on this list. Feast or famine. I sighed, picked up the phone and punched buttons. Bill Henley snarled into the receiver. That's Monday morning for you. Or homicide. Or both.

'Hey Bill, I'll buy you lunch.'

'Whaddya want, Kat?' But his voice was softer, almost pleased to hear from me.

'The pleasure of your company,' I said sweetly.

He snorted.

'And your opinion on a bunch of numbers,' I added hastily before I lost all credibility.

'You playing the lottery now?'

'Sort of.' I recited the numbers.

'Yeah?'

But he wrote them down, I could tell. 'I was wondering – if these were booking numbers, what would they tell me?'

He grunted, a friendly grunt. I smiled.

'Where do you want to meet for lunch?'

Another grunt. 'You heard of a place called Sumptuous Salad?'

So of course I busted up. I mean, who could help it? 'Bill, don't do this to me. You're a cop. You're meat and potatoes. Doughnuts. Fast food. You're not fiber and vitamins, you're grease.'

'Yeah, well. You know that, I know that, but the wife don't. She's got me on a friggin' diet. Again. I hate this crunchy green shit too. You?'

'Green stuff? I like it fine.'

'Huh. Hell of a deal.' He sighed heavily. 'Salad, twelve-thirty, that work for you?'

'I'm there.'

One down, three to go.

Delia or Johannsen? It was a toss-up in the Interest Department. I decided to go with Delia – she had sounded the most desperate, her soft whispery voice saying: 'Oh God, I'm so scared. I've got to talk to you. Please please call me. *Please*. Not today. Monday morning. I'll wait here for you to call. Oh please. I can't tell you how frightened

I am I wish— Oh God—' And she had hung up. And then called right back to whisper her phone number.

I had to nerve myself up to return the call. I recognized the tone, the desperation. It was a combination of confessional and I-need-you-to-fix-this-you-have-to-fix-this-right-now. And, though it is a combination I am familiar with, it is not one I am fond of.

'Delia, Kat Colorado.' My voice was hearty and upbeat, not that I thought for one moment it would do the trick.

It didn't.

'Oh my God. I'm so glad you called. We *have* to talk.'

'Okay,' I said, hearty, upbeat *and* agreeable.

'No, in person, I mean. Not on the phone.'

'Okay,' I agreed, acquiescing smoothly to the inevitable but not quite as hearty, upbeat, and agreeable, I admit.

'You can't come here. And I can't go to your office. Suppose someone saw us?'

'Java City?' I suggested.

'Oh *no*!' She sounded shocked. 'That's *way* too public.'

I thought for a moment. 'The Crocker Museum. Today is Monday so it's closed. I'll be parked across the street in front in a white Bronco. Twenty-five minutes.'

'All right. Thank you.'

I grabbed a diet Dr Pepper and a coat and was out the door. On the way I tried to figure the odds that she would show and settled, finally, on 80/20. Still, desperation is always a wild card.

I was a few minutes early but she was waiting for me, the candy apple-red Lexus coupe a bright Christmassy statement in the December gloom. I pulled up behind her, parked. Her door popped open and she skittered over to the Bronco like a waterbug on acid and clambered in. I had to concentrate on her features in order to recognize the woman I had met so recently.

She wore black jeans, loafers, and a heavy black wool coat. Her tight red sweater matched her car, and her lipstick and socks matched her sweater. Her face was a horrible lifeless white. Her eyes were the color of mud, as if despair had drowned there.

In an instant I saw a flash of a younger Madeline in this desperate and beautiful woman. And felt the hatred inside me. I had tried first to ignore the hatred, and then to leave it behind, when I heard Madeline's story. It is not good to have a personal stake in a case – much better to stay uninvolved, removed.

But not always possible.

Madeline's eyes. Delia's eyes. The blackmailer picked his victims well. The hatred was strong in me. The stakes high. And personal. Lindy's eyes had looked like that once, before I pulled her off the street.

'You can help me, can't you? I'm so afraid.' Delia pulled her coat around her and huddled down into it, her shoulders hunched up protectively.

'I'll do my best.' I spoke gently. 'Tell me what is upsetting you, what kind of help you need.'

Delia's shoulders came down a little, her chin jutted out. There were small spots of red on her cheekbones now. 'It's a long story.'

'All right,' I said.

'And you won't tell anyone. I can trust you?'

'Yes.'

She looked at me in silence and then nodded. Her eyes had little yellow sparks in them, were no longer mud. Desperation was on the run. Almost. I smiled slightly. She tried to smile back but it faded quickly.

'Do you know what it is to be dirt-poor?'

I nodded.

'*Dirt*-poor, not enough to eat? Bread fried in grease for dinner?'

I could have nodded to that too but I didn't, careful not to interrupt. She had fallen into her story. It was like falling into a well.

'White trash, that's what we were and it was a hopeless existence. There is nothing wrong with being poor, or even ignorant.' Her fierce voice dared me to disagree but I didn't. 'You can be born poor and ignorant but you don't have to stay there. That's what my mama always said.

'The thing that I remember most about my mama was how tired she was. She worked from sunup to sundown and beyond. Her hands bled from the hard work she did every day. She used to take me on her lap at night and hold me and sing to me. The old hymns and gospel tunes were her favorites. And she would tell me stories of

110

when she was a little girl and happy, when things were better.

'I remember one night how bitterly she cried when she was trying to comb out my hair and braid it with colored string we had saved. And she couldn't. Her hands were so rough and raw she couldn't. She worked every single blessed day of her life, was honest and loving in every thought and deed and she had to die to get some rest.

'I stood in the hot sun and watched as they lowered her coffin into the dirt and I swore to myself that I would neither live nor die as she had.'

Delia stopped. Staring blindly out the window she pushed her hands through her honey-blond hair, then turned to me and smiled.

'When I was growing up we heard tell that California was a land where the sun always shone and there were oranges everywhere just waiting to be picked. It's hard now to believe that in Sacramento in the winter.'

She paused and I waited patiently.

'What killed my mama wasn't the hard work and rough life, though God knows it could have. What killed my mama was the loss of hope. When hope dies you're a goner. You might just as well climb into that wood box, slide into the dirt and suck dust.

'I was fifteen when Mama died and I'm thirty-seven now. I won't bore you with all the years in between.' She looked at me and raised an eyebrow.

'Just the blackmail,' I said.

'Just the blackmail,' she agreed, and stared out at the fog. 'For seven of those years I was a call girl. I am not ashamed of that any more than I am ashamed of once being poor and ignorant or that I had a mama whose hands bled because she worked so hard.' There were tears in her eyes but her voice was fierce and hard.

'I never stole, I never took help that wasn't offered with open hands and a kind heart, and I never went on welfare. I am proud of who I am and what I have become. I am proud that I made something of myself.'

An elderly couple walked by, their arms linked together, their steps in easy synchronized rhythm, a melody of many years.

'But I am vulnerable. And I have made my husband vulnerable. Our future once seemed so clear, so open, so full of hope. My

111

husband's political career is going well. We were planning to start a family. Now all I can feel is fear. I see my hopes, like my mother's coffin, being buried in dry hard dirt. I am very afraid and I don't know what to do. You are my hope now.'

'Does your husband know?'

'No. I am afraid to tell him. I think, I almost believe, that he would accept me and my past, that he would understand me and love me and nothing would change. Almost. But I am not sure and I am not willing to take the risk. It is not just a risk, you see. It is hope dying in the dust and I could not bear that.'

'Blackmail is a crime. You should go to the police.'

'Of course I should. But you see the problem there and you know that I will not.' It was a statement, not a question. And I knew. She smiled at me. 'I am sorry I pushed you away at first but I was afraid and I had to think it through. You are my hope; I will help you in any way I can. You have already helped me; my heart is lighter now.'

Delia shifted in her seat. 'My mother loved rainbows. She said it was God's way of promising good things after storms and destruction. I always think of hope as a rainbow. Thank you, Kat. The phone number I gave you is my private line. No one answers it but me. Call me anytime.'

She was ready to go, having handed over the responsibility, but there were more questions. The same ones I had asked her before when she was scared: Did you know the blackmailer? Male or female? Method of contact? How much? To whom? The answers were the same too: No. I don't know, the voice was synthetic-sounding, deep. He phoned twice. Ten thousand. Hope For Kids.

She slid out of the car. Just then the sun struggled through the fog and glimmered weakly. Delia turned and waved. I almost stopped her. I would have if I had had more questions. But I didn't. Yet.

Or rather, I had too many. I still didn't know if the blackmail – okay, *presumed* blackmail, that's how shaky the ground I was standing on was – and Randolph's death were connected. Or if the blackmailer was the same in the cases that were turning up one after another like so much loose change. And I didn't have a clue as to the identity of the blackmailer.

Investigative work never happens in real life the way it does in the movies.

The Lexus blasted off in a red blur. I looked at the clock. And smiled. Nothing like lunch with a cop to perk a body up. Not to mention a chat with a lecherous minister.

CHAPTER 15

Here's Looking at You, Kid

'Why do you bother?'

'What do you mean?'

'Potato salad, pasta salad, chicken salad, Waldorf salad, pizza bread—' I was two-thirds of the way around Bill's loaded plate. 'Baked potato with everything, macaroni salad, cup of clam chowder. Not exactly the diet special.'

'I'm easing into it. This shit instead of a cheeseburger, what a deal.' He sighed, looked at my plate, looked quickly away. Too much green stuff, I guess.

'What gives, Kat?'

'James Randolph.'

'And?'

'Do you know J.O. Edwards?'

'No.'

'A reporter at the *Bee*.'

A pained look crossed his face. 'Persistent? In-your-face and a pain in the butt?'

'That's the one. He's looking for an angle, something ugly and unsavory, as sleazy as he can go and still get the *Bee* to print it. He showed me two photos; one was a copy of a booking photo, the other was of Randolph and the young woman in the booking photo. The two of them were leaving a building I'm pretty sure was the jail.'

'Not a big surprise there. Randolph was a lawyer, wasn't he?' Bill pushed his pasta salad around in a bored fashion.

'A probate attorney.'

'No shit.' The pasta slipped into second place and I took first.

'You guys find anything to indicate murder? Or a reason for the suicide?'

'No. You don't need a reason. It's nice if you get one – tidy, but not necessary. This seemed a pretty straightforward suicide. You come up with anything I should know about, Kat?'

'Not yet. I'm grasping at straws: that's where the photo comes in. The family's not satisfied with what's known.'

'Suicide's a tough one. You can't ever know what's in a person's mind, even someone you think you know well. You know that.'

'I know that. And you know that's not the only way to understand a situation.'

He nodded, finished off his potato salad, had a few bites of the Waldorf. 'Not a first offense. Nothing real serious but—' He shrugged. 'Shoplifting, passing bad checks, using a stolen credit card. Not your basic upstanding citizen.'

'This time?'

'Shoplifting. There were three of them working together.'

'Address for her?'

'Shit, Kat, you're pushing it already.'

I was, yes. I sat, quiet and immovable, so as not to seem too pushy. Not that Henley was dumb enough to fall for it. Kind enough, maybe.

He sighed. 'Lucky for you I'm a softie. Oak Park.' He gave me a street address. 'And for godsakes, watch your step. I've got enough on my conscience already. C'mon, let's go get dessert.'

We ambled over to the dessert bar, where Bill loaded up on frozen yogurt with granola and chocolate sprinkles and three kinds of cookies. And then ambled back to the table.

'Has your wife ever been here?' I was genuinely curious. I mean they had been married for thirty-two years and I was pretty sure she had him figured by now.

'Nah. I oughta keep it that way, huh?'

'Does she think you're eating lettuce and cucumbers?'

'Yeah.' He grinned. 'Garbanzo beans too. She says I gotta eat them for protein. Hell, what she don't know don't hurt her. That all you're having?'

I nibbled on a cookie. You know the kind. They look good but they taste like sawdust, only not as much flavor. I tucked it under my napkin, though decent burial was more than it deserved.

We parted in the parking lot.

'Watch your butt, Kat.' He said it crossly, which is the way he talks when he's fond of you and worried both.

'Scout's honor.' I held up my hand in mock salute as he grunted and walked off.

Oak Park was at one time a lovely part of Sacramento. Decrepit mansions and beautifully laid-out neighborhoods were still a testimony to the past. These days not too many people are old enough to remember those days. These days it is not a neighborhood many choose to live in, although it is easy enough to hit hard times and get stuck there. Gangbangers, hookers, guns, drugs? Oak Park: one-stop shopping.

I don't know my way around Oak Park very well so I looked it up in my Thomas Guide, got the picture clearly in my mind. It is not the best place to get lost in. Definitely at night but even in the day.

It was a cold bleak afternoon and I saw hardly anyone on the streets. The house I was looking for was an old one, a once-imposing Victorian that had been turned into apartments and then fallen into squalid disrepair. The weeds seemed almost attractive compared to the hubcaps, rotting mattresses, used condoms, and drug paraphernalia that filled the yard. The windows were boarded up. Nobody had lived there for a long time.

Gosh, a citizen had lied to the cops. Go figure.

I parked anyway. I was here, might as well give it my best shot. A small African-American child answered the door in the house to the left. Sucking a thumb, he stared at me in rapt and silent interest.

'Would you get your mommy or daddy, please?'

He removed the thumb and I anticipated an answer. Wrong. At least from him. A teenage girl with a severe haircut and expression appeared suddenly, scooped him up, and slammed the door in my face.

One down.

117

No one answered my knock in the house on the other side although I could swear I saw a curtain move. I knocked three times, waiting patiently in between each knock before crossing the street. There I struck out two more times before a door opened. By then I was so accustomed to failure I was almost startled.

'Yes?' I was greeted by an elderly woman with a leg brace and a cane. Neither hostile nor welcoming, she waited for me to state my business.

'I'm looking for a young woman going by the name of Mayan Nugen or perhaps Moon Nguyen. She is mid-twenties, Asian-American, slim and attractive, with straight, dark shoulder-length hair.' I stopped, not just to give her a chance to answer but because I was out of descriptive detail. 'Do you know if she lives in this neighborhood? Have you seen anyone answering her description?'

'I know of no one by that name or description,' she replied.

I could not read her eyes, could not tell if what she said was true or if she was merely declining to give me information. 'It is about an inheritance. There is a fifty-dollar reward to anyone who helps me find her. May I leave you my card?'

Dark brown eyes framed by deep brown skin and salt-and-pepper hair stared at me for a long moment. And then a nod. I handed her a card and left, framed then in her scrutiny.

I wasn't SOL yet; I still had the address Carter had given me. I hoped people were more honest about their whereabouts to lawyers than they were to cops. I climbed in the Bronco and headed for the freeway. From Oak Park to American River Drive. It was difficult to imagine a more stark contrast.

Cathi answered the door herself. Black leggings, black sweater, no makeup. Speaking of stark. And joyless.

'Hello.' her voice was soft, almost toneless. 'Come in.'

She stood aside so that I could enter, then carefully shut the door and headed for the little sitting room where I had first met her on the night of her husband's death. On the way we passed the music room and the Christmas tree. I gasped before I caught myself. Someone had toppled the tree and systematically smashed all the ornaments. The delicate glass angel that had graced the treetop lay by herself in the middle of the carpet, her wings and head snapped off and carefully

118

placed beside her. Cathi walked by, oblivious, and I attempted to match her demeanor.

Angel: DOA. *Joy to the world.*

Casablanca played silently in the sitting room. In black and white Bogie and Ingrid won and lost their love over and over again in Paris and North Africa.

Why was I not surprised?

Cathi seated herself on the couch and tucked her feet under her, taking up as little space as possible. Automatically her eyes turned to the screen. Her concentration seemed total to me, her lips moving in a silent whisper occasionally as she mouthed the lines.

Rick raised his champagne glass to Ilsa. 'Here's looking at you, kid.'

'Why are you here?' Cathi spoke but her eyes never left the screen.

Mine were on her. 'To check up on you, to see that you were are all right.'

'You expect me to believe that?'

'Why shouldn't you?' I asked reasonably.

'Everyone wants something. No one is just nice.'

'Cathi, Richard Carter hired me to work on the unknowns in this case.' I tried to stay vague and diplomatic. 'No one's paying me to be nice. I'm here because I'm worried about you.'

'Sure you are.'

We watched Rick at the train station as he read Ilsa's letter. There aren't any guarantees. And it's difficult – or is it impossible? – to believe in love when it's not in front of you.

'How can you do that to someone you say you love?'

The tears ran down her cheeks unchecked, unnoticed. Sam got Rick on the train. I tried to figure out what was going on. In Sacramento, not Paris.

'It wasn't love, it couldn't have been.'

I took a deep breath. 'Jim didn't commit suicide to hurt you, Cathi. He did it because he was desperate, because he could think of no other way to get out of the pain and confusion. Perhaps he even thought it was an act of love and that he was protecting you.'

'Why? *Why*? Nothing's that bad. Nothing! Whatever it was, we could have faced it together!'

Could they? Rick and Ilsa couldn't. Hank and I weren't doing a very good job of it. Divorce was common, staying together in hatred run-of-the-mill, but facing it together and with love? I covered my eyes with my hand. I was getting too close, getting tangled up in emotions – mine as well as Cathi's.

'Your husband loved you, Cathi. He never meant to hurt you. What he did hurt you and still hurts you a great deal, but that was not his intention. You must hold that in your mind and heart. You must believe it. Believe what you had together, all the minutes and hours, days and years. You cannot let one action, however horrible, negate everything else. You cannot.'

She stared at me, her eyes wide and terrible. 'It already has.'

'Jim's death has changed your life and your future. It does not change your past, the feelings and love and everything you experienced together. That can't change. You always have that.'

She shook her head.

I took another deep breath. 'Remember what Rick said to Ilsa at the end? "We'll always have Paris." But Cathi, they always did. Ilsa had acted out of love. It was Rick, not seeing that, who changed things in his mind. The reality never changed. Don't do what Rick did. Believe in your husband. Believe in your love. Cherish it. And then—' I took another gulp of air. It is very unlike me to use Hollywood as an example of how to live. Bad enough that politicians do it.

'And then?' Cathi asked me.

'Then, even though you are still in the fog, you can walk off into a new life with hope in your heart. Broken angels can be mended.'

Tears filled up her eyes and spilled over. Again. I see so much hurt, so much pain, and I can do so little about it. I wondered, again, if I was in the wrong job. But even in Hollywood the endings aren't always happy.

'Please go,' Cathi whispered. 'I need to be by myself. I'll be all right.' She answered my silent question. 'Thank you, Kat.' On the way out I picked up the pieces of the angel and placed them gently on the mantel. Tomorrow. Maybe the repairs, human and angel, could begin tomorrow.

I walked out into the fog but there the resemblance between me and Rick ended. Not love and hope and new beginnings but anger and sadness.

So many victims. Jim Randolph, Cathi, Madeline, Delia. Innocents. *Apparent* innocents, I corrected myself. And the guilty, who were also victims. Like Sid. And the unknowns. Like Moon.

Does a blackmailer count the human cost? Or even care? Does he see, not just the target, the blackmail bull's-eye, but the ripple effect of devastation, the casualties in family, friends, and associates? Perhaps he is blind. Or doesn't care? Or sees and takes a perverse pleasure in the pain? I shivered. People callous and oblivious to another's pain frighten me. People who take pleasure in the pain of others leave me speechless with horror. It is less than human. Not it — he? Blackmail could as easily be a woman's crime as a man's. No one sex, or race, or religion had the corner on inhumanity.

As I drove I tried to take the answer and sadness and change it to determination. Justice could be a product of all three but more likely, I thought, of determination.

The fog lifted somewhat as I drove out of town. American River Drive is so named because of its proximity to the American River. And waterways are conducive to fog. Still, my spirits lifted. I even took it, ever so slightly, as a metaphor. *Imagination is conducive to delusion.* I smiled to myself remembering the set of Rick's shoulders as he walked into the fog. Fog or sunshine, there is sweetness in life.

And I was on my way to see a sweet-talking, smooth-walking philandering minister. And kick ass. Talk about sweetness.

I straightened my shoulders.

Just like Bogie.

CHAPTER 16

Dear Charity,
The person I love most is very, very unhappy and I want him to
be happy more than anything in the world. What should I give
him for Christmas?

Wondering in Wichita

Dear Wondering,
Happiness is a gift you give to yourself, not a present you give
to someone else.

Charity

It wasn't déjà vu all over again, as Yogi Berra was wont to say.

Johannsen had a tie, a coat and a formal look on, and all were safely ensconced behind his desk. His look informed me that if he could have tossed up a barbed-wire fence on short notice he would have done so. Gladly. It was difficult to keep a straight face but I did – I'm good that way.

Johannsen half stood behind his desk. 'If you'll be seated, Ms Colorado.' Gravely he indicated a chair placed at a formal distance. Gravely I took it. And sat in attentive silence. It was his dime. (A mere technicality, I know, given the provocation I was dishing out.)

He cleared his throat. 'Well then, where are we exactly?'

Exactly? He was in deep shit, that was where. I didn't say that, of course. I smiled. A small enigmatic Mona Lisa-type smile was what I was shooting for. And I remained silent. Let-'em-sweat is the theory here.

'I, uh, see from your card that you are a private investigator, Ms

Colorado. This is your own business, I take it?'

'Yes,' I responded chattily.

'Running a business can be a difficult proposition, especially in today's uncertain business climate.'

'Yes.' The Great Communicator still.

It occurs to me' – Johannsen leaned back into his chair and laced his fingers together in an elaborately casual pose – 'that we might well have a common business interest.'

'Oh?' I dropped the serene Mona Lisa smile like a hot brick and did puzzled and unaware à la Little Orphan Annie.

'Yes.' He tapped his fingers lightly. 'It occurs to me that we could work together to our mutual advantage. And to your profit,' he added with a thoughtful finger tap.

I could hardly maintain my puzzled Little Orphan Annie expression. Even I, foolishly hopeful as I am, hadn't expected that he would be *this* dumb *this* easily.

'But I'm sure you understand me,' he added with a knowing smile.

'No,' I said, shaking my head and lying like a rug. 'I'm afraid I don't.'

'I would like to, uh, hire you to protect my privacy.'

'That is a very difficult thing to do. What, exactly did you have in mind?' Like I didn't know.

'I would want you to, uh, maintain silence.'

'That would, of course, be understood in any investigation I did. Standard procedure is to report only to the client unless otherwise instructed,' I stated smoothly. 'I am not, however, clear on the job you wish me to undertake.'

He looked exasperated. 'I don't want to pay you to do something,' he snapped. 'I want to pay you to be quiet. I want to make it worth your while to say nothing about what happened at our, uh, last meeting.'

'The meeting we had on Sunday, December eighth, here in the church office where you made physical and sexual advances toward me in the context of a counseling session?' I asked succinctly, if not delicately.

He squirmed. 'Yes, well, uh, that's not how I would put it.'

'How would you put it?'

'Oh for God's sake, can we skip this? Are you interested or not?'

'Very.'

He let out a sigh of relief. 'How does a thousand sound to you?'

'It sounds like a bribe, Mr Johannsen, not an offer of legal employment. And I'm not the only one who will be interested. Bribery is a felony.' I smiled again. Not a Mona Lisa or a Little Orphan Annie smile. Not even a Norman Rockwell kid-in-a-candy-store one. More like a smartass-private-investigator one.

'You little fucking bitch,' he snarled at me.

Key elements clearly missing in this man's education were the concepts of cutting your losses and beating a strategic retreat. Never mind learning from your mistakes. I played to these losses and smiled another smartass smile, the kind that translates to: *Gotcha, stupid.*

It inflamed him, as I knew it would.

'Bitch,' he repeated.

And I wondered if maybe ministers didn't get out enough to learn really good obscenities.

'I tried to settle this easily and nicely. Now I'll just have to take care of you.'

'You're threatening me? You are fond of felonies, aren't you?' Okay, that was an exaggeration; threatening isn't a felony. *Details.*

'You don't have a thing on me. Not a thing. Now get out. Let's see how you like playing hardball.'

I stood and walked to the door, Johannsen hard on my heels.

'Good day, Ms Colorado.'

He spoke in clipped and polite tones that were not, I was sure, for my benefit but for the church secretary's. She smiled brightly up at me.

'Good day, Mr Johannsen.' I turned to the secretary. 'Ma'am, could you tell me the time, please.'

She looked puzzled, since the clock was in easy view, but she told me.

'And do you happen to have the date?'

She told me that too. It was a nice touch and I congratulated myself. I had a tape of my conversation with Johannsen with his secretary establishing the date and time. Good work. Of course I couldn't have done it without Johannsen. Nothing like a loud youth, brains-in-your-crotch lunkhead, I reflected fondly as I took the tape recorder out of my blazer pocket and stowed it in the Bronco.

I was a little late for my next appointment but not ridiculously so. And the ex-Mrs Randolph had sounded easygoing and flexible.

She didn't use that name anymore, she told me firmly as we settled into the sumptuous leather love seats in her den. Her maiden name? I saw no wedding ring.

Her voice was clear and musical and she was a very attractive woman in her early forties. I wondered if Randolph had tired of her and turned her in for a younger, prettier, trophy-wife model, or if she had tired of him. Outpaced and outdistanced him perhaps? Lovely, poised, and intelligent, Lisa Gibbons was not a woman who could be easily fooled. I didn't bother to try.

'Rick Carter hired me to look into Jim Randolph's death.'

'It is, of course, strictly a business issue with him.'

'Yes.'

It sounded heartless, almost ugly and stark put that way, but it didn't seem to affect Lisa. Presumably she knew Carter well. Or the legal mentality.

'Jim meant a lot to me. How may I help?'

Surprise flickered briefly across my face. Lisa smiled in acknowledgment but her eyes were determined.

'Did you have much contact with Jim Randolph?'

'None at all.'

'He paid you alimony?'

'Yes.'

'And you benefit from his death.' I stated it; I didn't ask it.

She nodded her head. One-syllable answers, one-syllable movements. Economy in speech and body language is rarely helpful to a private investigator. Again I went for the direct approach.

'We could do this for a long time, I imagine, me asking you questions, you giving me answers I already know, but let's simplify the process. Either throw me out or tell me something.'

She laughed and the tension left her face and shoulders. Her beauty was radiant. Cathi had the allure and freshness of youth but Lisa Gibbons had something far more powerful. And I did not think that

Lisa had ever stayed home and watched the same movie over and over in the silence of a darkened room.

'And your angle – is it business as well?' There was an almost quizzical note in her voice.

'The police consider this a straightforward suicide. I disagree. As I have a passion for justice, nothing is ever just business for me. I am never quite sure whether I chose this profession or it chose me.'

'Nothing about a life is ever that straightforward.' Lisa leaned toward me, her hands clasped on her knees. 'And suicide is surely one of the most confusing of deaths.'

'And you are in a position to shed light on both.'

'Oh yes.' Her hands were clasped so tightly the knuckles were white. Something, pain I thought, was etched in the lines around her eyes. 'Jim was a man to whom duty and obligation were supremely important. It was an elemental factor in his life. You mentioned that I receive alimony and stand to benefit from Jim's death. I never asked for, nor cared about either. Financially I am quite comfortable.

'Still, it was I who supported us in the years when he was in college and law school. Financially, of course, but also emotionally. He never felt that debt had been paid, though I did. His system of honor was uniquely his and he was an extraordinarily loyal man.' She shrugged. 'I disagreed with him often but I long ago gave up fighting him on it. That was a battle I could never win.'

'You ended the marriage then?'

'Oh yes.' Her voice softened. 'When Jim said "until death do us part," he meant it.'

'And you?'

Another shrug. 'I am more pragmatic. Death is but one of the many things that can part people. Recognizing that, I left.'

'What was it that parted you?'

'Demons. Some he brought home with him from Vietnam. He could have gotten a student deferment but he refused. That was the first of many battles that I fought, and lost, before I gave up and acknowledged that duty was stronger than I.

'Some demons he collected elsewhere. Or perhaps they were updated versions of ones handed down by his family, I could never

127

really sort that out. When the day came that I finally, absolutely admitted I would never win and I knew I couldn't bear to live with the demons any longer, I left. I left loving Jim very deeply, as I always will, but leaving was an act of survival for me. The demons were consuming my soul as well as his.'

'Lisa—'

'No.' She shook her head in the smallest of movements. 'Don't ask me. I will not speak of them to you. That is too much and too personal. If Jim took his life without explanation, he did so with understanding and purpose and I will not intrude on that.' Her head fell back and she closed her eyes for a moment. 'It grieves me deeply that that was the only way he could find to vanquish his demons.'

'He left a widow.'

'Yes. Think how bad, how very bad it must have become for him to do that. He was not as good at fighting them without me. I am sorry for that but I could not and would not go down with him. I always hoped he would make it. I always believed he would.'

'Did Jim take any medication for anxiety or depression?'

'Not when we were together. He saw it as a weakness, as giving up, though I did not.'

'He drank?'

'Oh yes. That was his principal release though he never let it get out of his control. And it was a double-edged sword. Sometimes it would kill the demons, buy him moments of respite; sometimes it would release them.'

'Did you know Cathi?'

'No.' Lisa started to say something else, then changed her mind.

'But you know, of her?'

'Very little. It was difficult for me to leave Jim and, having done so, I needed to put it behind me. We both needed to start over. I am glad he found someone to share his life with.'

'But not a woman like you.'

'No. I think he chose not to ever love like that again.' She glanced at the clock. 'You must excuse me, I have an engagement soon.'

We stood. 'You never had children?'

'No.' Sorrow again. 'I could not. Jim was both saddened and relieved by that. He was afraid that he might pass on his demons.'

She hesitated a long moment. 'Is it something other than suicide?'

'More than, I think; maybe not other.'

'I hope you figure it out.' She spoke softly. 'Jim is worthy of that. And of justice.'

CHAPTER 17

Green Cards and
a Gray Christmas

I was tired, hungry, and cranky. I couldn't figure out this case or straighten out my love life. Forget: What was wrong with this picture? Try: What was right? Answer: Not much. Okay, I was *really* cranky. And I'd lost my perspective.

I had plenty of blackmail victims: Randolph (technically not proven but a pretty solid assumption), Madeline, Delia, and Johannsen. Victims with nothing in common in terms of background, education, profession, or social standing. Nothing in common but a generous donation to Hope For Kids elicited by extortion. And except for Madeline, who had figured that Randolph might be a victim, they were unaware of each other.

And the blackmailer? All victims assumed it was a he but all also agreed that 'his' voice sounded odd, possibly as though it had been electronically altered. Sex, age, physical description, personality? Zip. Nada. Hope For Kids was this blackmailer's charity of choice. That was it; that was what I knew.

Most blackmailers are in it for personal gain. A pattern of blackmail involves a communications system and a method of payoff. Both of these inevitably lead back to the perpetrator. The blackmailer is often personally known to his victims but feels secure and protected in the power he holds over them.

The blackmailer's MO in this case was, to date, foolproof: no personal gain or involvement, just a request for a check made out to an above-reproach local charity; no personal meetings or discussions; a one-shot deal rather than repeated acts of extortion; nothing in writing. Nothing, in other words, to identify, characterize, or lead back to the blackmailer.

Except for the fact that the victims I knew of were local, there was no particular reason to assume that the blackmailer was local. Much of the blackmail material was past rather than current, some decades old, and none of it had occurred locally. Johannsen was the exception here, but even without looking into his history, I strongly suspected that this was not a new pattern for him (a position solidified by profiles in similar crimes) and that he had a history as a sexual predator in other cities and areas. It was possible that this was a long-distance blackmailer considerably removed in both time and distance from the victims and their indiscretions.

It was like looking for a needle in a haystack. Or was that too optimistic a generalization?

I pulled into a minimart and bought a diet Dr Pepper and a KitKat candy bar, a wholesome snack that filled the nutritional requirements of two basic food groups: the caffeine group and the empty-carbo group. Then I drummed my fingers on the steering wheel and went for essentials.

Carter was my first client and top priority. My primary focus therefore was on Randolph and whatever had been compelling enough to drive him to suicide. I had an idea of what those demons, or at least some of them, were. True, I had no expectation that Randolph's demons would lead me to his blackmailer but the desperate can't be picky. That was the haystack; the demons were the needle, perhaps the irrelevant needle. I sighed and washed the last of the candy bar down with a slug of caffeine.

Off to visit Moon. Again.

As I was pulling out of the minimart parking lot a slick low-rider packed to the dash with a bunch of unappealing, hormone-hyped, body-pierced, leather-clad young males almost hit me. Not that they noticed. They had the windows of their car all the way down and were singing (screaming would be more accurate), 'Jingle balls, jingle balls!' at the top of their lungs. Gee. How festive and special.

The address Carter had given me was a ramshackle building in Alkali Flats on E Street, not far from where seven bodies had been found buried in the yard of a home rented by a 'sweet' little old white-haired lady who was in the business of luring in mentally incapacitated or elderly men and knocking them off for their Social Security, disability, or welfare checks.

Have I been in this business too long or what?

The house needed paint, a new roof, porch railings and steps. I looked up at the first floor. Ditto windows, curtains, and furniture. You name it, it needed it. I walked, carefully, up the steps and rang the doorbell. Hearing nothing, I knocked.

'Yes?'

The door opened on a vision of beauty. I know, I really do, what a dumb thing that is to say but I couldn't think of anything else. It was like being in a Hans Christian Andersen fairy tale. When you knock on the door of an ugly, evil, unhappy place you know that one of two things will happen. An ogre will answer the door and then your life is numbered in minutes. Painful ones. Or a beautiful but trapped maiden will be standing there, all dewy-eyed and innocent.

It was the maiden but she didn't look trapped. Or dewy-eyed. Or – I was remembering the video – innocent. But she was very beautiful, much more beautiful than the video or booking photo had led me to believe.

She had a compelling quality, a vibrant and physical charisma that was inescapable. I had no doubt that men would follow her to their destruction, in spite of judgment and survival instinct. And I had no doubt that she knew it and used it.

'May I help you?' There was a momentary (amused?) flicker in her young/old eyes and then it was gone.

'Moon Nguyen?'

'Yes.' A slight hesitation in her voice.

'My name is Kat Colorado. I have been retained by Richard Carter of Bradshaw, Bellows & Emerson in the matter of the execution of the legal affairs, more specifically the will, of the late James Randolph.' I deliberately spoke in legal gobbledygook.

133

'Please come in.' Her eyes were serious. There was no hesitation in her voice.

I followed the slim figure clad in a cheap knockoff of an expensive designer outfit into a house that was marginally nicer on the inside than on the out. Admittedly that wasn't saying much.

We seated ourselves in a living room that was, apparently, rarely used. The couch and easy chairs were threadbare and a thin film of dust lay on the coffee table and sideboard. The faded curtains were open but the windows were so filthy little light made its way in. There were no knickknacks or anything of personal note in the room.

Moon seated herself carefully, casually at ease with legs crossed at the knee and hands demurely in her lap. After a moment she tucked her abundant and beautiful hair behind her ears and then looked at me, eager but still demure.

Forget what I said about Hollywood needing me: it was Moon they would lust after. Outside a car backfired twice. And then a man yelled 'Goddamnit!' in a loud voice. Inside I could hear the drip of a faucet somewhere in the back of the house. And the wheels turning in Moon's mind? But that was my imagination. Or wishful thinking? I did not break the silence.

'James Randolph?' Moon queried at last.

'Yes.'

'When did he die?' There was no emotion in her voice and none on her face. The hands in her lap were still and calm.

'Are you surprised to hear of his death?'

She hesitated. Calculating what? Running through what answers? A foot started jiggling in the air. 'Well, uh, no. Ummmm. It was in the paper, wasn't it?'

'Was it?'

'Yeah, I guess. How else would I know?' Her eyes were young and innocent, open. But I had seen the old look in them before. And the videotape and booking photos. And those images were stronger than the present purported innocence.

'You knew Randolph?' I queried.

'No. Well, I—' She stopped and stared at me, her eyes speculative and hard now, all innocence gone. 'Why don't we just stop playing this little game.'

'It's not a game.'

'No,' she agreed. 'It's not. Give me the money and get the hell out of here.'

'What money?'

'He left me money, didn't he, and that's what this is all about?'

'That's not what this is about.'

Outside the hood of a car slammed down and something metal – a hubcap? – crashed, accompanied by more goddamnits.

'What *is* this about then?' There was a hiss in her voice and her eyes were thin slits. 'Make it good or you're out of here. I can go to Carter at Bellows and Whatsit myself.'

'What was your relationship to James Randolph?'

'That's none of your business.' Her voice was hard and insolent, like hubcaps crashing.

'I've made it my business.'

She thought that over carefully, then blinked and answered. 'We had no relationship. I just met him in passing and he took a friendly interest in me. That's all. He was a nice man. If you knew him, you know that. Why are people surprised when someone's nice?'

Why indeed? Surprised *and* cynical. Especially if extortion is involved.

'I've been very patient. There is absolutely no reason why I should have this conversation with you.' She had made her voice gentle and soothing. 'Leave me the name of the lawyer. I'll find out about the will myself.'

'You need to answer my questions first.'

'*You* need me to.' Her voice turned hard again. Her tone said: *Like I give a shit.* 'Well, that's too damn bad. Too bad for me because you're a waste of my time. Too bad for you because you're out of luck.' She stood and smoothed her skirt down quickly with her hands, never taking her eyes off me. Her right hand made a quick shooing motion. 'You're out of here. Out of luck and out of here.'

'It's tough to call, isn't it Ms Nguyen?' I leaned back in my seat. 'All the cards aren't out on the table and you have no way of knowing if the luck has changed.'

'All the cards?' Her voice was a whisper. 'What cards?'

'Randolph acted as your lawyer in getting you out of jail.'

Moon visibly relaxed, almost sagged in relief as she sat down again. 'Oh. That. Yes, that's true, he did. I, uh, made a mistake. He helped me take care of it. It was – what do you call it, you know, for free?' She waved her hand and dredged up a helpless vague look from somewhere. *Watch out, Hollywood.*

'Pro bono?'

'Yes.' She smiled at me as one would at a clever child.

'Hardly. Pro bono work is done within your field of expertise. Randolph's was probate work.'

'Oh really?' Surprise now. 'Well, that makes it even *nicer* of him then, doesn't it? I *told* you he was a nice man.'

She was relaxed though still very much on her guard. Wondering whether there were any other cards to come out on the table, wondering what they were. Moon looked at her watch and I got surprise again.

'Oh! It's so late, I had no idea! I've got to be somewhere and I mustn't keep you either. If you'll just leave me the lawyer's number. Oh! And your card too.' Winning smile. 'That way I can call you if I think of *any*thing that might help. Not that I imagine I will, but you *never* know.' She proffered a hand along with the smile.

Outside I heard children's voices, shouting in play or anger, I couldn't tell which. '*Step on a crack, break your mother's back!*' a gleeful voice shrieked, and then the shriek dissolved into laughter.

'The videotape, Ms Nguyen.'

Moon's smile dissolved, her face went white and scared.

'Videotape?' she whispered. 'I don't know what you're talking about.'

But the fear and knowledge was written on her face and we both knew it.

'You made Jim Randolph your lover. You called him your father. And then either you blackmailed him or you turned it over to someone else. Was he your father?'

'Oh God,' she whispered.

'Was he?'

'Oh.' She shook her head helplessly. 'No, I can't tell you . . . I . . .'

'How did you find out about Randolph?'

'Home. Vietnam. My mother . . .'

'She told you about your father?'

136

'Not my . . . It didn't happen that way. I . . .'

'Who made the tape?'

She shook her head, her eyes downcast.

'Who blackmailed Randolph?'

The same head shake. She looked like a terrified child. She played it well and I wasn't fooled.

'Leave me alone. Please. Don't make me hurt you.'

'You can't hurt me.' *How's that for bravado? And lying?*

'I can. My friends . . . Please don't make me. All I have to do is say something. I don't want to hurt you.' Her voice was a child's voice; her eyes were knowing and hard and filled with animosities as old as dirt. Animosity and knowledge. There was a glitter there too. Power is a drug and she was high. She stood and advanced on me.

I stood to meet her. And to fight back. We were playing dirty now; we were hitting below the belt. It was the only way I was going to get anything so I gave it my best shot.

'Moon Nguyen isn't your real name, of course. Are you here legally?' It stopped her, as I knew it would. I guessed there wasn't much about her that was legal.

She stood in front of me, frozen in body and in mind, and considered carefully before she answered, white-faced and whispering again.

'I have a green card!' She tried to make it sound forceful, even belligerent, but it sounded pathetic and forced instead.

'Randolph got you that, didn't he? A fake. Part of the payoff. What was the rest of the payoff? Money? Clothes? More green cards?'

She started screaming then. She was still screaming when I left.

137

CHAPTER 18

Dance of the
Sugarplum Fairy

I listened to screams as I picked my way down the rickety porch steps and climbed into the Bronco. By the time I'd rolled the windows down they'd stopped. Moon had sturdy vocal cords (not to mention violent mood swings and a volatile temper). I'd parked way down the block in a move that I call caution and Lindy claims is paranoia. There I settled in for what I hoped would be a short wait.

Settled in with props: a Giants baseball cap that I stuffed my hair into, oversized sunglasses, and a newspaper. In this neighborhood I looked like someone cruising through to make a drug buy. Well, except for the newspaper.

Fifteen minutes, that was it. A cab pulled up in front of the E Street house and Moon came tumbling down the steps. It was too far away to hear the swearing but I could see her lips move. She had lost the knockoff designer look and was in jeans, sneakers, and a sweatshirt, looking like an all-American kid going to a football game.

The cab pulled out with me right behind it. Zigzagging through town, we jumped onto Highway 50 where the signs informed us that we could go to Placerville and Lake Tahoe. I was betting we got off long before either.

It was a bet I would have won. And me with no money on it. Bummer.

We exited heading east on Folsom Boulevard in Rancho Cordova. Folsom Boulevard is one of those up-and-down streets, sometimes fine, sometimes not so fine. Rancho Cordova is an unincorporated area of Sacramento County, more not-so-great than great. Right now it was getting pretty cheeseball but not all that sleazy or dangerous. The cab pulled up in front of a small shop that advertised itself as Nails!Nails!Nails! in pink and orange neon. I pulled into a parking spot about five car lengths away, tipped my hat down over my eyes, and waited.

In half a minute Moon was out of the car and into the shop. Seconds and I was right behind her. I hate to miss the opening scenes, even the credits.

A little bell tinkled as I walked into the shop. Two faces turned toward me. One was slightly blank but welcoming, the other said 'Fuck!' in a loud voice.

The woman with Moon, a delicate attractive Asian woman in her mid-thirties looked shocked and distressed. Slipping herself in front of Moon, she smiled at me. 'May I help you?'

A torrent of words (abuse?) cut off any reply I might have made. Moon spoke rapidly, gesturing at me. Her companion seemed first puzzled, then distressed, then frightened. I could understand nothing of the conversation I guessed was in Vietnamese but the violence and anger in Moon's voice and actions transcended any language barrier. The woman, whose name was May – I got this from the name tag on the peach smock she wore – shushed Moon and addressed me again, her words polite and serene, her eyes frightened.

'May I help you?'

'I'd like to get my nails done.'

Moon exploded. 'She's not here to get her damn nails done.'

I looked at my nails carefully. 'I don't know. All this digging up trash and dirt is hard on them, don't you think?'

'Trash,' May said. 'There is no trash here.' But she was afraid. 'You should not bring people here,' she said to Moon. 'You will both please leave now.'

'All right.' I nodded, a little disappointed that I wasn't going to get a manicure. Dusty Rose, Georgia Peach, Vampire Red – what possibilities! 'Do you do red and green for Christmas?' I asked May.

'Glitter would be a nice touch.' May looked puzzled, and disinclined to answer. Moon muttered under her breath. And they say I have no fashion sense. Hah!

'May I use your bathroom?' I inquired politely.

May shook her head and started speaking at the same time. The words came out in sentences but they were all tangled up, English and Vietnamese together and impossible to understand. She was very frightened now.

'Thank you.'

I inclined my head graciously, shook off the frantic arm on my elbow, and headed for the back rooms. Moon made a grab for me, missed, and started swearing again.

I didn't find the bathroom. I did find a small room with tables that were almost completely covered with copying apparatus and green cards in various stages of production. The photos were of Asians; the names were, I thought, Vietnamese, though my understanding of Asian languages is far too limited for me to be sure.

Moon and May were right behind me, Moon still swearing. After that first comprehensive glance I walked past the table and knocked on a closed door.

'No bathroom!' May was emphatic.

'You can't use the fucking bathroom.' Moon was too.

'Okay,' I said, agreeably. I had what I wanted.

We filed out again, a little parade with me in the lead. May was silent now. Moon was still swearing. I was gloating but only on the inside.

'You go now!' May spoke to me.

I nodded and turned to Moon. 'Here's the deal, Moon.' I faced her down. 'We're walking out of here and down the block to my car where we are going to have a friendly little chat. If you take off, I'm not bothering to chase you. I know where you are; I know where your friends are; I know cops who will be as interested in this as I am. Are you with me?'

'Yes.' The answer was sullen and hostile.

'Let's go.' I led the way out of the shop without ever actually turning my back on Moon or taking my eyes off her. I trusted her as much as I did a rattlesnake. Less, actually.

141

On the way to the Bronco we passed a coffee shop and Moon turned into it. 'I want something to eat.' Sullen trying to sound assertive and in control.

'Okay.' I followed her in and pointed to a booth, watched her slide into the side away from the door before I sat down. Our booth looked out onto the street, into the fog and neon. Moon picked up a menu and flipped through it. I looked across the street at The G-String, which advertised *NUDE GIRLS*. How about that? You could eat, get your nails done and see a show and all on your lunch hour. Who says Sacramento is out of the culture loop?

A waitress plodded over to our table. She was almost as sullen as Moon but a lot more slovenly.

'Cheeseburger and fries, chocolate, milk shake.' Moon spat out the words like she had BBs in her mouth.

I shook my head when the waitress looked at me. I make it a policy not to eat in dives where the linoleum floors were last washed during the Truman administration and the waitress has large sweat stains in the armpits of her dress. Oh. And a dead fly on the table. The waitress shrugged and sneered. Translation: *Suit yourself, no skin off my butt.* And slouched off.

'Why won't you just fucking leave me alone?' Moon asked, still spitting words out.

'Did you research Life in Crime, Moon?' I asked pleasantly. 'Or just jump in?'

'Huh? What are you talking about?'

'Let me tell you how it works.' I spoke kindly, condescendingly. 'Crime looks good, pays big, seems like the way to go. Course that's on the good days and you can't count on them to roll around forever. The thing about crime is that you're breaking the law. Stop me if I'm going too fast here.' Moon glared at me. 'And that attracts attention, some of it from people you probably don't want to hang out a lot with – like cops and INS agents. And me, of course.'

The waitress slapped a couple of glasses of water on the table, only sloshing about a quarter of the contents out. The dead fly got caught in a brief ebb and flow and rolled around in a small tide pool.

'Shoplifting is one thing. But porn videos, blackmail, and running up green cards for illegal immigrants? That's getting big-time. Oh,

142

and incest, that's big-time too. Especially when it becomes a subject for extortion.'

Her face was white, her eyes dark and unreadable. 'You can't prove any of this.'

'Yeah? Try me.' And I smiled.

She said nothing. The conversational ball was still in my court. I tossed it out again.

'We're going to talk about James Randolph. 'We're going to talk about a lot of things and this time you're going to answer.'

Moon drummed her fingers on the table and then looked at me, ran her fingers through her hair, and smiled. Sweetly. Uh-oh, call me cynical but something was going on.

She confirmed that suspicion. 'Look, I haven't been entirely honest with you and I'm sorry. You're just trying to do your job—' She wrinkled her nose wryly. 'And I'm just trying to live my life. I'd be lying if I said I hadn't made some mistakes.' She spread her hands out, palms up, in a helpless and vulnerable gesture. 'My mother always said I should own up to whatever I had done and make the best of it, not run away or lie even though that may be the easiest thing to do.' She looked up at me shyly through half-closed eyes. Just like Di.

I said Hollywood, but forget about it. Maybe Stratford-upon-Avon. Ophelia, for instance. Or Desdemona. Wronged innocence and beauty, vulnerability – a poor young thing helplessly appealing for justice, compassion, and understanding. I felt myself buying in; I started feeling like an ogre.

That's how good she was.

Moon pushed her water glass around in the puddle in front of us and the fly ebbed and flowed. I took a deep breath. On the other hand, a dead fly is just a dead fly. I wondered what Moon was. What and who.

She smiled sweetly and winsomely at me. I saw moisture and the beginnings of tears in her eyes. 'So I'm going to help you and I'm going to tell the truth. I promise.' She did the Di look and shy smile again. 'And I'd like to ask you to help me and protect my privacy and—' She stammered to a stop there. 'And, well, you know.'

'Okay,' I said, smiling back. Not like Ophelia and Desdemona – if they smiled, which I kind of doubt – but like Iago, cunning and devious, motives well hidden. 'How did you know Jim Randolph?'

Her face became serious and still. 'This is *very* difficult for me.' A tear spilled out. '*Very*.'

I smacked a *very* concerned look on my face but remained silent.

'It goes back years, you know.' With her finger Moon drew water designs on the table. 'My mother knew him in Vietnam. Not just him but a lot of GIs. It was the war, you know. I never asked how she knew him but I guess I never had to,' she stated simply. 'As I grew older I understood. Those were hard times for many people and you did what you could, or what you had to do, to survive. I didn't pass judgment on her.'

She paused and we heard the waitress plodding and plopping – the plops were made by some hideous cross between sandals and bedroom slippers – over to our table, smacked down something that resembled a chocolate milk shake, and tossed a paper-covered straw into the puddle on our table, rearranging forever Moon's artistic creation. Art, like truth, is ephemeral. Moon went back to playing with truth.

'My mother tried to leave Vietnam. After I was born and after the Americans left, it was difficult for her. For both of us,' she said sadly, as she pushed and peeled soggy paper off her straw and stuck it in her milk shake, sipped delicately. 'She never made it.' She looked at me and bit her lower lip, blinking as if to hold back tears. 'She died before she could figure out how to get us over here. I was only eight. It was my uncle who got me out. My mother had left some money, you see, and that made it all possible. We came to America, to L.A., where I lived with my uncle's family. This is a good country, I love it very much. I am only sorry that my mother didn't live, couldn't start over with us, couldn't see me now.' She balled up her hands into fists and rubbed her eyes quickly.

I wondered how pleased Moon's mother would have been at some of her daughter's activities and interests. But perhaps Moon was a chip off the old block?

'LA. Have you ever been there?'

'Yes.'

'It is an exciting city. Fast. Dangerous.' Her eyes glittered. 'I liked it but my aunt and uncle did not. They traveled up here where there were others they knew and settled in this area. And I have come to like it here too. I was born in Vietnam but I feel like an American now.'

'James Randolph?' I nudged her back to the topic under discussion.

'Oh. Yes. Well, I told you. My mother knew him and other soldiers.'

'Is he your father?'

'I don't know. She never said. I think that perhaps she did not know. She had gone with more than one soldier and —' Moon shrugged. 'But he was kind to her and the others were not. She knew she was with child before he left, before he came home.'

With child. How archaic, how nineteenth-century that sounded, especially spoken by this old/young woman with flip modern ways.

'He gave her money and then later he sent us money. Every month. It would have been difficult for us otherwise. And it was because of the money that we were able to come to this country.'

I thought of the videotape. What an unexpected return that had been on Randolph's act of kindness. Or duty and responsibility – I corrected myself. But if Moon's mother had not known the father of her child, neither had he. It had not been his legal or moral obligation, though perhaps he accepted it as such.

'Were Randolph and your mother in touch? Letters? Phone calls? Anything?'

'No. He sent the money through a law firm.'

'Do you have any communication from Randolph – letters, pictures, a check, anything?'

'No. You are asking for proof, aren't you?'

'Verification, yes.'

'I have nothing. Nothing but these words which are the absolute truth.'

I nodded, though I thought that expecting the truth from the lips of a shoplifting extortionist was stretching it just a bit.

'How did you know about Randolph?'

'My mother told me. She gave me his name and address before she died. She told me that if I ever needed it he would help.'

'And you needed that help?'

'Yes.'

'And got in touch with Randolph?'

'Yes.' The Di look again, this time with a very shy, demure edge.

'And?'

'And he was nice – well, polite – to me but he refused to help.'

'You called him or saw him in person?'

'I called.'

'Why did he refuse?'

'He said I was over twenty-one and I was on my own. He said he had helped all those years out of a feeling of kindness for my mother even though he had no legal or moral obligation, had helped out of respect for her memory, but now that I was an adult that was over. He wished me well and asked me not to ever get in touch with him again. And then he hung up.'

She sucked at her milk shake and stared out the window. A plastic and tinsel Santa banged in the wind on a utility pole across the street.

'It's not the kind of thing I'd do, you know, if someone didn't make me.' She looked away from Santa and back to me.

'Make you?'

'Yes. I'm a nice person, really I am. But he wouldn't help me. He left me with no choice. He made me do something that wasn't very nice.'

I didn't respond. I couldn't, I would have lost it. Even though the world is full of people who don't take responsibility for their lives or actions it makes me wild every time. I watched Santa flop around on the utility pole while I got myself under control.

'What did he make you do?'

A floppy Santa, a demure liar – what a deal, what a choice.

'The video, of course. It's not the kind of thing I'd want to do. Not at all. He wouldn't help, he pushed me, he *made* me do it.'

Contempt rose in my throat like bile, ugly, nasty, and bitter-tasting. My diplomacy, limited as it is, was exhausted.

'You lying little shit.'

CHAPTER 19

Dear Charity.
I have a friend who won't be good, not even for Christmas.
What can I say?

Afraid Franny

Dear Franny,
Nothing. The world is full of people who would be happy and
secure if they worked as hard at being good as they do at being
bad.

Charity

The waitress slapped Moon's burger and fries down on the table,
then took a bottle of ketchup she'd tucked into her sweat-stained armpit
and smacked it down too. Both Christmas spirit and finesse had passed
her by.

Moon stared at me wide-eyed and hurt. I had seen a flash of anger
or hatred in her eyes but only a flash. Wide-eyed and hurt had shoved
it over almost immediately.

'How can you say that?' Her voice trembled. The tears were back.
She picked up a fry and nibbled delicately at it. Then reached out for
the ketchup bottle and poured. I shuddered. 'How can you even *think*
it?' Her voice was still hurt and quavery though she wasn't too
fastidious to eat ketchup that had been in someone's armpit. Stinky
armpit at that.

'Wrong question.'

She looked at me, hand holding a ketchup-dunked fry, mouth slightly
ajar.

'How could you think I'd believe it? That's the question. Randolph was an extraordinarily intelligent man, well educated and street-smart. And he was a lawyer trained to pick things apart and put them back together. You didn't call. You didn't even consider it. You would never have taken the risk that he would turn you down. You knew if you called him and he refused to help you there wasn't a chance, not a prayer, that you could entice him into a compromising situation. You never called him, you never spoke to him, all your efforts went into seduction.'

Moon took a big bite of her cheeseburger, chewed slowly and carefully, then blotted her lips.

'Well, okay, I guess it could have happened that way.' She spoke as though she had been corrected on something incidental and trivial, tying her shoes maybe.

I shoved my rage and contempt down again. 'How did you do it?'

'Get him, you mean?' She spoke in inadvertent honesty.

'Yes.'

'I found out where he worked – in an office downtown – and then I watched as he came out. Once or twice a week he would go to Biba's to have a drink. I followed him. Most of the time he – would go in by himself and leave by himself. Then I started going to Biba's a little bit earlier than he arrived. I'd get all dressed up and carry a briefcase and at the bar I'd act very, very . . .' She paused, apparently at a loss for words.

'Respectable?' I offered, trying to keep the irony out of my voice.

'Yes.' She nodded in agreement, a stranger to the irony.

'I think he noticed me right away but he didn't sit next to me or approach me or anything. He *was* respectable. It took me a little while to make the contact. This was before he got married, which was lucky, otherwise I probably wouldn't have had a chance. It wasn't all that easy, anyway.' She wrinkled her nose at the memory.

'It's usually a lot easier?'

'Oh, yes, much.' She caught herself and glanced at me through her lashes. 'Well, I mean, I wouldn't know. It's not the kind of thing I'd do, you know. *Ordinarily*, I mean.' She picked up her cheeseburger and munched away. 'Don't be mad at me, *please*. I was desperate. You understand, don't you?'

I looked at this beautiful, healthy, intelligent, talented woman who gravitated to criminal means to solve her problems and decided that no, I didn't. I didn't even want to try. I lied instead.

'Sure.' I nodded to punctuate my assertion and looked her right in the eye. Henley says it's true about the guilty being shifty-eyed and refusing to meet your gaze. 'You had it rough.' Something clanged outside and I looked out the window to see Santa banging around on his pole in the wind. Some of his tinsel was working loose, He had it rough too.

'It's funny.' She stared out the window and wandered around in the past. 'It was like he was attracted and repelled by the situation. I don't even think it was me, I don't think I mattered all that much. Somehow I reminded him of Vietnam or put him back into the past or made it alive again or something. Part of him didn't want to do it and part of him did. I didn't have long with him. I knew that, I'd seen it in guys before.'

Again she glanced covertly at me to see if I had noticed her slip. Again I pretended I hadn't.

'Anyway, I had it all set up, the video stuff, I mean. From the beginning, which was a good thing, it was only the one time. With him, I mean. He didn't call me after and when I went back to Biba's the bartender said he didn't come in anymore.'

'Who made the video?'

'It's nice, huh, a real work of art. A guy I know who works at a TV station. I could never have done that. I would've just sent the film and the photographs of my mom or something. I had to connect it, you see. I told him, Randolph I mean, that I'd been born and raised in L.A. So I had to prove it, show him pictures of me and my mother together – you can really see the resemblance and everything.'

'What's the name of the guy at the station?'

'Tommy—' She started to give his last name but caught herself.

'Was he in on the blackmail?'

'No. I gave him a couple hundred bucks for his trouble, that was it.'

'And Randolph?'

'I sent him the video and asked him again for help. I said that a thousand dollars would come in real handy. I said if he sent it to me I would destroy the only other copy of the video.'

'Did he?'

'Send money? Yes.'

'Did you destroy the tape?'

'No. I – uh – meant to but then I decided to keep it, kinda like insurance, I guess.'

'Did you hit Randolph up again?'

'No. I was going to, I guess, but then he died and it was too late. I was sorry about that.'

'His death?'

'Well, yeah, that too.'

She finished her cheeseburger and shake and I swallowed my rage.

'After he died I destroyed the tape. I really was sorry.'

'Does anyone else have a copy of the tape?'

'No.'

Wrong.

'Tommy?'

'Oh no. He just did it for the money, he said it was just a job.'

Wrong again?

'Would he work for me? I could use someone with his skills.'

'Tommy? Yeah, sure, he'd do anything for money. Well, not anything. You know what I mean.'

I nodded, though I thought she might have had it right the first time. 'What's his number?'

Moon pulled a small, ratty pink plastic address book out of her purse, flipped through it and shoved it across the table at me, pointing to the information. Tommy Turner. Two phone numbers. I jotted them down. And the number below them for good measure. I would have tried for more but I ran out of time. Moon tucked the notebook away in her purse.

'Jim Randolph could have been your father.'

She shrugged. 'Yeah, well, I guess. But I didn't think he was.'

'But he could have been?'

'Yeah, I guess. I didn't think about it much.'

'It didn't bother you, sleeping with a man who could have been your father?'

She shrugged again. 'I told you I didn't think about it.' She giggled.

'It was fun, though. He was really good in bed. I liked it a lot.' That giggle again. 'It's kind of cool and kinky, don't you think?'

I stood. I thought I'd get out of there before I smacked her. Moon stood too, a perverted smile playing with her mouth. The waitress plopped briskly over to us and handed me the check. Moon licked her lips. I handed her the check.

'Hey, this was on you, I thought.'

'No. Your idea, your meal.'

'I don't have any money. That was a *big* cab fare.' She started with the tears again. And the vulnerable innocence.

But I thought of her licking her lips, smiling over how kinky and cool it was to sleep with a man who could be your father. As I left the waitress was hollering and holding on to Moon, who was trying to scramble out the door after me. I caught a last glimpse of the dead fly.

Walking back to the Bronco I wondered if I had made a mistake in not pushing on the fake green card issue. I was willing to put money on Moon not having a legal immigration card and on May trafficking in them. Maybe I'd guessed wrong on Randolph being involved? Never mind. I could pull that ace out of the deck anytime I wanted to.

Santa banged the pole in a final goodbye as I drove off. I tried to comprehend what was kinky and cool about incest but I couldn't. I don't think I ever will.

Tommy Turner looked like a scruffy scumball to me. He was riding a Harley and wearing a leather jacket and chaps. A long ponytail hung down from the abbreviated helmet worn by bikers who think they shouldn't have to wear helmets but now, under California law, do. I saw him from the back first. As he parked his Harley I got a front view. Just as scruffy with an untrimmed mangy-looking beard. I could see the glint of metal that I assumed was earrings.

I wasn't positive, of course, that this was Turner but he matched the description I had gotten from some trusting soul at the TV station. And the address he was walking into matched the one in the phone book. I gave him a ten-minute head start.

It was an old house and he had a walk-up on the second floor. The place was clean but nothing to write home about. I could hear the TV blasting as I stood outside the door. I knocked twice before the door opened.

'Yeah?' He put a rude spin on that simple word. 'Can I help you?' That was after he'd looked me over and apparently decided I met with his approval.

'Tommy Turner?'

'Yeah?'

'I have a film job. I hear you're available and you're good.' I spoke loudly, over the TV.

He motioned me in, reached for the clicker and hit the mute button. I took in the scenery. He had acne scars, a huge nose, a receding hairline (why is it that guys with receding hairlines are so fond of long ponytails?), and a stained T-shirt. Oh, and a skull-and-crossbones earring with diamonds for eyes. Those were pretty much his good points. The apartment, except for the TV which was big and expensive, pretty much matched him.

'What did you have in mind?'

'Are you good?'

'No one told you?'

I shrugged. 'People exaggerate.'

'Yeah, I'm good. I'm the best.'

'Confidential?'

'Yeah. It'll cost you more then 'cause I gotta work after hours when nobody is around.'

'Fast?'

'Shit, yeah. You gonna get to it or are we gonna stand here all night?'

'I have some videotape, some photos, that kind of thing. I want it all put together. Packaged. I want it to look good, professional.'

'What's it for? You selling a product or something?' I didn't say anything. 'Hey, you in sales or what?'

'It's something personal. For a party.'

'Yeah.' He grinned. 'I get your drift. That'll cost you extra too.'

'My friend didn't say anything about that.' I made my voice outraged and pissed.

'Tough shit. Where you gonna go – Kodak? I charge what I can get. Life's a bitch – so what's new? Two hundred and fifty dollars for fifteen minutes or under, take it or leave it.'

'How do I know I can trust you to be confidential?'

'Professional courtesy.' He leaned forward and leered at me.

Jeez. On top of everything else he had bad breath. I backed up, heading for the door.

'You got the stuff with you?'

'No. I'll think about it and get back to you.'

'Suit yourself. I get busy, it'll cost you even more.'

For a scumball wannabe biker he definitely had a greedy mainstream capitalist attitude.

Turner reached for the clicker and hit the sound, then turned his back on me and started picking his nose. I walked toward the door, hesitated. I hated to touch the doorknob. The TV blared behind me as well-paid actors solved their 'problems' by drinking Coke. Right.

Before I could reach the door someone pounded on it. I jumped. So did Tommy. He beat me to the door and opened it onto another biker wannabe. This one wore an unbuttoned leather vest. No shirt covered his hairless chest or potbelly. At least these guys didn't let personal vanity or pride get between them and a fashion statement.

'Hey man.' Biker number two leered. 'You busy?'

I walked by them both.

'Naw, I guess not. I got some beer. You got some stuff?'

Tommy's reply was lost on me as I headed down the stairs and out the door, desperate for fresh air. I sat in the cold Bronco for an hour but no one came or left. And, finally, I was too cold to care.

You can come up with a lot of possibilities in an hour in the cold. I thought Moon was a straightforward small-time con artist. While there was definite potential to go big-time I didn't think she had yet. I thought I was looking at the same blackmailer in all these cases – Randolph, Madeline, Delia, and Johannsen. And it wasn't Moon. He – I found myself calling the blackmailer he – was a pro. Big-time. He covered his tracks well but there were tracks. Links.

Tommy Turner was one, I was pretty sure of it. Had he sold the tape and information to the blackmailer? One-shot deal? Regular business sideline? I didn't know. And I didn't see a way to make Tommy spit it out. Yet. I toyed with the idea of following through on the entrapment 'blackmail' video. Too time-consuming for now, I decided.

The other thing I was sure of was that there were more blackmail victims. A lot more, is what I was betting on. And, sooner or later, there would be a lead back to the blackmailer.

Nobody's perfect.

Not even a smart criminal.

CHAPTER 20

WANTED: Volunteers to help children. Please
apply in person at Hope for Kids.

Madeline seemed the logical place to start. That tactic also required a
minimum of explanation and no subterfuge (i.e. lying). Both were
attractive options. She was pleased to hear from me but that pleasure
wore off pretty quickly. This is another aspect of my job that makes
me wonder if I belong in a different line of work.

'You want me to *what*? Kat, I don't know. I mean—' She stopped.

'Madeline.' I made my voice patient. Or I tried to – it was a little
difficult because it was the opposite of how I felt. 'It's discouraging,
I know, but since I'm not psychic our only other option here is to fall
back on basic investigative tactics.'

'Well, yes, I see that but – but we're prying into things.'

'No.' Still patient, in voice at least. 'Charities routinely list their
donors. We are not prying into people's private lives, we are looking
at donor lists. I need you to get me into the office so I can go through
the files.'

'But how would I do that?'

'For godssakes, Madeline, you sound like a feeble, helpless little
old lady – which you are not. You are a firecracker, a *fighter*.' Okay,
I lost it. Patience never was my strong suit.

The phone line was silent; then I heard her take a deep breath. 'All
right, I'll get us in. Do I have to stay?'

'No. It's probably easier and quicker if you don't.'

'When?'

'As soon as possible. Tonight even.'

'All right. I'll call you back when I know more.'

I worked at my desk for the next hour hoping Madeline would put it together quickly. And she did. I answered the phone just as quickly.

'Can you meet me there around six-thirty?'

'Yes.'

'I'm going in at five-thirty but someone is often there until later. Usually not past six-thirty though. If it's not clear I'll call you by six.' She took a breath. 'I told them I was thinking of planning a social get-together. Maybe a donor and volunteer appreciation night, and I needed to take notes on who should be included and featured.' Her voice sounded flat and sad.

'Madeline, cheer up, this has got to be stopped. The blackmailer is not just injuring you, he has targeted numerous others. And he is using Hope For Kids. This is precisely the kind of thing that can destroy an organization. Never mind that – Hope For Kids does a great job and is not involved, the scandal could still bring it down. You are doing the right thing.'

'Yes, all right, I believe that.' Her voice sounded a little bit better.

'Six-thirty, then?'

'Six-thirty,' I confirmed.

I was there early, once again watching on a cold night from a cold car. At exactly six-thirty I made my way up the steps of the building with a Midtown address that was the office of Hope for Kids. I knocked on the heavy glass-paneled outer door, then watched as Madeline made her way down the corridor toward me. In the high-ceilinged old building she looked small and fragile. She smiled wanly at me through the glass panel as she turned the dead bolt.

I smiled back, my heart clutching slightly. Happiness is such a tenuous thing and the pursuit of it often so arduous and uncertain. I answered Madeline's soft greeting and followed her down the hall. The office of Hope For Kids was well lit and cheerful with photographs of smiling children; everywhere there were framed drawings, poems and essays by children. A small space heater was working overtime in a doomed attempt to take the chill out of the heavy damp cold that was seeping in from the outside. A filing cabinet with an open drawer beckoned invitingly.

'Would you like a cup of tea? I made some for myself.'

'No. Thank you,' I added quickly. I hate it when I forget my manners. 'Please show me around. Then I'll walk you back to your car and get to work.'

Madeline nodded, looking relieved at hearing such a straightforward and simple plan. 'Can you work a computer?'

'Yes.'

'Oh, good. I'm not very competent at it yet, though Amy's trying to teach me. Everything of course is in the computer. Here's a list of file names, or whatever they're called. Here are donors – individual and corporate, the volunteers, the professional volunteers, grant histories and so on. Everything is cross-referenced. If a doctor donates her services, is part of a medical group that made a corporate donation, and volunteers to mentor a child she would appear under corporate donor, professional donor, and volunteer. Each category would refer you to the others.'

I nodded, glanced at the printout on the desk and began playing with the computer. 'Got it.'

Madeline looked relieved. 'The filing cabinets hold hard copy of the above, backup files, copies of grants, et cetera. The organization is basically the same, although the cross-referencing is limited – and it is alphabetically done.'

I nodded. 'Everything is here at this office?'

'Yes. At least everything that I know about. This filing cabinet holds informational brochures, newsletters, publicity packets, applications for inclusion in the program and that sort of thing.'

'Mailing list, tax files, personnel files?'

Madeline frowned. 'Oh my, I haven't any idea. It didn't occur to me to ask even, not that I really could without sounding nosy and looking suspicious.'

'Never mind. If it's here, I'll find it. Explain to me the lockup procedures.'

'Here are the directions.' She pointed. 'It's dead bolt locks and then setting the alarm.'

I nodded. 'Does anyone else have a key? The director, board members?'

'I don't know. Jackie, the director, must. No one else was expected in tonight though. Her office is through that door but she always locks up when she leaves. I would assume that sensitive and private files are kept in there.'

I nodded, then smiled. 'Don't look so worried, Madeline. Everything's fine. Let's get you back to the car, and me back to work.'

'All right.' Again she looked relieved. 'Please call me later and tell me how everything worked out.'

I agreed to it, in a hurry to scoot Madeline off, in a hurry to snoop. Madeline had turned all the available lights on. After she was safely stashed in her car I turned off everything I didn't need. No point in being wildly obvious.

I started with the computer files. Since all the donations were legitimate, entirely aboveboard, there was no reason to think they wouldn't be duly recorded and noted. So far so good. Unfortunately I didn't know what I was looking for. When you don't know that, your job is both harder and longer.

The blackmailer's pattern so far had been to hit up victims only once. Still, a small sample was hardly conclusive; I decided to go with the premise that repeats were at least possible. In a minute and a half I pulled up repeat donors for the last five years in amounts of a thousand or more. God I love computers! Do you have any idea how many snoop hours this would entail without a computer? I printed that list, then pulled up and printed a list of all donors of a thousand and more – just in case Charity and I had missed something.

The information in the computer was abbreviated and coded. I was curious to see who, if anyone, had recruited these donors, how they had found out about the organization, what had sparked their interest and so on. Anything, in other words, that might lead me back to a (nefarious) source.

Scanning the list I eliminated anyone who was cross-referenced as a service provider or volunteer. Given that the charitable instinct of the donors I was searching for was motivated by extortion, I thought it unlikely that they would be involved to the point of providing free professional services or mentoring a child. Twenty names. I eliminated those who hadn't donated in the last year. Twelve names. I headed for the filing cabinets and hard copy.

Hard copy is one of those terms that sounds very full, complete, and businesslike. Hah. As with many organizations that rely on volunteer labor and a dedicated but overworked and underpaid staff, the files ranged from pretty good to a shambles. I flipped through each – again looking for something I couldn't put my finger on. A few quick observations and notes: Sam Gunther and Jackie Anderson both had excellent track records here, Gunther easily in first place – no surprise there since he worked fulltime at fund-raising and Anderson had numerous other duties as director. Their notes were concise, orderly, and businesslike. A number of donors mentioned other donors both as informing them of the program, and as their impetus to contribute. A few were apparently motivated by a vague sense of do-unto-others. Several claimed a need for a tax write-off. Nothing was jumping out at me. Phooey.

I went back to the computer and pulled up and printed corporate donors and professional donors. Nothing jumping out there either. I scanned through files to see if donors were referenced by how they found out about or joined the organization. Nope. Or what their long-term commitment was. Nope. Or favorite sport. Or toothpaste. Or the price of tea in China and hog shares in Kansas.

Rats.

Nothing was jumping anywhere.

Okay, change-of-pace time. I exited the computer and headed for the director's office. The door was, as Madeline had said, locked, but the lock was a piece of junk – I'd noted that when I walked in. A piece of junk that I could open in a heartbeat. Jackie Anderson's office was strikingly different from the outer office. No photos, no children's art. Instead tastefully framed reproductions of abstract art, plants, and objets d'art dominated. The hues were subdued and harmonious, not the vivid slash of primary colors that was so evident in the outer office. The director's office spoke of good taste, elegance, and money.

I pulled out Jackie's incredibly expensive black leather chair and slid into it. The desk was a heavy antique oak. Luckily for me either the locks didn't work or the small keys had been long since lost. The top of the desk was pristine, graced only by a computer, a Mont Blanc pen, and an exquisite glass paperweight. I started through the drawers: office hardware and supplies; paper supplies, stationery, and cards; folders with notes for possible fund-raising projects;

publicity releases; copies of laudatory newspaper articles – one with a note to forward on to *60 Minutes*.

I began to lose heart. Let's face it, breaking in and snooping around really isn't as much fun if you don't come up with something good. The bottom drawer – last chance – had a box of chocolates. Nut-and-caramel chews, my favorites. I had to hold myself back. Snooping is one thing, stealing another. Also a large bottle of mineral water and a glass jar of pistachios. Another favorite. All of this reminded me that I hadn't eaten for what seemed like weeks, maybe months – not that I was cranky about it. Yeah, right. An expensive silk scarf was tucked away in the back of the drawer. Underneath it was an oil-stained chamois cloth. Scary stuff. I closed the drawer with a sigh.

And opened it again. Something was wrong. What? A quick once-over told me nothing. Ditto a long thoughtful one. *Whoa!* Not the old false-bottom drawer trick? *Yes!* I found a letter opener in the top drawer and eased the false bottom back. It slid effortlessly in nearly invisible well-used grooves.

Well, well. Who would have thought? Ms Director had brought her nonprofessional side to work. I looked at – but didn't touch – a slim vibrator, a set of small metal balls in a box, and a black and red lacy something-or-other. I closed the false bottom and then the drawer feeling a little smarmy. I often find out things I don't need to know, don't want to know, and would be better off *not* knowing.

The score so far? One down, two to go: the filing cabinet and Jackie's computer. The former was disappointing. No personnel files, no tax records, no intriguing letters from attorneys, no commendations from the President. It was largely empty except for the bottom drawer which housed a well-worn pair of athletic shoes, a dressy pair of high-heeled pumps, and backup panty hose still in its original packaging. The computer was my last chance. I headed for it, my hopes foolishly up.

They were quickly dashed. With the exception of a correspondence file, the records here were apparently identical to the ones I'd already looked through. On impulse I went back to the supply drawer, found an empty disc, and copied the correspondence. While the computer was copying its little heart out I took a quick look around the office. One of the plants was desperate for water. And I was puzzled by the three-panel bamboo screen in the corner. For elegance? For quick changes à la Superman? For vibrating moments?

The computer finished, I exited and pocketed the disc. I must remember to send in a small donation, I reminded myself, what with helping myself to office supplies.

Instinct is built on survival and training. As with the false-bottom drawer it is difficult to say what tipped me off. I took a last quick look at the desk to make sure I'd left it as I found it, turned the desk lamp off, and glided over to the corner and the bamboo screen.

Shit!

I raced out again, closed the office door – the click of the lock all too audible – and dashed behind the screen, tripping on my shoelaces and almost toppling me and the screen over. Quality suffers badly under time pressure.

In time, but barely.

I heard her before I saw her.

'Damn it all! How many times do I have to tell them to turn the lights out when they leave? Ooops!' I heard the crash of something that sounded like a metal wastebasket bouncing off a desk. And then a giggle. 'And how many times do I have to tell myself that three double martinis is too many?' She giggled again.

She was the only one giggling. I was alternating between despair and silent curses. At myself, at my job, at my stupid hardheaded I'm-too-good-to-get-caught attitude. I wondered what the bail was on illegal entry.

I heard the fumbling of metal against metal and then the key turning in the lock. I quit swearing under my breath and just despaired. Okay, and considered prayer.

Jackie wobbled over to her desk – I could see clearly through the woven bamboo of the screen – and tumbled into her chair. People wearing two-and-a-half-inch heels should probably resist drinking three double martinis. There she giggled again and reached for the phone. Punching out a number, she leaned back, swung her feet up on the desk, eased off her shoes and wriggled her toes.

By then I was holding my breath as the bamboo screen had turned out to be a big-time dust trap. I hoped I wouldn't sneeze. *Really* hoped I wouldn't.

161

'Well, *hey*.'

Jackie's voice seemed sweet and friendly but there was, I thought, something ugly and awful woven into it. I shivered.

'Imagine my disappointment, will you?' She paused. When she spoke again the friendliness was gone, the ugliness stark. 'You know, I really can't be bothered. I'm not interested in what you call reasons and I call excuses. When I pick up the mail I don't want to be disappointed. I want to see a check, a nice . . . big . . . fat . . . check, and I want to see it now.' She slammed the phone down.

Another giggle. And more numbers being punched out.

'Hey, Big Boy.' Her voice was slow, lazy, and seductive. I braced myself for the coming threats and ugliness.

'You're working late? *Me* too. You want to know what I'm doing now? Hmmm? I'm thinking about you. Well . . . not *just* thinking.'

I had lost all urge to sneeze and was now desperately trying not to gasp. You know how some people indulge in hyperbole, especially on the phone? Yeah. Well, *she* wasn't. I looked away; listening was bad enough. I'm the kind of person who doesn't go to X-rated films.

'I'm thinking about you and I'm playing with myself. I *could* get out my vibrator but *you'd* be better, Big Boy.'

She listened to Big Boy, giggling and playing, and I was never ever *ever* going to break in *any*where again. Not even my own house if I forgot the key. Not even a burning building if I—

'Well, all *right*. Ten minutes. I'll be waiting.'

She made a bunch of sickening kissy sounds on the phone and then hung up. I peeked through the bamboo screen again, hoping it was safe. She was standing by her desk, smoothing down her skirt and smirking.

'Bathroom,' she said to herself as she giggled and wobbled off.

I gave her a small lead but basically I was right behind her. No giggling. No wobbling. Just getting the hell out of there.

I was out in a heartbeat.

And down the street, into the Bronco and breaking speeding laws in a flash.

Okay, that's a lie. That's what I *wanted* to do. That was Plan A, triple-starred, triple-rated. Every cell in my body urged me to get lost, to go home to a nice hot bath and a fried egg sandwich.

Plan B was to wait for Lover Boy.

Waiting in my safely locked and secure Bronco was another Plan A but once again it was Plan B. Sacramento's side streets are not graced with adequate lighting. Sitting in the car I would see only a shadowy figure in a coat going up the stairs and in the door. Not good enough. I sighed. It would have to be lurk and pounce.

I leaned against the shady side of a tree – trees are something we have plenty of in River City – and stuffed my hands in my pockets, thinking longingly of the toasty leather gloves in the warm winter coat in my closet at home. I wasn't far from the building that housed the Hope For Kids office. Lover Boy would either pass me or I would walk out and cross his path.

So where the hell was he? The damp, cold night was turning me into a Popsicle; I was shivering almost uncontrollably now. Headlights swung around the corner and I snuggled up to the rough-barked sycamore I was hanging out with. Lover Boy parked down the street on the other side of Hope For Kids. He doused his lights and climbed out of a silver Mercedes that chirped cheerfully at him as he walked away.

His heels sounded on the pavement, my sneakers were silent. He looked up, startled, when we passed. I was startled too, I just didn't show it.

Lover Boy was Adam Howard, a local TV news anchorman.

And a self-described happily married man.

CHAPTER 21

Nutcracker Waltz

That night on the eleven o'clock news I fancied there was a certain sated and content look about Adam Howard. His eyes had a sparkle to them and he seemed a little more smug than usual. Not a hair was out of place, his tie was straight and his collar unsmudged. His voice throbbed with emotion as he told of a small child who had dashed out into the street after her puppy and been struck by a UPS truck. The child, the puppy, and the driver – a father of three who had held the little girl in his arms and sobbed – were all doing well.

I turned the sound down, finished my fried egg sandwich, sipped on my wine, and played with the computer while my mind played with possibilities.

Like the conversation I'd overheard in Jackie's office. 'I want to see a nice big fat check, and I want to see it now.' In a threatening voice. This was the way directors of reputable charities addressed their donors? Difficult to believe. Was I was out of the polite business loop? No, probably not.

Jackie Anderson, director, as blackmailer?

Talk about a new twist on an old theme.

I glanced at the TV and at Adam Howard's smug smirk. Big Boy? It was a stretch for my imagination. Ranger stirred at my feet, then stood growling, his hackles up, his nose pointing in the direction of the front door. I stood too, slipped through the house to the bay window

165

in the living room where by peeking through the curtains I could see the porch and the front door.

'Son of a bitch,' I muttered under my breath. This was a description, not a random expression. Ranger started barking when the pounding on the door began. I turned a light on in the living room, walked to the front door and opened it.

J.O. lounged against the doorframe, hands behind him, hair tousled, shit-eating grin in place. His shirt was wrinkled and buttoned lopsidedly, the collar higher on one side than the other. He looked like Robert Redford the morning after. And he was playing it for all he was worth.

'For you, Kat, a peace offering.' He held out hands filled with presents, a bunch of baby roses (only slightly wilted), a bag of pretzels, a sack with twisted licorice whips, and a bottle of wine.

'Gosh, J.O., you sure know the way to a girl's heart.'

His grin widened. 'May I come in?' His feet followed his words in without waiting for an answer. Ranger growled and showed his teeth. The feet stopped. The growling didn't.

I signaled to Ranger and stood back to let J.O. in. Ranger stayed close to me, his hackles still up; he rarely gets like this. Ranger and J.O. both followed me to the kitchen where I stuck the flowers in a crystal vase, opened the pretzels and wine, a nice merlot.

'Licorice whips?' I raised an eyebrow.

'Isn't that your favorite?'

'No, I hate licorice. Is it yours?'

'Yeah.'

I got a sheepish, impish, boyish grin which almost had me in abandoned thrall until I reminded myself that J.O. was at his most deadly when he was at his most charming.

'Cheers, Katy.' He held up his wineglass in salute. 'To success.'

'We drank – to something different, I bet – then I picked up the pretzel bowl and headed for my office. I waved J.O. into a seat and set the pretzels down next to him. Then I turned the computer off.

On the TV the weatherperson, a diminutive, chubby-cheeked cherubic little man, assured us that we could expect more of the same chilly, damp weather with, maybe, a nasty winter storm blowing in by the end of the week. He smiled cherubically at us and J.O. snorted.

'What the fuck? I thought all the Munchkins were long gone.'

'Your warmth and sweetness are so endearing J.O., not to mention politically correct.'

He grinned at me. 'Open your mouth. Pretzel toss.'

I ignored him. Naturally. Adam Howard came back into focus and filled up the screen with his charm and smile.

'Do you think evil is visible, J.O.?'

J.O. looked from me to the TV screen and back again. 'What brought that on?'

'Do you?'

'No.'

'Wickedness? Felonious intent? A bent toward crime?'

'No.'

'Why not?' It's not that I really expected him to have the answers, I was thinking aloud now. 'Poor physical health, even if it's hidden – an internal ailment, say – is visible in the body. Why shouldn't psychological or spiritual imbalance—' I frowned. 'Not that I think that exactly defines evil, but you know what I mean. Anyway, why shouldn't that be visible?'

'You ask the wrong questions, Katy. Drink your wine. Eat your pretzels.'

'Remember *The Picture of Dorian Gray*?'

J.O. thought, then shook his head. 'Photograph? Painting?'

'A novel by Oscar Wilde about a very beautiful young man who had his portrait painted. He never aged or changed but his portrait did. It became old, dissipated, and ugly, reflecting the way he was and lived. Every day he would admire his own beauty and stare at the hideous portrait which by then he kept in a closet.'

J.O. finished his wine and reached for the bottle. 'You not only ask the wrong questions, you read the wrong stuff.'

I turned the TV off, the news over. 'Maybe he made a deal with the devil.' It had been a long time since I'd read the book.

'We all make deals with the devil.'

'No.' I dismissed that as a stupidity. And then I thought about Nazis, about baby-faced murderers, handsome debonair rapists, and fatherly child molesters.

167

'What did Adam Howard do?'

J.O. caught me off guard, way off guard, and I gasped. Good reporters, like investigators, have to have that quickness, that sense of things that is almost intuitive.

'Your question about evil didn't come out of nowhere.'

'No. But your last question did.'

He shook his head. 'You don't watch TV, I know that. It wasn't a particular news item or you would have turned it off then. Or the weather, or you would have turned it off after that. That leaves us with Adam Howard. You turned it off when he said goodnight.'

'I don't know why you don't spend more time with fiction, J.O., you seem to have quite a flair for it.' I gave him my big innocent smile.

'Hey, to hell with all that.' J.O. put his wine down, hitched his chair across the floor to mine and reached out for my hands.

I had a wineglass in them. And no intention of putting it down. 'I thought you came offering peace?'

'I did. It could be a package deal though. How about I throw in a piece of ass?'

'Jeez J.O., how do you *ever* score? Lacking in finesse doesn't even begin to cover it. I have a boyfriend, remember; and some of us are faithful to our commitments. Also, I don't like you.'

'You're attracted to me though, be honest.'

'That's true but so what? Even if I didn't have a boyfriend I wouldn't sleep with someone I didn't like.' The phone rang in the other room, my home line, and I got up to answer it. 'Don't bother to pour yourself any more wine, I'm throwing you out.'

It was Alma, Alma on a roll. It took me two minutes to cool her down and agree that I could call her back. I walked into my office to find J.O. standing over my desk and computer. The computer is programmed to resume, which, in computer language, means that when it's turned on the cursor is flashing in precisely the same place as it was when it was turned off. Two minutes. J.O. had had enough time to go through the file, see both what it was and what I'd noted. As of course he had.

'You son of a bitch!' I was furious.

He grinned at me. 'Hope For Kids, huh? I thought they were on the up-and-up. We talking scam here? Is Howard somehow connected to this?'

'Get the fuck out of here, J.O.'

He downed the rest of his wine. The bastard had poured more. Talk about adding insult to injury. I crossed the room swiftly; hitting him over the head with a wine bottle was a really tempting possibility. He put his glass down and backed around my desk heading for the door.

'C'mon, Kat.' He made his voice placating. 'It's nothing you wouldn't have done. Cut me a little slack.'

'Not in a friend's house, I wouldn't have.' I was right behind him and Ranger was right behind me. Growling. The anger in my voice had definitely aroused his territorial instincts. I did nothing to hold Ranger back. J.O. picked up the pace another notch. 'Not that I'll ever consider you a friend again. I wouldn't cross the street to spit on you if you were on fire.'

J.O. got to the door and slid out, pulling it shut behind him. I shot the dead bolt and Ranger growled some more. Then I went back to the office. There was, as far as I could tell, nothing missing. J.O. had confined himself to spying and resisted stealing. It was small consolation. He'd had time to flip through the file I'd taken from the director's office as well as the notes I'd made and the hard copy I'd printed out from Hope For Kids' files.

Shit!

It took me a long time to appreciate the irony here – the do-unto-others and what-goes-round-comes-around angle.

I was up late that night. Since I was way too angry to go to sleep I figured I might as well work. I went through the correspondence first. A few things caught my eye but nothing really sparked me, never mind set me on fire. Not for the first time I wished that real-life investigation unfolded in the same neat and tidy way it did on TV. How nice to trip over clues and bad guys. How convenient to fall into revelations and airtight theories.

I turned away from the computer and pulled out the hard copy of the files I'd printed. It was two-thirty before I found something that struck me as a possible. Okay, a remote possible. And by two-thirty, after hours of searching, maybe I wasn't as picky as I would have been in another situation. You know what they say about beggars and choosers.

What I noticed was a pattern of donations that stretched out over four years: ten thousand the first year, nothing the second, twenty thousand the next, and then back to ten. Why the skip? Why the makeup? A dedicated philanthropist who had a bad year? A victim of blackmail? If it was the latter it was a break in the hit-'em-once pattern that, so far, had been a trademark of this blackmailer. Dr Hiram Grant had no cross-references. He didn't volunteer his professional services, nor was he involved with the mentoring program; he just signed checks that averaged out to ten thousand a year.

I put the doctor at the head of my To Do list.

Tommy Turner was right behind him.

That night as I fell asleep a stray thought crossed my mind. Cops will sometimes refer to a person as an Adam Henry. This is not a real name but their way of designating someone as an asshole either on the radio or in the presence of citizens. Adam Howard. Close enough.

Was he an asshole as J.O. was a Jerk Off?

CHAPTER 22

Dear Charity,
Suppose you do what you think is the right thing for the right
reason but then it turns out to be the wrong thing for the right
reason or the right thing for the wrong reason or even God
forbid the wrong thing for the wrong reason?

Worried Sick

Dear Worried,
All you can do is your best. Speaking of doing your best – do
you know what a run-on sentence is?

Charity

The doctor, the receptionist stated in a cheery voice, had no
appointments available for two weeks and did I want a morning or an
afternoon slot?

I explained, again, that I was not making a medical appointment,
that I was a private investigator and that I needed a short consult with
the doctor on a legal issue. I was happy to fit into his schedule if he
could please see me immediately.

She (predictably) asked what kind of a legal issue? I (predictably)
said it was confidential. She asked half a dozen more questions that I
also wasn't going to answer. I merely requested again that she convey
my request to the doctor.

She said she would call me back. The cheeriness was gone. Her
call came in fifteen minutes later and there was a note of triumph in
her voice. 'The doctor does not do legal consultations and suggests
that you look elsewhere.' The cheeriness was back.

I said I hoped he would reconsider as it had to do with Hope For Kids, a charitable organization.

She said she couldn't bother the doctor again and I said, in a definitive tone, that I thought it would be less of a bother for her to check with him than for me to come to the office and insist on seeing him. She processed that, made a harrumphing sound and then hung up. I decided to give her forty-five minutes. She only took twelve, then called to inform me, cheerlessly, that the doctor would see me in his office at twelve forty-five and hung up on another harrumph.

One down, one to go.

I called the TV station and was told that Tommy didn't come in today until two. So I called Tommy, who took eight rings to answer and then sounded like he'd just woken up. When I asked for Gretchen he yawned and said I had the wrong *fucking* number.

I hung up and was out of the door in a flash. Ten minutes later I was standing on his doorstep. Again, it took him a while to answer and when he did he definitely had the look of a man who had just gotten up.

'Yeah.'

No welcome there. 'Hey Tommy.'

He squinted at me. 'I know you?'

'I talked to you the other day about a job, about making a film.'

'Oh yeah.' He hid his enthusiasm well. I could see goose bumps on the scrawny arms poking out of the faded Raiders T-shirt. He yawned. 'Gonna cost you more now. Gimme the stuff.' He looked around vaguely, finally noting I had no stuff with me. 'You got it with you, right?' He shivered in the morning cold and tried to turn it into a muscle flex. It didn't fool me or his goose bumps.

'You going to invite me in to discuss it?'

Tommy stood back, unenthusiastic in the extreme. I followed him into an apartment that looked a lot less appealing in the daytime than in subdued evening light.

'Did you know that extortion is a felony?' I asked politely.

'Huh?'

I waited him out, hoping that his brain cells would eventually start firing.

'What the fuck you talking about?' He leaned forward and tried to look aggressive.

Pheeew! Morning breath of a really ugly variety.

'Extortion,' I repeated patiently, 'is a felony. A felony is when they throw you in the slammer.'

'The fuck you talking about?'

'An example of extortion is making a film to threaten someone for the purpose of obtaining money from them.' Still patient.

'I do a fucking job, that's all.'

'If you do a job and discover it's for an illegal purpose it is aiding and abetting. Which brings us back to the felony. And to the slammer. You'd get free dental care though, that would be a plus. And haircuts. Another plus.'

'You fucking bitch, you never did have a job for me, did you?'

'New clothes too. Of course they're orange.' I frowned slightly. 'Not ideal for your coloring actually, you're a bit sallow.'

'You *fucking* bitch.'

'You want to brush up on your human relations skills and PR, Tommy; they're a little short. Your vocabulary could use improvement too. And your manners.' I was on a roll, no doubt about it. Nothing I like better than jerking a scumball's leash.

He was getting hot.

So I smiled. Might as well add insult to injury.

'Get the fuck outta here, bitch, before I throw you out.' He clenched his fists and he and his bad breath advanced on me.

'I doubt you could.' I smiled again. 'Black belt in karate,' I lied. 'But go ahead and try.' He stopped.

So I laughed in his face. 'Not much of a man are you, Tommy. No taking people on openly or fighting fair for you, no siree. Not when you can come up from behind and stab them in the back or play tattletale. Sissy tactics,' I sneered. 'Baby stuff,' I said derisively. It was amusing to watch him turn red, his face especially dramatic, all mottled and lumpy-looking.

'You figured you were safe, didn't you. You think you're the only asshole playing this game, the only one willing to sell someone out for money. Well, guess again Tommy boy. The world is full of assholes like you who will do anything for money. They'd sell out their

173

grandma, never mind a two-bit sleazeball operator like you. The price wasn't even that high. Not that I care, I'll turn you over to the cops for free and have a good time doing it.' I smiled in a satisfaction that wasn't feigned.

Tommy got even more mottled, red and lumpy again. 'The son of a bitch sold me out?'

Hot damn, he fell for it. So I dished out some more. 'You're a bright boy, Tommy, and you got it.'

'That son of a bitch told you where to find me?'

'Two for two.'

'Goddamn mother-fuckin', shit-eatin', cock-sucking son of a bitch.'

I waited in silence for a name, a gender, a direction. For anything. Nothing. I decided to push some more. 'A smart son of a bitch though. He saved his skin at the expense of yours.'

'Wait just a goddamn minute. How do I know you're not lying?'

'Why would I bother? It's not like you're fun to talk to. Or nice to look at. Or anything at all,' I baited him. 'You're nothing, Tommy, not even interesting. And not just to me.'

'Get the fuck out. I ain't talking to you no more.' Tommy was not the brightest light on the Ferris wheel but he'd finally figured out that there was nothing in this conversation for him. He yanked open the door and advanced on me giving menacing his best shot.

I stopped him by raising a hand. 'Cover your butt, Tommy. Watch your step. You're on my list now,' I made my exit on that line. Tommy bravely muttered obscenities to my back.

Throw out shit and see what hits the fan. Talk big and see what jumps. These are not sophisticated investigative tactics. I didn't have the luxury of sophistication. I didn't have the luxury of time either – I wasn't the only one tossing shit and talking big. J.O. was very much in the picture. The blackmailer was elusive but not invulnerable. And not unknown. Tommy was one possible link to him. And Tommy was running scared, stupid, and mad – a highly volatile combination and one given to dumb moves. I had my money on Tommy for that. Big money. I didn't think he'd disappoint me.

Back in the Bronco I pulled on my Giants baseball cap and scrunched down in my seat. On top of everything else this job is really lousy for your posture.

It took Tommy twenty minutes and he was still mad. I could tell by the way he walked, by the frown and mottled pattern decorating his face. The Little Merry Sunshine concept had, once again, eluded him. He hurtled down the stairs and swaggered – well, tried to, it's really hard for skinny little twerps to swagger – over to his bike. Oooops, hog. I wondered idly how dangerous he was. I had made the mistake of underestimating nasty little twerps before.

Tommy buckled his helmet on and swung his leg over the Harley. He practiced that, I thought, until he could get the strut and macho just right. Punched the starter button, rode it down off the bike stand and roared and revved it for a while. He had yet to give any consideration to his surroundings, never mind check to see if he was being followed. Good news for me, of course. *Don't get cocky*, I reminded myself. Cocky people do just as many stupid things as scared and angry people. I started the Bronco and watched Tommy pull on his gloves. A last rev and he was off. I was right behind him. Almost.

It's hard to tail a motorcycle. They have much more flexibility in traffic than cars and trucks if they choose to ignore the California Motor Vehicle Code. I was pretty confident that this was a choice that Tommy could easily make. It wasn't an issue right now; the midmorning traffic was minimal. I dropped back slightly.

We cut through quiet midtown streets, crossed P and turned on Q which is one-way and feeds into several major freeways. I stayed back a bit, though close enough to make all the lights. Tommy turned on 29th and headed for I-80 West. Me too. On the freeway traffic was smooth for a quarter of a mile and then it slowed. And stopped. Ahead of us a big rig had jackknifed, a minivan and a BMW were in various stages of dented and crushed, and the place was swarming with California Highway Patrol cars, fire trucks and ambulances.

I watched helplessly as Tommy roared between lanes of stopped cars and disappeared. I stayed right where I was. Duh. Hours later – I could have taken a course in Spanish and become semi-fluent, knitted a sweater, or redesigned the Sistine Chapel – the cops cleared out one lane of the freeway and started funneling us through. With luck I would make it to my twelve forty-five meeting with Dr Hiram Grant. Lunch, of course, was out of the question.

I reversed direction going east on 80, off at Madison, over to Dewey and on to Mercy San Juan Hospital. Anywhere there is a hospital you will find the usual clutter of doctors' offices, medical clinics, and labs. Mercy San Juan was no exception and Dr Grant was part of that community. I knew nothing about Grant, was walking in cold – which was neither great nor my first choice but this morning's unscheduled activities had preempted my research plan.

Grant's office was in a modern, recently built two-story building. He was listed on the directory as an internist. I climbed the stairs to the second floor and walked into his office, a pleasant place with muted seafoam colors, real plants, tasteful art, and quiet music. A smiling receptionist greeted me.

I felt instantly soothed, especially after my less than perfect morning, though I hesitated to give my name to the receptionist, preferring to savor the warm, welcoming, and healing atmosphere.

'May I help you?' She smiled with her eyes as well as her mouth.

'Kat Colorado to see Dr Grant, please.'

'Ahhhh . . . yes.' She drew out the 'ah' a little too long. The smile faded and the eyes became cold. I was not a patient but an annoyance. 'Please sit down. The doctor will be with you in a moment.'

And, surprisingly, he was. The receptionist ushered me down a short hall, tapped on a door, opened it and waved me in. The doctor was seated at his desk writing up what looked like a chart. He glanced up as I entered, removed his glasses, and stood in formal and courteous greeting. He was a good-looking man of about fifty-five, five foot eleven and stocky, with thick black and liberally graying hair. He was slightly tan and looked fit and healthy. His smile was warm and friendly but there was, I was sure, something alert and wary in his eyes.

'Good afternoon, Ms Colorado. Please come in.' I returned his cordial greeting. 'Won't you sit down and tell me how I may help you?'

I sat, paused. It was as difficult for me to imagine that he might be a victim of blackmail as it had been to comprehend that Madeline was. Pillars of society: that is the kind of term that comes to mind with people like Madeline Hunter and Hiram Grant.

'I came on an unpleasant and difficult errand, Dr Grant.'

'Surely not.' He smiled the same open, kind smile but his eyes were wary and hooded now. 'I understand you made reference to Hope For Kids, which is a fine charitable organization, one, in fact, that I support.'

'Unfortunately I have reason to believe that someone is using Hope For Kids in a blackmail scheme.'

'Ah.' The smile had vanished. His eyes were dark and unreadable, his hands folded and still on the desk. 'That is indeed unfortunate but I do not see how I can be of any help.'

I looked out the second-floor window at the stripped and bare tree branches profiled against a cold, darkening metal-gray sky. There was both a delicate beauty and a stark and uncompromising winter harshness there.

'The blackmailer has been targeting people whom I would uniformly characterize as good people, people of integrity and kindness, people who, like all of us, have made mistakes. And who have a lot to lose, or feel they could lose, should these mistakes come to light. Again, a fear that we all share.'

I looked at the doctor, his face bleak and drawn now. I thought I could see the outline of his skull beneath the flesh. I looked away, looked at the skeletons of the trees instead.

'Interestingly, the blackmailer in this case does not seem to be in it for personal gain. Monetary gain,' I qualified. There was no question in my mind that the blackmailer was getting something out of this. 'He, or she, targets the victim, usually only once, and indicates that a single contribution to Hope For Kids will resolve the issue. And that, usually, is the end of it.

'This method of operation makes it extremely difficult to trace the blackmailer. He or she makes one or two contacts to the victim by telephone, the contribution is made, then it's over. Hope For Kids, unaware of the extortion, is grateful for the support; the victim is thankful the situation has been resolved; the blackmailer moves on. Except it's not just blackmail now; a death has been connected to this. The hidden costs of blackmail are very high.'

I looked at Dr Hiram Grant, at the dark eyes in dark sockets in a face that was like a skull. His eyes met mine. 'As I believe you know, Dr Grant. I believe you have been a victim on at least four occasions; I also believe you know who the blackmailer is. I am working for another victim, trying to end the blackmail. I am not threatening you and will not threaten you in any way. I want your help in this.' I paused, searching for the right thought.

He beat me to the punch. 'For the sake of discussion, Ms Colorado, let us say that I have made myself aware of your reputation and I believe that I could trust you. That is quite a bit to allow but it is not enough. The threat is not ultimately from you but, as in any extortion, in public knowledge, in exposure by the blackmailer. And that is not something you can control.'

'I can do a lot but I can't promise that, no,' I acknowledged. 'I would hope to accomplish that.'

'Hope is a thin thread to hang from, Ms Colorado.'

I thought of all the times I had hung from that thread and I agreed that it was. Thin and unreliable both.

'I can't answer that, Dr Grant. I can only tell you how important I believe this is. There are deaths on many levels: of love, honor, and pride, of dignity and delight. But the loss of a human life is different from all of these, is final. You know this far better than I.'

He was silent for a long time. 'Jeremy Treacher is a friend of mine. You helped him.'

'Yes.'

'He has nothing but good to say of you.'

'And I of him as well. I do not work for people whom I cannot respect.'

He nodded. 'May I tell you a story? I ask in the understanding that all you hear today will be taken in absolute confidence.'

'Yes.'

He picked up the fountain pen that lay on his desk and clicked the top off and then on again. The skin on his hands, as on his face, now seemed parchmentlike. I thought I could see the delicate tracings of intricate finger bones.

'My wife and I have been married for many years. We have three children. Do you have children, Ms Colorado?'

I shook my head.

'It is a sacred trust. And that is something I learned long before I had children.'

I could tell by his eyes that he was lost now, in the past and in the

178

story. His eyes had a spark in them but it was passion or sadness or something besides happiness and trust.

'I had a twin sister, and with her I had a closeness that I have never known with anyone, not even my wife and children. She died at seventeen at the hands of a back street abortionist. He botched the abortion, then loaded her into a car, dumped her in an alley and left her to die. She hemorrhaged to death, alone and cold on filthy urine-soaked concrete. They never found the abortionist.'

He stood and walked to the window, looking out, hands clasped behind his back. Perhaps he did not want me to see clearly what I had glimpsed only briefly in his eyes.

'It is amazing to me now that I got through the next year. I had been an A student, a letter athlete, the class president. I walked away from it all, almost walked away from life. For a long time I blamed myself. For a long time I blamed my parents and the coldness and aloofness that made it impossible for my sister to turn to them. Finally I walked way from blame and it was then that I decided to go to medical school. I wanted to dedicate my career to saving lives and I vowed that I would never forget to listen with an open and compassionate heart and mind.'

Grant turned away from the window and faced me. 'Abortion is a legal procedure now, thank God, but it was not when I first practiced medicine. I performed many abortions. Young women like my sister came to me, desperate and alone; older women unbearably burdened by the number of children they already had; victims of rape and incest – they came to me in numbers I couldn't begin to handle. But I did what I could and always in a clean and sterile environment. I never accepted monetary payment, just asked for their promise that they would get birth control.

'I could do nothing about my sister's death but, in this way, I found some peace. Her life was gone but I saved many others from abortionists like the one who had killed my sister.' He ran a hand through his hair. 'I have not performed an abortion in many years, not since the procedure became legal, and I hope never to perform another one. I am now, and always have been, dedicated to the practice of medicine. To healing.'

Grant returned to his desk and sat. 'Four years ago the blackmailer

– as you call him or her – got in touch with me.' A wry smile twisted his mouth. 'And then I became, as you so astutely noted, a regular contributor to Hope For Kids. I was afraid that the revelation of the past would be very damaging to my present and future; I was afraid of the impact it would have on my family. And I was afraid that the demons I had buried so long ago would be set free.'

Our eyes met. I know about demons, I have shared that fear. In that moment we recognized it in each other. As Madeline had in Jim Randolph.

'I cannot do what you are asking of me. I'm sorry.'

'Do you know who the blackmailer is?'

'No.'

'But you could find out?'

He hesitated. 'I believe so, yes.'

'He? She?'

'I don't know.'

'Ten thousand one year, nothing the next, then twenty thousand followed by ten the following year.' It was a question. Grant didn't miss it. He looked and me and said nothing. I waited it out.

'The blackmailer was stronger than I was,' he said finally.

I let it ride. 'If you change your mind you will call me?'

'Yes.'

He walked me to the door where we shook hands, soldiers in the trenches still but formal again.

'What was your sister's name?'

'Eloise.' He smiled, the smile belying the sadness in his eyes and voice. 'Thank you for asking.'

I knew from the tone in his voice he would not call.

CHAPTER 23

Santa Claus Is Coming to Town

Winning isn't everything, it's the only thing.

I don't believe that. The human wreckage left in the path of winning at all costs is devastatingly high. But sometimes I wondered. The human wreckage this blackmailer had created, and could yet create, was also devastating. Hiram Grant was my key, the way to the blackmailer. I could break him, I was sure I could. *Guilt. Pain.* I could force him to tell me what he knew, which would lead me to the blackmailer.

Any means to an end?

And then I would be doing the same thing the blackmailer was doing. And be on the same moral plane.

I picked up a sandwich on the way back to the office. I had long ago lost my appetite for lunch – and for this case – but my body needed food. Back at my office Lindy was propped up against the door, books piled around her on the floor.

'Well, *finally*. Did you forget?'

'Forget what?'

'*Katy!* Today's the day we go Christmas shopping.'

'Today?' I had forgotten. I climbed over Lindy and unlocked the door.

Lindy followed me singing:

> *'You better watch out,*
> *You better not cry . . .'*

'Lindy, I—' I broke off as her smile disappeared and her face fell. I improvised like crazy. 'I'm sorry I kept you waiting, it's been pretty hectic. Give me ten minutes to catch up and then we're off.'

'Sure.' She grinned big-time. 'Anything to eat around here?'

'Probably not but check the minifridge.'

'Jeez, Katy. A six-pack of diet Dr Pepper, that's it.'

I heard a tab pop. 'May I have one too? Here.' I shoved my paper bag in Lindy's direction. 'Have half my sandwich.'

'Yum. Thanks. What is it?'

'Vegetarian. I have an urge to live a clean life when cases get ugly.'

'Not the tofu, bean sprout kind?' Her worried voice.

'No.' My soothing voice. 'The lettuce, tomato, cucumber, Swiss cheese kind. Eat your sandwich, revise your Christmas list, and shush for a moment so I can catch these messages.'

'May I put a CD on?'

'Sure.'

I unwrapped my half of the sandwich and punched the message retrieval button. Mariah Carey's voice filled the room; Bill Henley was a bass chord. 'Kat, the gal you asked about, Moon Nguyen, someone beat the crap outta her. You know anything about this? Get back to me.'

And J.O. 'Well, well, Katy. Your boy Adam Howard leaves quite a trail. Thanks for the tip.' I growled. Mariah sang that she couldn't live if living was without her love.

The third message was Hank, who asked me to call him. In his serious voice. Lindy noticed and frowned. 'Are you two fighting again?'

I shrugged, not to push her off but because I wasn't sure.

The fourth message was Jackie Anderson. 'Kat, I would like to invite you and your godmother to join me and Sam Gunther for drinks at the Rio City in Old Sacramento. Would tomorrow at four-thirty work for you?'

'What godmother?' Lindy asked.

Good question. I shrugged again.

I finished my sandwich and took a sip of Dr Pepper. Some days you long for a break, for messages that are hang-ups and wrong numbers and trivial junk. Not that longing has anything to do with reality. I dialed Bill Henley's number, got his voice mail, told him to try me later at home. Then I smiled at Lindy.

'You ready? Great!'

'Theoretically. I don't have an idea in the world about what to get *any*one for Christmas. I hope you've been thinking for two.' I picked up my keys and purse. I was very aware of our surroundings as we left the building, of people and cars and movement. *Someone beat the crap outta Moon*. I walked Lindy to her car, followed her home, then drove us to the mall from there.

Lindy was excited, chattering away like a parrot on methamphetamine. I tried to listen, tried not to think about death and beatings, about blackmail and secrets.

'Katy, I have to write a paper and I can't get started.'

'About what?'

'Whatever it is that we value most. At first I thought it would be really easy but now I'm not so sure. I was surprised about some of the topics the other kids chose too.'

I braked sharply as a black BMW slashed across two lanes of traffic and cut in front of me. An outraged little old lady in the lane next to me honked, and the BMW driver – a blond bimbo bombshell – made an obscene gesture. Is it just my imagination or are almost all BMW drivers complete jerks?

'What are they writing about?'

'Security, like getting through school and getting a good job with medical/dental, retirement, stock options. Or material things – houses and cars, clothes and stereos. One girl said happiness was the most important thing, but then she defined happiness as marrying a rich guy. Katy, all these things are outside you. Shouldn't what you value most be what comes from inside?'

'Yes. It should.' I could see clearly the shadow of the damaged teenager that Alma and I had taken in and loved and sheltered, the child/woman who had never been valued and who had nothing in her life then to value.

'Like love and respect for yourself and others. And doing work – not just for the money but because it's what you want to do and it's what you're good at and helps the world somehow.'

'That's what it's all about, yes.' I smiled at her. Love and respect.

The end does not justify the means.

'Except for someone like Tricia,' Lindy added.

I was lost and said so.

'When they took the port-wine stains off her face it changed her life. That was something from the outside that changed her on the inside. That's important, I don't mean it isn't, but it's very different from expecting a fancy car or something like that to change your life.'

Way different, yes. I exited I-80 at Arden and headed for the mall. It was packed, naturally, cars and people stacked in like cordwood. We joined the barely moving Christmas throng.

'I can't really write about that though, can I? Isn't it too vague?'

'Not if you use examples from your experience, or that of others, to show what you mean.'

'Like Alma?'

'Yes.'

'And you.'

'And you and Tricia.' I responded.

She smiled at me. 'What are we going to get Alma?'

'I haven't a clue. I was *really* hoping you'd have an idea.'

'You know about her latest plan, right?'

I groaned. Really, you *never* know with Alma. She volunteers at the zoo and is a mainstay of the Granny Hotline, a resource for at-risk children. So far, so good. She is also ferocious at pool, bingo, and poker, drinks Manhattans and loves to 'whoop it up' with her semidangerous bunch of gray-haired cohorts.

'You *don't* know?'

I shook my head. We were in the south forty of the mall parking lot now and I still hadn't spotted a parking place. A heavily laden shopper made her way down the lane in front of me and I puttered along behind.

'She wants to start her own business as a greeting card writer.'

'*What?*'

'Yeah. Here's the kind of thing she comes up with: "I love you so/ that the memory of you/ sticks to my heart/ like dog shit to my shoe."'

Lindy and I looked at each other and lost it. The shopper heaved all her packages into a brand-new pickup and climbed in after them.

'Love and *dog shit*?' I hiccuped finally.

'Yes. She thinks it's a profound combination of the earthy and the sublime.'

'*Love* and dog shit.' Another hiccup.

'So I thought maybe we could get her some poetry books. *Good* poetry, not Rod McKuen junk, which is what she's been reading.'

'That's a great idea.' I pulled into the now empty space.

'And maybe a fountain pen since she refuses to learn how to use the computer.'

'Thank goodness.' I shuddered. 'Imagine Alma on the Internet.'

'True. So how about Charity? Perfume? Lingerie?'

We climbed out of the car.

'Nah. She has all that. What did we get her last year?'

Lindy and I have been shopping as a Christmas team from the git-go. I thought it over. 'Antique china cups and saucers.'

'Oh right, that was a good one. Let's get something else like that, okay? And a lace runner too, I know she wants one. And then there's us.' We get our presents together too, then pretend to be surprised on Christmas morning. 'Do you know what you want, Katy?'

'A new purse, maybe?'

We looked at my shabby bag.

'Bo-r-r-ring,' Lindy drawled.

'Okay, a silk scarf, a really bright one.'

Lindy looked at me, surprised. I don't usually wear scarves. The fog and blackmail were getting to me this year, I guess.

'Okay, good, a purse and a scarf.' She was writing as we walked. 'How about you?'

'I need new jeans and I would love some nice boots but—'

'But?'

'But I would really love some gold earrings and maybe a necklace, if it's not too much, I mean,' she said shyly.

'Phooey on jeans. Boots, earrings, and necklace coming right up,' I exclaimed cheerfully, and waved away the objections I could see starting. 'No buts. I've got a bonus coming up,' I added, hoping it was true.

She hugged me. We were close to the mall now and caught up in the lemminglike surge of humanity flowing in.

185

'And there's Dakota and Granny and Rafe.' Dakota and Rafe are close friends, family really. 'And Hank,' she added, looking at me sideways. We get him something little together but I always get him something separate. And special. Only this year I was filled up with blackmail and the ghosts of lives past and fresh out of special.

'I don't know. Help me figure it out.'

'Okay, what shall we start with?'

This was not a shopping question but a food one. Part of the Christmas shopping tradition was junk food. I pushed the ghosts and blackmail out of my mind as we walked into the dazzling Christmas scene in the center of the Arden Fair Mall.

The phone was ringing as I came in the door. I had empty hands and a wallet stuffed with credit card receipts. Lindy had taken all our loot home with her to wrap.

It was Henley. Speaking of Christmas cheer. I had called Henley back not out of enthusiasm but courtesy and respect. He always treats me fairly and has helped me on numerous occasions. I wasn't really looking forward to the conversation though and I wasn't in a position to spill the beans, at least not all of them.

'Something's going on, Kat. Why do I have a feeling you're involved?'

Uh-oh. Not even a *Hey, how you doing?* So I didn't bother to joke around. 'Not involved, no, but I can make a few educated guesses.'

'Do that.' His tone was terse.

'Did Moon say anything? Identify her attacker?'

'Said it was an ex-boyfriend. Wouldn't give his name. Wouldn't discuss why he allegedly beat her. Basically told me to fuck off.' His voice intimated that it would be better if *I* didn't consider that as an option.

Okay, I didn't. 'I spoke to Moon yesterday afternoon. Her name turned up again in the Jim Randolph case. I have reason to believe that she moonlighted on occasion using sex either for favors or as a leverage point.'

'Leverage point?'

I knew by his tone he had a good idea of what I meant. Still, he wanted me to define it. 'Either to get something she wanted or as an opportunity for blackmail. I have reason to believe that she took pictures and/or made videotapes of the men and the sexual acts.' Henley started making question noises. I knew what was coming and tried to head him off at the pass. 'But I can't prove any of this. *Yet.*'

He grunted. It was his pissed-off grunt – I've known him long enough to tell. I knew what was coming next too: he was going to let me have it. *Hi-ho, Silver.* I headed for the pass again.

'I stumbled on something else which could also explain the beating.' The noise on his end died down. 'I followed Moon to a business establishment in Rancho, a beauty parlor. No,' I corrected myself. 'They just do nails. It is run by an Asian woman who goes by the name of May. I was unexpected, unwanted, and nosy.'

Henley snorted. 'You? Nosy? You're kidding.'

I ignored that. Naturally. 'I snooped around a little, managed to gain access to a back room where I saw a stack of green cards. I'm guessing the same thing you're guessing: she's involved in illegal production and/or distribution. All the names and photos on the cards that I was able to see appeared to be Asian or Asian-American. I was tempted to swipe one but I figured it would be better to turn the information over to you guys. Or the INS, I wasn't sure. How would you like me to handle it?' I asked in my cooperative and compliant voice.

'I'll handle it.' He answered in his gruff but not real mad voice. 'Don't think for a goddamn minute I've forgotten the shit about Moon.'

'No. I didn't have anything concrete to bring you, Bill—' I tried not to think of the compromising videotape so that I could consider my last statement a harmless little white lie. 'You know the minute I did, I'd be there.'

Okay, we both knew that wasn't necessarily true.

'Yeah, right,' he said, meaning he'd let it go for now. 'Give me the name and address of that shop.'

I gave it to him.

'You got anything else on that?'

'No, it was all I could pick up at the time. I told you I didn't want to interfere.'

He grunted. All right, maybe the last statement was stretching it a little. Okay, a lot.

'Where is Moon? What hospital?'

'Anything you find out you're bringing to me, right Kat?'

'Right,' I agreed. 'I do not pass GO. I do not collect two hundred dollars until I talk to you.'

He grunted again, not entirely believing me, but mollified. 'UC Med Center. You got the picture, right Kat? Whoever did this is no fucking choirboy. He beat the crap outta that little gal. He'd beat the crap outta you too – no problem – if you get in his way.'

'I got the picture.'

'Okay, call me in a coupla days and tell me what the hell you're up to. And cover your butt.'

I promised.

Talk is cheap.

CHAPTER 24

Adeste Fideles

It was too late to visit a patient at the UC Med Center but not too late to call J.O. It was never too late to call him. It was tough for me though. I was still mad. Big-time. Of course being pissed off and pouting is not what breaks a case. I swallowed mad. And a chunk of my pride.

He wasn't at work. He wasn't at home. I tried the cell phone next; he's never far from that.

'Yeah.'

'I'm going to overlook your utterly despicable, contemptible, and totally unprofessional behavior and you're going to tell me everything you've got on Adam Howard.'

He laughed. 'You think so?'

'Yes. You are going to cough it up; you are going to smile doing it; you are going to tell me everything without me having to dig and you are going to do all this right now or – and I am not kidding – I am not only cutting off communication with you, I am going to do everything I can to fuck up your life in this town. And, believe me, I can do a lot.'

'Only for you, Kat.' The laughter was gone. 'Where do you want to meet?'

'I don't want to meet. I don't ever want to see you again. Just tell me what you've got.'

'On a cell phone? Tsk, tsk. We're meeting. We're drinking.'

189

I sighed. 'Just for once, J.O., spit it out sober.'

'What? And spoil a lifetime record? Naw. You're buying, so we'll make it somewhere nice. How about Mace's?'

I agreed without enthusiasm although Mace's is an excellent restaurant with a good bar, a place I would enjoy going with almost anyone – J.O. being the obvious exception. 'Thirty minutes.'

'I can't wait.'

I hung up in the middle of his next sentence. Maybe he meant it but ask me if I cared.

Mace's is an upscale restaurant with an upscale bar. But, as in almost all of Sacramento, you can find a mix of people and attire – suits to jeans, designer labels to Levis. Not surprisingly, both J.O. and I fit into the latter category.

Also not surprisingly, J.O. beat me to the bar. Not only was he closer geographically, he was a lot more eager for a drink. Not to mention that drinking on someone else's dime really works up his thirst. A half-consumed double martini sat on the bar in front of him, as did a bar tab. I pulled up a stool and sat down, then pulled away as he hugged me around the shoulders. Nobody has ever accused J.O. of being overly sensitive to others.

'A drink for the lady,' J.O. said to the bartender, who was politely waiting for my order, and he waved grandly at the bar tab as though he, not I, were paying. I almost admire him sometimes. It's difficult to get away with being such a cheeky, phony son of a bitch. I ordered a glass of wine and got over my admiration.

'So, what you been up to, Kat?'

'Cut the crap, J.O., I'm in no mood for games.' My wine arrived and I thanked the bartender.

'How did you get onto Howard?'

I shook my head. 'You're doing the talking. This is your story, not mine, remember? So talk.' I thought about Moon, beaten up and in a hospital bed. I thought about crawling into my bed, curling up and drifting off into oblivion. 'Talk fast.'

'Howard's been linked to a number of women.'

'No! *Really?* You amaze me. A good-looking man in the entertainment business is a womanizer? Imagine!' I shook my head in a mockery of disbelief.

'A cliché, a dime-a-dozen kind of guy, huh? More usual for LA than here, but not exactly unknown here either.'

I sipped at my chardonnay and hoped that the conversation was going to get interesting soon.

'Howard's pretty open about his past. The key word here is past. He's one more professional figure caught up in the trendy twelve-step confessional crap. He talks about how he was a foster child brought up in a home long on hard work and lickings and short on love and respect. All of which made him afraid to love and trust and blah blah blah.'

Looking disgusted, J.O. tossed down the rest of his martini and signaled for another. 'You know, the usual load of crap about the fear of really caring about another person so instead you fuck around a lot feeling empty and alone inside, always hoping you will meet that special someone who will change everything. That crap.'

'Good line.'

'Yeah, works really well. Women fall for that one hook, line, and sinker.'

'You would know.'

He grinned at me. 'Yeah, I would. Every single goddamn woman thinks she's the one whose love will change you, settle you down, turn you into a new man. So you use 'em – fuck 'em and enjoy 'em until you get bored or something more interesting comes along.'

'Then you just drop them like a hot rock?' Ooops. I'd gotten curious in spite of myself.

He shrugged. 'Whatever. The best way is to say that you've fallen totally in love with them though you never meant to, and that you just can't handle love in your life right now. You say it's work or something like that and then you let them draw it out of you that it's really that you're afraid of love and you've never loved like this before. More crap.'

He shook his head. 'They lap it up. They cry. Maybe you even squeeze out a few tears, women love that. Then they screw your socks off, trying one last time to change you with their love. The best thing about it is that when you leave – and you always do – they don't hate you. You've been a total shit but they feel sorry for you. And they love you still.'

J.O. looked across the bar and into the mirror where he met my eyes and then laughed. 'You can even go back, Katy. Tell them you couldn't forget them, tell them you hate yourself for coming back because you're a no-good shit with nothing to offer them. That's probably the first honest thing you've ever said – not that you hate yourself but you're a no-good shit – and they don't believe you. They open their hearts and beds to you all over again. And you fuck them and leave them all over again.'

I made a disgusted sound. 'I hate it when women are so dumb.'

He shook his head. 'It's not dumb, not exactly.'

'What is it then?'

He thought it over. 'First of all you really deliver in bed. You concentrate totally on them. You give them sex they've dreamed about but never had. Women confuse sex with love because they don't want to open themselves sexually like that unless they're in love. Then you play on their insecurities. You make them feel that if their love were strong enough, good enough, it could reach you. You make them feel it's up to them, so they give you everything.'

He looked at me again in the mirror. I met his gaze, choking back the contempt and disgust I felt. We were a long way from Adam Howard. Or maybe not. Maybe this was the way he manipulated women too.

'Insecure women don't believe in themselves. It's only when someone loves them and needs them that they believe they're real. You're not like that, Kat. That's why I like you. This shit would never work on you.'

'Does it work on men?' I was fascinated by J.O.'s take on things.

'Oh yeah. We're different though.'

'How?'

'Guys like to fix things, rescue women. The bird-with-a-broken-wing routine is good. A lot of guys can't resist that. Guys want to be needed and appreciated. A woman offers that, a guy will fall for it.'

'And sexually?'

'A guy wants to feel that he satisfies his woman, that he's the best. His fantasy is an angel in public, a whore in bed. And blow jobs.'

J.O. laughed a harsh unpleasant mocking laugh. The bartender looked over at us briefly from where she stood fifteen feet away. For a moment my attention focused on Jim Randolph. What had reached him: sex, memories, demons from the past? Randolph was not a womanizer yet Moon had stepped into his life. How many categories had she filled for him?

'The man you spoke of, the hypothetical womanizer, was that you or Adam Howard?'

He shrugged, smiled his hard cynical smile. 'Take your pick. Two of a kind.'

'You documented this on Howard?'

'Woman after woman. I tell you the boy kept a busy schedule. It was a veritable bonanza, a reporter's dream come true. And a lot of women were willing to talk. After a while a broken heart turns bitter. And talkative.'

'None of this is news. Or newsworthy.'

'Yeah. It is. Four years ago Howard was in a well-publicized sex scandal involving a married woman, a jealous husband, a suicide attempt and then a murder. That was when he started with the twelve-step confessional crap. Soon after, he met and married a young woman, a relative unknown, and publicly renounced the life he'd led, the man he'd been, blah blah blah.' J.O. looked and sounded bored.

'All very laudable.' I thought about Jackie Anderson, vibrators and crotchless underwear. *And implausible.*

'All very untrue.'

'You have proof?'

'Yes. He cleaned up his act considerably, discretion is his middle name now. LA, San Francisco, San Diego, Seattle, Santa Fe, Sacramento? The west is littered with hearts he's broken. Broken hearts on the sleeves of bitter, talkative, vengeful women.' He grinned.

'Nice combination.'

'This is inquiring-minds-want-to-know stuff, J.O. You're a serious journalist.'

'You're missing the news angle, Katy.' His everyday grin widened into the shit-eating variety. 'Howard's public persona is two things, news anchor and do-gooder. He's involved in a lot of charities, almost all having to do with young people; he's set himself up as a role model.'

His expression toughened into a sad and serious set. 'How do you feel knowing that this man is a role model for our children? And not just as a remote figure, either. No, he comes into daily and close contact with susceptible and impressionable youth.'

Looking at J.O. it was difficult to believe that he didn't care. But of course he didn't, except for the story.

'I dug up some really sleazy sex stuff too.' The shit-eating grin was back. 'And the new wife is sweet, good, lovable, all that kind of shit. It's a hell of a story. I'm really going to bust some chops on this one. Enjoy it, too.'

I opened my mouth and he shook his head. 'Don't even bother, Katy. Nothing you say will make a difference.' He tossed the rest of his martini down, stood, dropped a kiss on the top of my head. 'Watch for my byline, kiddo.' And was gone.

I sipped at the almost full glass of wine in front of me. The bartender drifted my way. 'God, your boyfriend is so good-looking and sexy. I wish I could meet a guy like that. He *is* your boyfriend?' she asked, an insecure woman looking for trouble in pants and J.O. fit the part.

I let it stand, though I know nothing can stop someone looking for trouble. If it wasn't J.O., it would be someone else.

It's easy to find trouble when you're looking.

It's easy to run into trouble even when you're not looking. I thought about men like J.O. and Adam Howard, who prey on women. And women, like Moon, who prey on men. And those who prey on anyone who is vulnerable, like blackmailers.

I should have called Hank that evening when I got home. I meant to, but I didn't.

CHAPTER 25

Eight Maids a-Milking

The UC Med center is at Stockton and X across from the old Coca-Cola bottling plant. It is a boring multilevel beige concrete building with brick stripes. If you don't have health insurance or money this is where you end up. I parked on Y and crossed the street.

I caught myself holding my breath and squinting slightly as I walked through the hospital – as though I could shut out the sights and smells and pain. And I promised myself I would take my vitamins. And eat less junk. And exercise more.

The room I was looking for had two beds, although only one was occupied. I stared at the sleeping figure for a long time before I was sure. Moon had been a very beautiful young woman but none of that beauty was visible through the cuts, bruises, swelling, and bandages. Her eyes were round and puffy, her mouth bruised and swollen. Her face was the worst but I could see bruises and cuts on her arms as well. She slept deeply, her fragile chest barely moving under the light covers. An occasional wispy, poofy sound escaped her swollen lips.

Moon looked very young, very alone, and very vulnerable. I saw no cards or flowers or personal items of any kind. I sat down in the chair not far from her bed. The young forget how vulnerable they are, or the cockiness of youth hides it from them. I tried to remember the physical beauty that had been there and couldn't. Not with this reality staring me in the face.

Outside the uncurtained window the December day was black and gray. Inside it was harsh and white, sterile and unforgiving. Ugliness. There was nowhere pleasing to look, nothing pleasant to think. Moon stirred and muttered, started to lick her lips and then moaned slightly as her eyes fluttered open. I leaned forward in my chair. Her dark empty gaze drifted around the room before it landed on me.

'Who are you? I know you, don't I?' Her usually melodic voice was heavy and slow, beat-up and drugged.

'Kat Colorado.'

'Who?' She moved her head slowly from side to side as if that would clear it.

'Who did this to you?'

'Are you the police?'

'No. Who did this to you?'

'I told you – them – I don't know. Or no . . . it was my boyfriend. We had a fight and . . .'

'You don't have a boyfriend.' Risky guess.

'I remember you. The restaurant. And at the shop. May was mad at me. I remember you. Go away.' She turned her head from me. One hand picked fretfully at the light spread on the hospital bed.

'I hope you're scared.'

She turned back to me. 'What do you mean?'

'Whoever beat you up wasn't fooling around. And there are no guarantees that it won't happen again.' I saw the fear move in her eyes and across her battered face. 'You are afraid. Good. Let's start over. Who did this to you? And why?'

No answer. Her fingers were frantic now, picking and pulling at the coverlet.

'Okay, let's start with why. This was a warning. You did something or someone is afraid that you will do something. There are a couple of possibilities here. Fake green cards and May – or one of the thugs she works with.' Moon's face went white and blank, not fear but stark terror. 'Or something to do with Randolph. You tried to put the squeeze on someone.'

I considered Rick Carter but discarded that notion. Lawyers have their ways of beating up on people; this wasn't one of them. 'Maybe someone else knew about the blackmail, was in on it even, and you threatened to blow the whistle if you didn't get paid off. And maybe this time you threatened the wrong person.'

White blank face. Terrified eyes.

'It's not going to go away, Moon. They got to you once, they can get to you again.'

'I don't know who it was. I really don't. It was dark. He wore a ski mask.' She whispered the words.

'He?'

'Yes.'

'What did he look like?'

'I don't know. I couldn't see his face. Or hair. Medium tall, I think. And strong, very strong.' She was trembling.

'Did he say anything?'

She nodded.

'What?'

'What you said. That it was a warning and I'd better shut up and mind my own business. He said that he knew just how to do this, to beat people up, and that he was not only good at it, he liked it. He laughed when he said that, about liking it.' A shudder ripped through her body. 'He said that this time he wasn't marking me, that I would still have a pretty face, but that next time it would be different. Next time I wouldn't be pretty.'

She held out a trembling hand. 'Could you get me that water?'

I handed her a plastic glass with a bendable straw.

'I think I'll go to LA for a while. As soon as I can get the money.'

'What did his voice sound like?'

'I don't know. I couldn't tell. It was all in a whisper. Like hissing. He scared me.' The glass trembled in her hand as she gave it back to me to place on the hospital tray.

'Was it someone you knew, someone you've met before?'

'I don't know. I don't think so, but I don't know.'

I left the who and picked up the why. 'What were you doing that provoked this?'

She shook her head.

'You did something, said something, talked to someone.'

The head shake again. 'I don't want to talk anymore. I've said too much. You'll have to go, I'm so afraid.'

'Moon—'

'I'm calling the nurse.' She pushed the call button. 'Go away. Go away!' There was a hysterical edge to her voice.

I put a business card and fifty dollars on the tray. 'This will buy a bus ticket to LA. Call me if you need help. Call me if you change your mind.'

'Go *away*!' She pushed her hands, palms out, in the air at me. But she kept the money and the card.

I walked out, the hospital smells assailing me again: antiseptic, bleach, the residue of excrement, the smell of fear and death. An old man was strapped in a gurney in the corridor, skin and bones and almost gray. And he looked dead. They didn't leave dead people in the corridor, did they?

And I wondered if the beating was something I'd provoked. Maybe Tommy Turner had spilled the beans. Maybe he was the connection back to a blackmailer who badly wanted to scare Moon off, out of town. Or maybe it was the phony green cards, an Asian gang, and a brutal warning.

I pushed the last hospital door open and walked out into the cold damp morning wishing I had a job with a lot fewer maybes in it. A Salvation Army volunteer sat by his donation bucket and rang a bell tonelessly and unrhythmically.

Merry Christmas.

No dinner last night. Nothing to eat this morning. I needed food. I headed for La Boulangerie, picked up a newspaper on the way, queued up with the rest of the crowd, and ordered a ham and cheese croissant and a lemonade. I even managed to find an empty corner table by the window.

J.O.'s story got top billing on the front page of the Metro section. So did a picture of Adam Howard. J.O. had accumulated a lot of material in a very short period of time. I was impressed. Howard – I was willing to put money on this – was undoubtedly dismayed. J.O. hadn't missed much and, of course, had shown no restraint, an admirable trait in a journalist if not in a human being.

First came the affair in San Francisco four years ago: the married woman, the jealous husband, the philandering seducer Adam Howard. Then the woman's suicide attempt and, shortly after her release from the hospital, the death of her husband in an episode of domestic violence.

J.O. spared no details. The police claimed the woman faked the suicide attempt and then murdered her husband to be with Howard. She claimed that the suicide attempt was real and that she had killed her husband accidentally when he tried to take the gun away from her in another suicide attempt. The police arrested her and hauled in Howard for questioning, believing that he too was involved. Howard was never charged and steadfastly maintained his innocence.

We've never heard that line before, right?

The DA's office declined to press charges against the woman, citing a lack of evidence. Everybody believed she did it; most believed Howard was involved. He – surprise surprise – turned out not to be a stand-by-your-woman kind of man and left town, pretty much washed up in the Bay Area TV market, where people now regarded him as news rather than a reporter of it.

He surfaced next in LA, again as a news anchor, and began dating a very pretty, very demure, very wealthy young woman. This relationship culminated in a marriage surrounded by bulletins announcing Howard's involvement with Alcoholics Anonymous, with Human Growth and Potential training and marital counseling (Philanderers Anonymous?). Since then he had kept a low personal profile although his public appearances were numerous. After moving to a station in Sacramento he had become the champion of several causes involving children – a literacy campaign, a sports program and Hope For Kids. He and his wife had one child and were expecting another.

He then became as public about his marriage and family lifestyle as he had been about his playboy career. There had been nothing to contradict that until now. Until J.O. Well, until J.O. and me. And now maybe Jackie.

As it turned out, Howard had been a busy boy and a liar, not a devoted husband and family man. J.O. was specific about it although I noticed he'd left the sleazy sex stuff out.

Melanie (he didn't use last names for the women in this list) was a very attractive young woman – only slightly younger than his new wife – who had worked at the LA TV station in a summer college-

199

intern program. News was not their only project in common.

Joanne was a cocktail waitress at a popular downtown San Francisco watering hole. Howard was known to frequent the establishment for food and drinks and an occasional business meeting. And good times. She, too, was young and pretty, a divorcée with one child, who was trying to get ahead.

Judi was a Sacramento supermarket checker. Howard, the perfect family man, was given to dashing out for diapers, baby food, Handi Wipes and groceries. 'He was just something,' Judi gushed. 'I was used to seeing him on TV and there he was, just like a *real* person, buying bread and milk and diapers. Wow!'

And condoms, I hoped.

The *Wow!* had worn off pretty fast for all three. Howard's seduction tactics had been standard, especially from a middle-aged man to a young woman. 'Let me show you the ropes, help you get ahead, use my influence on your behalf. I really care for you and I'd like to help you out.' Good, huh? Although it did sound better than: 'Sleep your way to the top. Start here.' They had all fallen for it; it's hard not to when you're young, hopeful, trusting, and dazzled. And maybe even a little bit in love.

That was the first thing they had in common. The second was that even though they had fallen for the line, it hadn't gotten them ahead. It had gotten them laid. Big difference. And one they were not slow to appreciate. *Hell hath no fury like a woman scorned.* Adam Howard had overlooked that. Turn back the clock? No. Clean his clock? They had, with J.O.'s help.

The quotes were in a sidebar. The first was boldface and dated three years earlier. His wife, newly wed and gushing. 'I knew from the moment I met him he was the man of my dreams. He was so kind and loving, so willing to help me get ahead, be someone. I know there've been problems in his past but that's all behind us now. The future is ours and it's wonderful!' And then Melanie, Joanne and Judi had their say.

The portrait was clear: Adam Howard, dirtbag. The future his wife looked forward to had been a replay, albeit a more discreet version, of the past. The present was damning. It was a riveting story. *Not to mention a perfect example of the pot calling the kettle black.*

I had to hand it to J.O. I wondered whether the scandal would make Howard's ratings plunge or soar. My money was on the former. What would charities, like Hope For Kids, who had previously cultivated Howard as a prominent supporter and spokesperson do? Drop him like a hot rock?

The smart money was probably on that one too. J.O. had devoted a fair amount of his story to the charity angle; it fit in beautifully with his 'innocents abused' theme. I felt sorry for Mrs Howard. The innocent, gullible, and vulnerable have a tough row to hoe. Of course, she was also rich. Here's hoping she was smart enough to have an airtight prenuptial agreement. I finished the last of my lemonade and tossed my trash. On my way out I succumbed to temptation and bought a chocolate chip hazelnut cookie.

Sure it was better to find comfort in life, but hey – food is not a bad backup plan. I headed over to my office in the mood for trouble. That's the problem with guys like J.O.

Jackie Anderson was in a meeting, so I left a message with her secretary confirming drinks at Rio City at four-thirty this afternoon. And I said I was bringing my godmother. Then I called Alma.

'Want to go drinking?'

'What's the catch?' She sounded suspicious. Alma and I do a lot of things together but drinking is not one of them.

'No catch. I'm doing an investigation and I need you as a prop.' Okay, and as a distraction. 'You're my wealthy, eccentric godmother.'

'Does that mean I'm supposed to buy drinks?' More suspicion.

'Nope. Free ride. Jeez, Alma, how did you get so suspicious?'

She snorted. 'Do I have to dress up and look wealthy?'

'No. Dress however you want. You're eccentric, remember. Be yourself,' I said grandly, although later I would, of course, regret it.

'What time?'

'I'll pick you up at four. Oh, one more thing. You're supposed to be very interested in Hope For Kids and considering becoming a major donor.'

'That's easy, I *am* interested in Hope For Kids.'

'Good. See you at four.'

'I can't wait, dear. We'll really whoop it up!'

That should have been a clue too. *Clue*? Hey, try warning.

CHAPTER 26

Do You Hear
What I Hear?

I couldn't rouse J.O. at work, at home, or on his cell phone, which was odd. Of course life is way too short to worry about guys like J.O. They always land on their feet anyway.

Instead I called the UC Med Center with a cheery, friendly get-well message for Moon. Who had checked out. *That* worried me. She should have stayed in the hospital under medical supervision for at least a couple of days. One more indication of how scared she was. I hoped she'd had the sense to go from the hospital to the bus station — no stops, no pauses, no dillydallying.

O for 2.

I called Hank at work. A formal and unfamiliar voice told me he was unavailable.

Three strikes, you're out.

I made myself a cup of herbal tea, which I hate. Unfortunately I was desperate for something warm and soothing and out of everything else. Soothing eluded me. Again. A little before four I drove over to Alma's to collect her. She's always on time, usually chomping at the bit, so it was a surprise to find her in the bedroom smoothing down the gray hair she had twisted into a knot at the nape of her neck and pinning a stunning ruby and emerald brooch the size of a small town on her freshly ironed pearl-snap plaid flannel shirt.

'You look lovely,' I said, kissing her cheek. 'Is that pin real?'

'Oh heavens no, I got it on sale at Mervyn's, but these days who can tell? My goodness, Katy, I don't know what's the matter with people.' Alma spoke in a cross tone. 'What about these earrings? I mean I am supposed to be eccentric.'

'Perfect. Nice touch the way the rubies and emeralds match the red and green in your plaid.'

She smiled complacently. 'I thought so.'

'What people? What's the matter with them?'

'People who would sleep with their wife's sister or mother. For goodness' sakes, isn't there any sense of common decency?'

'Have you been watching the talk shows again?'

'One man slept with his wife's *twin*. Can you imagine! She, the wife I mean, was devastated, although really I think she was much more upset about her twin's behavior than her husband's. And do you know what the husband said when he was confronted?'

'What?' I always try not to get sucked in by this. I always fail.

'He said neither of them was worth a hill of beans in bed and that their mother was much better, that she could suck the chrome off a— And then they bleeped the rest. Off a what, Katy?'

'I don't know. Why were you watching the talk shows? They *always* upset you.'

'I wish you wouldn't be so overprotective. Off a what?'

I sighed. 'Trailer hitch. Why the talk shows?'

'Trailer hitch? Oh. I get it. My, how coarse. That was just like him though, coarse to the bone. I hope his wife leaves him. And takes him to the cleaners too.'

'Are you ready, Alma? What jacket are you going to wear?'

'My warm coat. The red one. I don't think I'll carry a purse, dear. Eccentric people can do whatever they want, after all. I might even have an hors d'oeuvre with my drink. I had a *very* small lunch today.'

By now Alma was ahead of me, trotting down the street toward the Bronco. 'Knock yourself out,' I agreed cheerfully.

'Did you read the paper this morning?' My question.

'I always do, you know that.'

'And you saw the article about Adam Howard?'

She gasped. 'Oh my, wasn't that something? I felt so sorry for those poor girls. I was going to mention it but that dang talk show got me all in a bother. He looks like such a nice man too, so gentlemanly. It just goes to show you can't judge a book by its title.'

'Cover,' I said absently.

'Cover what?'

'Will you do something for me?' I moved on.

'What?' Her eyes sparkled in anticipation.

'When I give you a sign, I want you to bring the article up. Discuss it in great detail. Talk about the girls, talk about him, talk about anything you want.' This is like inviting a shark to lunch with mermaids.

'Really go to town?'

'Really go to town,' I agreed.

'Let 'em have it?'

'Let 'em have it.'

She sighed in anticipation.

We were a few minutes late to Rio City. Jackie Anderson and Sam Gunther had a lovely table overlooking the river. *Río* means river in Spanish. Sacramento is informally known as River City – both the American and Sacramento rivers flow through our area making us a city of water and trees and parks. There was no fog this afternoon; the sun was struggling to break through the clouds. We could see the Sacramento River and the Tower Bridge, a local landmark. Old Sacramento – around here we say Old Sac – true to the historical beginnings of our city, is right on the waterfront.

Sam Gunther rose when he saw us. Alma looked at him and tossed a silent question at me. I nodded, then followed in her wake as she crossed the room heading toward them. We all exchanged greetings and I introduced Alma, who inclined her head regally to one side.

God, she is such a ham.

Jackie was surreptitiously eyeing the brooch and earrings. Sam pulled out a chair and graciously waited to seat Alma. She had declined help with her coat. I seated myself so I had a river view, wishing this were the kind of day where I could just watch the currents in the river, the boats, the Tower Bridge going up and down with the approach of a large vessel.

'What will you have to drink, Kat?' Sam Gunther's voice snapped me back to reality, like a rubber band snapping on my arm.

Jackie and I ordered white wine, Gunther had a beer and Alma had a Manhattan on the rocks, double, extra sweet, two cherries. This can still make me shudder, even after all these years. I watched Alma graciously accede to Jackie's suggestion of appetizers then went back to looking at the river and tried to think of words that would describe how much I hated this case.

And couldn't, not really.

Blackmail was more than mucking about in people's dirty linen. There, you see? That's a perfect example of how words fail to capture reality. Dirty linen is a minor housekeeping problem. The issues here had torn up people's lives like a psychotic jackhammer operator on uppers. Blackmail dragged the past into the present and made the future fearful. And it gave control to someone else. Randolph hadn't been in control, nor was Madeline, or Delia or Hiram Grant; the blackmailer was. I contemplated control.

'They say you never look at the same river twice.'

Sam was eyeing me intently, smiling. His gray eyes were deep-set and attractive. 'With each moment the river becomes something different.'

I smiled back.

'I suppose every moment in life is like that, if only we were to focus on it,' he continued. 'I remember squatting in the jungle hunched over an M16 and looking at the way the sun splashed through the tropical canopy and drifted down dappling the leaves. Little drops of water shimmered like strewn diamonds. I thought I had never seen anything more beautiful in my life.' He shrugged. 'Of course in special Forces you saw a lot more ugliness than beauty.'

I thought this was interesting and philosophical but not helpful, and I remembered that I was supposed to be working. 'And Hope For Kids? How did you get from there to here?' I inquired.

He shifted in his seat. 'Children are often the innocent victims of circumstances. Sometimes those circumstances can be changed. I do not believe that the sins of others should be laid upon children.'

'Sins?' I had lost the connection here.

He laughed, a rich full sound. 'Religious hyperbole. We are not talking about sins of course, but about poverty, malnutrition, neglect, inadequate medical care. These are social and economic conditions. At Hope For Kids we try to come to the help of children trapped by such conditions.'

Our drinks arrived.

Gunther lifted his glass in salute: 'To a better future.'

Alma lifted her glass politely.

Jackie countered with: 'Hope For Kids.'

I drank to both.

And shivered as though, in Alma's words, someone had walked over my grave. Blackmail was about control; murder was the ultimate assumption of control. There was no appeal after death. This worried me: Desperate people do desperate things.

'Alma – may I call you that?' Jackie queried politely, and Alma inclined her head in gracious assent as she made a definite dent in her oversweet double Manhattan. 'What else may I tell you about Hope For Kids?'

Ah. That accounted for Alma's glazed expression. While Gunther and I had been waxing philosophical, Jackie had been unloading detail on Alma – a process for which Alma has an extremely short attention span.

'Do let me go into greater detail on our plans for the future. Our goal is to serve—'

Jackie broke off as the appetizers arrived; Alma sipped her drink complacently. Clearly she had shown no restraint when ordering. Stuffed mushrooms, calamari, roasted vegetables, and deep-fried mozzarella were arranged before us. I could hear Alma's satisfied sigh across the table. I smiled at her fondly and winked.

Alma was the first to pile her plate and the first to pick up the conversational ball again.

'My my, wasn't that something in the paper this morning? About Adam Howard, I mean. All those women.' She spoke with relish and gazed around the table in anticipation.

With Alma the issue is not will she rise to the occasion but how soon will she hit overkill? I put a bite of cheese and a roasted pepper on a round of sourdough bread and gazed at Jackie. So did Sam and then he caught himself and looked away.

Jackie's face went white and still. Her hand, calamari and all, froze in midair. After a long moment she put the food down and reached for her wine.

'I *couldn't* believe it,' Alma babbled on cheerfully and (apparently) obliviously. 'My goodness me, where does that man find the time and energy? It sounded like he had a new woman every month or so. And those girls! Goodness knows I feel sorry for them but really! Where were they when God was passing out common sense – at the end of the line?'

Jackie choked on her sip of wine and began coughing. Alma leaned over and pounded her on the back, which made it worse. I ate a bite of mozzarella. It was fair to say that I was totally focused in the moment.

Jackie recovered slightly and sipped on a glass of water. She had pasted a wan smile on her face in a brave-little-trooper effort. 'Well, I certainly don't think we can take that story at face value. You know how reporters are – they just love a scandal. In fact, they'll do *anything* to create one. I really don't think we can jump to conclusions.' She spoke cheerfully. It was the oddest thing – those bright cheerful words coming out of that white, unhappy face.

Alma snorted and helped herself to more food. Gunther spoke in measured, considered tones. 'Jackie, this is the *Sacramento Bee*, not the *National Enquirer*. I think it's fair to assume that the research and facts are reasonably solid.'

Jackie stared at him, looking like a department store mannequin, only with less animation.

'I know this comes as a great shock to you.' Gunther's voice was soothing and he spoke to Jackie alone. 'To all of us.' His gaze swept around the table including Alma and me. 'Adam Howard has helped us on many occasions as an informal spokesperson and MC for various fund-raisers. He has been a valuable ally and advocate as well as a generous donor. Naturally, although our concern is certainly for any pain this may cause him and has family, our primary focus must be what effect it will have on Hope For Kids. We cannot afford to let our work or goals suffer because of an association such as this.'

Jackie took a deep breath and followed up on Gunther's save. 'Exactly. The whole thing has been very upsetting. *Very*. But the issue, as Sam so aptly put it, is damage control.'

Alma glanced at me, read my look, glanced back at Jackie.

'I *do* hope, Alma' – Jackie had injected a bright, cheery tone into her voice – 'that this unfortunate occurrence won't—'

'What I wonder,' Alma announced, again apparently oblivious to the conversational dynamic of the table, 'is how many more of these poor girls there are. I bet this is just the tip of the iceberg. They'll probably be falling from the skies and popping out of the woodwork now.' Alma is unparalleled in her adeptness at mixed metaphors. 'I bet it's just like those Catholic priests and all the children they molested. The *minute* it became public, victims were everywhere.'

Jackie had gone white and still again. No amount of money, I was sure, could ever entice her into having another drink with Alma.

'I hold him totally to blame, *totally*, but at the same time you can't help but ask why those girls didn't use the brains that God gave a box of rocks and figure it out. I suppose he told them that they were the ones he loved and he was only staying with his wife for the children's sake. Hah! He probably told them that he never slept with his wife, even though we all know she's expecting. Goodness me. *She's* the one I feel sorry for.'

I thought Jackie was going to lose it. The waitress's timing was a perfect interruption, one that probably saved her. Gunther declined another round and asked for the check even as Alma opened her mouth to order a drink.

'You must excuse us. We have another meeting. Damage control,' he acknowledged wryly. Jackie nodded mutely, whitely, blankly.

We stayed so that Alma could have her second drink and finish the food.

'You did great, Alma.'

She nodded. 'Are you going to tell me what this is all about?'

I shook my head.

'Not that I can't guess.' She snorted. 'Damage control indeed. She's one of his floozies, isn't she?'

That Alma, what a way with words. I wondered if the greeting card industry was ready for her.

CHAPTER 27

Dear Santa,
You can give me a Mercedes for Christmas. A black one with
gold wheels. Loaded. And don't cheap out on me with a Lexus
either.

Lant

Reviewing things is inevitable. A book, a movie, a life, a case – you get my drift here. I wouldn't exactly say that the word shambles leapt to mind but it did creep right in there. I guess the conversation with Gunther had put me in a philosophical mode. Make that a downer philosophical mode.

I had put an enormous amount of legwork into this case and it had been productive, no question. I had established that Randolph had been the victim of blackmail and found the probable issue. I had found a number of other blackmail victims – Madeline Hunter, Delia Melton, Sid Johannsen and Hiram Grant – and established, with a minor deviation in Grant's case, a consistent blackmail pattern and MO. I had uncovered a probable green card scam (May) and turned it over to the cops, flushed out secondary blackmail schemes (Moon and maybe Turner), pulled the metaphorical covers on an extramarital affair (Jackie and Howard), and been the unwitting lead into the low-minded exposé of a leading public citizen (via J.O. and his journalistic endeavors).

Looking at it that way, it was pretty darn impressive. I was pleased. Well, almost. Of course the way to look at it was to ask whether I had accomplished what I had been hired to do.

And the answer was no.

211

Impressive evaporated just like that.

Okay, maybe I could stretch it into a yes-and-no answer.

Rick Carter had hired me to find out if Jim Randolph had killed himself and, assuming my findings concurred with the police finding of suicide, why. At issue here was not a dispassionate thirst for knowledge but a desire to protect the business interests of Bradshaw, Bellows & Emerson.

I had the information they wanted. So far so good. But I couldn't deliver it without possibly injuring innocent people, one of whom was another client, Madeline Hunter. So far so good went the way of impressive – right into the garbage.

Madeline wanted me to stop the blackmail. So did Delia and Grant. And, no doubt, Johannsen – but I didn't give a shit about him so that definitely fell into the moot point category. In order to stop the blackmail, I had to uncover the blackmailer. Score so far: Blackmailer 5, Kat 0. Nothing moot about that point.

This is the spot in the review, after the analysis and conclusions, that you come to Follow-up strategies.

I was there; the page was blank.

Well, shit.

When the phone rang I jumped. If this were TV or the movies it would be a clue. For sure. No. Forget clue. It would be a break. A big one.

'Kat Colorado?' a businesslike voice inquired.

I agreed, though I was a little puzzled. I was at home, not at the office, and very few people have my unlisted home number.

'This is Julie Sender at Sutter Hospital. We have a patient here, John Edwards, who asked us to call you.'

'John Edwards?' It took me a shocked minute to put it together. 'J.O.? In the hospital? Is he all right? What happened? How long has he been there?' I ran out of breath on the questions but my mind kept racing: Car accident – DUI? A definite possibility. His liver gave out? No. He was probably too young still. A woman's husband or boyfriend caught him with his pants down? Another definite possibility.

'He has been here for several hours. His condition is stable but serious. He asked that you visit him, tonight if possible.'

She had cleaned it up, I could tell. J.O. would have said: 'Tell her to get her butt down here now.' Or, oh God, if he really had been polite, it was a lot more serious than the tactful Julie had implied.

'What is it? What's the matter with him?'

'I am not at liberty to give out that information.'

I thought about arguing and gave it up. I've argued with hospital personnel before and lost pretty consistently. 'Tell him I'm on my way. What room?'

Once again I was in a hospital staring at something that was unrecognizable to me. The face was puffy and bruised, the eyes either closed or swollen shut, the mouth distended and unrecognizable. I could see bandages and stitches and hear labored breathing. An IV dripped into the patient's arm. I wasn't at all sure that it was J.O. I walked out and looked at the room number again. I'd gotten it right. I still wasn't sure it was J.O. It didn't look like a person, it looked like pulp.

I drifted down to the nurses' station and asked for the name of the patient in room 613. It was J.O. all right. Robert Redford had never looked like this, not even on a bad day. I pulled a chair up to his bed and sat, watching J.O. sleep a sleep that was drugs and pain.

J.O. and Moon.

I didn't like this at all.

'Cherry, it wasn't a girl that looked just like you, it was you, wasn't it? You were the one sitting on the terrace drinking champagne with Brad. You were the one dancing barefoot in his arms at midnight. You were the one in his bed the next morning.'

'No, I told you. I would never do that. You know I wouldn't.'

I shifted in my chair. I couldn't see the TV screen of J.O.'s room companion but, like her interrogator, I didn't believe Cherry either. How can you believe someone named Cherry anyway?

'I know Cherry wouldn't; it's Charlotte I don't know.'

Violins fiddled wildly up into a crescendo that involved saxes and French horns and lots of timpani and, presumably, the pitter-patter of pulses racing wildly.

'Charlotte?' Her voice wobbled at the end telling all of us in TV land that she was new in the bad-girl gig. *'I don't know what you're talking about.'*

213

'*I think you do. Charlotte Ames embezzled from the family business, stole her stepmother's jewels and her stepbrother's heart before she mysteriously disappeared, then reappeared as Cherry.*'

'Kat, is that you?'

I snapped my attention back to the human pulp that was J.O. 'J.O.?' *Damn!* I couldn't get the question out of my voice.

'That bad, huh?' He made a weird sound that, maybe, could pass as a chuckle. 'You bring some whiskey?'

'Aw shucks, I left it in my other briefcase.' That weird sound again. We both know I don't carry a briefcase. 'What happened, J.O.?'

'Someone jumped me. Beat the shit outta me. I was walking home from the Sacramento Bar and Grill. Not paying attention. Got jumped from behind.' His voice drifted off and he made panting noises as though it was difficult for him to breathe and speak.

'*You're a little slut, that's what you are, Cherry, a cheating, lying slut in Ferragamos and knockoff designer clothes.*'

'*At least I can keep my clothes on,*' Cherry hissed. '*I'm not dropping my panties for every Tom, Dick, and Harry with a Rolex and a Lexus.*'

There was the sound of a slap and then a scream. And then a girl named Gretchen got her disbelieving dad to eat Firehouse Chili because she'd gotten him a new antidote for heartburn. I listened to J.O.'s labored breathing and thought he needed an antidote too. But for what?

'Katy, you still here?' J.O.'s head didn't move but his voice searched for me.

'Yes.'

'It's the drugs. I'm floating in and out. Wasn't a mugging. Wallet, everything still there. Guy knew who I was. A professional. I'm a street fighter. Mean. I didn't have a chance.'

'Do you know who it was?'

'No.'

'What he wanted?'

'He warned me to mind my own business. "Keep your fucking nose clean," that's what he said.'

'Was he referring to Howard?'

'Don't know. Been working on a story about a developer for months.

214

Pattern of payoffs and bribes to local officials, illegal contributions to favored candidates, destruction of protected habitats—' The labored breathing again. 'Coulda been that, coulda been a lot of things. Lotta enemies, lotta bad blood.'

I looked at J.O. He was an asshole and a jerk, true, but I was still fond of him. There was someone or something, maybe way inside, that I cared about. I looked at the swollen, beaten human pulp in front of me and wished him well. And was afraid. That beating translated into a lot of anger. Or fear.

Maybe he was pushing the right buttons. Or I was.

'Katy.'

I could hardly hear his voice.

'Yes, J.O.'

'Be careful. Guy said something about you. Can't remember. Hard to fucking remember when your head's bouncing off a brick wall like a melon. No chances, promise me.'

'I promise.'

'Don't leave alone. Knows what he's doing, this guy.'

'Okay.'

'I'm losing it, Katy. Pain and drugs. Come back?'

'I'll be back.'

'Good. Bring whiskey.' His face moved in a tortured expression that I took to be a smile.

I dropped my hand lightly on his leg and walked out the door. I didn't leave by myself, I had hospital security with me. I didn't go right home either, not until I was sure no one was following me.

J.O. wasn't given to exaggeration or nighttime fears. And he had made an extraordinary effort to warn me.

I didn't take it lightly.

That night when I got home I wished – and not for the first time – that I had an attached garage. I live in an older part of Orangevale where barns and livestock are common. There are no sidewalks. The older houses, like mine, have carports or freestanding garages. Ranger and Kitten were both there to meet me – they have a swinging pet door and beds in the garage – and we all trooped over to the house together. *Safety in numbers.*

I knew the minute I walked in. I just didn't know what it was. I snapped my fingers softly and Ranger heeled, looking at me questioningly. Something was pushing my button but not his. *Odd.* We stood there in darkness and silence for a long time, Ranger at my side, the front door – AKA Emergency Exit – open behind me. Kitten had long ago padded off, food his only concern. I could hear the crunch of cat biscuits in the kitchen.

Other than that, nothing. The house was very cold, almost as cold inside as out. Ranger was obedient but not on the alert – his sense of smell and hearing, so much keener than mine, had not told him anything. I turned on the lights finally, closed the front door. Nothing was out of place. Nothing looked wrong.

False alarm?

Something had spooked me. I walked through the house looking. When I snapped on the light in the kitchen I saw the back door standing wide open. That was it; the house had been much too cold when I walked in. I shut and locked it. There was no evidence of a break-in.

A shiver ran through me. Not the cold. The message. The vulnerability. I didn't know if someone had been in the house; I didn't think so. But the message was very clear: I can get to you anytime I want.

How had the intruder gotten past Ranger? I would have sworn nothing could. My half-acre of property is completely fenced and Ranger has the run of it. He is territorial and protective. Hank, Charity, and Lindy all have keys to the house. Ranger would let them come and go but they would never leave a door open. Or come by without leaving a note of explanation. There was nothing.

'*Be careful, Katy. He's a professional.*' J.O.'s tortured whispery voice filled my mind. '*He said he liked his job, he liked beating people up.*' The memory of Moon's voice, also in a frightened whisper. I shook myself. Paranoia. There was no connection. Except that both thugs were professional and both victims had associated with me and . . .

When you're afraid, the downhill skid is a fast one. I didn't sleep well that night, one nightmare after another. Big surprise.

CHAPTER 28

Jingle Bells,
Jingle Bells . . .

No kidding. I was in the semifinals for Ms Popularity by the next morning, the phone ringing nonstop from seven-thirty on. My pigeons, Alma would say, were coming home to roost.

Or poop.

I am definitely not an early-morning person.

Alma knows this too, not that it stops her from calling. The freedom of being elderly and eccentric has gone to her head.

'Katy, that was such fun yesterday afternoon. To think that you get paid to sit around and drink and eat yummy food like that.'

'Amazing, isn't it.' I yawned. 'Alma, it's seven thirty-two. I thought we agreed that you wouldn't call me before eight-thirty.'

'Unless it's important, dear. This is important.'

Oh right. This is exactly how Alma's logic works. I yawned again. 'Okay, shoot.'

'After sleeping on it I decided that that Jackie person is as guilty as sin.'

'Of what?'

'Well, it's obvious that she's having an affair with Adam Howard – that's what the whole conversation was about, wasn't it?'

'Alma, have I ever mentioned that an essential quality of a good investigator is discretion?'

'Yes, many times. In fact, you get quite long-winded and boring on the topic. Anyway, Jackie is having an affair with Howard so we know she's no better than she should be. *And* if she would do that, she would do *anything*. A person who will lie and cheat will stop at *nothing*. Remember what I said about Richard Nixon? Hah! And I was right, wasn't I?'

'For Pete's sake, Alma, you said he looked like a sleazy two-bit unshaven used-car salesman. Big deal. *Everyone* said that.'

'Tsk, Katy. That sharp-tongued cynicism is *very* unbecoming. Is Hope For Kids financially stable? Have they had an audit recently? She reminds me of the butcher's wife at the shop we patronized when I was a child. That woman always had a heavy thumb on the scale. It wouldn't surprise me one . . . little . . . bit if she – that Jackie woman – had her hand in the cash register.

'She's no natural blonde either,' Alma stated darkly. 'Right out of a bottle is where that color comes from. What was this case about again, dear?'

Alma's 'logic' is long on non sequiturs and short on order. I stifled yet another yawn. 'Blackmail.'

'Right down her alley, yes indeedy.' The satisfaction was heavy in her voice. 'I wouldn't be one bit surprised if that diamond ring on her finger was real. Did you see the size of it?'

I'd noticed the ring. I certainly didn't get Alma's point.

'Ill-gotten gains, I bet.'

Oh. There it was. 'Hmmmm.' I tried to sound noncommittal.

'Think about it, dear, it'll come to you. Ooops, there goes the teakettle. Gotta run. Let's go drinking again soon!'

Over my dead body, I thought, the phone line hollow in my ears. I hoped I'd have as much energy as Alma when I got to be her age, but at the rate I'd been pushing it lately that seemed highly unlikely. I thought of Jim Randolph and Moon and J.O. Jeez. It was beginning to seem highly unlikely that I'd even reach old age, never mind enjoy it.

Charity was next. She's another early bird who refuses to believe that everyone's not up chirping away with the dawn's early light and the first go-getter birds.

'Katy, you're up. Great.'

218

I let it go. It was too early for snappy comebacks and witty repartee.

'I've decided we need a change and should take a trip. Travel is so broadening. We should go somewhere where there is culture and history. Oh, and good weather, cute guys, and margaritas. What do you think?'

'Good idea.' I was back to yawning. Jeez. I needed a shower and caffeine. Big-time.

'Great. We'll leave next Monday.'

'In my dreams. Sorry, but I'm in the middle of a case. And a rocky love affair. And it's almost Christmas.' I thought that one through. 'Charity, what's with you? You never leave town at Christmastime. You love Christmas.'

'I know,' she sighed. 'It's this damn fog. And my stupid life. Everything looks gray and bleak to me. I need to get away. Desperately. Say you'll come. *Please.*' The entreaty in her voice was real.

I was nonplussed. 'I can't. Not now. Maybe in January.'

'Oh Ka-a-a-aty! *Please.* Pleasepleaseplease! I'm *desperate*, I really am. I'm not kidding. *Please do this for me!*'

'I can't, I'm sorry. I would if I could.'

Charity hung up on a wail.

I stared at the receiver which eventually started beeping at me. What was going on? That was totally unlike Charity. I hung up and ran for the bathroom, determined to have a shower and get dressed before the phone nailed me again. I made it. Actually, I was eating peanut butter on toast – very grumpy about it too, I might add – and drinking diet Dr Pepper by the time the next call came in. This is a lousy breakfast, I know, but there was no coffee, tea, juice, cereal, milk, eggs, or fruit. The only reason there was peanut butter is that I can't stand it, so one jar lasts me a really long time – basically until Lindy cleans it out on a binge.

I thought about women who work full-time, take care of a husband and children and run a house. How do they do it? I can't even manage to work and keep my refrigerator full. I struggled with a mouth full of peanut butter and stale toast. Yuck. This was definitely putting me in a cranky mood.

When the phone rang again I wasn't even surprised. Just resigned.

'Kat, is that you?'

219

'Yes,' I mumbled.

'What's the matter?' Hank sounded concerned.

'I have a mouth full of peanut butter. I think I'm stuck.'

'Why? You hate peanut butter.'

'I'm hungry and desperate and you're not here to do the shopping.'

He laughed, his old lighthearted happy laugh. I wondered, with a pang, how long it had been since I'd heard him laugh like that.

'I will be soon. This weekend, all right?'

So that was something to look forward to. Mostly.

I got to work a little before nine – one stop on the way to pick up tea, juice and an apple – and the message light on my phone was already blinking. Apparently my headlong hurtle for the finish line and the Ms Phone Popularity award continued.

I should have taken the time to drink my juice, eat my apple, and sweeten my mood – peanut butter definitely starts me off on the wrong foot – but I didn't. So when Rick Carter snapped at me, I snapped right back.

'Kat, I expected to hear from you before now.'

'I told you I'd call when I had something to report, Rick.'

'It's been a little over a week now.' Impatient and testy.

'If this case were simple you would have figured it out yourself. If you don't care for the way I'm handling it you are certainly free to make other arrangements.' Testy and foolhardy.

'Now, now . . .' He was backpedaling, perhaps having thought it through and realized that no one but me was dumb enough to take these cases. 'I just meant I'd like to hear from you, be brought up to date on what you've found.'

'Will do,' I agreed without coming up with anything.

I ditched him just in time to take Madeline's call. Two disgruntled clients in a row. What fun.

'Good morning, Kat. May I inquire how things are coming?' At least she was polite, even diplomatic about it.

I took a deep breath. 'I'll be darned' – I yanked 'damned' back at the last moment – 'if I know, Madeline. Blackmail's a tough one. As you know. No one wants to talk and everyone's got a lot to lose so I'm swimming upstream the whole way. I know a whole lot about this case but nothing about the identity of the blackmailer, so even though I am incredibly informed, I am getting nowhere fast.'

Her soft voice *tsh*ed in my ear. 'Please don't think I'm getting impatient; I didn't mean it that way. I know how very difficult this is. Nothing would have induced *me* to speak out about my experience had I not been desperate. Please don't give up. Is there anything I can do? If it's a question of money?'

I sighed. 'I wish there were something you could do. It's certainly not a question of money.'

'No,' she sighed, echoing me. 'If only it were so easy.'

Exactly.

We hung up, but on a pleasant note.

I dialed the phone quickly before it could ring again. A sleep-fogged woman's voice answered in a groggy hello.

'Cathi, it's Kat Colorado.'

'Oh . . . hi.'

'How are you?'

'Fine, I guess.'

She didn't sound fine. She sounded like the last kid on the playground, still waiting – kicking her shoe in the dirt – to be chosen for a team.

'Really? You don't sound fine.'

'Oh.' Same kid, watching the teams play without her.

'Are you getting out at all, doing anything?'

'I'm thinking of going to Paris.'

'Cathi, that's *wonderful*. Do you have friends there or are you going for the shopping and the museums?'

'Rick and Ilsa found love there. And peace even in wartime. I thought I might too. Peace, I mean, not love. I've lost the only love I'll ever know. They say Paris is a very romantic city. What do you think?'

'Sounds good to me.' I tried to think of a tactful way to get from Paris to hell and I couldn't. So I just jumped in. 'Cathi, did Jim ever speak of his demons?'

'Demons? What on earth do you mean?'

'Nightmares, negative thoughts, bad memories from the war, anything.'

'No!' Her voice was loud, shrill. 'It wasn't something like that that killed him. It wasn't. It couldn't have been! Where did you hear that? Those are lies.' Her voice died down.

I waited for a moment. 'Had Jim made any new associates in the months before his death? Maybe someone he had business meetings with, perhaps at odd times? Or played golf with?'

Silence.

'Was there anyone like that, Cathi?' I tried once more.

She hummed a few beats of a tune I didn't recognize, then her voice slid haphazardly into melody:

'*I love Paris in the springtime,*
I love Paris in the fall . . .

Is it still fall, Kat?'

'Do you have a passport, Cathi?'

'Passport?' Her voice was vague. 'I don't think so. Why?'

'Are you taking the medication the doctor gave you?'

'I . . . I don't remember. Wait, maybe I am.' Her voice was low and cunning. 'Yes, I am. I have to go now. See you around.' She hung up.

I dialed her doctor's office immediately. Carter's office too. Red flag time. Emergency road service time.

I barely had time to catch my breath before the phone rang again. Sam Gunther. Pretty much the last person I would have expected to hear from. His voice was warm and gracious, modulated and deep. It was difficult to imagine a more stark contrast than the one between this call and the last.

'Kat, glad I caught you. I wanted to thank both you and your godmother for joining us for drinks. Also to apologize.'

Apologize? The surprises continued. 'What on earth for?' I was genuinely puzzled.

'Jackie wasn't herself yesterday. I think there have been family problems. She is too private to discuss them and too proud to ask for help – it's a difficult situation. I regret that it wasn't a more social gathering. I hope you'll take a rain check?'

'Gladly.'

'Good.' And he rang off.

'*Rain check?* No. Gunther's call was not about rain checks. And I remembered the little boy who cried wolf. His cries for help had sounded loud in the still night air.

But they were false.

Apology? Or cover-up?

CHAPTER 29

Better Not Cry

When the phone rang again I almost didn't answer. And that would have put me in the world of what-ifs and who-knows.

'Kat?' The voice was slurred and husky.

'Yes?'

'Is it really you? You sound so funny.'

I could barely understand the words. 'Cathi? Are you all right?'

'I can't go to Paris. It's the law.' She made a sound that started off as a giggle and turned into a sob. 'You have to be in love to go to Paris.'

'Cathi, are you drinking alcohol?'

'A little bit. Just a glass of wine. Or three.' The same slightly hysterical giggle.

'Did you take any pills, Cathi?'

A long silence.

'Cathi, answer me about the pills.'

'Who will take care of my baby when I'm gone? The poor little thing. No mommy. No daddy. Just a big empty house with no love in it. Will you help it, Kat? For me. Nobody should be alone. It's too hard to be alone, don't you think?' Her voice was drifting off.

'Cathi!'

'What?'

'I'm coming over right now to help you. I'll be there as soon as I can. I want you to unlock the front door for me. Don't sit down,

Cathi. Walk around. Keep moving. Promise me.'

'I'm so tired . . .'

I heard a soft thud as though the receiver had hit the carpet. I broke the connection and punched out 9-1-1, was out the door, flying down the steps three at a time, when I saw Lindy. She looked at my face, said nothing, just turned and ran with me to the alley in back of my office where I park the Bronco.

'Katy, can I help?'

'No. Yes. Maybe.'

She nodded, climbed with me into the car. We spoke very little as I crossed town, breaking traffic laws with abandon.

I tried to explain: 'A woman whose husband committed suicide not long ago just called me. She's been drinking and taking pills.' This is not the kind of thing I want to expose Lindy to, I thought. 'You shouldn't be involved in this, I'm sorry . . . but I might need your help. You know CPR, don't you?'

'Yes. Did you call nine-one-one?'

I nodded and wondered if it was true – that Christmas was the worst time for suicides.

We were fast.

The Sacramento County Rescue Unit had been faster.

I found Cathi puking up her guts in the downstairs bathroom surrounded by paramedics. She finally stopped – half collapsed on the toilet, vomit in her hair and on her face – crying. Someone slapped a blood pressure cuff on her arm and pumped. Cathi looked at me, tried to say my name and couldn't. The tears continued, trickling down her face through the vomit trail. The medic took the cuff off her arm and held Cathi under the chin – her hand slipping slightly in the saliva and vomit – and shined a light into Cathi's eyes.

'Ma'am?' a polite voice addressed my ear. 'You family?'

I turned and faced a pleasant-looking young man in his late twenties. 'A close family friend,' I replied. 'She called me for help; I called you. How bad was it?'

He shrugged. 'I'm not a doctor. My guess is that she was serious, both about the attempt and about getting help.'

'Did you induce vomiting?'

'No, it was spontaneous. Again a guess, that she's not used to

226

either the drinking or the pills and that induced her vomiting. According to her she only took a half-dozen pills. They'll tell you more at the hospital.'

There were crying and gagging sounds in the background. 'No, oh God no, I don't want to go to the hospital. Please, Kat, don't let them take me. Please! *Please.*'

There were bubbles on her lips, vomit and saliva, and her voice was desperate. I saw pain and sadness in Lindy's eyes. She's seen this before, I thought, years ago on the streets with hookers who were addicts. I turned away from both Lindy's and Cathi's pain.

'Is her medical condition stable?' I asked the polite and talkative medic.

He shrugged again. 'Seems to be. She should still go to the hospital though.'

Cathi moaned. Lindy covered her face with her hands.

'I'll take responsibility,' I stated firmly. 'I'll get her doctor here immediately, have him decide what is best for Mrs Randolph.'

Cathi was crying again. I could hear the words 'pills' and 'Paris.' And 'Jimmy.' The female paramedic who had been helping Cathi stood, looked around at the expensive tile bathroom with gold fixtures and designer towels and then stared at Cathi with contempt in her eyes. She made no attempt to hide it from me, meeting my eyes as she stripped off her surgical rubber gloves and dropped them into the trash can at her feet.

'Merry Christmas.' I spoke in a low tone as she walked past me. She looked at me again, eyes startled. I followed her into the hall. 'Her husband died a violent death a few days ago. They'd only been married a short time; they wanted a child. This was her dream come true – she had never had anything loving in her life before this.'

The paramedic started to walk away from me, then turned and walked back to Cathi, who sat on the cold tile floor with her arms wrapped around her drawn-up knees, and her head down. The woman spoke in a low voice. 'Don't give up, it will get better. God bless you.'

Cathi sat silently, without acknowledging the words, without looking up, and began gently rocking back and forth. I lifted my eyebrows at Lindy, who nodded so I left the bathroom, walked down the hall and picked up the phone. As I waited for the call to go through to Cathi's doctor I watched the last of the rescue personnel leave. Then I shut the door firmly on the small knot of nosy neighbors who had gathered on the doorstep like a vulture choir of the damned.

After I spoke with the doctor, Lindy and I pulled Cathi's clothes off and got her into a tub of warm water where we soaped and shampooed her, then dried her off and wrapped her up in nightclothes and a robe. She rinsed out her mouth and brushed her teeth – but only because I stood over her – then sat apathetically as I blow-dried her hair. She was drinking tea and watching a silent *Casablanca* with blank eyes and tears streaming down her cheeks when the doctor arrived. He helped her to bed and stayed with her for half an hour. I noticed his step was heavy and tired, his eyes sad, when he came down.

'She'll be all right. Physically,' he qualified his statement. 'She'll sleep now. I'll send over a nurse as soon as I can. You'll be here until then?'

I nodded, feeling as though we were all trapped in a time warp, a Been-There-Done-That kind of place. Lindy was strangely silent. Every time I looked at her my heart clutched and time stood still in another kind of warp. Her eyes had a haunted look I hadn't seen for years.

'She doesn't need a nurse.' The doctor's voice was full of resonance and common sense. 'She needs a friend, someone who will stay with her and care.'

I held out my hands helplessly. 'She says there's no one. Maybe you know someone, a therapist, or a group she could join?'

He nodded. 'I'll look into it.'

At three o'clock the house was empty and quiet. We could hear the measured tock of the grandfather clock in the hall and I couldn't seem to get away from the sadness in Lindy's eyes. I smiled at her.

'Take the Bronco home. I'll grab a cab and head on over as soon as the nurse arrives.'

She shook her head. 'I'll stay with you. I wanted to talk to you. Something important, not Christmas. Do you think it would be okay if I made us a snack or something? I'm starving.' Lindy piled food words on her serious words.

'Sure. Whatever you can find. Cathi won't mind at all. Or you can call out for pizza.' This I said to Lindy's retreating back. Her step was brisk and purposeful and headed for the kitchen. Following in her footsteps fifteen minutes later, I walked into a swirl of activity. And good smells. On the table I saw chicken salad, deviled eggs, assorted cheeses and pâté, pickles, olives and bite-sized vegetables. Lindy was slicing what looked like a loaf of pumpernickel.

'Wow!' She spoke almost reverently. 'You should see all the goodies in the refrigerator. I've *never* seen anything like it.'

It was after our snack – when Lindy was making tea and putting away the food – that I spoke. 'What did you want to talk about?'

'There have got to be cookies around here somewhere, Katy. She's got everything else. Where are they, do you suppose?' The kettle whistled and Lindy poured hot water over our tea bags. She was whistling too – a high tuneless sound.

'What's important, Lindy?'

'Hmmmm . . . Oh goody, here's some ice cream. Want some?'

'No thanks.'

'It's Häagen-Dazs.'

I looked at her.

'Oh God, Katy, I got the strangest phone call.'

And I knew. Immediately.

Her face was young and frightened but the look in her eyes was old and experienced. *Been-there-done-that* knowledge. Awareness of the way evil works.

'It wasn't anyone I knew and he didn't give a name. I guess it was a he. The voice was funny, electronically altered I think. He called at lunchtime today. It was a funny time to call. Usually I'd be in school but my biology class was canceled.'

Her voice ran down. We were running out of safe territory, out of descriptions and general comments. Soon there would be nothing left but blackmail.

'He seemed to know a lot about things, Katy, about my life and yours. He knew about Alma.' Lindy sucked in a breath of air. 'He said to tell you to drop the case. He said . . . right now . . . immediately. He said it wouldn't be a good idea at all for you to go on.' She looked at me directly. 'He didn't sound nice, Katy. He didn't sound like he was kidding. I'm worried.'

I nodded. 'Was that all?'

Slight hesitation. 'I think so. He repeated a couple of times that you should stop.'

There was more, I knew it. 'He threatened you, didn't he?'

She gasped. 'How did you know?'

'It's the way he works. Tell me everything.' My heart constricted. 'Don't protect me.'

'It wasn't that, not exactly. I just didn't want to mess anything up for you.' Her voice was worried as well as scared.

'You could never do that.' I smiled at her, hoping I looked natural and relaxed. 'He can't either. Tell me everything this time.'

'He knew things about me, a lot of things. Katy, it was scary. He knew I was going to Davis and running for president of my class. He knew Alma adopted me years ago.' She took a deep breath. 'He knew I used to be a hooker. He said that if you didn't stop he would send all that stuff – about when I was on the streets – to the Davis school paper.'

I looked at the fear in her eyes and the vulnerability in her face. She was smart and successful and whole now. She had started her life over, left the garbage behind. Her friends and professors at Davis knew her as the young woman she was now, not the child hooker she had been. She had dug herself out of the trash once. She shouldn't have to do it again and again.

'Katy, I didn't tell you because I didn't want you to do anything different. I didn't want you to stop because of me.' Her face was white and still, her eyes large and dark, young and ugly – like a Keene painting. Her beauty was gone; just the fear remained. I felt cold suddenly in Cathi's warm kitchen. And I felt the hatred and anger fill me.

'Katy?'

I turned back to Lindy.

'I've thought a lot about this. Not just today but long ago. I've always known it could happen. I hoped it wouldn't, but I knew it could. Too many people know. And it's not a secret. We don't bring it up but we talk about it if it does come up. I'm not going to let someone threaten me and make me afraid. If I let it happen now, it could happen again and again. And each time it happened it would be worse, because the more you cover up, the more you have to lose.'

Lindy played with the spoon in her melting dish of Häagen-Dazs. And I thought how wise she was and how sad it was that she had had to learn such wisdom so young.

'Katy, it's not that I'm proud of what I did – but I won't be ashamed either. My stepfather abused me sexually and my mother didn't protect me. I ran away. I ended up on the streets and into prostitution. Was that worse than what I faced at home? I don't think so. I was fighting to survive. I didn't give up. I know – you've taught me – that that's a really good thing. And then I met you. And Alma. And my life changed. I really am a survivor.'

'Yes. You are.'

'I want to show you something.' Lindy pushed back her chair and left the kitchen, returned shortly with her backpack. She pulled out a notebook and then a neatly printed essay. 'Read this. I spent all afternoon working on it.'

There were tears in my eyes when I finished reading and looked at Lindy.

She spoke softly. 'It's my story, the same one the blackmailer threatened to tell. I won't let him have it or tell it his way. I'm taking this to the editor at the Davis paper tomorrow. Nobody is going to take my life from me. Not now, not ever.' Her voice was proud and strong. Her face was still scared.

I thought of Rick at the end of *Casablanca* when he said that he and Ilsa had Paris again. And forever.

'Good for you, Lindy. That's a very brave thing to do.'

'It's very hard,' she acknowledged. 'I know it's right but it's still very hard.'

'Everybody else paid,' I said softly.

'What do you mean?'

'This blackmailer has found a number of victims. They all paid. In money and in self-respect. And still they live in constant fear because he holds their future hostage.'

Lindy dropped her eyes, stirred her melted ice cream, a puddle now in raspberry and vanilla. 'It's hard not to hate, isn't it, Katy?' she asked.

I couldn't answer. The anger and hatred filling up my heart and mind made it difficult. The victims, the numbers filling up this case, made it even more difficult.

'Does everyone have a secret, Katy?'

'Something big you mean? Not just something embarrassing?'

'Yes. Do you? Do you have a dreadful secret, as they used to say in dime novels?'

I shook my head.

'Does Alma? Or Charity?'

'I don't know.'

We looked at each other in wonder, realizing the secrets, the hidden dark sides possible even in those you know best and love most dearly.

Everyone has something to protect.

And lose.

The blackmailer had realized that before we did.

CHAPTER 30

Dear Charity,
I want lots and lots and lots of things for Christmas. Do you
think that's way too greedy?

Christmas List Kelly

Dear Kelly,
I don't know about greedy. It may not be very realistic though.

Charity

When you drop in on your friends in the hospital it's supposed to be
for humanitarian purposes. And it was. Mostly.

Okay, sort of.

J.O. was feeling a lot better. I could tell because when I arrived he
was giving a nurse a hard time. She was obviously young and must
have been inexperienced because she was blushing.

'What do you say, darlin', put on your dancin' shoes and I'll pick
you up at eight.' He winked broadly at her, his southern accent as
thick and gooey as chunky peanut butter.

'Now, now, Mr Edwards. You're not going to be dancing for a few
days yet. You *know* what the doctor said.'

'Sweetheart, the sight of you has restored me to good health and
turned me into a dancin' fool.'

She blushed a deeper shade of red and giggled. I tapped my foot in
poorly disguised disgust. J.O. winked at me. Was it possible that
someone had been dumb enough to bring him whiskey? I thought
about his friends and associates. Duh. Not only possible but probable.
The nurse exited on a final giggle.

'Hey, Katy.'

'Glad to see that you're back to your old self, J.O.'

'Yeah.' He grinned. 'Suave, debonair, and charming.'

'I meant ornery and obnoxious. Not to mention thinking with your zipper down. Who brought you booze?'

'Hey, hey, hey, Katy. Like I would break the rules.'

I snorted.

'What did you bring me on this mercy visit? Beer? Cigarettes? Glad you didn't waste your money on chocolates and flowers.' He stared pointedly at my empty hands.

'I brought you an idea, J.O.' I pulled up a chair and plopped into it.

'Something twisted and mean?'

'You got it.'

'Well, spit it out, girl.' He grinned, the interest written large on his face.

'Got an opinion on blackmailers?' I thought I'd take my time on this one. And use the indirect approach.

'Scum. Well, shit, that's the best side of a blackmailer, the scummy side. It goes downhill from there.'

'Exactly. I want to see a story in the paper; I want to flush a blackmailer out.'

He gave me the pointed-stare routine again. 'Tell me it's a coincidence: you wanting to see a story in the paper and me being a reporter.'

'My gosh, that *is* a coincidence, isn't it?' I asked brightly. Not to mention innocently.

He made a disgusted sound. 'For godssakes, Kat, you wouldn't fool a day-old baby. Goddamn, there are first-graders that lie better than you.' He arranged his bruised, swollen features into a patient and patronizing look. 'Reporters don't make up stories, they report actual events; you know, news. That's why it's called a *news*paper. Made-up shit is called fiction. Hey, feel free to jump in anytime and say you're clear on the concept. *And* that you apologize for being dumber than a post.'

Jeez. Talk about nerve. *J.O.* asking *me* to apologize for a remark – that was the pot calling the kettle black. 'You see the problem here,

J.O. It's blackmail. If the victims were going to come forward they would have done so, and gone to the police. But they didn't. And they aren't going to. Names and stories are changed slightly all the time to protect the innocent.'

'You've been watching too many *Dragnet* reruns,' he said sourly.

'Phooey, you know I'm right.'

'How "slight" are these changes?'

'Well, I can't take any chances that someone will recognize the victims.'

'So – change the name, gender, age, physical description, place of residence, and make up something out of the blue?'

'Hey! Great idea.'

'I fucking knew it.' He laughed. 'Does the name Janet Cook mean anything to you?'

I flipped through my memory bank briefly. 'Reporter for the *New York Times* – no, *Washington Post* – who won a Pulitzer for a story?'

'Yeah. That's the first half. How about the second half?'

'Big party. Everyone had too much champagne and then she lived happily ever after. C'mon, J.O., don't be such a wet blanket. You're the man who prides himself on breaking the rules, remember?'

'Kat, Cook *made up* a story. Got busted for it too, after winning the Pulitzer. Big scandal. Up to then she was a good journalist with a very bright future. God knows what she's doing now. Probably flipping burgers in a Peoria Wal-Mart. You don't do what she did. Period.'

'Don't give me that. You have no honor, no ethics, and no morals. And you lie and cheat all the time.'

He flipped his hand in my direction as though I were an annoying mosquito. 'Shit, Kat, that's with women, creditors, and guys at the bar. That's with things that don't matter. I wouldn't do it on a story.'

'Okay, you're not going to. We're going to be up front with everything, with your editor and with the reader. We're going to be clear that the stories have been changed to protect the victims.'

'Changed? Made up.'

'Whatever.' I saw no need to get bogged down in detail. 'And there's a nice hook, J.O. Real nice.' I smiled. Let him beg.

'What?' he asked finally, reluctantly.

Hah. I knew he couldn't resist. 'The blackmailer isn't in it for personal gain. The money is funneled into a local charity.'

'No shit?'

'No shit.'

'Man or woman?'

'Don't know. He or she establishes minimal contact, always by phone, always using an electronic device that alters his/her voice.'

'No shit. What's your angle, Kat?'

Good. I had him hooked. Now it was just a question of reeling him in and working out the details.

'I want to bust him. He's playing a good game – good hand, good moves. I want to turn up the heat, pile on the pressure. Then I figure one of two things could happen. Other victims surface, maybe with new information that could help me nail him. Or he gets rattled, even scared, and stupid. Either one would work for me.

'Even without the names and exact situations it's still a good story. Innocent people with a mistake in their past, reputable – although unnamed – charity, local angle and color, discreet but gutsy ball-busting reporter. Jeez, J.O., what more could you want? This is made to order and I've *handed* it to you. Didn't your mama ever tell you not to look a gift horse in the mouth?'

'Yeah, right. Let me think it over, run it by the boss.'

'Strike while the iron is hot. I'm sure your mama taught you that too,' I said brightly. 'As a matter of fact I just happen to have my laptop with me.' I pointed to the computer I'd stashed by the door on my way in.

He stared at me, his face expressionless and blank except for the colorful bruise tattoos now starting to go green and yellow. 'How about you get lost, get a cup of coffee or something, for fifteen minutes. I'll see if I can interest my editor. You going to give me any names?'

'No. Not unless a victim publicly comes forward.'

'Name of the charity?'

'Same answer. Neither case is likely.'

'And if you get him, do I get the story?'

'Yes. The story, his name, everything I can get on him. Or her. Ditto with anyone who is willing to come forward. All yours, J.O.' I unabashedly appealed to his greed as I backed out the door. He was already pushing phone buttons. 'And don't trade my laptop for a roll in the hay.'

He grunted, waved me off again. I gave him ten minutes.

When I got back his face was stoic, grim. My spirits crashed, not even an SOS on the way down. 'News was that good, huh?'

He tried to smile. It was an effort. 'It was, yeah. Ring for the nurse, will you, Kat? I feel like warmed-up shit. No, not that good.' He shifted slightly in bed, winced, sucked in a breath.

I punched the call button.

'Goddamn, I ain't been beat up this bad since a frat party in college. And I was a lot younger and tougher then.'

'Now, Mr Edwards, what's the problem here?' The nurse smiled perkily at him and frowned at me, deciding I was the problem, I guess.

'Hey darlin', rustle me up some drugs, will you? I'm hurtin' pretty good.'

She consulted his chart and her watch and marched stiffly and whitely off. Rustling up drugs, I assumed. I bit my tongue, aware of J.O.'s pain and impatient to know what was going down with the story.

'Kat.' His lips were drawn back in a ghastly smile, his discolored skin stretched across the bones in his face. Like a barely covered skull. Like Hiram Grant.

I leaned forward and took his hand. It was warm and sweaty. 'Jeez, J.O.' I squeezed it and held on.

'Katy.' His voice was harsh and hoarse. 'For godsake, remember what I said. This guy is one mean motherfucker. I don't like it that he said your name. I wish to hell I could remember what he said. You take care now, you hear.'

I could hear the southern in his voice, soft and liquid now, like a smooth twenty-year-old bourbon. I could hear the concern. I could hear the fear.

'I hear, J.O. Maybe I'd better come back tomorrow when you're feeling better.'

'Kat, did my getting beat up have anything to do with this story?'

'I don't know. I can't see the connection, but I guess it's possible.'

'Stick around.' That ghastly grin, again. 'I got it going for this guy now. Like to make the payback one goddamn sweet son of a bitch. The drugs here are fast. Good. Just give me a minute.'

Right on cue the nurse showed up. She frowned at me. Apparently I was still the problem.

'If you'll step outside, ma'am.' The hypodermic needle on her tray looked large. Ominous. Like something out of a Stephen King novel.

'Aw shucks, darlin'. This little gal has seen a naked butt before. Just load up and fire away.'

The nurse frowned but complied. Presumably she had figured out that with J.O. it was, in the long run, the easiest way to go. I averted my eyes. J.O.'s butt would undoubtedly have made for pleasant scenery but the needle had me nervous. The nurse rustled out and I looked back at J.O. His face was still drawn but looking like a face now, not a skull.

'Better?'

'Soon. Ten minutes. It's not so much the pain, it's the feeling that it'll never end. Life without hope is fucked.'

'Like life with blackmail.'

'Yeah. Good angle. You going to get that laptop out? We going to get a move on here?'

I smiled affectionately at him. 'I never thought I'd be pleased to hear you in your usual obnoxious and ornery form. But I am.'

'C'mon, girl, let's get crackin'. You a fast typist?'

'You bet,' I said proudly. 'I can do nineteen words a minute, easy.'

He groaned. 'Don't tell me. Another smart gal who was damned if she'd learn how to type.'

I ignored that – it annoys me when people can read me so easily – and pulled the computer out of its case, hit the power button. 'Ready when you are.'

'Let's do it. Son of a bitch. Let's *really* do it.'

It danced across the paper a day later. In bold. Huge letters. 'BLACKMAIL: THE HIDDEN NIGHTMARE.' And it was good. Really good. We'd pulled out the stops and thrown in some historical tidbits: sex and spies, marriage and illicit romance, politics and strange bedfellows. Pretty riveting stuff.

But nothing to the realization that it was happening here. Now. In Sacramento. J.O. even worked in, basically with cunning innuendo, that he was writing from a hospital bed where he was recovering from severe injuries due, he implied, to his ruthless pursuit of this story. A lot of things went without names in that story. Me, too, which was fine. I didn't want to look out at life from a hospital bed.

I wriggled my toes under the bedcovers. Kitten was stretched out next to me purring like a small freight train. Ranger was curled up on the rug at the side of the bed. I was sipping tea as I read the morning paper, the house warm and cozy. I not only felt safe but as though nothing could touch me. Of course J.O. had felt like that just before he got beat up.

I had a gun.

Maybe I should be carrying it?

CHAPTER 31

Dear Santa,
Please bring me a Walkman, a computer and a lot of fun games,
a baseball glove, Rollerblades, a swimming pool, a pony, Nikes,
a gun and some bullets, firecrackers and some money for other
stuff. My mommy and daddy can't afford this but I know you
can. I promise cross my heart and hope to die I'll share!
                                                          Jason

I couldn't lose what Alma said the other day about Jackie. Jackie who reminded her of the butcher's wife with the heavy thumb. Alma is often right. Often wrong, too, I reminded myself. Not to mention that she watches soap operas religiously and thinks of them as true to life.

A hunch is worth a phone call though, no question.

Madeline sounded pleased to hear from me. 'Well, Kat, and how are things?'

'I'm up to my usual no good,' I replied cheerfully. 'And I need your help.'

Measured silence. Thoughtful silence. 'Are we breaking into something again?' She spoke carefully.

'Whoa, Madeline, you can't expect to have that kind of fun every time we do something together. A lot of my job is boring and law-abiding.'

She chuckled but I don't think I was imagining the relief behind the chuckle.

'What is it then? How may I help?' Her voice was light and cheerful now.

I considered being tactful and discreet but then figured, what the hell, why start now?

'Remember the big scandal with United Way?'

'Ummmm.' She drew out her *m*'s into a pause. 'Was that the one where one of the CEOs had a young mistress and was living the life of Riley with her at United Way's expense? Or, no, was it someone draining off charity funds for personal use and investments, that kind of thing?'

'Close enough,' I agreed cheerfully.

'You're not talking about the United Way, are you?' The lighthearted note was gone.

It's depressing, the effect I seem to have on people. 'No, I'm not. Who does the bookkeeping for Hope For Kids?'

'I was afraid you were going to say something like that.' She sighed. 'I can't really be sure without checking but I believe someone comes in part-time – a day a week, or is it every other week? Anyway, she works with the figures Jackie keeps. I guess Jackie has a very good program of some sort on her computer and she makes the everyday entries.'

'Everything goes through Jackie then?'

'As I understand it, yes. I can check for you.'

'Will you please.'

'Kat.' Her voice was sad. 'Are you suggesting . . .'

'No. I am gathering information. I am not in a position to draw any conclusions. Don't you either.'

'All right.'

But she was, I could hear it. 'Is a regular audit conducted within Hope For Kids?'

'Regular audit?' A sad little echo. 'I don't believe so. I've never heard of one. I'll have to ask about that as well.'

'All right. Good. And the name of the software program please.'

'Is this . . . uh . . . Am I supposed to be secret about these inquiries?'

'Not at all. Most charities open their books to public scrutiny as a matter of course, as well as publish financial statements showing what comes in and how funds are allocated. These days many potential contributors want that information.'

'I mean, am I seeking information on my behalf, for a potential donor, or what, exactly?' She sounded confused.

A vision of J.O. – bumps, bruises, and broken ribs – danced in my head. This was, in part, a trap. I was trying to lure a blackmailer out into the open. And you always bait a trap.

'Say that I'm the one who's interested.'

Bait.

'Say that it's for a job I'm working on.'

Tempting bait.

Visions of bumps and bruises, cuts and scars, danced in my head again. Wrong picture, of course. It should have been sugarplums; it was that time of year.

After talking to Madeline I called Bee Search again and put in a request for anything ever published on Jackie Anderson or Hope For Kids. I asked that they follow Anderson back twenty-some years, far enough to pick up anything from high school or college in case she had been in the area at that time.

By afternoon information was trickling in. Madeline called to say that no, there had never been an audit in the five years of Hope For Kids' existence; yes, Jackie did all the entry data, and all checks etc. went through her hands; the data was then passed on to MaryJane Mueller, whose phone number she gave me.

There are lots of bookkeeping programs out there. As I listened to the phone ring I wondered if the one Hope For Kids used had the asset protection feature that indicates whether figures have been tampered with. That was worth a phone call too. A diffident hello interrupted my thoughts.

'Ms Mueller?'

'Yes.' The diffidence deepened.

'Kat Colorado. I am doing an internal investigation that involves Hope For Kids and I would like to ask you a few questions please.'

'Oh. Well, all right. Let me just turn something down on the stove.'

I listened to sounds of silence and then, again, sounds of diffidence tempered by cooperation. She was with me all the way: no questions, no checking up on me. People are way too trusting.

'Your bookkeeping job involves how many hours a week, or a month?'

'A half a day a week, about twenty hours a month.'

'And you work at the office of Hope For Kids?'

'Yes.'

'Do you receive checks, do any of the banking, write checks for outgoing expenses?'

'Oh, no. Well, I do write the checks for basic monthly expenses: rent, utilities, office supplies and so on, but they must all be cosigned by Mrs Anderson. Checks are not valid with my signature alone. She is the only one authorized to write checks with a single signature. Mrs Anderson receives all contributions, does the banking. and enters all such transactions. I merely pull everything together to produce monthly and annual statements for the board.'

'You never see the original checks?'

'No.'

'Or pledges?'

'No.'

'Do you deal with the banking records?'

'I keep track of them, yes.'

'Who writes the acknowledgments that the IRS requires for charitable contributions?'

'Mrs Anderson.'

'You use bookkeeping software?'

'Oh yes.'

'Does it have an asset protection feature?'

'No, I don't really know what that is but I don't recall anything like that at all.'

'Do you have bookkeeping training, Ms Mueller?'

'I learned on the job,' she said with a small note of pride.

'Do you have any other bookkeeping jobs as well?'

'No, this is the only one.'

'Is there anything else you do that I haven't enquired about?'

'I make the coffee,' she said meekly.

It was clear, I thought, as I hung up, that Jackie Anderson ran the show at Hope For Kids. The term 'alert financial watchdog' did not leap to mind in thinking about MaryJane Mueller. Cowering puppy was more the term. Or kicked cur.

I want to see a big fat check and I want to see it now.

I wondered how many attractive thirty-five-year-old women were blackmailers. It was difficult, though not impossible, for me to imagine it. It was much easier to imagine a butcher's wife with a heavy thumb.

The fax from Bee Search arrived while I was still imagining. It was a long one, with reprints of a number of articles. Nothing exciting, nothing interesting, nothing new. The clippings were in chronological order beginning with the most recent – the trail got colder and colder. *Rats, I'd struck out.* I picked up the last page. *All right. Still in the game.*

Picture, too. Jackie was a beautiful woman now, more beautiful than in her younger version. There her features were soft and unformed, a blandly attractive young woman. The one thing that stood out was her innocence. That was gone, long gone I suspected. There were three coeds in the picture and about a dozen children; all the children were physically challenged. And smiling. The girls were smiling too. The article lauded them as young women who were making a difference in the lives of others. Everyone in the picture was named. *Bingo!* I was flipping through the phone book in a heartbeat.

One hit out of fifteen names. Not bad at all. I dialed Doreen McAlistor's number. It had been Dorie in the article but she was a coed then. Now, fifteen years or so later, a CPA with her own business.

I was in luck. She was in and she took my call. Unlike MaryJane Mueller, she was cautious and she had questions. The vague mention of an inquiry in progress didn't cut any ice with her.

'Could you be more specific, Ms Colorado?' Her voice was kind but it was firm.

I could of course, I just didn't think it would get me anywhere. Ms McAlistor was a shrewd customer. I dropped the truth like a hot potato.

'I am a private investigator, Ms McAlistor. A number of prominent Sacramento citizens have been nominated for a civic award for their contributions to our city. Ms Anderson is one of them, in recognition of her charitable work with Hope For Kids. I have been asked to verify the candidate's work history and past so that the commission may make an appropriate recommendation. I understand that you are a longtime friend and associate of Ms Anderson's and I am hoping for your help in this endeavor.' I spoke briskly and professionally.

'I see.' We were both silent as her abbreviated response echoed through the phone line. 'Would it be possible for you to come to my office, Ms Colorado? I should prefer to speak with you in person.'

We agreed that I would be at her Carmichael office in half an hour. I was prompt and she received me equally promptly. I was also surprised. The laughing, buoyant coed had metamorphosed into a gray-suited unsmiling sobersides. We shook hands and I tried not to wince at her grip. Make that a gray-suited, unsmiling sobersides who worked out. Her office matched her gray appearance. I seated myself and looked at her – there was little to distract me in the room.

She measured me with her eyes, as I imagined she measured rows of figures. Apparently I added up. 'How may I assist you, Ms Colorado?'

'I know relatively little of Ms Anderson's background. I am hoping that you can fill me in, not so much education and training, but personal and anecdotal detail. I would be particularly interested in the work you both did with children, as well as other charity work.'

'I see.' She smiled a tight thin-lipped smile at me. 'I find it somewhat difficult to move back in time that way. It seems so very far off now. We were so young, so idealistic then.' The thin smile implied that the idealism had died with their youth.

I smiled back, trying to look serious and encouraging at the same time.

'It was Jackie's idea really. Or at least that's the way I remember it. She decided we should do something for kids who didn't have much. She was a very generous person with a big heart. Not just in that way, with the kids I mean, but in any way. She would always lend you her tennis racket or a sweater, whatever it was that she had and you needed.

'Her heart just went out to those kids. I guess that was true for all of us. They were brave little kids who had had a pretty darn hard time of it. It felt good to help. Maybe you know what I mean?'

I nodded.

'It went on for a year, our little group. We took the children to the zoo and the park and the museum. We went miniature golfing and swimming and fed the ducks at McKinley Park. It was pretty neat, and then it just ended.' She stared out the window.

I took a risk. 'It just ended or it ended because of embezzling?'
And I waited in silence while she worked through something.

Finally her eyes strayed back to the room. She glanced at the adding
machine, then touched it. Very few things add up as neatly as a row
of figures. Especially in my job.

'Embezzling? Has that come up in connection with Jackie?'

I nodded.

'This is difficult for me to talk about. You won't use the information
I give you if it is not important?'

'No.'

'It's just – just that it might be important.' She glanced at me. 'I
guess that my idealism isn't quite dead yet.'

I smiled encouragingly at her.

'There are two sides to everything, of course. Jackie's generosity
was a really nice, really special quality in her. It's just that it wasn't
only *her* things that she was generous with.'

I snapped to attention just like that.

'But you already know that, don't you? About Jackie I mean. She
seemed to feel just as free about borrowing as she did about lending.
And not just things.'

'Money.' I jumped to conclusions again.

'Yes.' Doreen ran out of steam and stared blankly out the window.

'She borrowed from you? Or other students?'

She looked back at me. 'A little, yes. Never much. Quarters for
the phone or the Coke machine. Or for laundry. Maybe a dollar for
lunch. And she always mentioned it and paid you back. The thing
was she didn't ask. It didn't bother her to go through someone's desk.
Or wallet.'

'It bothered you though?'

'Yes. It did. I guess maybe she'd been brought up that way but I
sure wasn't. I would no more do that than I would fly to the moon.'
She finished lamely but her discontent was very clear.

'You're being very kind.'

She looked at me, puzzled. 'What do you mean?'

'The term for taking something without asking is stealing, not
borrowing.'

She nodded. 'You're right, of course you are. It's just that we all liked her so much. And we knew she meant well . . . so we just let it go.' Her voice drifted off again.

'And then it got more serious?'

'Yes. Yes, it did. How did you know?'

'It usually does,' I answered gently.

'You know, I never did figure it out, whether she understood what she did was unacceptable. Well, *wrong*. She seemed so sure of herself. You know, so clear that what she was doing was just borrowing, that everything was okay. She said – she always said that she would return it.'

'How much was it?'

She shrugged. 'It seems so little now, but it wasn't then. It was a couple hundred, maybe more, we couldn't really tell because no one kept good records.' The wry smile again. 'That was my first lesson in accounting.'

'Records?' I wanted to clarify this. 'She took another student's money?'

'No. Money for the children. They came from all different backgrounds, you see. Some couldn't afford the zoo or the movies so we paid for everyone. We didn't want to make anyone stand out. People would give us money, and groups, like the Lions were very generous. Jackie handled the money. It had been her idea, after all, and anyway she was so good at everything. No one ever questioned it.

'No one ever questioned anything until the day she was sick and someone else went to get money out of the bank for that day's project. There was nothing in the account, just five dollars or whatever it took to keep the account open.'

'And that left two hundred missing?'

'Yes. Maybe more. We never knew. She really wouldn't say. It got out, of course. We had ten very unhappy kids that day. And we were unhappy too. And so was everyone who had given us money. And after that everything kind of ended. It was really too bad. We didn't get to tell the kids properly or anything. I still feel kind of crummy about that.'

'What happened to Jackie?'

'Nothing. I guess she got her hand slapped and she was supposed to pay the money back but I really don't know if she did. Maybe it was just another one of the things she pretty much got away with.'

'There were others?' Of course. There always are.

She shrugged. 'That's what I heard. I don't know for sure so I can't speak to that.'

'Who would know?'

She hesitated. 'I'm not sure but I'll give you a name. After that, it's up to you. I really liked Jackie, I hate doing this,' she said miserably.

'Stealing is against the law.'

'Yes.' She looked at her perfect mauve nails. 'Yes, it is.'

CHAPTER 32

Dear Santa,
My mom and dad give me all the stuff I want so what I want for
Christmas is to get even with Jimmy and Burt. Please kill them
for me or at least hurt them real bad.

Your friend Steve

I have never understood a football pileup. The squashed player with
the ball at the bottom of the pile is not going anywhere with one or
two big guys on top of him, never mind six or eight. But I understood
the theory: Stop the play at any cost; get the ball.

I was working under the same theory. Same technique too, pileup,
because when you don't know what will stop the play, throw everything
you've got at it and figure out the details later.

J.O. was still in the hospital but looking a lot better. Also producing
articles in the blackmail series at the rate of one a day. I was not
eager to see him leave the hospital. Protective custody is pretty much
how I viewed it.

I had looked for Moon and been unable to find her. This pleased
me. I hoped she had had the sense to go to L.A.

Lindy's article had been printed in the university paper and
reprinted, with her permission, in the *Sacramento Bee* as part of J.O.'s
series. I had been against it but no one listened to me. A college paper
was one thing, a major paper tied into a wire service something else
entirely. I didn't want Lindy in the pileup.

The violence had been escalating steadily and that trend wasn't
over, I was sure of it. *Thud.* The sound of a body hitting the pile. Or
bodies.

Jeannette Danver was next on my list. Doreen McAlistor had given me the name but nothing else. I found her in the Folsom phone book. She was surprised initially at my request but eager to meet with me and eager to talk. This is a pleasant change of pace for a private detective.

'One o'clock,' she said. 'At Hacienda. I love Mexican food, don't you? Meet me in the bar.'

The lunch rush was over by the time I arrived and I found her easily. Plump, smiling, and cheerful, she was the only woman at the bar. The margarita in front of her was half gone and she was licking salt from her lips. I tried to see her as one of the coeds in the long-ago picture I had but I couldn't. Time changes some people more than others.

'Hey!' She waved across the room at me. 'Ready to eat? I'm starving.' Her handshake was margarita-cold and a little salty, her smile open and eager. She talked – well, babbled – all the way to the table.

'Are you in this photo?' The old news photo, smiling coeds and children. I pushed it across the table to her.

'Oh yes.' She grinned and pointed to a slim figure with a happy face and a hand on the shoulder of a child on crutches. 'That's me. This is Dorie and that's Jackie.' Her glance lingered on Jackie. 'Has it caught up with her finally, then?'

'What do you mean?'

'Dorie said you knew about the money she stole from the kids. Did you know about the blackmail too?'

I let my breath out slowly. Chips, salsa, and water arrived along with the blackmail. 'Tell me,' I said.

'I think it all started at the same time, I really do. I have this theory about people, how some people are honest because they really are and some only because it's convenient or they never figure out anything else. Jackie is that kind of person. Only she figured it out. I believed her back then when she said she only wanted to borrow the money, that she was in a bind and was going to pay it back. Who would steal from kids? I remember her asking me that.

'I wonder if she believed what she said. Maybe then, but not for long. She saw how easy that kind of stuff was to do, and how easy it was to get away with. She saw how you could make money without lifting a finger. Jackie was always one to keep her eyes open, she was.'

Jeannette played with the salsa, pushing a chip around and around the bowl and finally, absentmindedly, eating the chip and starting the process all over again. 'People like that don't look dangerous, you know, but they are.'

'Yes.' I remembered the ugly note in Jackie's voice the night I had eavesdropped.

'Especially when they're out to get their own way.'

'And Jackie was?'

She nodded, sipping at her margarita. 'Jackie was. Jackie liked to win. She'd never gloat, not in public, but winning was everything to her.'

The waitress appeared with Jeannette's second margarita and took our orders.

'What did she do to you?'

Jeannette licked the salt off the rim of her glass, then sipped. 'It's that obvious, huh?'

I nodded. It was that obvious.

She sighed. 'I hated her then. I guess I still do a little. I've never been real good at forgive-and-forget.'

> *'Frosty the Snowman*
> *was a very happy soul . . .'*

The music assaulted us. Jeannette ate chips. I watched and listened in silence.

'She was the secretary/fund-raiser at another charity event that year. They raised a lot of money but in the end there wasn't as much as they thought there would be. Overhead was higher than they thought. I didn't say anything although I knew about Jackie's new clothes and the gold charm bracelet. Jackie was the overhead. I caught her; I was looking, you see. I said she would have to pay it back or I would tell.'

The silence stretched out. Frosty the Snowman had thumpety-thumped off and now the little drummer boy was ram-pom-pahing in our ears.

'Kat, it was the most amazing thing. She just smiled at me. And then she said that would be a really stupid thing to do. I didn't get it.

Can you imagine? I just didn't get it. She said if I said anything at all she was calling my parents. It sounded so stupid, so childish, and of course I ignored her. I took the proof I had of her stealing to the organization. They fired her but it was all hushed up. And then she called my family. She told them she was *so* sorry to interfere but she was doing it because she cared and was *so* worried about me.

'She said I was staying with my boyfriend on the weekends, that I'd gotten pregnant and had an abortion, that I was cutting classes and doing drugs. None of it was true. They believed her, not me, and it really messed up my life. I had to move out of the dorm and back home. My boyfriend broke up with me. Everything was really shitty for a long time.'

Our food arrived and Bing sang about how he was dreaming of a white Christmas.

'Jackie had already figured out about stealing. That was when she learned about blackmail. Every once in a while after that I'd hear something that made me think she'd gone into business but I never paid attention or followed it up. By then I'd learned about blackmail too.' Jeannette pushed a bite of enchilada around her plate for a long time before eating it.

When I left she was on her third margarita.

A couple more loose ends to tie up and I was ready. Pileup. And Jackie Anderson was going to be on the bottom of this pile.

The financial records I had pulled off the Hope For Kids computer and files had told me nothing. This was not a surprise. It confirmed what I suspected but it didn't prove it. Not a chance. And I needed proof before the next body hit the pile.

The approach would be tricky. Howard would be gun-shy now and besieged by the press. I didn't think he'd be real excited about talking to a private investigator either. Appointments were out, the men's room was out. I sighed. Back to wait-and-pounce. It was two hours – cold, dark, foggy hours – before Adam Howard came out of the back door of the TV station. He didn't notice anything until he had almost reached his car.

And me.

'You got a raw deal. I'd like to help.' I didn't gush or smile or move in on him. I stood there. And I sounded sincere, even to me.

True, I felt pretty much like a worm. And I'd had to psych myself up with wronged-woman stories before I could get into the role. I met his eyes with a strong, steady, sincere gaze. For the record, it's pretty hard to overwork sincere; I wasn't even close yet.

'What do you mean?' He wasn't falling for it but he wasn't walking away either. His voice was hard. So were his eyes. This is the way you get when you're on the bottom of the pile. Right then and there I promised myself I'd quit my job before my eyes got like that.

'True or not, it's still only one side. Nobody said a thing about the other side, about your side. About going to church and about the kind of loving father and husband you are. About the Little League team you help coach and the kid you tutor after school. About the hundred-thousand-dollar donation to Hope For Kids and the innumerable other donations you've made in time and money to local organizations. About the Adam Howard who's a good guy, not a playboy. I'd like to write that story.'

He smiled, not a sincere, happy smile but a cynical smile, and hit the automatic door opener on his Mercedes.

'I'm not real interested in talking to the press right now, I'm sure you can appreciate that. If I change my mind I'll let you know.'

'You want to know how to get in touch with me?'

'No.' He stopped at the Mercedes. 'Your research needs work. It was seventy-five thousand, not a hundred.'

Not research, educated guess. The next question was research. 'But it was Hope For Kids?'

'Yes.' He turned his back on me and reached for the door handle.

'Is it a relief now that everything's out?'

His hand rested there. Still life in the fog. His back was to me but the set of his shoulders changed, tensed up. 'What are you talking about?'

'Now that it's out you're free of the blackmail. Or is there more? Does the blackmailer have something else on you?'

There was a long silence before he turned and faced me. 'I don't know what you're talking about.'

I couldn't read his eyes, his face, or his voice. He was an actor. Training tells. But he was lying and we both knew it. If my accusation had been empty he would have shrugged and walked off.

255

'What is your source?' His voice was harsh.

'He has something else on you, doesn't he? You're still afraid. Still paying?'

Howard climbed in the Mercedes, slammed the door, then powered the window down. 'I hate the fucking press.' He said it wearily, as though rancor was too difficult to summon up. I watched him drive away and thought of J.O. and agreed with him. Sometimes at least.

My appointment with Jackie Anderson was at eight-thirty the next morning. Ordinarily I don't like early appointments, especially on a weekend, but this was not ordinarily and I was looking forward to it. Big-time.

Jackie was smiling and relaxed when I arrived. We had the whole place to ourselves. She offered me coffee and then we went into her office. Doughnuts too. I had neither.

Jackie bit into a powdered doughnut with relish and then flicked sugar off the Christmas-red dress she wore. The silk scarf on her shoulders was red, yellow, and green Christmas trees. Miniature green Christmas balls hung from her ears. Her red-lipped smile was welcoming.

'It's so nice to see you! How is your lovely godmother? This is a wonderful time of year, isn't it? I love Christmas. Are you sure you won't have a doughnut?'

'I have a coincidence.'

She frowned, not seeing the connection between doughnuts and coincidences.

'More than one. Let me explain.'

Jackie looked puzzled still but took a bite of doughnut and nodded at me through the puff of powdered sugar.

'Your background is an unusual one. Stealing from a charitable organization that helped handicapped children, blackmailing friends—' I was ticking items off on my fingers.

The doughnut hit her plate in a cloud of sugar.

'I became interested in your past when I unearthed a pattern of extortion victims who had "contributed" large sums of money to Hope For Kids. Coincidences are fascinating, don't you think?' I inquired blandly. 'Then I became aware that many of the donations do not show up in their entirety in your records. For example—' I had ticked off several more fingers by now. 'Three one-hundred-thousand- and one seventy-five thousand-dollar contributions all showed up in your accounting as fifty-thousand-dollar contributions. The math here – stop me if I'm going too fast – is one hundred and seventy-five thousand dollars. Missing. Who receives, records, and acknowledges donations? You. *Talk* about coincidence. See? Isn't this fascinating?'

Jackie was the color of her powdered sugar doughnut, lips standing out in an ugly red slash. I didn't ascribe it to fascination.

'Here's another coincidence: Extortion and skimming are both felonies. Of course it's pretty difficult to prove extortion as victims often refuse to testify.'

Jackie's color was a little better. Her spunk was coming back. She took a bite out of her doughnut and licked her lips. 'You are *way* out of line.' Her voice was cold and hard. I think. It was a little muffled with the doughnut.

'But guess who's really good at paper trails?' I continued. 'And very interested in undeclared, undisclosed amounts of money?'

Jackie looked at her nails. Bored to tears was the attempt. 'You're an amateur.' She stretched out her talons and yawned. 'You don't have a rich godmother either, do you?'

'No.'

She pointed her nails, nails that matched the Christmas red, or blood red, of her dress at me. 'Get out of here.'

'Okay.' I didn't budge from my chair. 'Here comes clue number two on my question: They don't care how you make your money, they don't even care if it's a felony.'

She advanced on me.

'And they love anonymous tips. Got it?' I stood, pushing back my chair. 'The IRS. Good riddle, huh? Oh, and did I mention that they love stuff like a missing one-hundred-and-seventy-five-thousand-dollar chunk of change. Missing *before* taxes.'

She was speechless.

I don't think it was admiration.

And I liked the way the bodies were piling up.

Of course, the thing about piling up bodies is that it's way too easy to end on the bottom.

CHAPTER 33

Blue Christmas

'Roses are red
Violets are blue
Friends are special
Stick to 'em like glue.'

I said nothing. Alma is blunt to the point of rudeness but try that with her and you're in big trouble.

'What do you think, dear?'

'Nice.' I swallowed my lie with difficulty. And hoped to God that Alma wasn't sinking her pension into her greeting card venture.

'Thank you.' Her voice was complacent. 'Katy, could you take me to the mall? I know you're busy but I really must pick up some things. Goodness me, Christmas is right around the corner.'

'No.' I didn't even think it over. And then I changed my mind. A case is a case and a grandmother is a grandmother. I could also use a little Christmas spirit. 'Okay, but only if you promise that I don't have to listen to poetry.'

'Philistine,' she chided cheerfully. 'Thirty minutes?'

'I'm there.' And I almost was; ten minutes late was all and that was the traffic, not me. There were a lot of people out there with that festive ho-ho-ho spirit.

'Where do you want to go?'

'Nordstrom.'

259

I groaned. Arden Fair Mall. *Again.*

Alma ignored me. 'Katy, Charity's very upset. She called me and I know she was hoping I'd talk to you.'

'What?' I was drawing a total blank. Total. I thought everything was fine.

'Well, I don't know exactly but she was upset. She didn't tell you?'

'No.' That is very unlike Charity. She is a big believer in the Blurt-It-Out-and-Get-It-Off-Your-Chest philosophy.

'I think she wants to talk to you. I know she wants to get away. To someplace warm, she said, just for a break and a change of pace. She's hoping I can persuade you. I think it's a good idea, dear.' Her look was pleading. So was her voice.

Both Alma and Charity are very persuasive, although not necessarily about the right things. I have learned to ignore them a lot. I shook my head.

'The timing is bad. I'm in the middle of a case. It's almost Christmas. I don't like the situation Lindy is in. And there's Hank. Any one of those reasons alone would be enough to keep me here, never mind the whole list. I told Charity all this.' I frowned. 'It's not like her to be so selfish.' Or undefined and vague. Or tricky? 'Are you and Charity in this together somehow?'

'No.' Alma spoke adamantly and a bit too quickly. 'Of course not. Not at all. What do you mean anyway?'

I snorted. This would not have been the first time my family (Lindy, Alma, Hank, Charity – take your pick) had been in cahoots, to use Alma's phrase. 'Who is this getaway supposed to be for, me or Charity?'

'It would be good for both of you, I'm sure,' Alma said diplomatically. 'It's always fun to get away.' Her tone was perky and hearty.

I glanced at her. 'The mental health tour guide strikes again. Hi yo Silver, awa-a-ay!'

'Oh for goodness sakes, Katy. Grow up!'

Hah. Look who was talking. I thought this. I was *way* too smart to say it.

'Why are you sitting at a green light? Go on now!' Her voice was cross and cranky. 'C'mon, c'mon, we don't have all day.' I could hear her foot tapping impatiently on the floor of the car. 'C'*mon*. Oh . . .' She let out her breath in a whoosh.

The long black hearse motored majestically by, drawing numerous cars along in its wake. Headlights were on, faces were somber. Alma bowed her head in respect as a Saab came barreling through the green light, horn blaring. The middle cars in the procession scattered in confusion, then regrouped. Alma muttered under her breath, then caught herself and pursed her lips.

The procession was a long one.

'It's so hard to lose a person at this time of year.'

I nodded but really I thought it was hard anytime. Maybe spring would be the most difficult, new life and loveliness all around. Sunshine, flowers, the warm earth and the coldness of death. I felt Alma's hand on my sleeve.

'I'm sorry, dear, I shouldn't have snapped like that.'

'It's all right.' I smiled at her, my heart tightening at the thought of losing her some day. Life is chancy and unpredictable. I never forget this.

'What do you think of a greeting card with a snapping turtle?'

I would have laughed but she was serious, so I drove in silence while she prattled along. Remember the congestion and traffic at the mall when Lindy and I went? It was like that only worse. The desperation edge was a little sharper with each day that we got closer to Christmas. I lucked into a parking space, which was a very good start, and Alma whistled and stomped her foot like a little kid.

Christmas spirit was with us again. Tiny Tim scuttled off smiling.

Alma tried to ditch me as we approached Nordstrom, threading our way through white reindeer made of intertwining branches. My favorite had huge antlers and a tossed-back head, a red Christmas ball in his mouth. Wrapped boxes and ornaments were scattered around, like nuts on ice cream, on a bed of 'snow.' People were everywhere, jam-packed in, package-laden and mostly jolly although the Santa with two kids on his lap and a long line waiting was looking a little ragged around the edges.

'You go ahead, dear. Why don't I meet you back here in, say, an hour or so?' Alma was edging away from me toward Nordstrom.

'I'll come with you,' I said cheerfully. 'You'll need someone to carry your packages.'

'I'll be fine.' She sidled. I stuck like glue, enjoying myself big-time. 'Really, Katy, go *on* now.'

'Nope. You dragged me here, you're stuck with me. Where to?'

She sighed. 'Mmmmmph department,' she mumbled.

'What?'

'Men's department.' She sailed off with her head held high.

'Oh?' I happen to know that she buys most of her Christmas presents at Nordie's summer sales. Monogrammed handkerchiefs for Hank, socks for Rafe, etc. etc. 'What are you looking for?'

'A dressing gown.'

I thought that one over. 'A dressing gown? For whom?' And what *was* a dressing gown anyway, a bathrobe?

She tossed her head. This means that she's not going to 'fess up. Or not without a struggle.

'What is a dressing gown, a hoity-toity bathrobe?' I nudged her in the ribs. 'My, my, he must really be something. Regular price at Nordstrom. Phew.'

'It's on special,' she said tartly. And blushed. *Blushed?*

My curiosity zoomed up another notch. And that was nothing to what I felt when I saw the burgundy satin robe she picked out. Navy-blue and hunter-green piping, no less. Size medium. Gift box and bow. Alma was blushing continuously now. This was getting *really* good.

I started improvising and singing, 'I'm dreaming of a red satin Christmas . . .'

'*Katy!*' Alma hissed at me, I swear it, even though there are no s's in my name, so you wonder how it could be done. Alma can be very snaky – okay, rattlesnaky – sometimes.

'A loaf of bread, a jug of wine and a red-satined thou,' I intoned in a low voice. 'To robe or disrobe, that is the question.'

The saleswoman turned her back to us and Alma jabbed me in the ribs with her elbow. Hard.

'Ouch!'

The saleswoman turned. Alma smiled beatifically and I rubbed my side. Little old ladies can be unexpectedly vicious. And vindictive. It took us two hours at Nordstrom to get through Alma's list.

'Home?' I queried as we reentered the mall at ground level, me, as predicted, laden with packages.

'Oh no, dear, let's window-shop. You never know when you'll find the perfect stocking stuffer.'

I moaned. 'You're a fragile and frail eighty-one-year-old person. We should get you home, tuck your feet up, and put a cup of tea and a cookie in your hand.'

'Piffle.' Alma took off briskly, declining to dignify my comment with further reply. I followed closely, afraid to lose her. We threaded our way around trees and rock gardens and the cart shops in the middle of the wide mall aisle. Lights blazed and Christmas voices and noises engulfed us on their way up past the second story festooned with planter boxes and into the high vaulted skylight ceiling.

Alma waltzed past Casual Corner and Scribners without a glance, paused at Frederick's of Hollywood.

'Something for you in black satin?' I queried.

'You're the one who needs it,' she replied tartly.

That silenced me as it was dangerously close to the truth. Well, not the black satin part, the needing help part.

Past J.C. Penney's and Warner Bros., FAO Schwartz and the Banana Republic. Almost to Macy's and then back again, lingering in front of Eddie Bauer, an outdoor clothing and back-to-(trendy and expensive)-basics kind of store. The window was filled with mannequins in graceful, headless postures wearing jeans and khakis and colorful layers of turtlenecks, sweaters, vests, and scarves.

'Would Lindy look good in that sweater?'

'Yes.' This was a no-brainer. Lindy would look good in absolutely everything, up to and including sackcloth and ashes.

'Would you wear that with a blouse or—'

It was arresting, the strength of the image in the window in front of us. In the glass, not in the window – it was a reflection. Most of the reflections were a blur of motion, back a bit, background. This was close, very close and out of the traffic pattern. Like we were.

Exceptions.

The richly toned black hair looked like a wig, the features were strong, odd somehow. The clothing was loose and bulky. The hand moved up, reached over and then down.

'Katy, are you listening, dear? I asked you if—'

The hand came up again. There was something dark in it. Metallic. Alma's hand was on my arm, gently insistent. I shoved her violently away, heard her cry out.

Slow motion.

I whirled, crouched – the floor was marble, large squares of black and white interspersed with variegated geometric patterns, everything even, fine, beautiful – and dove, aiming with my head for his – her? – gut.

Slow motion. The slight crack in the marble square was a feather-white delicate thread beneath me. a brand-new black athletic shoe, unscuffed, unworn. My head slammed into soft flesh. The first gunshot. The sound of glass shattering. Screams. The second gunshot. Christmas voices, songs, and noises gone now in the screams, the stampede of feet and voices. Something hard slammed down on my shoulder. I grabbed and held on. Soft flesh staggering, toppling. Bodies all around, pounding on me, pushing on me. On us.

'Who?

Grabbing, trying to hold on. Dark blue clothing in my hands, my grip. Close to flesh and muscle.

The gun? Where was the gun?

He kneed me in the thigh, again in the side as I started to reel, to fall. Too many people, noises. Fear everywhere. Falling. Bodies piling up. Next to me. Around me. On me.

I was the bottom of the pile.

Dark clothing still gripped tightly in my hand. Savage slash on my wrist. I lost it. Went under. Bottom of the pile. Bottom—

He – she – was gone by the time I struggled to my feet. I didn't follow, didn't even try. It was pandemonium, people running wildly, madly. There was no way I could have picked out the shooter, one runner among many. A purposeful runner who was by now, I was sure, long gone. I caught a glimpse of Alma, looking dazed and frightened sitting on the marble floor surrounded by Christmas packages. Safe.

First things first.

It was easy to get into the Eddie Bauer store. Everyone had gone the other way, out into the mall and toward the outdoor exits. It was easy to get to the phone too. It was difficult to ignore the young woman on the showroom floor. And the blood, the red that is death, not Christmas. I picked up the receiver and punched out 911. 'There has been a shooting at Arden Fair Mall. There is at least one victim. Send an ambulance to the Eddie Bauer store.

'The shooter could have been a man or a woman. Five foot eight to ten. Very short black curly hair, possibly a wig. Stocky build.' I thought about the soft fleshiness of the body when I had connected. The slight 'ooof' and stumble backward. I hadn't hurt him, not seriously, and I had hit hard. 'The stockiness could be padding or clothing. Dark complexion.' Another quick mental review. 'Could have been heavy makeup.'

I paused again. Every time I paused the 911 operator bleated quietly frantic questions at me – all of which I ignored.

'Clothing was navy blue. Sweatshirt and sweatpants, something like that. Black athletic shoes, brand-new. Small handgun. Two shots fired before the gunman took off on foot.' The operator squawked at me until the receiver settled into place. One more quick call. That one to Rafe.

There was a cluster of people around the fallen woman. She was on her back now, her eyes wide open, her face pale. In shock. There was blood oozing from her left shoulder, a rapidly widening pool of it on her clothing. The medics hadn't arrived yet but she was attended by a woman who apparently knew what she was doing. She was the victim I could have been, was supposed to have been.

Only at short range I probably would have been dead.

I headed out into the mall for Alma. She sat there on the floor docilely, quietly, still dazed and frightened-looking.

'Alma?' I knelt down next to her. 'Are you all right?'

She nodded, putting her hands on my arms and moving them up and down my body. 'I couldn't see you. I thought . . .' Her face crumpled up.

Oh God, I hadn't considered that, hadn't realized.

'Katy, you're all right. Katy . . . Katy . . .'

I held her tightly, kissing her cheek. 'I'm all right,' patting, soothing. Finally she heaved a big sigh and pushed me away. 'Where are our packages? They better all be here, by gum.'

I collected the few that had spilled out of the shopping bags and repacked them, then picked up Alma, dusted her off and walked her over to a nearby wooden bench.

'Let's rest here for a moment.'

'I want to go home.' Her voice was querulous and tired.

Old, I thought, with a sudden pang of sadness. 'We're waiting for Rafe,' I explained.

Rafe, six foot two of gorgeous lean and mean. Alma and I are two of his favorite people. There isn't anything he wouldn't do for us and in a tight situation Rafe's a good one to have on your side. He was exactly what I needed now. Good good guy, *bad* bad guy. You've watched Clint Eastwood movies, you know the type.

The shooter could be out there still, I knew. Waiting. Gunning.

Two minutes. That's what it would take to pull off a wig, rub off makeup with premoistened towelettes, climb out of an oversized sweatsuit – jeans and a nice sweater, say, underneath – and become a completely different person. Except for the gun. That would be the same. And this time maybe it would be me. Or Alma.

'I'm sorry I hit you so hard.' I was holding her hand tightly. 'I was frightened and I wanted you out of the way. I didn't stop to think. Are you hurt?'

'Bruises. Bumps. Nothing that won't heal.' She shook it off. 'He shot a girl?'

'Yes.'

'Will she be all right?'

It took me a long time to answer. 'Maybe.' That meant it was touch and go and we both knew it. Alma's face was pinched and white. I hugged her and hoped that Rafe would get here fast. 'Alma, did anyone know that we were coming here to shop tonight?'

'I don't think so, no.' She sounded bewildered and sad, so I didn't press it.

We waited for Rafe and I watched miniature teddy bears wave and ride a little train over bridges and rivers and up and down mountains in the window of FAO Schwartz. The crowds had thinned out. The police and medics had arrived. How did they get the bears to wave? I wondered. Little brown bears with red scarves. Red like blood.

And Elvis sang about his blue, blue blue blue Christmas.

CHAPTER 34

It's a Wonderful Life

Rafe finally arrived and bundled Alma up and off to safety after bundling me up in a huge dark, dirty parka and a weirdly horrible knitted scarf and cap. Rafe and I are not exactly masters of disguise. Or fashion. I did look different though, like a pudgy person with really poor taste in clothes and no washing machine.

I saw nothing suspicious on my way out. Big surprise there. Not, to be honest, that I was enthusiastically combing the crowds or the increasingly deserted parking lot for bad guys. I wasn't really up for a replay of the shoot-out at the OK Corral. Plus I had no gun which pretty much cast me in the dead guy role, not the survivor role. The funeral procession of this afternoon slipped through my mind again. It was sort of like being in an Ingmar Bergman film, only not as cheerful.

That was still pretty much my mood by the time I arrived home. Most of the lights in my house were on and a car was parked in the driveway, blocking access to the garage. I let myself into a blast of heat and followed the trail of light, noise and smells.

'Oh *God*, Katy!' Charity sounded genuinely shocked. 'Look at you. That is *just* terrible. I can't believe you'd dress like that in public. Those clothes aren't even fit to rake leaves in. That's it, we're going shopping.' She held up a hand. 'I am *not* kidding. Do not argue with me, the case is closed. There is no way you can go out looking like that. *No way!*' She sipped at what looked like a gigantic martini –

actually, slurped is probably a better description – and frowned at me while standing in the middle of my living room and whup-whupping something around in a mixing bowl. *It's a Wonderful Life* was playing on the VCR. It was the part where Jimmy was in his morose down-in-the-dumps stage.

I started shrugging off layers of clothing. It felt like about 80 degrees in the house, my heating bill of course – speaking of morose and down in the dumps. 'These aren't my clothes, they're a disguise. Some guy is gunning for me. I was hoping he wouldn't recognize me like this.'

'Well, thank God you have a reason for wearing that dreadful outfit. As opposed to losing your mind, I mean.'

I nodded glumly. Call me a baby but I was kind of hoping for something more in the Concerned Response category from my best friend.

'Make yourself at home,' I said, with just the merest hint of sarcasm and bitter disappointment.

'Mmmm.' She sniffed as Jimmy threw himself into roiling water. 'This part always makes me cry.' I thought about what an odd word roiling was. I mean, when is the last time you, or someone you know, plopped that sucker into a sentence, never mind a conversation? And I thought of the blood burbling out of the young woman on the floor in Arden Fair Mall. Burble is another low-frequency-use word. Where was her angel? I wondered, as Jimmy's angel hoved into view. Hoved? Jeez. I needed to spend some time with my thesaurus. Or I needed a life that wasn't roiling, burbling and heaving.

'Would you like a drink?' Charity asked politely, as though we were in her home, not mine.

'Yes.' I looked at her economy-size martini. 'But not a martini.' She shrugged disdainfully, indicating that I was on my own. I wandered off to the kitchen and got a diet Dr Pepper and checked the back door, which was unlocked. Rage and fear both flooded me for a moment. I took a deep breath, locked the door, then leaned over to pat Ranger, who was lying on the floor in front of the preheating oven. He thumped his tail languidly.

I went upstairs and got my gun, stuck it in my waistband and pulled my shirt over it. Better to be prepared than languid, I thought grimly.

On my way back to the kitchen I turned the heat – it was on seventy-five – down to sixty-eight. Then I put my untouched soda back into the refrigerator and poured myself a glass of wine. An empty brownie mix box was on the counter along with a package of chocolate chips and a bag of chopped pecans. I drifted back into the front room where Charity was still watching the TV and whup-whupping away.

'Why so hot in here?'

'It's freezing outside.'

'Forty degrees actually.'

'Also to get us in the mood for Hawaii.' She started doing a hula step that I'd never seen. Not that there are a lot of hula dances that use a bowl of brownie batter as a prop.

'I'm not going to Hawaii.'

Charity burst into tears.

Disappointment? *It's a Wonderful Life*? Whatever. I sat down – the gun digging into my waist – unmoved. Blood was one thing, tears another, especially over something like this. I wiped the sweat off my forehead. I would have opened a window, or ten, except for guns and fear and paranoia.

'Ka-a-aty,' Charity wailed at me, making the *a* last a really long time. 'You ha-a-ave to.' Ditto on that *a*. She slapped the bowl down on the coffee table.

'No I don't.' Callously I sipped my wine and dunked my finger into the brownie batter. Yum. I love raw batter.

Charity sat on the couch next to me, put her face in her hands and sobbed. I ate more batter and did some simple math in my head.

'Have you considered the possibility of early menopause?' I asked in a brief break between sobs. 'More and more women are—'

'Oh *shut* up!' Charity said crossly. 'I am *not* menopausal.'

'Really? Then why are you acting like it?'

'I'm not. I'm upset. After Lindy and all – I want her to come to Hawaii too – and now you tell me someone's gunning for you. So I'm worried sick about that and about everything.'

I just stared at her. Her worry about me definitely fell in the Way-Too-Little-Too-Late category.

'I think all this blackmail stuff is just horrible. And so is J.O. I hate it. I hate all of it.' She had been snuffling but the last riff worked

271

her right up into another burst of tears.

I ate some more batter and took another sip of wine. If early menopause was out, what did that leave? Concern for me? Concern for Lindy? On the TV Jimmy walked through his hometown looking at the same old everyday things in a new way. It is easy to be blind to what is closest to us. Did you know that psychiatrists have one of the highest rates of divorce? They probably never say, *Tell me about it*, or *How do you feel about that?* to their spouses.

Blind.

Ten thousand dollars. Hawaii.

Dumb.

'You're being blackmailed, aren't you?'

Charity stopped crying in midsob and stared at me, then hiccuped and wiped her nose on her sleeve. She looked about ten. And very scared.

'Yes.'

'Do you really want to go to Hawaii, or just get me away from this case?'

'Yes.' It took her a long time to get that out.

'Which one?'

'Get you away.'

'You were threatened?'

'He told me if I didn't get you off it he would give it to the tabloids.'

I reflected on the number of pronouns in that sentence without references, then picked one.

'He? You know who it is?'

She shrugged. 'No. I just *said* he. I think of it as he. I always have.'

'The ten thousand three years ago to Hope For Kids – was that a blackmail payment?'

'Yes. He said that he would never bother me again. And he never has. He's been a man of his word.'

An unreasonably high expectation to have of a blackmailer, I thought. Call me cynical.

'He never bothered me, not until now. And it's not for money. It's about you. He said I had to get you to stop. Katy, you have to stop.

You *have* to. He'll ruin me. My career will be over. My *life* will be over.'

'He did this to Lindy too.'

'I *know*. She told me all about it. I read her article. It's not fair, you know. You can't make us suffer for something you're doing. You *can't*. People don't do that to people they love. It's not my fault, or Lindy's fault. We're innocent!'

'If you're innocent you have nothing to worry about.' That sounded terrible to me, even as I said it; and I knew it wasn't true. Cops say it all the time too and they know it's not true. Innocent people have a lot to worry about.

Charity's face went white.

I spoke gently. 'Lindy was the only one who didn't pay up.'

Charity stared at me for a long time, large eyes in a round white face. 'I hate you,' she said finally, softly.

She is my best friend. I love her dearly and would do just about anything for her. Just about.

'"Dear Charity,"' I said, winging it like crazy, '"I am being blackmailed about something in my past. To stop it I have to put pressure on my best friend. I know it's not right but I'm desperate.'

'"Dear Desperate, that would be moral blackmail and you would be doing the same thing to her that the blackmailer is doing to you. Do what you know is right. There's more than one way to—"'

'"—to skin a cat,"' Charity finished in a whisper.

She looked away from me, looked into a corner where, apparently, a spider had set up housekeeping months ago and was complacently sitting in a web the size of Cleveland, surrounded by children and grandchildren and dried-out pieces of bugs. One of the offspring was working on a suburban addition, a duplex, I think. I glanced at Charity's white, closed-up face, picked up the brownie batter and headed for the kitchen.

I opened a couple of windows – the eighty-degree heat and the oven were now more overpowering than my paranoia. Then I dumped the chips and nuts into the batter, scooped it all into a baking dish, and tossed it into the oven. I didn't think a batch of brownies could pull Charity out of this but it was worth a try. Almost anything was.

The brownies were out of the oven and cooling by the time Charity came into the kitchen.

'Katy, it's really bad.'

'Do you want to tell me?'

'No. I don't want to tell anyone. I don't see how anyone can know this and not hate me.'

'"Dear Charity,"' I began again.

'Stop it.' Her voice was weary. 'I know what you're going to say, that I undoubtedly think it's worse than it is, that we all exaggerate and overdramatize, that no matter what, the people who love me will stand by me. But Katy, it's really bad.'

I opened my mouth to speak but she shook her head at me, so I didn't.

'I'm not going to ask you to stop. I know I can't do that. I don't want to be a blackmailer, to make myself into something worse than I already am.'

'Good for you.'

I said it with pride and encouragement in my voice – which is how I felt – and then I remembered how Jim Randolph had dealt with a similar situation, and my mouth went dry with fear. I could feel a trembling starting way inside me. *People in pieces don't need your help, did you know that?* Cathi Randolph's words echoed in my mind.

For the blackmailer the stakes were higher now, higher than then. I was not a randomly targeted victim at the mall. Lindy and Charity were not random targets either. The blackmailer wanted it to stop and would do whatever was necessary to make that happen. To stop me.

I licked my dry lips and hoped the words would come out as words and not as the sound of dry dead leaves crumpling underfoot. 'Please tell me. Please let me help you.' I was entreating, pleading, begging. 'I can't imagine anything that would change the love and respect I have for you.'

'But you don't know.'

'No. I can't know the specifics but I know who you are and who I am and I trust that. I know that you are not a Goebbels or a Manson or a Dahmer. You've made mistakes, yes, we all have.'

Jimmy Stewart's family was probably embracing him by now. He was seeing life in a new way, like Rick at the end of *Casablanca*. Of course, life is not the movies. (No, no – forget the Ronald Reagan and Newt Gingrich take on that.)

'You should tell me; you should tell the whole world. And you should definitely beat the blackmailer to it.'

Charity shivered. Maybe my words, maybe the cold air breezing in. I got up and shut the windows, then cut up the brownies. Charity was still shivering.

'Let's go into the front room.' I thought about calling Madeline, about asking her to come over, that it was important. I thought about Lindy's question: Does everyone have a secret? Does Alma? Does Charity? And I thought about the hidden side of someone you think you know well, and love dearly.

Is it a wonderful life?

I picked up the plate of brownies and walked into the living room, Charity and Ranger docilely following.

CHAPTER 35

Christmas Cookies
and Martinis

'Have you ever seen someone who has hanged themselves?'

'No. Only autopsy photos.'

'It's not the same as the real thing. The dead thing.'

The house is silent now except for Ranger snoring at my feet. We have turned off *It's a Wonderful Life*.

The brownies have not helped.

'I was one of the people who found her in the dorm room. There were three of us. I honestly didn't recognize her at first. I looked at the face and it didn't seem human. I couldn't recognize the features, couldn't find anyone I knew in there. All I could see was this horrible purple face and bloated tongue, the eyes bulging out and the head at an angle that wasn't right.

'So many things weren't right, Katy. Walking in a room and seeing the bottoms of feet at the top of your nose. They looked so small and vulnerable, little toes in clean socks pointing down, dangling there. Swinging slightly. And then that horrible face. We cut her down. We couldn't untie the knot, not with the weight of the body on it, and we couldn't bear to hold – to take the weight off the rope. We knew she was dead – it was just turning cold, the body. But it didn't seem right to leave her hanging there, not for another minute even. I covered her face as soon as I could.

'I kept wondering why it took so long for help to come. Maybe it wasn't really that long but it seemed like it. Did you know that there was a code out here in the West that you didn't leave your dead? There's something so wrong about that, about leaving them. You either buried them or you sent for help. And someone had to stay with the body so the animals wouldn't get to it, couldn't violate the body. It's a gesture of respect, I guess, as well as protection. So I stayed there while the others went for help.

'I sat on the end of the bed as far away as I could get from the body and I tried not to look at it. I tried to say a prayer for her and to think of other things. But, hard as I tried, I kept looking at it.

'It. Her name was Judith Elaine Hanaford Clark. We called her Jody. And now she was an "it", a body, a horrible dead thing with a swollen tongue and bulging eyes and feet that pointed in an odd way. Her hands looked small and sad and as though they should have done many more things in life, but instead they had tied a knot and that was that.

'The seconds dragged on like minutes and the minutes like hours and days and somewhere in that ugly dead desert of time I saw the note. And I read it. Why? I shouldn't have. They never made it public. Not the family or the authorities. But it was there and I read it.

'After that incident they changed the light fixtures in the dorms. The old ones, like the one in Jody's room, were strong and would hold a lot of weight. Not the new ones. They would pull right out of the ceiling, dragging down wire and plaster.'

'The note?' I asked.

'Jody said she couldn't bear the shame of everyone knowing.' Charity was tipping her martini glass back and forth, watching the liquid intently as though there were a truth, a future to be read there. 'I found out later that she was pregnant. She had been planning to leave school and get married quietly. Her family was very proper – proper Clarks and proper Hanafords – and she didn't know any other way to handle it.

'The thing is' – Charity put her drink down – 'no one knew she was pregnant. Jody just thought they did and she thought that because of something I had written. She killed herself for nothing. No, she killed herself because of me.'

'She killed herself because she was pregnant?' I tried to keep the incredulity out of my voice.

'It was almost twenty years ago, Katy, and her family – they were so proper, so religious and righteous. It was a different time and they were different people.'

'What had you written?' I was having a difficult time seeing Charity's culpability in this.

'I wrote a gossip column for the school paper. And I was good at it, very good. It wasn't important stuff, just who was seeing whom, or sneaking in after hours, or getting awards and honors or barely squeaking by – that kind of thing. It was mostly for laughs.' She winced. 'No. That's not really true. It had a mean, nasty streak running through it. A lot of gossip columns do. That's why we like them so much. We like it when other people are nasty in ways we don't dare be. And clever. I was very clever and funny, my column was the talk of the campus.

'It went to my head.'

Ranger snored and Kitten prowled around looking for excitement and I waited for the ugliness.

'I was so taken with my cleverness, wit, and charm that I got careless with the truth. Here and there I exaggerated or implied something that wasn't, or was sly and suggestive about basically nothing. I did that with Jody. I talked about her naughty little, soon-to-be-much-bigger, secret. The irony is that I didn't even suspect she was pregnant and now I can't remember what unimportant little thing I was needling her about. It didn't matter, it doesn't matter, except that she took her life over it.'

I shook my head. 'That's a big stretch, an unbelievable, unprovable assumption – one you made with death staring you in the face and guilt hollering your name out. Perhaps that was understandable when you were a college student but it hardly makes sense now. Jody's proper background and religious beliefs, her sense of fear and desperation – that's what makes sense. Or perhaps she didn't really like the boy or want to get married. There are a million possibilities and no way that you can know the truth.'

'You didn't see the body. Or what was clipped to her note.'

I had a sudden, bad feeling about what was coming next.

279

'It was a copy of my column with the line about the dirty little secret getting bigger circled. After I read the note I pulled the paper clip off and put the column in my pocket. The paper clip too. I left the room and sat outside the door until help came and I could slip away in all the commotion.

'Later, when they interviewed us about finding the body, I said nothing about the note or clipping. I thought no one else knew of it. The other girls didn't see it, I know they didn't. They were hysterical after we cut down the body. Oh God, it was horrible, Katy. I can still remember the feel of that cold/warm flesh under my hands. How can someone have known? How?'

She shook herself. 'That's the wrong question, the wrong issue, I know. I've lived with that death for all these years. I'm always trying to make up for it. It's been difficult enough to live with until now – you're the only one I've ever told. How can I possibly live with it, go on in my career, if it becomes public?'

'No sensible person will believe you had anything to do with her death.'

'Yes they will. There was even talk at the time. Not to my face but behind my back or just out of my hearing. It was horrible. I left at the end of the year. I haven't forgotten. Why should they? They believed it then, why shouldn't others believe it now?'

I shook my head. 'You were upset and your judgment was impaired. You never heard anything directly, just the innuendo. Perhaps they felt sorry for you, you and the others, because you were the ones to discover the body. Surely that's more plausible?'

Charity was unaffected by my reasoning. 'It doesn't matter. Even if you were right, which I doubt, it doesn't matter. Somebody knows.'

'No.' I tried reasonable again. Quiet persuasion. 'How could they? That means someone found Jody before you did, read the note, then left the room without saying anything, and all without anyone noticing? How likely is that in a dorm? How likely is it that someone would have been so cold and calculating about the suicide of a dorm mate? Charity, it's crazy.'

She looked at me, unconvinced. It was my voice. I had figured out something that wasn't crazy, that made an appalling sense.

I want to see a big, fat check and I want to see it now. Jackie and

Charity were about the same age. Had they both been in school at the same time? The same school? Or had friends in common? Visited back and forth? Jackie was an embezzler and a blackmailer who was capable of putting the squeeze on her own lover. She was capable of using this against Charity. Easily. But why now? Why wait so long?

'Katy?'

'What did the blackmailer say to you? What did he or she know?'

'She?' The fear in her voice had fallen into a trembling, wavering vibrato.

'It's just an expression, Charity – he or she because we don't know for sure.' I made my voice as soothing and gentle as I could.

'Oh.' Scared and unconvinced. 'She, or he, said, "You've gotten away with this for a long time but I know the truth about Jody. She committed suicide because of what you wrote. And now you're an advice columnist. That's pretty funny, isn't it. Ha-ha." That's what he said, Katy. It wasn't a real laugh, it was words, horrible mean words. And then he said, "I wonder if anyone else would think that you giving advice is funny? Funny or fatal?" And then this ghastly voice started laughing.

'It was like something out of a horror movie, not like something human. It was very frightening.' She was visibly trembling now. 'I could just see my career, my column, everything I love going down in flames. *Every*thing, friends and – Oh God!' She looked at me, question marks in her eyes, as easy to read as a cartoon character with a balloon over her head.

'I said I wasn't going to ask you this but I am. Please stop this, Katy. Please. If you don't everything will come out. Please don't let him take me down. I couldn't bear it! Nothing would ever be the same. You're my friend. You can't do this to me. You *can't*!' She ended on a long drawn-out wail.

I waited for it to subside.

'Did you know Jim Randolph?' I asked.

She nodded.

'And you know he committed suicide?'

'What does this—'

'Did you know that?'

'*Yes!*' She sounded mad, impatient.

'Randolph was a victim of this blackmailer. He was set up, either by the blackmailer or someone the blackmailer knew. Randolph acted in innocence but the setup was good.' I thought of Jim Randolph's demons. 'It was the perfect thing to bring him down, to drive him to suicide. And it was very carefully planned. Technically it was suicide, but there was murder in there. Do you see that? Do you see the difference between the two suicides?' My voice was harsh.

Another nod. Her eyes had lost the wildness, the questioning. On the floor Ranger stirred and twitched in his doggy dreams and Kitten swatted lazily at his tail.

'You did what we have all done. You made a mistake, an error in judgment – the kind we are likely to make when we are young. Had Jody been a different person, a stronger, more balanced person, she would have shrugged the column off, ignored it completely or told you to go to hell. The decision on how to live her life, or whether to take her life, was hers and hers alone. It's that way for everyone. It is a foolish arrogance to think that one small thing you did was that important in someone's life and death.' My voice was still harsh. I waited for her to hear me.

'Katy!' She gasped.

'It's true. Stop this emotional wallow in guilt and what-ifs and responsibility that isn't yours. You paid ten thousand in extortion; you've been paying in guilt. Both were unnecessary. This is guilt and extortion built on supposition and fiction and you must stop it. Now. Jody's death was suicide, not murder, and you are not to blame.'

Charity sat there, her mouth flopping foolishly around like a fish out of water. She looked confused, but not desperate.

'Charity, how can I stop work on this case? Jim Randolph's suicide was the result of someone's murderous planning and intent. You know how well the blackmailer does this. It is not just you and Lindy and Randolph, there are others. And it won't stop, extortion rarely does. No one will go to the police. No one ever does. If I stop, there is nothing between him and more victims. More pain. More destruction.'

'Katy.'

Her voice pleaded with me. I did nothing to make it easy for her. Life is not easy.

'Katy, I'm not brave like you. Like Lindy. I wish I could do what

Lindy did, but I can't. I'd rather die.'

'Lindy did the right thing for her. Prostitution is a crime. Her past actions were a matter of public knowledge and record.' Technically she was protected because she was a minor, but I was being realistic. 'You have broken no law, committed no crime. You were thoughtless, indiscreet, and used poor judgment. That is not criminal, that is human. There is nothing here, Charity. The blackmailer is playing on your fears. It is a bluff.'

'You really believe that?'

'Yes.' And I did.

'And you think I should . . . should ignore the latest threat?'

'Yes. But not because it is a bluff. Because it is the right thing to do. Because, like Lindy, you have a lot of courage. More than you know.'

I have known Charity for a long time. She is not a cream puff. I thought of the gunshots flying around Arden Fair Mall and the young woman lying in a pool of red red blood while Elvis sang 'Blue Christmas.'

I am not a cream puff either.

Good thing.

Charity reached out for a brownie. 'Get the bastard, Katy.' It wasn't her tough-guy voice, not quite, but it was pretty close. It was pretty good.

CHAPTER 36

Be Good for
Goodness' Sakes

'Who the hell are you anyway and what the fuck do you think you're doing?' Words snarled into a phone.

'I'm fine thanks. How are you?' I replied – urbanely, I hoped – and tipped my chair back to put my feet up on the desk. Eight-thirty in the morning. Early for me to be at work. I'd gotten sucked in again by that early-bird-gets-the-worm junk. I reached for my mug of tea. 'Your name? You forgot to mention it.'

A polite inquiry on my part, wouldn't you say? Not that I didn't know her name. Not that she was going to give it either. Not that I cared. And I had caller ID. I was smug in that knowledge. She wasn't smug, she was pissed. Big-time.

'You fucking, meddling, two-bit bitch!'

Two-bit bitch? I tried to figure how insulting that was and decided to go with fairly insulting, definitely unimaginative. Hah. I wasn't the only one who needed to spend some time with her thesaurus.

'Whoops, you're having a bad day, I can tell.' I said, egging her on.

Jackie Anderson made a low, snarly sound, the kind of sound I imagine hyenas make although I've never actually known a hyena. You can't really count the ones in *The Lion King*.

'You don't have a rich godmother *and* you're a fucking private investigator.'

285

'Bingo,' I said cheerfully. 'Aren't you good. Do you play the lottery?'

She sputtered. I figured – what the hell? – I'd gamble and play the odds. It was time for focus, for direction. Okay, for uncontrolled and – one could only hope – indiscreet rage. On Jackie's part, not mine.

'What punched your button, Jackie? The fact that I set an audit of Hope For Kids in motion or that I pulled the covers on your lover boy's past and tossed him, like meat scraps to a pack of starving hounds, to the press.'

'You did WHAT?' The 'what' was in capital letters, the rage was muted by incredulity but catching up fast. 'That was *you*? You goddamn bitch!'

Somebody needed to explain to Jackie that only lazy people relied on profanity to express themselves. Somebody besides me. She didn't seem all that receptive to my suggestions.

'Listen.' Her voice hissed viciously over the wires. 'You keep this up, you're going to be sorry. Back off now while you still can. Back off fast. I mean it.'

She hung up. Before I could say: *Ooooooh, I'm so scared.* And I would have said it, just to piss her off and because I'm a smartass. It was also true. Jackie was involved in this, although I didn't know how deeply. I did know her connections seemed good and I could count on her to send out informational bulletins. Do bulletins equal bullets? They had at the mall, that's why I was scared. I didn't want a bloody Christmas. Or a blue one.

Time to call Hiram Grant and J.O. But not necessarily in that order.

J.O. was home. I think it's the only time I've ever caught him there. Eight-thirty in the morning and he sounded slightly drunk. I looked at the clock. Ooops, my mistake, it was almost nine. Still, the principle was the same.

'Jeez, J.O., a little early to be in the bag, isn't it?'

'I'm not drinking just to drink, Kat.' His voice was slow, paced, the way drunks talk. 'There's a principle involved here: I'm celebrating.'

I let that idea – that sticking to a principle should necessitate alcoholic celebration – whiz right past me without comment. 'What are you celebrating?' I inquired instead.

'I'm out of the hospital.'

'Just until your liver transplant.'

'Ha-ha.' His voice was mirthless, cheerless, his tone grumpy. 'Hey, Kat, gotta run. Watching my ice cubes melt is more fun than talking to you.'

'More fun than writing your series?'

'What do you mean?'' His voice was wary.

'You didn't have an article in the paper yesterday and there wasn't one today. What gives?'

'Nothing much.' He made his voice light. 'Shit, you know I'm not up to my usual fighting form. No biggie, I'll pick it up as soon as I feel a little better.'

It took me a long time to process that all the way through. And then I could feel a hard knot of fear in my belly.

'I've never known you not to finish something, J.O. – you're like a rabid terrier with a rat. Drunk, stoned, sick – it doesn't matter, you still write. Something's wrong. What?'

'Nothing.' He sounded pissed off. 'Don't be making a big deal out of this. I just got the shit kicked out of me and I don't feel so goddamned great, that's it.'

'You wrote three articles in the series feeling like that. What's different now?'

'Fuck off, Kat.'

Two hang-ups in a row.

Was I on a roll or what?

I called Dr Hiram Grant, who was in consultation and would return my call, the receptionist informed me distantly but almost politely.

It got to me a little.

The thing is I'm not used to being the bad guy. The reason I do what I do is because I like dropping dimes on bad guys. *Really* like it. Naturally I don't care if bad guys don't like me. Or get mad, scared, etc. (Actually, my theory is that bad guys don't feel like that often enough and every little bit counts.) But in this case *everyone* was mad at me. Or scared. Or unhappy. Especially the victims, and I was on their side. They were understandably afraid of what I knew and what could come out, aware of how quick people are to judge, and how slow to forgive.

Have you ever seen a police target?

There are different kinds. The bull's-eye and a human silhouette from the waist up are popular. *Shoot to kill*, not wound. *Go for critical mass* – torso, not limbs. This is what cops are taught. Randolph, Madeline, Delia, Lindy, Charity – good guys lined up with bull's-eyes on their chests.

Me too.

It took me a long time to track down the names and numbers. I almost gave up at several points, especially since there was a good chance I was sprinting down a dead-end street. Almost. I wanted to be sure about the last possible target.

In case you're wondering, there are eighty-three people named Edwards in Dallas. I called sixty-seven of them before I hit pay dirt. The drawl on the phone was heavy, the voice low. A cigarette voice, a whiskey voice. A down-and-dirty voice. My spirits shot up. Maybe it wouldn't take me that much longer. I hoped I was right about the down-and-dirty.

'Mrs Edwards—'

'Call me Marnelle, Kat. We won't stand on ceremony. Kat, that's a funny name, isn't it? You northern girls have the oddest names.'

I let it go, not the part about the odd name, which is true, but the part about the North. California is west but maybe it's the same thing to Southerner.

'Marnelle—'

'So, do you see that low-down son of a gun much?'

I had the distinct impression that the word gun was a last-minute substitution. And I was beginning to understand why it was his godmother and not his mother that J.O. had been close to. I could hear Marnelle dragging deeply on her cigarette, sucking in a nicotine breath.

'A fair amount, mostly in work situations.'

'And are you at all personally—' she made the word last forever with extended vowel play— 'involved with him then?'

'No. We are business associates. Marnelle, I—'

'Well, honey, I think that's a fine choice, a helluva fine choice.'
Another drag.

I sighed and gave up. My original plan was to keep this conversation
direct, short, and sweet. Well, short anyway, maybe bitter instead of
sweet. But obviously this was not going to happen. I followed
Marnelle's lead.

'What do you mean?'

'Why, I can't believe he's changed that much, I surely cannot.
That boy was set in that way from the beginning.'

'What way?' *A sports fanatic? A newshound? A cross-dresser? A
womanizer?* What *way?*

'Set, yes siree, like a piece of marble or a chunk of concrete.' I
heard the tinkle of ice cubes against a glass and another deep drag.
And I decided I'd better settle in for the long haul.

'That's how set the boy was.'

I made a murmuring, encouraging sound.

'A pretty little thing in a skirt, J.O. was right after her. I knew it
would happen. I always said it would. You ask anyone and they'll tell
you, yes ma'am, Marnelle saw that one coming a long ways off.
Why, it was as plain as the nose on your face that he was going to get
a girl into trouble. And sooner, not later.

'There wasn't hardly anyone who was surprised when it came to
pass. Certainly not me, not by a long shot.' There was a grim
satisfaction in her voice. 'It was a nice girl too, even though I had
told him not to go messing about with nice girls. Goodness knows
there was trash around and plenty of it, there always is. No one would
have much noticed that.'

No wonder, I reflected sadly, that J.O. was a little short in the
principles-and-ethics department. No wonder, either, that drinking
and smoking came so easily.

'Did J.O. marry her?'

She snorted in derision, dragged on her cigarette, and made the ice
cubes in her drink clatter around.

'Lord,' she laughed. 'If that don't tell me plain as day you really
don't know J.O., nothing in this world would. Bless you, anyway.
No, Kat, he sure enough did *not* marry her. He did not even think
about it, not for one small minute. He was gone. Shoot, he made

289

better time than Sherman's army through Georgia.'

'How old were they?'

'Seventeen. They were nothing but seventeen, the both of them. Honey, you hang on for a minute now, will you. I got to freshen up my drink.' The phone thunked down on a hard surface and I hung on and felt sorry for the seventeen-year-olds that J.O. and his girlfriend had been. And hoped her parents had been more understanding and compassionate.

'All right now, where were we?'

I heard the scrape of a match and then Marnelle dragged away on her cigarette and took a pull off her drink.

We were in deep shit, I thought.

'What happened to the girl and the baby?' is what I asked.

Silence broken only by smoking and drinking sounds. Uh-oh, was Marnelle going to go discreet on me all of a sudden? I should have stuck to encouraging murmurs.

'I don't know as I should tell you that. Not that it's any big secret in these parts but out there, why, if J.O. hasn't said anything, I reckon I shouldn't. A person deserves a chance to start over.'

'I would never say anything,' I assured Marnelle. 'I was just worried about her and the baby and I wondered if J.O. ever saw them.' Them. The young woman who would be middle-aged by now and the baby who was a grown man. Or woman.

'It was bad, real bad. No one expected anything like it.' Her voice was serious, sober. 'She took an overdose of pills and washed it down with ninety proof. They didn't find her in time.'

'She died?' I could hear the tightness in my voice.

'No. She lived, but she was a vegetable.'

'The baby?'

'It lived too. Severely retarded. I never saw it but once. It was just a little lump of a thing. It didn't even look human; its features weren't in all the right places. I couldn't bring myself to touch it, never mind pick it up.'

I let out a breath I hadn't realized I was holding. Sadness, for the girl and the baby and J.O., choked me up.

'Until I saw that girl I always wondered what folks meant when they said someone was a vegetable. What kind of a vegetable? A tomato, a string bean, an onion – what? Or maybe it was just a figure of speech, like saying someone was a long, tall skinny drink of water. After I saw her I didn't wonder any more.

'She looked like a turnip. You know how they are? Round and white with a little pink and purple coloring. That's what she looked like. And she had been a real pretty girl before, real pretty and slim.'

'Are she and the child still alive?'

'Oh my yes. They tell me she could last for years. They say she's in real good health, except for being a vegetable of course. And the child too, I guess. I don't think anyone goes out there anymore, not even her people. They did, for a real long time they did, but then they gave up too.'

'Did J.O. ever come back?'

'Yes, he did, I'll give him that much. He came back right after it happened. He went to visit her and he stayed at that hospital day and night. The nurses told me he wouldn't hardly leave her at all, not to eat or sleep, barely to go to the restroom. They said he talked to her all the time, talked to her and sang to her, held her hands and stroked her forehead.

'They said he talked about all the things they were going to do together when she got well. They were going to get married and get a little house and play with the baby and have another if she wanted. How he was going to take her to Atlanta and New Orleans like she'd always wished and even to New York and Boston. They were grand places he said, different from anything they'd ever known. He promised it would all be different, he'd be different, they'd have a good life together. And all she had to do was open her eyes and smile at him and get well.

'But she never did. She never opened her eyes once. He stayed with her for a month. I never saw anyone so changed in all my life. Why, I almost didn't recognize him. For a couple of years he came back and spent time with her. I think he only went to see the baby but once. That baby was pretty hard to take, I'm telling you. But she never changed. After a while he quit coming back. I never saw him since. Never hear from him either. Nobody back here does. He's dead to us, that's what he is. Dead as if the good Lord had taken him.'

'What was her name?'

291

'Her name?'

'The girl.'

'Oh. Joyce Ellen Burdett. Everyone called her Jossie.'

'And the baby?'

'It never had a name, not that I knew of anyway, though they tell me it was a boy. It was hard to think of it as a person. Now it's hard to think of her as a person too. Sweet pretty Jossie died, leaving nothing but a turnip behind. Don't you think?'

She dragged on her cigarette and I thought two things: that J.O. thought of Jossie and the baby as people in spite of all the bourbon he poured on the memory, and that the blackmailer knew what I did about J.O.'s past.

Knew it and used it.

CHAPTER 37

Dear Santa,
My daddy's always saying he's fed up with his life. Can you
please bring him a new one? And can I have a teddy bear? I
love you.

Mandy

Rick didn't do this, I thought as I banged on the door again. He didn't
get involved; he watched out for number one. Shoot, he wouldn't
even let people buy him drinks. It was wartime Casablanca: Don't
get involved, don't be beholden. He knew those things. I pounded the
door, kicked it for good measure, the bottom of the pizza box warm
on my hand.

I'm not Rick.

Even Rick wasn't Rick after Ilsa came back into the picture. Love
changes things. Or friendship. 'I'm not leaving,' I hollered. 'Open
the door.'

The door opened and I blinked. To say that J.O. looked like shit
would be sugarcoating it. Gaunt face, haunted eyes, three-day growth;
slovenly, slightly smelly clothes. I've seen better-looking homeless
guys. Way better.

He leaned against the door frame, not casually but for support.
'How many times do I have to tell you to fucking go away? Goddamn,
you're a slow learner.'

'Yeah. You going to move or do I have to push you out of the
way?'

'Get lost, Kat.' He started to close the door.

I kicked it open and pushed him out of the way. He staggered back

293

and thudded onto an antique armoire. I kicked the door shut. His eyes were hostile, hating. Not hatred directed at me, just hatred that had filled him to capacity and was spilling out.

'Can you walk into the kitchen or shall I drag you in after I put the pizza down?'

He snarled.

'Yes or no?' I sliced the words into the stream of vituperation he was spewing. 'It's going to be my way. You're no match for me right now.' I let my eyes travel over his body, his face. 'You're no match for a six-week-old kitten.'

'I can walk,' he said sullenly.

I marched down the hall and through the swinging door into the kitchen, which wasn't as bad as I expected. No filth, no food. Just liquor bottles and dirty glasses. I threw two empty bottles away and piled the glasses into a sink of hot soapy water.

Plates were easy to find, pristine but dusty. I wiped them off and set them on the small wooden table where the pizza sat. I looked for juice, milk, even soda, then gave up and made coffee.

'Sit down. Eat. If you don't I'm coming back with a doctor who will sign you into a detox center. I'm not kidding, J.O. Hop to it. You've got thirty seconds to get started.' I put two pieces of pizza on his plate and set down a cup of coffee. Black. There was no milk or sugar.

'I can't eat.'

'Get your coat then. I'm taking you to a medical facility.'

'Go fuck yourself.' His face was tired. No life, no spirit. He looked at the pizza. 'I need a drink to get this down.'

'No.'

'Just one.'

'No.'

He sipped at the coffee, made a face, made a choice, drank some more. Ate some pizza. I watched over him like an anxious mother bird, cooing at his bites and sips and small successes. Three pieces of pizza and two cups of coffee later he was starting to look almost human.

But not sound it – that was a little too much to expect.

'Okay, you made your point. Now get the fuck out of here.'

'Soon. Get into the shower first. Clean clothes too. There are pigs that smell better than you. Lots of them.'

He started swearing at me. Talk about a predictable, boring routine. I waited it out. When it didn't stop I interrupted him.

'I am perfectly capable of throwing you fully clothed into the shower.'

I was, too, and he knew it. And he wasn't strong enough to push me off. Not now. I waited until I heard the bathroom door slam and the water run before I poured all the alcohol I could find down the drain. Even with two bottles in each hand it took me a while. Then I took the trash — okay, evidence of my perfidy — out and tidied up a little. I was just putting the pizza away when J.O. appeared, clean and sweet-smelling, looking only slightly run down and unshaven but more or less like a human being. Looking sheepish too. Good sign.

'I'll be okay, Kat.' He mumbled some words that might have been thanks or appreciation. 'I'm going to bed now, haven't been sleeping that great.'

I made him change the sheets. I even helped, practically holding my nose. Then I pushed him out into the front room before he could topple into bed.

'We have to talk.'

'Later, Katy. Goddamn, have a heart.'

'Now,' I said, feeling heartless and humane both.

He groaned but gave in. Rubbing his eyes with his fists like a little kid he wandered into the front room and sat on the couch.

'What?' His tired, cranky voice, also like a kid.

'The blackmailer got to you, didn't he?'

'What the fuck you talking about?' An adult voice, angry, evil.

'I know about Jossie, J.O. And the baby.' I met his eyes, looked at him with sadness and compassion but not with pity. Pity, like alcohol, eats away at you. Enough of J.O. had been eaten away already.

'Yeah. He got to me.'

'Jossie?'

'Yes.'

'Money?'

'No.'

'He wanted you to shut up, to stop publishing the extortion series?'

'Yes.'

'Go to bed. We'll figure out something when you're stronger. Just eat and sleep now. Give me a key. I'm sending someone over with groceries.'

He started to protest, then nodded. When I left with a key he was already in bed. Before I left I called Grant.

And made an appointment to see him at two-thirty.

Dr Hiram Grant was looking rumpled but not cadaverous, which was good news for me. I'd seen enough – make that more than enough – of the walking dead lately.

'How's it going?' he asked me.

We didn't, either of us, think he was inquiring about my health.

'I know a lot, it's just not getting me anywhere.' I thought that one over. 'Or rather it is, but I don't know where. Blackmail is a bitch.' I added the obvious and irrelevant; I was feeling a little bitter.

He nodded without speaking. *Tell me about it*, is what his expression said.

'I've uncovered three more blackmail victims, one of them very recent. He was working with me to stop this. The blackmailer wanted to stop him.

'Did he?'

'Yes.'

He said nothing. There was nothing to say to that.

'There was a shooting the other day at Arden Fair Mall. Perhaps you heard about it on the news?'

'Yes. A random shooting, wasn't it? A young woman was the victim.'

'It wasn't random and I was the intended victim. I got out of the way, she couldn't. In the chaos that followed, the shooter got away. I didn't have a chance at catching up to him. Or her.'

'I'm sorry,' he said. It sounded lame. 'Is she going to be all right?'

'They've upgraded her condition from critical.'

He nodded.

I was going to have to drag it out of him. 'You see, of course, what I'm getting at?'

'Yes.'

'You're not very forthcoming.'

'No. Fear does that.' There was no apology there, just an explanation.

'The stakes are high now. He's taking risks now – wild, at least, if not foolish. There will be more moves like this and they will be equally dangerous. To me, to others as well. This is where the death toll of innocent bystanders could go up.' Innocent and not so innocent, like me.

'You don't know any of this.'

I noticed a skull the color of yellowed ivory on the top of a glassed-in bookcase that was overfilled with medical tomes. It was a small skull; I guessed that it was an old one. I wondered why I hadn't noticed it before and if it had belonged to someone Grant knew. No, that was foolishness. I shook myself mentally. 'Alas, poor Yorick . . .' drifted through my mind. 'I knew him . . .' Hamlet had reflected over ivoried bones.

The blackmailer knew a lot of very different people very well. How? It was not the first time I'd asked the question.

'Yes. I do know,' I answered Grant's question finally.

He gave me the bemused look that people with scientific training are so fond of, the one they use when they think you're reaching.

'I have irretrievably set things in motion. Either I stop the blackmailer, or he stops me. These are the only possibilities. If I get him, it will be without violence. *Talk about boundless optimism.* 'If he gets me . . .' I shrugged.

I was focused on Grant but my eyes kept trying to drag my attention back to the skull. *Fear does that. Death does that too.* His eyes wavered, looked out the window at the bleak gray landscape. Marginally better than yellowed ivory, I reflected.

'What do you want from me?'

'You know something about the blackmailer. I need to know what that is. I will make every effort to see that it does not come back to you.'

'I know nothing.'

'A supposition, then.'

'Yes.'

The silence stretched out. I could have – if I remembered it – recited Hamlet's soliloquy to Yorick's skull. Or drafted volume one of my memoirs. Or finished up an unambitious plumbing job. I waited, though I am not a particularly patient person. And getting less so daily, I might add.

'I always wondered how he, or whoever the blackmailer is, found out about me. The women I helped with abortions did not know me by name, did not come to my office. They did not even know me by sight, as I always wore a gown, a mask, and a cap. Voice, perhaps? But I consider that farfetched, especially since they were often upset, nervous, and afraid in spite of my best efforts to put then at ease. How then?'

I shook my head. I had plenty of questions myself. The commodity I was short on was answers.

'Some years ago my wife and I came home from a weekend away. It was summertime and the children were not around.' He smiled wryly. 'Which meant that we returned to the same orderly house we left. Or almost the same. I was convinced that someone had been in it, had been through our things. Some items were not in quite the same order or places.

'There was no evidence of a break-in, and we found nothing missing. My wife, who is not by nature either as orderly or as observant as I, pooh-poohed my supposition. Perhaps she was right. But perhaps not. Shortly afterwards the blackmail started.'

'The blackmailer had accurate information?'

'Remarkably so.'

'And there were records, medical notes, a journal, something at your home that contained this information?'

'Yes.'

'And they were still there when you returned from your weekend away?'

'Yes, but I would have sworn that they had been moved about.'

'Where is that material now?'

'I destroyed it.' The wry smile again. 'You are of course familiar with the concept of locking the barn door after the horse is gone?'

'Very familiar. And your theory is?'

'Theory is too dignified a term.'

Yes. There was no data here, nothing for a medical expert to base a theory on.

In lieu of a theory, I speculated. 'It is possible that someone entered your house looking for information rather than material things.' *Stealing secrets, not electronics, guns, and jewelry.* 'And it is possible that the blackmailer entered other homes in search of personal and potentially damaging information.'

'That is the possibility that had occurred to me, yes.'

'How would he know?' I asked, thinking out loud. 'We don't go around with scarlet letters pinned to our chests.'

'Many people have something to hide, though not necessarily something they could be blackmailed on. And few of us are as clever as we think in hiding our weak or vulnerable spots. The balding man who combs his hair over his head fools no one but himself.'

I thought of killers who keep 'mementos' from their victims, child molesters who keep damning pictures, lovers who hold on to love letters and photos from previous loves.

'Do most people keep such records?'

'I don't know. Perhaps. I did.'

Dinosaur bones are everywhere. Skeletons take a long time to crumble.

'You know something more.'

'No. I wish I did but I don't.'

I wished I did too.

CHAPTER 38

Better Watch Out

It was possible I could walk out my front door and trip over the blackmailer but, realistically, what were the odds? Hey, might as well ask for him to be hog-tied and gift wrapped as well.

Time for a setup. I sighed inwardly. I hate this kind of stuff. *Hate it.* I mean, the only way a trap is going to work is with bait. And what's the bait? You guessed it, me. Not that I wouldn't do everything I could to make the trap safe, foolproof. Again, what are the odds?

The thing was, I didn't see that I had a choice. I needed something to take to the cops in order to stop the blackmail. That something was the identity of the blackmailer and evidence of extortion that would stand up in court. I didn't have either. Right now I didn't even have a reasonable expectation of getting either. And that left me with the trap.

How do you get in touch with an unknown blackmailer? An invitation? A personal ad? Oh sure. It would have to be more of the same, more of what was getting to him already. He had used Lindy and Charity to try to stop me. He had shut up J.O. He had tried to kill me. I didn't know what, specifically, was working so well but I could do more of all of it. A lot more. I also knew he was watching me closely. The shooting at Arden Fair Mall had told me that.

I called J.O. and left a message on his machine. I wanted him to get the paper to print that he was ill but another writer would be taking over. This (unnamed) writer would be working closely with sources in the investigative community. Translation: Me.

Then I called Madeline and asked her to convene a formal, and highly publicized, board inquiry into possible financial irregularities at Hope For Kids. I asked her to use my name as both a present and future source.

I was enunciating well and speaking carefully, just like a kid in speech class. Or in case my line was tapped. Wouldn't want him, or her, to miss a word. I made a mental note to get an electronic whiz kid I knew over here to look around.

Finally I called a friend I knew was out of town and left a message asking her if she wanted to grab a quick bite today. I told her to call me back in half an hour as I was heading downtown to the Sheriff's Department and the courthouse to wrap up a case.

By then I was having fun, even had to force myself not to get too theatrical.

After that I ambled over to another office in my building and called the whiz kid, who was in and salivating at the thought of a tricky little job.

'I can't promise you tricky,' I warned.

'Let's hope,' he said, sounding slightly disgusted. 'I mean, *any*one can go to Radio Shack. I'm on my way now, I'll get in touch with you later today. You got an okay line somewhere?'

'No guarantees. I'll call you.'

'Roger. If I don't hear from you and I have to go out I'll call you at home and leave a message like I'm Bob the plumber. If I say the water heater is running fine and you got plenty of hot water it means I found something. If I say you got nothing but cold water you're fine. Get it? If you got hot water, you're in hot water, if—'

'I got it.' I sighed thinking, and not for the first time, that his was a generation that had watched way too much TV. Then I left my keys, as per arrangement, with the receptionist in the front office, jumped into the Bronco, and started waltzing around town. If it could make a bad guy nervous I was there. With bells on.

My first stop was downtown at Bill Henley's office. Ooops, second stop. First was really good coffee and sinful cookies. I carried the cookies in an official-looking briefcase that I keep for just this kind of occasion. No point looking like I was going to a picnic. I spent an hour in the Homicide Department drinking coffee, consuming a gazillion cookie calories, and shooting the shit with the guys who were there and not busy.

Not that they were any help – 'Hell, Kat, the only kind of extortion we see is the straightforward kind. "Give us money or we waste your kid," that kind' – but we all agreed that extortion is a shitty crime. Nobody likes a blackmailer. That perked me up but naturally I didn't leave with a smile. No way. This was theater – I had a sober, serious expression glued to my face when I left.

It's a short walk from the Sheriff's Department on 7th and G to the courthouse on 8th between G and H. I trundled on over with firm purposeful stride, official briefcase and serious – now verging on grim – expression in place. My first stop there was in the records office, where I looked up some stuff as a courtesy to an out-of-town investigator. Then I headed up to the fourth floor, chatted with a bailiff and a deputy DA I knew, and rearranged my serious expression. At that point the expression part was easy since I was pretty sure my meter had expired and parking tickets in this area are expensive.

I beat the meter maid by two lengths – she looked a little surly about it too – and headed on over to the *Sacramento Bee* at 21st and Q. There I killed another hour, and drank some *really* bad coffee, piddling around in files and shooting the breeze with a reporter I knew. He didn't know anything about extortion either but we also had a good time agreeing that extortionists were pond scum. This time when I left the building I allowed myself a lighter step and a slightly smug and self-satisfied expression.

On the way back to my office I stopped at a lawyer's office, an accountant's office, and a real estate office. These were quickie stops, ten or fifteen minutes at most.

My last stop was another private investigator's office. That was supposed to be a quickie too but Zeke is an old friend of mine so we played catch-up for an hour or so. I emerged from his office with a definite spring in my step and a quietly pleased look on my face. Translation: *I had scored big-time today.* And the corollary: *I was closing in for the kill. Time to get nervous, sucker.*

I went home then but not to stay. To get the animals out. I might be part of a setup but they weren't. I wanted to assure their safety and also to provide easy access for the intruder I was expecting soon (knock on wood). I came home with a briefcase and I left with a dog, a cat, and an overnight bag. No briefcase. Translation: *The house was unprotected, the goodies were there.* I didn't leave the back door unlocked. I mean, no point in being ridiculously obvious, but the house wasn't tied up like a fortress either. I also made a very careful mental survey of where things were and how I had left them. We are talking exact here. Fortunately I hadn't dusted for a long time. Good, huh? How often does slovenliness pay off like that?

I dropped the four-footed guys off at Charity's ranch, which is where they often stay when I'm out of town. She spoils them in a sickening fashion and they come home fat and sassy with an I-am-a-spoiled-pet! attitude which always takes them an annoying couple of weeks to get over.

The minute we walked in Charity started yammering at me. Subtle is not her middle name.

'What's going on? You're not leaving town, I know you're not. You'd never leave at this point in a case. Did you find out something? What? Tell me, tell me, tell me. I *promise* I won't say anything. Is it almost over? Who is it? I *deserve* to know. Katy, spit it out *this* minute.'

She was yammering to the whir of an electric can opener. Kitten was about to dine on tuna – expensive people tuna, not pet food. Ranger was having wildly expensive doggie sirloin laced with leftover meatloaf, mashed potatoes and gravy. You see why they're so snippy when they get home again. And chubby.

I tossed the Bronco keys on the counter and grabbed the last slice of meatloaf before it went into Ranger's bowl. Then went searching for bread and mayo. 'I'm trading cars for a day, okay? I need the four-runner.'

'Don't talk with your mouth full, Katy.' Charity spoke crossly, undoubtedly because I hadn't answered her questions.

'I wasn't. This is *really* good meatloaf. I wish you hadn't given it all to Ranger.'

'What's going on?'

'This and that.' I shrugged.

'Why won't you tell me, Katy?' Really cross now.

'I will, I promise, as soon as possible.' I gave her a hug, then raided the refrigerator for an apple and a diet Dr Pepper. 'Where are your keys?'

Nobody noticed when I left. The guys had fat bellies and had crashed into post prandial nap heaps and Charity was still pouting.

Have I mentioned the lack of appreciation in my job recently?

My next move was a tough call. Part of me wanted – okay, want is too weak a verb here, lusted maybe – to stake out the house and catch the sucker red-handed, then nail his hide to the barn door. Shoot, as long as we're going vigilante here, might as well string him up like a horse thief.

The wiser part of me prevailed. It was, after all, only step one of a complicated setup. The pyrotechnics had just begun. I wanted to watch though, and I'd figured out a safe distance and a reasonable plan. Well, reasonable if you didn't count the weather. Not only was it cold, it was supposed to rain. I had my fingers crossed for a mere drizzle.

This time I was prepared – a heavy sweater, my Gore-Tex jacket, a scarf, gloves, the works. Also a backpack with hot tea, sandwiches and cookies, binoculars and a camera. My gun was in a clip-on holster. Timmy was almost as hard to shake as Charity. Maybe harder; he had youth and tenacity on his side.

And it *was* his tree house.

My part of Orangevale, like most of the Sacramento area, is pretty flat. It doesn't take much elevation to give you a view of the neighborhood. A tree house twenty feet up wasn't exactly ideal but it wasn't bad, not in an area where almost all the houses are single-story. Charity's 4-runner was parked in Timmy's driveway – the family driveway actually, since Timmy is eleven – and I was parked in the tree house. Binoculars and camera (zoom lens, night lens, the works) at the ready.

It was a long, cold wait which meant I had way too much time to think. This was my shot at identifying the blackmailer. Once I had the ID I would compile evidence. I shivered – it wasn't just the cold. I had an uneasy feeling that compiling evidence would involve something really unpleasant – like breaking into the blackmailer's home or office. Okay, not only unpleasant but illegal. I had stayed out of jail so far but, I reflected glumly, my luck could change at any time.

And the blackmailer? Panicked was my fervent hope. After all, I'd spent all day in a major endeavor to create that state of mind. Okay, not just panicked but desperate to see what I had and how damning it was. And desperate to stop me before I started spilling the beans.

The clock was ticking.

I shivered again. It was not only cold now but wet. The drizzle, as promised, had arrived. I was just starting to feel really bitter about Gene Kelly singing in the rain in such a happy, chirpy way when a vehicle with the headlights cut pulled up between my house and my neighbor's. *Hot damn*, it was a possible.

I forgave Gene just like that.

And scrambled lickety-split down the two-by-fours nailed to the tree as a ladder and hightailed it across an empty field, using trees and shrubbery as cover. The weather had long ago eliminated the issue of long-distance surveillance. I gave my house a wide berth – too easy to scare off the bad guy before I had the necessary detail – and swung around toward the street. Almost swung. The rain slick and mud patch pretty much spoiled my style, just as the mud on my butt and legs spoiled my fashionable prowler look.

I checked the license number of the vehicle, a new dark-colored four-wheel-drive Ford Explorer. The car was remarkably clean except for the license plates, which were muddy. *Talk about a tired and stale old gambit*. Correction: had been muddy before the rain started. They were smeared now, but legible. I jotted the number down.

And smirked. Even the cold and wet couldn't make me feel bad now. My Gore-Tex jacket was holding up really well. The rest of me was a sodden, muddy mess, the rain coming down in a slow, steady gray curtain. It would be difficult to see anything but I waited on the off chance. Investigation is full of gambles.

I am here to tell you that standing in the bushes in the driving rain – well, crouching really, I was doing the old hide-in-the-shrubbery-and-spy bit, and yeah, I know that's a more shopworn cliché than the bad-guy-with-muddy-plates bit – anyway, time passes very slowly in situations like this. It's like being at the dentist, only there's more fear involved. That bad.

It felt like I'd been there for two hours, or weeks or decades, but when I looked at my watch only twenty-four minutes had passed. I started to feel bitter about Gene Kelly again. Another ten minutes and I was not only bitter, I'd pretty much promised myself I'd never again watch *Singin' in the Rain*. All this and I still didn't know for sure whether it was the blackmailer or just a friendly (undaunted-by-the-rain) person visiting a neighbor.

I didn't see him leave the house or cross my driveway. I heard nothing but the rain. I picked him up visually as he approached the Explorer. Like me, he was dressed in dark colors (the hue of choice for sneaks). Unlike me he was wearing a ski mask and gloves. *Talk about another tired old cliché*. No physical characteristics or distinguishing marks at all were on view. While not unexpected, it was still a bummer. He opened the Explorer door and swung himself into the vehicle. No interior light. Another bummer. A moment later the brake lights flashed and the car pulled forward. I watched it leave. Getting wetter or muddier was, by now, a moot point.

I didn't try to follow. This guy was good and would have picked me up in a heartbeat. It didn't matter. I had what I wanted. More of a description: medium height, stocky, male. The walk, the carriage, the set of the shoulders, the way he swung himself into the car – all had told me that it was a man.

And that was just the beginning. Did I mention that I'd asked the electronic whiz kid to stop by the house before he checked the office phone line? Not just to check the phone line there but to set up the well-hidden cameras.

Hot shower, popcorn and videos. Good program, huh? I caught myself singing in the rain. Jeez. I headed for my house; picking up the car could wait until tomorrow. And I was excited, though knowing your home has been broken into is never a good feeling. Even if you set it up.

I moved carefully through the house, checked it out, checked it thoroughly. I wasn't the only one who could set up a setup.

CHAPTER 39

Silent Night

The whiz kid was good. Not that it was Oscar material; the tapes had the same level of character interest and plot action as the tapes at a 7-Eleven or an ATM machine. But they had a bad guy. I got little more in the way of a physical description, although the clothes seemed similar to those the mall shooter had worn – dark, nondescript sweatsuit. The intruder wasn't stocky/chunky but stocky/well-built and he moved with grace and ease.

He evidenced no interest in the usual – electronics, jewelry (not that I have any worth stealing, but the point is that he didn't even look), or other easily ripped off and fenced items. He headed for my office and went through it, briefcase, desk, files, computer. He was methodical, thorough, and careful. And apparently found nothing that interested him.

This was not surprising. There was nothing there, or in my office, that was relevant to this case. He went through the whole house. The whiz kid hadn't set up cameras everywhere; I could tell by the way things were moved or sightly out of alignment. He was very good. If I hadn't set it up, I wouldn't have noticed.

Of course, this guy had had a lot of practice.

The whiz kid's phone message told me that I had hot water and plenty of it, which meant that both home and office phones were bugged. I'd told him to leave the bugs in place.

I'd had a lot of practice too.

* * *

I wanted to catch Henley so I was up early the next day.

'Hey Bill, I need to cash in on that favor you owe me.'

He snorted. 'I owe you? Shit, Colorado, you owe me.'

'Yeah? Okay, whatever. I just happen to have—'

'I hate sentences that start out like that,' he said glumly.

'Really?' Ever agreeable, that's me. 'Okay, how about: Run this plate for me, would you?' I rattled off the California license plate number.

He sighed. 'And I really hate it when you ask me to do shit like this. You know that's illegal.'

I made a sympathetic sound, the kind that acknowledges what's been said without withdrawing the request. I was pretty sure I could hear his computer clicking in the background. I started whistling under my breath, only stopping when I realized the song was 'Singin' in the Rain.'

'Amazing how many vehicles are leased, not owned, these days.' Bill spoke conversationally. 'Capitol Leasing is a popular company, I understand.'

I blew him a kiss through the phone line. 'You're a peach, Bill.'

'Yeah. And you owe me *big*-time now.'

Capitol Leasing got all excited the minute I walked in the door. Enthusiasm was their middle name. Unfortunately it wore off pretty fast when I identified myself as a private investigator and not a potential sucker. I was passed on down the line and finally dumped into the manager's lap.

Dave Garrison was a little oily and smarmy but not too bad, especially considering it was the car business. I flipped out my investigator's license and he took a two-second look-see. *Whoa*. Hope he didn't write up contracts like that.

'How may I help you, uh . . .' His sentence trailed off unpleasantly, like snail slime. He hadn't looked at my license long enough to remember my name.

'I'm representing a client who was involved in an accident. One of the vehicles in question was described as a dark-colored, recent-model Ford Explorer. Your company was listed on the registration. We need the name and address of the lessee.' I rattled off the plate number.

It zipped right past him. 'The license number again?' he asked, his eyes uninterested.

I gave it to him. He wrote it down, studied it for a minute, then pushed his chair back and walked out of the office. Through the fishbowl windows I watched as he spoke with a young woman working at a computer, who listened attentively, clicked away briskly at her keyboard, then jotted something down and handed bored, slightly smarmy Dave the note.

He returned to the office and handed it to me, standing next to me and now looking bored to tears, I guess so that I couldn't possibly assume this conversation was going to continue.

No problem. I had what I wanted. I was history.

'Is there legal action? An accident should have been reported to us.' The querulous voice in the too late query followed my quickstep exit.

'Very preliminary,' I said in my fake official and definitely vague voice. 'You'll be notified if and when further action is taken.' It was an exit line. I was gone.

The name printed neatly on the paper smarmy Dave had given me was another exit line.

But not mine.

It was odd, I thought, as I popped the sliding glass patio door and entered the house, that someone who regularly broke into other people's homes could be so careless about the security in his own home.

Not that I was complaining.

I had skipped the ski mask but otherwise I looked like your standard intruder: Dark sneakers and socks. Ditto jeans, sweater, the knitted cap I'd stuffed my hair into and the small backpack that held the tools of my trade. Oh, and surgical gloves.

The house was small, beautiful and spartan. Leather couches, Oriental rugs, keynote Asian art (à la Gump's, not Cost Plus), a bonsai tree with that hundreds-of-years-old and thousands-of-dollars'-worth look. I caught all this on a cursory glance – no time for an extended art appreciation tour. His obliging secretary had told me he was out of town on business for two days. His phone machine message reiterated that. Not that I assumed that an extortionist told the truth. Or a secretary either for that matter.

I moved quickly through the living/dining area, master bedroom, and spare room. Getting caught in the act had no appeal. Neither did a court date. The home office, while still stark and spartan, was the most cluttered room in the house.

Easily my best bet.

I had my hopes up for hard copy, not computer copy. Blackmail material comes in a variety of shapes and sizes, including documents, photos, letters, clippings, all that kind of thing. Not that hope isn't an iffy proposition; it is.

First stop was the filing cabinet; it took me a while to get it open. Everything seemed to take a week longer than usual. Of course that's the way of things when you're working with a flashlight in unfamiliar territory. And when you're working scared and nervous.

I was halfway through the filing cabinet when the silken touch caressed my neck.

No words, no sound of any kind.

No gun.

I had no gun, I mean – not the blackmailer, who was probably armed to the teeth. The thing is, burglary is a felony and carrying a weapon in the commission of a felony is big-time trouble squared. Not, I have to admit, that it seemed important at that moment. More like one of those good-idea-at-the-time things.

Soft, silken caress.

My flashlight was purse-size, almost useless as a weapon. I slowly straightened up.

Yellow, feral feline eyes gazed at me from the top of the cabinet, a silken paw reached out and batted my cheek. Jeez. If I were a cat I would have lost a life or two in the last four seconds. I willed my heart to stop thudding, my pulse to toddle instead of race. And I swore at the cat under my breath. Not that it was her fault, but it did make me feel better.

When my hand stopped shaking I patted the cat and refocused the flashlight on the files. The kitty, who still had me nervous, stood, stretched and sat down, head erect, paws primly and exactly planted in front of her. She looked like an Egyptian cat. Ancient Egypt, now there was a country that really went over the top on death. I shivered, desperate to be gone.

None of the files I was flipping through looked relevant or even interesting until I came to 'High-End Donors.' I pulled it. *Bingo. Bull's-eye. Advance to GO*. The shiver again. Maybe the sense that I could use a *Get Out of Jail Free* card too. The file was a full one, the first of a series. I slipped off the backpack and pulled out my portable fax. Speaking of high-end.

Getting it all would have taken a good part of the evening but I got enough, a lot of meat 'n' potatoes and send-'em-to-the-slammer kind of stuff. My current career as a burglar had lasted over forty-five minutes now.

My nerves were shot.

No real aptitude for the job, I guess.

I packed up my stuff and put everything back exactly as I found it. I wanted the element of surprise. And suspense. Then I patted kitty, who was still regal and Egyptian-like, one last time, relocked the patio door, and exited by the back door where there was no dead bolt to contend with.

Remember the PIs in B movies, the ones with a bottle of bourbon in their bottom desk drawer? I was still shaking by the time I got back to my office. There is a reason for that bourbon. Unfortunately I didn't have any.

My phone line wasn't secure; neither was my office. I made copies of everything, placed one set in an envelope with an overkill amount of stamps on it and mailed it to myself at the PP box I use as a drop. The other I took home to study. I was a little stunned at the wealth of information there, not just on my clients and the other victims I'd dug up but on a number of additional victims. Or soon-to-be victims. And on the blackmailer.

A lot of skeletons.

A lot of rotting, decaying flesh.

CHAPTER 40

It Came upon
a Midnight Clear

Dark alleys and offices in the deserted after-hours of the night were out. Really out. I hate it when they do this in books and movies. I mean – except in fiction – let's hope that no one is *really* that dumb.

So we were at Piatti, a lovely restaurant – though answering the phone in Italian is a little over the top, especially for Sacramento – in the Pavilions, which is a shopping area as upscale as we get around here. Winding roads, brick and stone work, gorgeous landscaping, outdoor sculpture, you know the kind of place. The Pavilions is also the place to eat and drink. You could munch away at David Berkley, the Terrace, Mace's, and Piatti for days and never get bored. Broke, maybe.

I parked and drifted past store windows filled with thousand-dollar suits, a boutique with nothing but socks, and a Sharper Image store with a gumball machine only slightly smaller than the Sears Tower and a robot the size of a small gorilla. *Drop by here for those hard-to-please holdouts on your Christmas list.*

A gazillion little lights were sprinkled in the bare winter branches of the trees. The rain had stopped and the night was clear and sparkly with stars, the air fresh and clean. The stone statues of a woman and children seated on a concrete bench not far from Piatti were festooned with Christmas decor, elfin hats and scarves, bells and

315

mittens. A trio of carolers right out of Dickens laughed and smiled and called out cheery greetings in between their songs. They passed me singing 'It Came upon a Midnight Clear' and a young man in top hat and tails and round apple-red cheeks blew a kiss at me. It was the kind of night that made me happy – that Christmas was coming, that I was alive.

That I got to drop the dime on a blackmailer.

I hadn't had Christmas cheer in mind when I chose the restaurant. What had attracted me was the hustle and bustle in the restaurants and shops and in the walkways and roads. *Safety in numbers. Stay in a crowd. Don't be in a hurry to get clobbered.* Great concepts. I regarded this area not just as neutral territory but as safe territory.

At almost six on a weekday Piatti was crowded with the after-work mix of drinkers and diners. I was early for my appointment. I found a seat at the bar, ordered a bottle of mineral water and cased the joint. (Okay, I was in something of a *Maltese Falcon/Thin Man* detective-movie mood.) What I saw was a lot of well-dressed people with time on their hands, money in their pockets, and Christmastime wishes that had nothing to do with being good. *Hey Santa, take note.* I sipped my water, then smiled as he approached – smiled in the nonchalant way they do in the movies.

'Good evening, Kat.' He smiled back at me, slid onto the vacant stool on my left. 'Isn't it a shame to spoil a lovely holiday evening like this with threats?'

'Merry Christmas,' I said, in a lovely holiday way.

I spoke softly and he leaned in to hear me – tenderly, gently, as though we were lovers. I noticed the small scar that nipped his cheek like a dimple, the smooth dark line of his eyebrows, the quirky little laugh lines at the corners of his mouth. It's not just in the movies that the bad guys are suave, debonair, and charming. And I was charmed – in spite of myself. It's not just in the movies that the bad guys are dangerous. I reminded myself of this.

'Hello Gunther. I brought you a Christmas present.'

He laughed and ordered a bourbon and water. 'A real drink, Kat?' he asked me.

So I ordered a chardonnay.

'And will I like it?' he asked.

'One can only hope,' I replied modestly. 'You will, I think, be intrigued.'

'Ah, not the same thing at all.'

The bartender set our drinks in front of us. He raised his glass, clicked it against mine.

'To intrigue.'

'Do you think like Santa all year round?' I asked in what I hoped was an intriguing fashion.

He raised an eyebrow in query, let his eyes look puzzled.

'You knew who had been good or bad, who had better watch out?'

He sipped at his drink. Not nonchalant, not exactly, but not worried either. My present hadn't gotten really good yet though.

'You are speaking in riddles.'

'The bad list was a long one: Jim Randolph, Madeline Hunter, Delia Melton, Sid Johannsen, Hiram Grant. There were more, I know, but these are sufficient to illustrate my point.'

He offered me a glass filled with bread sticks, which I declined. He sipped on his drink. He did not enthusiastically join in our conversation. 'Go on,' he said finally.

'You knew about Madeline's early marriage and the divorce later when she could afford it. You surmised, from a long article in the paper as well as personal mementos, about the death of a child.'

'Murder is not the same as death.' He spoke not to be argumentative but to set me straight.

And it is not, of course, not even close, but for then I let it go. I was pursuing another line of thought.

'It was remarkable to me how here, as in other cases, people let themselves be blackmailed on such old and, in many cases, tenuous evidence.'

'Guilt and fear are very powerful.' He signaled for another drink. I had barely touched my wine.

'Sid Johannsen had a record. There were sexual molestation convictions against him in several states. He had served some time, lost his counseling license and so on. All this was a matter of public record. Hiram Grant? That must have been more of a challenge. The only extant records or paper trail were in his possession. Fortunately it was the kind of challenge yóu relished. Illegal entry. Search. And you are good at it. Few of the victims suspected that you went through their houses; certainly none could prove it. I would not have known that you entered and searched my house had I not set it up. That and the evidence from the surveillance cameras.'

The eyebrow shot up again. And he laughed. It sounded joyous and happy, not forced in the least.

'I don't know if you had a hand in making the video that drove Jim Randolph to suicide. Perhaps. Or perhaps you just happened upon it. Either way it was devastating for Randolph, perfect for you. Delia? She is hard to figure. No paper trail. No record. And she was silent, discreet, and circumspect. I assume someone else was not. Unless you were once with her?'

'No.' He looked amused. 'Except in a business sense, hookers do not interest me. One evening I was sitting at a bar, very much like this one, with a man heavily involved in politics and women both. We were watching the evening news and drinking. The news covered a political fund-raiser for Robert Melton, his wife smiling by his side. She, according to my companion, was a former call girl. I was fortunate that he had photos.' Gunther sipped at his drink and finished a bread stick.

'And Randolph? Was the tape your work?'

'Ah. Beautifully done, was it not? I wish I could take credit for it but I merely took advantage of the situation. Someone who has done occasional work for me tipped me off.'

'A low-level puke named Tommy Turner.'

He stared at me in silence. 'You are better than I thought. And you surprise me. Come, finish your drink and let me buy you another.'

My wine was almost untouched. Business is business, partying is partying. And drinking with bad guys is not a good idea.

'How did you pick your victims, Gunther? How could you know their secrets?'

'Everyone has something to lose, although not everyone is foolish enough to keep a record of it. I picked people I wanted to bring down and then made it my business to find something on them. I relished the challenge, the building of a case if you will.' He smiled. 'I had my failures as well but I always enjoyed the search and I rarely gave up.'

'How much of it was natural talent, how much training? Special forces training, those tours in the Rangers. I noted the medals and commendations in your military record. They taught you how to watch and wait, to stalk, to—'

'To kill. Don't forget that.' His voice was gentle in admonition. 'Natural talent? Training? I had both.'

I thought how much nicer it would be to be outside listening to the carolers sing 'It Came upon a Midnight Clear' and 'Joy to the World,' to be singing along with them under my breath. Instead I was drinking with an extortionist.

'Extortion? Is that a talent?'

'A predilection.' He smiled.

'The money not for you, but for a charity to benefit children. Curious.'

He shrugged and started another bread stick. Now he was nonchalant.

'Was it something twisted in you?'

'What?' Blasé as well as nonchalant.

'A common thread that linked your victims was sexual: the death of a baby born of forced marriage, and rape, the seduction of a man by a woman possibly his daughter, a call girl, the sexual abuse of women by their minister, abortion.'

A woman tapped Sam Gunther on the shoulder. 'Don't I know you from somewhere?' She spoke in a flirtatious come-on voice. Her hand rested on his shoulder a moment too long, then slid down his arm.

The disdain, revulsion and contempt were naked in his face.

'I—I guess not,' she stammered and walked on quickly without a backward glance.

'Exhibit E and I rest my case on the sexual and twisted,' I murmured dryly. 'Childhood, I suppose?' It's a cliché but prevalence is what creates cliché.

'Childhood.' He laughed. The nonchalance, the ease, was gone. 'Did you have a happy childhood, Kat?'

'Not particularly.'

'But not bad?'

'How bad does it have to get before it qualifies as bad?'

'Witnessing the deliberate destruction of a soul.'

I was silenced.

319

'My father was a cruel man. It wasn't until I was almost an adult that I recognized how extraordinarily cruel and vicious he was. Then I remember viewing in amazement other families where there was love and encouragement, not blows and ugliness. I was not the primary target of this viciousness, my younger brother was. And to a lesser extent, my mother. He beat my brother almost to death; emotionally, spiritually, psychologically – the attack was ruthless and relentless.'

'Your brother, not you?'

'Yes. My brother was deformed, I was not. Or that was how my father characterized it. My brother was a kind, loving, and intelligent child who was born physically imperfect; there was nothing deformed about him. My father, who called himself a religious man, said these imperfections were a mark of the devil and that it was incumbent upon him to beat them out of my brother.'

Such a long list of evils, I thought sadly, that are committed in the name of God or love.

'My mother did not interfere. The few times she tried my father beat her as well. I have nothing but contempt for women who do not protect their children.'

Madeline.

'I tried to protect my brother as best I could but it is impossible for one child to protect another from an adult. Or for a child to protect an adult. What my father did to my mother was contemptible as well.'

Johannsen.

'Still, it was nothing to what he did to my brother. Bringing a child into this world is a sacred trust, one not to be broken at any cost.'

Hiram Grant and his patients.

'To violate a child, your flesh and blood, is a heinous crime.'

Jim Randolph.

'My mother sold herself to my father for money, for the financial security he provided. She sold – prostituted – us as well.'

Delia Melton.

'At sixteen I was big enough to stand up to my father. I beat the crap out of him, told him that if he ever again laid a hand on my brother or mother he would answer to me.' Gunther shrugged. 'The simple solution of a child. It didn't work, of course. He ran me off with a shotgun, told me he would kill me if I ever came back.' He paused for a long time, staring at his hands.

'And?'

'I lied about my age and joined the Army. A sympathetic chaplain there was my confidant and with his assistance I turned my father in and got help for my brother. He was placed in a foster home.'

Gunther stared at the ice melting in his glass. 'I have not spoken of this before. It amuses me' he looked at me but he did not look amused – 'to tell you this. All of it. I do so knowing how safe I am. None of the people I have worked with—'

Worked with? 'I take it that worked with is a euphemism for extorted?'

He smiled. 'None of them will involve themselves in a legal case, not even to bring me down. Guilt and fear, remember?'

'Your brother? What happened to him?'

Something in his eyes shifted. 'I do not know the details of what happened, either in foster care or in the institution in which he was placed. Only later was I to find that he was abused in both places. When I was in a position to help him he was gone. He had retreated to a world within his mind. I have never been able to reach him.'

'What you couldn't do for your brother you try to do for other children through Hope For Kids?'

'Yes.'

I thought of his beautiful and starkly spartan house. And I gazed at the huge garlic bulbs, the tomatoes and eggplants and verdant leafy branches that were painted on the walls at Piatti. Bread sticks and wine in front of me. The staff of life, if shelter, food and drink were enough. But they are not.

I looked at the scar on his cheek and the deep dark eyes and spoke words into the warm food-fragrant air and Christmas cheer that surrounded us.

'It has to stop, you know. All of it. I imagine you have lived with these lies, or others, for a long time.' I took a deep breath.

'In truth your mother was a prostitute. She was the support of the family when your father, a heavy drinker, was out of work. There were many nights when you and your brother were left alone with your father, many nights when he sexually assaulted you. When he was sober he was religious and he beat you; when he was drunk he

321

sodomized you. You could not protect yourself; you could not protect your brother. And it marked you, as you now mark others.'

Gunther signaled for another drink, picked up a bread stick and broke it in half. When he looked at me he was calm, unruffled. And his look was amused. 'I was wrong then, about your being good. That is fancy, not fact.' He sipped at the drink in front of him.

I gazed at his handsome profile. 'It's interesting that I learned about you in the same way you learned about others. I broke into your house, as you broke into mine, as you broke into the homes of many who were your victims. I saw your beautiful spartan home with the Asian art, the bonsai tree, the cat with the gentle paws. I saw the military medals. And I saw the files.'

I turned away.

I heard the bread stick snap although I didn't look at him. Not until I spoke again. 'I saw the evaluations the social worker wrote, the letters your mother wrote to you, the letters your brother wrote before he died. He did not go into a catatonic state. He was a male prostitute who died of a drug overdose. I looked up the police reports and the coroner's report. And your father's trial for child abuse.'

The bread stick snapped again.

'I saw all of this and I am beginning to see how it made you into the man you are. You have no close relationships. You have never been married or fathered children. Your life is devoted to assisting vulnerable children.

'And to vengeance. Like your father, you decided to play God. To pass judgment on others and execute punishment.'

'Not on good people. On bad mothers, on whores, on the strong who abuse the weak, vulnerable and defenseless, on those the law doesn't catch up with.'

'You play God.'

He shrugged. 'The defenseless, the weak, and the innocent have too few defenders. Those earrings, they are quite nice.' His hand reached out as if to touch my earlobe.

Earrings?

Too late I tried to pull away.

His fingers pressed into my neck, into the carotid artery.

Special forces training.

322

Too late I tried to call out.

They taught me how to kill.

The pressure was unrelenting. Faint and far away now – like a foghorn on a sunny day – I heard him call out: 'Please help me, my girlfriend has fainted.' And I felt – or did I learn it later? – him gently put one arm around my shoulders and the other under my knees and pick me up and carry me out. 'Out of my way, please. I've got to get her to the hospital. Get the door. Hurry. Please hurry!' And he held me ever so gently.

The gentleness was gone now.

He was laughing and pleased with himself. I was struggling to climb back into consciousness. We were moving. In a car? I felt his fingers dig into my neck again. I couldn't get away from them.

And then I lost it. Again.

CHAPTER 41

And a Partridge
in a Pear Tree

I had been tossed into a chair. Like a rag doll, I thought. And, like a doll, I stayed where I was placed. Without moving, except to wriggle my ankle a little. Just checking. And I peeked through slitted eyes and lashes.

It scared the shit out of me.

I sat upright, bolted out of my chair.

'Good.' He smiled benignly. 'Having you in action, fighting back, makes it much more fun.'

Fun? I skidded to a stop. Not just the words, the gun. And the fact that it was pointed at me. Gunther wasn't the kind of guy who would miss.

'Hark, the Herald Angels Sing' floated through my mind. Gunther smiled at me. Why couldn't angels play in *his* mind? *He* was the one who needed them.

'We're in Jackie's office.' I spoke conversationally, not confrontationally. I prefer conversation to a shoot-out any day.

'We are,' he agreed. 'She was next on my list. This way I kill two birds with one stone. I shoot you in her office with her gun. She stands trial for your murder. And goes down. You caught her skimming, which gives her a very strong incentive for getting rid of you. She'll go down for skimming too, of course. Our little Jackie is looking at a lot of time in fact.' There was satisfaction in his voice.

'And you get to play God.'

He tried to look amused but I was getting to him.

'Jackie not only interfered with your program, your plans for the children, she—'

'Interfered?' His voice was cold. 'She stole from them. She embezzled money that could have, would have changed the lives of innocent children.'

'And she was promiscuous. You wanted to nail her for that too, didn't you?'

He stared at me. There was surprise in his eyes, I thought. And the gun was no longer pointed directly at me, it was pointing at the ground. Headway, however dubious.

'You knew about Adam Howard, surely? The philandering philanthropist? He wasn't just a financial supporter and spokesman for Hope For Kids, he was balling Jackie every chance he got.'

I was pleased to note that Gunther was looking unpleasantly flushed. So I went for it, adding insult to injury.

'Of course you know about the kinky sex?' I sat down in the chair I had so recently vacated and crossed my legs, putting my ankle on my knee.

Gunther's flush deepened to an apoplectic crimson. He looked, as we said when we were kids, like he was about to bust a gut.

'The lower left-hand drawer in Jackie's desk has a false bottom to it. That's where the kinky sex stuff is. Wear rubber gloves,' I added on an inflammatory, not a cautionary note.

It was too much. I knew it would be. He looked down, reached for the drawer. I reached for my gun.

Ankle holster.

'Well, well, this is a little more exciting than I anticipated.'

Jackie drawled the words out in a deliberately blasé fashion, the gun in her hand the only contradiction to the blasé. Gunther slowly straightened up. I sat tight, not about to take unnecessary chances. Jeez. What *was* wrong with this country that we didn't have strict gun-control laws?

'He's got a gun, Jackie. Shoot the fucker! I'm with you, I'm cheering you on.' I tried to sound peppy and cheerleader-like.

'All in due time, Kat.' She laughed. 'The setup's a little different now, you see. Like Sam, I can appreciate the idea of killing two birds with one stone. And I never really did care for you, Kat – so prying and nosy. A shoot-out between you and Sam would be nice, wouldn't it? You're about to nail Sam as the blackmailer and he nails you instead. A shoot-out with no survivors. Tsk, tsk. I believe you said that once to me, Kat? Tsk, tsk.' She shot the snotty, snippy little words at me, no doubt as I had to her.

I ground my teeth.

'I never liked you either, Sam. Oh sure, you were a great fund-raiser. But such a stuffed shirt. No, worse.' She wrinkled her nose. 'A prude, a moralist and a self-righteous asshole. Always that holier-than-thou crap. What a jerk-off.' With one hand Jackie held the gun on us, with the other she made an obscene gesture to accompany the word 'jerk-off.'

Gunther had gone cold and hard. Jackie was much better at adding-insult-to-injury stuff than I was. No kidding. Gunther's gun hand was still at his side, not in view. Jackie was still not scared.

'I knew I was next on your hit list, Sam. And I know how much you like playing God. That's the perfect expression for it. Thanks, Kat.'

I didn't bother with a polite *You're welcome.* Manners slide when someone has a gun on you.

'You would have nailed me, Sam, for the skimming or the sex. Sex with a married man is a no-no in your book, isn't it. *Hah.* You have no idea how delicious, how exciting it is – the element of danger, of risk. It's *yummy.* I'm surprised you never tried it. Oh, but you get off, you cream in your jeans when you sneak around and spy on people. That's *your* kinky little twist.'

Gunther's face was cold, the face of a killer. It was the kind of thing that would have worried me but it didn't seem to slow Jackie down. Slow her down? It didn't even make her pause.

'We did it on your desk, you know. Not just once but lots of times. Naked and sprawling and coming and creaming on your desk. We played around with your pen and paperweight—' She licked her lips. 'I fucked with you, Sam, and I loved it, you uptight asshole playing God, I loved it.'

Gunther wasn't the only one playing God now, Jackie was too. Sam looked like a bad-guy cardboard cutout. And like he could blow anytime. Playing God goes to your head: It's a dangerous game and Jackie had forgotten that. And that Gunther was a trained killer.

They had both forgotten me. My .22 was out of the ankle holster now, out of sight between my legs. We were all armed, although I was the only one who knew about my gun. *Jeez, I hate this stuff.*

Having a gun in your hand, maybe that's playing God too.

'This is *so* sweet.' Jackie spoke. 'I see what you mean, Sam. I know what people mean now when they say revenge is sweet. It's yummy, it really is. But you've always known that, haven't you Sam?'

'You're a fool, Jackie.' He was forcing himself to stay in control, doing pretty well now too, doing much better.

'Finesse. Did you notice his finesse, Kat? Tell her about it, Sam.' She waved her gun. Foolishly, I thought, but I said nothing. I stayed in the background unwilling to draw anyone's attention. Or gunfire.

Sam said nothing either. He was doing his imitation of an Easter Island statue playing a comatose butler. Very convincing. Except he had moved. Very slowly. He was almost out from behind the desk now. Jackie didn't seem to notice – too busy playing God maybe.

'You know what Sam once said to me, Kat? He said that most people are "architects of their own destruction." That's poetic, isn't it? I guess it means that character is destiny, not biology. But Sam took it one step further. It was like a Greek tragedy or something where the characters sealed their own fate.' Jackie took her eyes off Gunther but only for a moment. It was the kind of thing that could seal her fate.

I waited for Gunther to make the move I knew was coming. My move was second. If I made the first move I was a dead duck. They could take out the first one, I would take out the second.

That was Plan A.

'You said, Kat, that Gunther liked to be the executioner but it wasn't quite like that. It was better than that, wasn't it, Sam?'

'Much better.'

He smiled. *I was starting to really dislike that smile.* He was also closer, his gun still not in view. Jackie hadn't noticed. Apparently having a gun and playing God lulls one into a false sense of security.

'I started things but it was they who made their lives a living hell. I couldn't do that. No one can. They used their minds and imagination. All their creative energy went into fear and guilt and what would happen if the world found out. It's the kind of thing that makes men crazy.' Gunther was still smiling.

'Or drives them to suicide.' I spoke softly.

'Yes. That was nice.' He answered without looking at me. He was closer to Jackie.

Nice? Is this how the banality of evil begins?

'No one could torture or twist Randolph the way he did. He made his life unbearable and then he threw it away. I counted suicides amongst my biggest successes. There were others.' He was talking to both of us but looking at Jackie.

I was ready.

'Don't come any closer, Sam.' She spoke pleasantly but firmly.

'Let's rush her, Gunther,' I urged, changing sides without a qualm. 'She can't get us both.'

She would go after him, we both knew that – she knew he had a gun and she didn't know about mine. I thought he would shoot, not rush, and that the odds were that he was a better shot than she.

Much better.

'What are you doing here, Jackie?' Gunther was biding his time, waiting for his moment. I saw him shift his weight, rebalance.

'I've been spying on you, Sam, just the way you spy on other people. And you're right, it's fun. It's fun sneaking around in people's lives and secrets and wondering how you can use that information. It's fun reading people's memos, appointment calendars, and correspondence, listening to their phone conversations. It's fun going through cars and briefcases and anything else you happen on.' She looked thoughtful. 'Not as much fun as kinky sex, but fun. Definitely.

'So I knew you were going to meet Kat and I was almost positive that you were going to bring her back here. You went out of your way to find out what my plans for the evening were. It was clear you didn't want me here. And so I told you I had a hot date.' She winked. 'An all-night date. But I lied.' A complacent smile played around her lips and settled in for a catnap. 'That's another thing that's fun, lying.

Of course I've known that for a long time, I didn't need you to teach me *that*.

'Second-guessing you was fun too. You think you're smarter than you are, you know. Like last week you 'worked late,' but really you went through my desk and checked out my gun, checked to see that it had been cleaned and oiled and loaded and was ready to go. But you didn't put it back just the way I do, so I knew. I put it all together, how Kat had figured you out and you were going to get rid of her and set me up.

'It was a good plan, Sam, except for one thing; it's not going to work.'

'It'll work.' He spoke pleasantly. 'Only instead of standing trial, you'll be dead. You and Kat. Murder/suicide.' He shook his head in a lousy and unconvincing imitation of sorrow.

Plot. Counterplot. It would have been entertaining except for the fact that no matter who plotted, I was the one who was dead. Have I mentioned how much I like happy endings? The kind where you live happily ever after, not the kind where you hark to herald angels singing.

'You know what always happens in *Murder, She Wrote*?' I asked.

They both focused on me, not in interest but as though I had completely lost my mind.

'Okay, I know it's a dumb show – well, except for Angela Lansbury. I like her, don't you?' I asked briskly as they gave me the have-you-lost-your-mind? look again. 'Well never mind. The point is that in show after show, just as Jessica is about to get it, the cops show up. Like now.' I pointed toward the office door with the hand that didn't have the gun in it.

They both looked.

I shot Gunther. So did Jackie. She thought he was shooting at her, so she emptied her gun into him. While Jackie was shooting I jumped her. I didn't care if she turned Gunther into Swiss cheese but I didn't want to be a target.

Gunther grabbed for my ankle when I went for his gun.

I kicked him. Hard.

'Goddamn fucking bitch.' But he was bleeding badly. Red blood and a blue Christmas.

'I'll get you. You think it's over but it's not. I'm smarter than you

330

are, smarter and better and—' Jackie was whining.

I had her gun too and she wasn't a good sport about it. Ask me if I cared. She deserved a red and blue Christmas as merry as Gunther's.

I trained my gun on both of them.

Then I called the cops. They weren't really there, I lied. That kind of thing never happens in real life, only on shows like *Murder, She Wrote*.

Jeez.

Talk about *gullible*.

CHAPTER 42

The Hopes and Fears
of All the Years . . .

Around here a lot of people go to Reno or Tahoe to drop their change.
Not me. I like to drop it at home.

Dimes are my favorite.

Sam Gunther was my first stop. Okay, technically I wasn't dropping
a dime; I'd already dropped it. Clean up, that's closer. It took an okay
from Henley to get me in. Sam was in the hospital; he was also in
police custody and he was, considering all the bullets Jackie had blasted
around her office, in pretty good shape – shoulder wound, thigh and
arm wounds. No rearrangement of internal organs, nothing permanent
or fatal.

Jackie was disappointed. So, I know, were a lot – no, probably all
– of his extortion victims. Gunther was not a man with a big fan club.
I was relieved; there was enough on my conscience already. My shot,
the one that took him down, was the one in the shoulder. A few more
inches would have done it.

He looked good too, I thought, alert and perky staring out the
window with a preoccupied, maybe sad, expression.

'Hey, Gunther.'

'Kat.' He turned to me and smiled. *Smiled.* I ruled out Christian
forgiveness. Maybe special forces training. Camouflage or something.
Or painkilling drugs.

'Good run but it's over.' No chitchat. I got right to the point.

'Nothing lasts.' He smiled again, a little ruefully this time. 'I did a lot of what I set out to do.'

'What?' I asked. 'What were you trying to do?'

'Even up the odds.' His voice was soft – not gentle soft, evil soft. 'Too many have in abundance what they don't deserve to have; too many have nothing at all.'

'Let me guess: *Robin Hood* was your favorite book as a child.' *And playing God your favorite game.*

He grinned. 'No, he didn't cut the line fine enough. I didn't steal from the rich, just the rich and morally depraved. And I didn't give to the poor, but to the innocent, the kids who didn't have a chance, who had no help.'

'Like the child you were.'

'Yes.'

'And now?'

He shrugged. 'I have no now. You must have talked to the cops.'

'Yes. Assault with intent to kill, kidnapping, extortion. I understand a number of your victims agreed to testify.'

He nodded. 'And burglary, wiretapping, being armed in the commission of a felony. Hell, Kat, I forgot to brush my teeth and straighten my tie that morning and they threw the book at me for it.' He tried to grin again but it was pretty forced.

'Poster boy of the criminal justice system.'

'Poster criminal.'

'I don't feel sorry for you, Gunther.'

'No. I don't feel sorry for myself. One of the many things I learned in Nam. And it was, as you said, a good run.' He leaned toward me, winced – shoulder wound, I guess – and fell back. 'I'd like to give you a gift, and ask a favor of you. No, hear me out.' He raised a hand as though he thought I would interrupt, would say I couldn't accept a gift or do a favor for someone like him.

But I wouldn't say that. Life is full of gifts and favors and some of them involve people like him.

'I have many beautiful things, as you know.' That wry look again. 'But only two that I care about.'

I thought of the valuable rugs, antiques, and artwork.

'Both of them are living. That is what matters after all, life.'

I thought about it and was puzzled. 'The cat and—?'

'The bonsai tree. It is very old, very valuable. Please accept it with my compliments.'

I was silent. Something was hanging on this but I didn't know what. 'Thank you, but I can't accept. I *really* hate bonsai trees. To me they're not beautiful but stunted, misshapen, and twisted.' *Like the soul of this man.*

'The cat? Maybe you would take her? She is a sweet and loving animal.'

I remembered the silken paw on my cheek. 'Maybe.'

It was the last time I spoke to Sam Gunther.

A day later he pulled off the chest lead hooked up to the cardiac monitor, making it appear that he were dead or dying. The hospital responded by sending in a crash cart loaded with drugs and emergency supplies. In the confusion, no one noticed that he lifted a knife from the cart. He waited then, until they took him off the monitor.

In the early-morning light they found him in a pool of blood, his throat sticky and slit. His face was contorted, determined, a nurse told me, as though his body had fought to live in spite of what his mind had decided.

He died as he had lived, playing God.

Jackie's joy at the news of Gunther's death knew no bounds. I heard this, I didn't witness it; she was having nothing to do with me. Or with her previous attitude. She'd dropped the hard-line, hardball, go-after-'em-gal routine. Gone was the woman who used and manipulated people, who enjoyed emotional blackmail and playing tough guy, who reveled in seeing others bend to her will, beaten and crawling and craven. I knew that side, of course, and would testify to it but she figured that with Gunther dead it was my word against hers – her sweet-tongued, pillar-of-the-community word.

She figured wrong on several counts.

Gunther made a complete (damning is too mild a term here) confession. So it was her word against his, the cops', and mine, and the cooked books at Hope For Kids. Not to mention the clothes, jewelry, and Tahoe vacation home she couldn't afford on her salary or explain. *Ooops*. Her strategy? Self-defense in the shooting of Gunther, lousy-bookkeeping skills (you know what they say about girls and math) in the skimming, and a mysterious but generous relative she couldn't produce.

It was naive and desperate. Nobody fell for it. Not to mention that the DA and the IRS had heard way better in their time. I hoped jail orange was a good color on her. But I doubted it, it makes everyone look like shit.

So that was the clean up. Back to dimes. Sidney Johannsen, Tommy Turner, May and company, Moon – forty cents right there.

Apparently Sid had decided to wipe his slate clean and not bother to register as a sex offender, which is against the law. *Tsk, tsk*. I started the ball rolling, the cops picked it up. I also wrote a letter to the board of his church, detailing the past (his record) and the present (my experience and the police investigation). The board was not pleased. In a decision that was eminently sensible, if not Christian, they decided not to turn the other cheek and fired him.

Turner was fun too. I gave Henley what I had on him and his involvement in the making of the extortion tape. That was enough for them to get a warrant. It turned out that Tommy was a very nasty little piece of work. He made, even starred in porno films, Bad Boy Biker movies (heavy on S and M), and his stand-by, blackmail tapes. They nailed his ass.

Henley had, he told me, turned May and her green card scam over to the 'appropriate authorities.' And 'things were progressing accordingly.' That's all I could get out of him. God, I hate it when he goes tight-lipped cop on me.

Moon? She was, like her namesake, in a dark phase. No one had seen her in Sacramento. This pleased me no end, as I was reasonably sure that gangbanger goons had beaten the tar out of her for inadvertently helping to tip me off on the green card scam. I hoped she was in L.A. turning over a new leaf. Of course, what are the odds? And hope, as Hiram Grant once said to me, is a thin thread to hang from.

But it is a thread.

I dropped by Grant's office with his Christmas present. It was only a stack of blurred and hasty photocopies – everything Gunther

336

had had on Grant – but he was pleased (although the police wouldn't have been if they had known). His face stopped looking like a skull with skin stretched over it and I saw tears in his eyes as he gave me a Christmas hug.

I had pulled everything on Charity and Madeline too but there was no way I could keep Jim Randolph out of it. Too many people, the cops included, knew pieces of the story. And he was dead, beyond hurt, the demons silenced at last. I never did learn more about Jim Randolph, his past and his demons, but I hope he is at peace. The cops said they had enough. So the others – those who didn't choose to come forward? It was okay.

Jim Randolph's story never went further than the cops and Rick Carter. Nobody in their right mind wanted Cathi to know. Carter didn't want it out either; it wasn't the kind of publicity that helped a law firm. His gratitude knew no bounds. He paid me double what I asked and refused to listen to my demur.

Delia also chose silence. So did Charity. J.O.? He wouldn't talk to me about it and neither would the cops. He wasn't talking to me about much lately but I heard, on the grapevine, that he was drinking more than ever. I called him a couple of times and he told me to fuck off.

The hopes and fears of all the years
are met in thee tonight.

Not in J.O. It was almost Christmas but the spirit of the season had passed him by.

And maybe me as well.

CHAPTER 43

Merry Christmas!

'No?!'

'It's *true*, I swear. Anyway, how could I make something like this up?' Lindy giggled. 'Not that we have to make up anything about Rafe or Alma. The truth is way more than enough. Are those waffles *ever* going to be ready, Katy? I'm *starving*.'

Since she had arrived unannounced, roused me out of a sound sleep and demanded waffles for breakfast – her favorite as well as Hank's – I thought that ignoring that last comment showed great restraint on my part.

'Have some more juice. Or an apple. So then what happened?'

'Tricia, Cathi, and I picked up Amy and Madeline on our way to the hospital. We wanted to be early, the kids were so excited. Oh Katy, it was really something.' Her voice faltered. 'Some of those little guys had no one who cared, not even at Christmas! They couldn't believe we were having a party and presents and everything just for them. And, jeez, what a party!'

I poured batter into the waffle iron and waited. Expectant didn't quite cover it. Nervous too. It involved Alma and Rafe, after all.

'Rafe was Santa. He wore red long johns with the seat dropped revealing boxers covered with little red-nosed elves.'

'They weren't obscene, were they?' This was not an idle question.

Lindy laughed. 'No. Alma hid those. He had a really fake-looking bushy white beard dripping with bells and ornaments and his padded tummy kept slipping under the red coat. The kids loved him. Almost as much as . . .' She stopped, teasing.

'As?' I egged her on.

'Alma, who had three strings of blinking multicolored Christmas lights wound around her body and plugged into a battery pack at her waist. At first the kids were speechless and then they made wishes on her, as though she were Star Light, Star Bright. Actually, I think they thought, she was the Christmas fairy.'

Alma as a Christmas fairy. What a concept.

'Madeline came dressed as Mrs Claus and she really got into it. Did you know that she can sing? She'd found a lot of silly songs and the kids loved them. Amy was wearing fake reindeer antlers and a blinking red nose and gave all the kids a ride in her wheelchair. Oh, and a really impressive demonstration of wheelies. She was a big hit too. We all were.' She laughed happily again.

'Even Cathi?'

'She's a lot better now, Katy, you won't believe it. Remember when she refused to go to counseling or join a bereavement group?' I nodded. 'That was the first time I took her to the hospital, to the children's ward, I mean. I thought it would help but she didn't want to have anything to do with the kids. Not until she saw the babies. She goes there a lot now to hold the crack babies, the ones nobody wants. She's a different person. She'll be okay now . . . What's that smell? *Tell* me you didn't burn the waffle.' Her voice was ominous.

I snatched the lid of the waffle iron up. 'It's not burned, it's . . . toasty.'

'Burned,' said Lindy in a slightly disgusted voice as she drowned it in butter and syrup and ate it anyway. 'And then there was Elmer.'

'What?'

She swallowed her mouthful of waffle and washed it down with milk. 'Elmer. Have you met him?'

'No. I don't even know who he is.'

'He's the reason Alma bought black lace underwear and a man's satin dressing gown.' She giggled again.

I shook my head in awe. 'You are good. How did you find out?'

'I came home from the library really early one night and caught them necking on the couch.'

Okay, we both giggled.

'Alma pretended she had something in her eye but even Elmer laughed at that one, so she 'fessed up. He's a really nice guy, I like him. He came to the Christmas party dressed as an elf. Have you ever known anyone named Elmer? What an odd name.'

'Elmer Fudd. Does that count?'

She ignored me. 'He used to own a hardware store and does plumbing. Alma says he's a really great kisser.'

We lost it again.

'Oh God! Katy, the waffle!'

Just in time. Lucky for me too.

'Put chocolate chips in the next one, okay?'

So I did. It was almost Christmas after all. And they are good that way. Just butter though, or whipped cream. No maple syrup.

'Katy, have you read the paper yet?'

'No. Why?'

'Look at this.' She held the paper out to me. 'Isn't that your friend?'

J.O. And blackmail. It was a belated finish to the series. I sat down to read, Lindy leaning over my shoulder dripping butter and syrup onto the newspaper.

'Wow,' Lindy said, 'he didn't leave much out, did he?'

That was an understatement. With the exception of the blackmail victims who had chosen not to come forward, it was all there. In gripping Technicolor detail. J.O. and Jossie and the baby too. He had been a newsman first and told the truth, not cutting himself any more slack than those he wrote about. The article was harsh and pitiless, angry and ugly. And very powerful.

I walked over to the phone, dialed, spoke fast when he answered. 'J.O., it's Kat, don't hang up.'

'Why the fuck not?' It sounded like he was stuck in harsh and angry.

'You need me.'

He laughed his ugly dregs-of-humanity laugh. 'The fuck I do.'

'After that last article I'm the only one in town who won't be slobbering sentimentally over you, who will still give you shit.' I waited out his silence.

'You buying?'

'Yes. Driving too. I'll pick you up tonight at seven.'

'All right.'

He hung up before I could answer.

I was home well before ten. J.O. and I had had fun – I'd even gotten in a quick hug and a congratulations – before a gang of people arrived. I guess they were friends; J.O. seemed glad to see them anyway. Drinks started arriving very quickly then, so after the second round and my third mineral water, I said goodnight. No one noticed.

Not until I got home.

Ranger was ecstatic, Kitten phlegmatic but pleased, and the new kitty delicate, dignified, and enigmatic. Gunther said her name was Phoenix, a mouthful of a name for the small, sweet creature she was. She had adjusted well to our household, mostly by deciding that she was queen and we her lowly and humble servants.

I had a long hot shower, washed my hair and then my clothes. The smoke from J.O.'s nonstop cigarettes had been thick and ugly on me. Then I sat in front of the fireplace and dried and fluffed my hair as I watched *Casablanca*. Now that Cathi had a life and had stopped watching it, I had started.

Maybe that was a bad sign.

Many things were clear-cut in wartime Casablanca. The bad guys (Nazis) were really bad; the good guys (almost everyone else) were pretty good. But then there was Rick, who was ambivalent and torn, although not between good and bad. And Ilsa. And Victor. Even Sam.

And me.

Not about Casablanca, but about Hank. Was love enough? Fear could destroy love. Many things could destroy love. Hope and love – was that enough? No, hope and love and hard work? Hank would be here tomorrow and I had promised him an answer.

Ranger started barking before I heard the car, the knock on the door, the key in the lock. Hank is no more predictable than love.

'Katy!' He picked me up and swung me around.

I buried my head in the shoulder of his flannel shirt. He smelled vaguely of outdoors and sweat and dog and cheeseburgers. When he opened the bottle of champagne I was taken aback.

'I'm not assuming.' He smiled gently at me. 'Just welcoming the future, whatever it is.'

We held our glasses high for a moment, then drank to the future. Hank smiled at me still and I thought, as I had thought so many times before, how much I loved him.

'Yes.'

He raised an eyebrow.

'Let's get married.'

We drank champagne for a long time. The first bottle was not, as it turned out, the only one Hank had brought. Fears and doubts sometimes chased through my imagination but I pushed them from my mind, as I did Casablanca and Rick and Ilsa.

Love is always a beginning.

And tomorrow, as Scarlett said, is another day.

Alley Kat Blues

A Kat Colorado Mystery in the bestselling
tradition of Sue Grafton and Sara Paretsky

Karen Kijewski

Tough-talking, soft-centred PI Kat Colorado's latest
case is really getting to her. It was Kat who stopped
her car to rescue the mangled body of a young woman
in the middle of the road, apparently the victim of a
terrible hit-and-run disaster. But the victim's mother
turns up in Kat's office, convinced that her daughter's
death was no accident.

And with that investigation not only plaguing her
waking hours but invading her dreams too, Kat is in
no shape to cope with her policeman boyfriend
Hank's apparent infidelity as well . . . It looks like this
time Kat's bitten off more than she can chew and with
feelings of insecurity and frustration, not to mention
a complete lack of clues for the case, Kat could be near
breaking point . . .

0 7472 4838 9

HEADLINE

When Death Comes Stealing

A Tamara Hayle Mystery
'A riveting, emotional page-turner of an
ending. An excellent debut novel' *Booklist*

Valerie Wilson Wesley

'Wesley is one of very few black women writers writing in
this genre . . . a welcome new voice and a fresh point of
view' *USA Today*

Tamara Hayle fell in love with DeWayne Curtis when she
was too young to know any better. The result was a
disastrous marriage and Jamal, now fourteen. A private
investigator, the last thing single mother Tamara wants
back in her life is her shady ex-husband, but when he begs
her to help him through some serious trouble she can
barely refuse. For his eldest son has died a violent death
and DeWayne's sons are the only humans he seems
genuinely to care about, apart from himself. Then five days
later there's another killing. And Tamara realises that
unless she does something, and quick, her own son is next
on a killer's list . . .

'Quick and often funny . . . reads like a successful
collaboration between Terry McMillan and Sue Grafton'
Kirkus Reviews

'Grips you by the throat and never lets go until the last
spine-tingling word . . . a well-created novel with a poignant
message that resonates long after the mystery is solved'
Bebe Moore Campbell

0 7472 4759 5

HEADLINE

A selection of bestsellers from Headline

All Headline books are available at your local bookshop or newsagent, or can be ordered direct from the publisher. Just tick the titles you want and fill in the form below. Prices and availability subject to change without notice.

Headline Book Publishing, Cash Sales Department, Bookpoint, 39 Milton Park, Abingdon, OXON, OX14 4TD, UK. If you have a credit card you may order by telephone – 01235 400400.

Please enclose a cheque or postal order made payable to Bookpoint Ltd to the value of the cover price and allow the following for postage and packing:

UK & BFPO: £1.00 for the first book, 50p for the second book and 30p for each additional book ordered up to a maximum charge of £3.00.
OVERSEAS & EIRE: £2.00 for the first book, £1.00 for the second book and 50p for each additional book.

Name ....

Address ....

....

....

If you would prefer to pay by credit card, please complete:
Please debit my Visa/Access/Diner's Card/American Express (delete as applicable) card no:

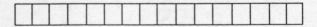

Signature .... Expiry Date ....